J.S. Breukelaar's work has appeared in *Spinetingler*, *Juked*, *Fantasy Magazine*, *New Dead Families*, *Prick of the Spindle*, *Opium*, and others, and in the *Women Writing the Weird* anthologies (Dog Horn Press). Her collection of short stories and poetry, *Ink*, was published in 2012 (Les Editions du Zaparogue). Born in Berkeley CA, she now lives in Sydney, Australia with her family. She writes for online literary and culture magazines such as The Nervous Breakdown and PopMatters. You can also find her at www.thelivingsuitcase.com. *American Monster* is her first novel.

American Monster

by J.S. Breukelaar

To Michael & Carolyn,
So great hanging out with
two of the coolest people I've
yet met on this road.
Hope to see you soon!
JS

Lazy Fascist Press
Portland, Oregon

Lazy Fascist Press
an imprint of Eraserhead Press
205 NE Bryant Street
Portland, Oregon 97211

www.lazyfascistpress.com

ISBN: 978-1-62105-135-0

Copyright © 2014 by Jenny Breukelaar

Cover Art Copyright © 2014 by Matthew Revert

Edited by Kirsten Alene

Proofread by Jamey Strathman, Ross E. Lockhart, Andrew Wayne Adams, Shane Cartledge, Amanda Billings, and Dustin Reade

All rights reserved. No part of this book may be reproduced or transmitted in any form or by any means, electronic or mechanical, including photocopying, recording, or by any information storage and retrieval system, without the written consent of the publisher, except where permitted by law.

All persons in this book are fictitious, and any resemblance that may seem to exist to actual persons living or dead is purely coincidental. This is a work of fiction.

Printed in the USA.

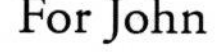

For John

The goddess can be recognized by her step.
—Virgil

La charité est cette clef. —Cette inspiration prouve que j'ai rêvé!
—Arthur Rimbaud

PART I

KALI I8

It is said that even in the Before there were those who fell. The curse of their fall was to become Brainworlds. Sentient and eternally celestial, they were unable to generate or sustain life. They were not so much planets as conscious Wholes.

Over eons of formation these Brainworlds finally took their place around dying stars at the edges of the Entirety. The Brainworlds were all thought, all brain. Their awareness was indefinite yet they could not conceive of the mind of another. Cursed with eternal awareness, they were entirely alone.

In the time of the Before, a small voyager ship crashed on the surface of a giant Brainworld called Kali I8. Kali's sun, WD 236-10, was in its death throes. The ship was filled with First Beings from an unnamed galaxy. These beings had wings and they had horns. They had life, and unlike the Brainworld, an intersubjective awareness limited to their own mortality. They crashed onto the Brainworld with their wings and their horns and they were magnificent beyond anything that Kali I8 had ever dreamed of, or dreamed it dreamed of.

As a result of the imminent violent death of its sun, the temperatures on Kali I8 had become too high for the beautiful beings, who perished screaming in the lethal winds and whose cells shriveled in the gamma ray assault from the dying star. The leader of the alien beings was the strongest, and he held out after his people had all died. He attempted to repair his ship's communications, he prayed for salvation, he wept for his comrades. The leader was, in Kali I8's conception, a perfect being. Kali I8 watched him with his tremendous horn and shimmering black wings that filtered the cosmic rays out of the air and bounced toxic rain and sand off their surface like arrowheads off a Sherman tank. But even such a being could not withstand the toxic atmosphere of the Brainworld, who loved him all the more as it killed him.

After the leader of the First Beings perished, Kali I8 was again alone in the Entirety, but this time its awareness extended to that of its own solitude. It mourned its affliction. In an eternal lie, it denied its role in the death of the Beloved so that it could mourn him, and blamed the Entirety for the loss of the horn. There could be no other.

(Fascicle 25.4 Nilea AQt., trans. L. Shay 2656)

1//: teeth

Here you are.

She'd known it as soon as she opened her eyes on the train. His head silhouetted against the orange square of sky, neon popping out like veins over the blurred expanse of shanty towns. Everything orange, that's what she'd take from this place. The orange sky. Toxic and ravishing.

The guy's horn, truth be told, was no more than a crumpled bulge in his jeans, nothing to write home about. Plus, he ignored her, or pretended to. He was riding backwards and seemed absorbed in a weathered deck of Harry Potter cards he'd worked into a Klondike array that she'd seen only once before from the old Salinan gardener up at San Miguel. There was something both frail and tensile about him. And so pale. A shock of wheaten hair matched his pale-ale eyes. Long legs that ended in cowboy boots—dusty lizard skin and a metal heel.

Norma shook off her exhaustion. Mentally palpated the inner edges of a perpetual hangover. She looked around at the other passengers. Across the table from the guy sat another man, riding forward. He was big and shyly smiling. She felt caught between the two of them, the warmth of the big man's smile and the cold diffidence of the skinny blond.

– You okay? said the big man. We didn't want to wake you.

Norma's eyes slid between the two men and she tried to gauge what ran between them. She felt bleary from sleep and parched, ran her tongue over her lips. The big man reached into a backpack on the floor, rummaged for a plastic water bottle and tossed it to her. She caught it and let the water run down her throat, wiped her mouth and tossed it back.

– Little bitty inside voices, said the big man, pinching his thumb and finger together. So we wouldn't wake you.

The blond guy continued silently with his game, eyes downcast, so Norma figured that by 'we' the big man meant the clustered strangers around them who'd struck up one of those wayfarers' conversations to pass the time. The couple behind her were Consortium militia on furlough to celebrate their wedding. The girl and her mother were planning a quick family ceremony in Spill City before returning to active duty. Norma could hear the mother's voice issuing from the girl's army-issue console, something about flowers.

– Where from? said the big man who looked part Native American.

And Norma, careful to keep to human registers, said, Australia.

It was what Mommy had told her to say when anyone asked because it was one of those places, according to Mommy, that everyone always said they wanted to go to, but never actually went.

– They have seasons there or what? said the girl, looking up from her mother. I heard they just have summer. And rain.

– Same everywhere, said the girl's fiancé, staring out the window.

The train's whistle moaned.

– I figured you were Australian, said Gene, approvingly.

– I would of said Canada, said the girl coyly. With that thick dark hair.

Norma felt the eyes of the big man on her but she attributed the dentata's pulse to the presence of the blond, the way his hat half-covered his face. Multiple piercings. Across one visible cheekbone was a confluence of small scars, like the bed of a dead river. He folded tightly into himself, his fulvous eyes lifting only once to take in the man across the table from him, and then dropping back to his cards, the soft slap and shuffle, his fingers tentative and seeking. Norma crossed her legs, the dentata throbbed.

– I'm Gene, said the big man, still staring at her. Where you headed?

– LA, she said and wrenched her eyes away from the blond guy. She glared at the man who called himself Gene, and flushed in spite of herself. She knew what she looked like—burned-out drifter, will fuck for food.

– City of Angels, yeah, said Gene. Something both infectious and exhausted in his exuberance. His long black hair was tied into a messy ponytail. His eyes were the color of Mission coffee—deep brown and rippling with warm lights. Huge scarred hands and a nose bent out of shape. It turned out that he had a wolf. This impressed the marines. He showed them a leather cord wound several times around his thick wrist, at the end of which hung three vanilla-colored teeth. They were from his wolf, Gloria. Her baby teeth—a canine, incisor and molar. Gene explained that in some states the regulations regarding enclosures and papers did not apply if you were First Nations.

– Where from? said the soldier.

– East, said Gene. Haudenosaunee on my mother's side.

– How the what? said the soldier.

– Iroquois, said Gene.

Mommy had warned that the only thing a Slash ever really wanted to know about you was where you were from. It was the most important thing to them, Mommy said, as if by affirming one's origins one could guarantee a safe return. It was very human, Mommy said. Very Slash. Slash was the old term for Human. It was from the Before, and Norma found it weirdly dating, but she could never tell Mommy that.

Norma felt rigid with lust. She crossed her legs, little shivers of delight. The more Gene talked with the blond guy's cards softly slapping on the table, the stronger the dentata pulsed. She sat up in her seat, tried to make herself look out the window. Behind her the girl's mother, who ran a Korean food truck at the market, was complaining about noise from the New Westborians who'd set up a chapel near the train tracks. Travel tales wrapped around them, the binding clack of wheels, the pale man silently absorbed in his game. She watched his probing fingers, mesmerized by their imagined touch. A kid came through the train selling fruit and chewing gum. The noodle man too, with his steaming contraption that looked a little like an accordion. The framed trailer parks and smokestacks and the ocean in the distance unreeling around them, like a universal zoetrope. Gene went on to tell stories from his boyhood. Crazy words that webbed around Norma and the others, the train wheels clacking out a chorus, the marine on her console now talking in Korean to her mom, the hiss of the pale man's cards. Reservation stories, houses with no rooms, how his Auntie used to chase him with a devil puppet when he'd been bad. Gene's upper lip was fuller than his lower, not quite an overbite, and not quite a smile, but almost. Norma found herself smiling back, not quite, but almost.

That puppet was bad mojo, said Gene, waving away the memory with his big hand so that the teeth danced on his wrist.

The card player sat back in his seat and stared out the window. Gene just shook his head and smiled his goofy smile. Within the Haudenosaunee are a number of clans, he explained, the bear, the turtle, the wolf and so on. Gene was a member of the wolf clan, and he got his first wolf-dog when he was fourteen and still on the rez up in Ontario, had them ever since, until the last one, Gloria, who he'd buried up at Bakersfield, got his Chevy as far south as Santa Barbara then decided to get on the train to LA, where some friend of his had a squat.

Norma was half-listening, half watching a movie running on a holo in one corner of the carriage. The Slash got around, you had to give them that. The great wash of distance, the rush of years. What were they looking for? Had it ever been theirs? Gene kept talking, answering questions and asking more. His auntie had a farm in Bakersfield, anyone been there? Norma smiled to herself at the mention of Bakersfield. If she had been a wolf, one ear would have swiveled around on her head at the very mention of the place.

VIPr: (abb.) (n) Vantage Insertion Point or Viewpoint (V). A built-in (unremovable) receptor/instrument panel/implantation device encoded at the genetic level for communicating with the NORMAS. The activator has two ports, an external bioswitch often manifesting as an adornment such as a headpiece or item of jewelry, and an internal (dentata) for transferring intelligence from the Viewpoint (V) to a horn via the neural host. The VIPr's stored information contains a failsafe code so that if it is not transferred within a certain time frame, the 'intelligence' begins to multiply within its host, causing side effects that can include but are not limited to bleeding hands, loss of memory, heightened libido, abdominal pain, prodigal strength, fits of anger and free-floating paranoia, periods of immeasurable and inexplicable suffering.

(Saurum Nilea, AQ., trans. L.Shay 2656)

2//: the trap

First was Barstow, where the ship landed. Well, Rainbow Basin, to be exact, but even that was a false start. You could go back and back, further and further, as far away as the dying sun.

To retrieve the creature who had fled it in the Before, Mommy created a hunter and logically, if unimaginatively, called it Norm. Mommy had had many Norms, all named after the set of algorithms slash prohibitions that constrained the hunter and each identical but logically discernible from the next. For this mission a Norm was selected for its appetites, its sensory acumen—in particular, its sense of smell—and its physical stamina. But, in the misguided notion that it would take one to know one, Mommy had given the horn hunter a horn of its own.

It transformed en route. Assuming male form, it emerged from the wreckage naked and crouched, the transmitter fiery around its neck. The lonely canyons racked by its screams. It killed a restroom pederast for his clothes, fled the Basin, and spent the first few days at Barstow getting the hang of things. Long limbed and haunted, wrong in this flesh, not knowing what to do with itself. Nothing worked like it should.

– The form doesn't mesh with its function, the hunter observed. Look at this.

– It's a horn, said Mommy. You are a hunter, looking for the horned being who fled in the Before. When the First Being came to me in the Before, it was horned. Magnificent.

Mommy hadn't meant to kill the beautiful horned being in the Before.

Norm (as she'd been then) tried to explain that human males, generally speaking, don't hunt with their horns.

– They think with them, don't they? said Mommy. Hehe.

There was no point in arguing.

– So think, said Mommy. And find the Being with the perfect horn. Return him to me.

– Roger that. But being throttled by a trucker for looking at you the wrong way in a Wendy's restroom, saving a cross-dresser of sixteen from a New Westborian flaying, and having your face licked by an off-duty mail woman is enough to confuse anyone. Just saying.

– Your point?

– Maybe I should try being female for a while.

Mommy thought about it. Entirely unconvincing sounds meant to approximate human rumination came over the line. Mommy was nothing if not careful.

– You're a horn hunter. It seems to be a disadvantage to have one yourself.

– Bingo, said Norm into the broken cellphone, trying not to yell. It just seems a little redundant, that's all. And the costs outweigh the benefits on several levels. Even before Secession, appetites that restricted themselves to the same gender tended to come under a great deal of social and cultural scrutiny in the Zone.

– But the females didn't have horns in the Before, whined Mommy.

– You're living in the past, Mommy.

Mommy sharply said, The horn is crucial. You have to implant it with the VIPr. It's the key. The dentata, in other words. The hole in your Whole.

– Well. I was selected for the mission because of my appetites, right?

– And your stamina, said Mommy indulgently.

– I'll cover a lot more ground if I don't use a horn to attract other horns.

– Meaning?

– Meaning, you catch flies with honey, not with pictures of other flies.

More grinding and gnashing on the line.

Norm took that as a yes.

But Barstow was too much a risk. It was a small place, and there had already been contact with too many people. Norm caught a bus a hundred and thirty muddy miles to Bakersfield. An older woman got on at Tehachapi Springs, started talking about how a relative's Motel 6 went from being Cartel-run to being taken over by Er and she ended up out of a job.

– Er? said Norm.

The passenger looked part Salinan and had dirt under her nails. She fidgeted with a small diamond ring on her finger, nailing Norm to the seat with her coal-black eyes.

– What planet are you from, honey? said the woman. Er is what the Consortium is, is what Er is. Buying the state up in chunks is what Er is. Selling it back to the Cartels in slivers.

The woman spat a brown stream on the floor of the bus, leant in closer and Norm could smell the opiates on her breath.

– I'm Salinan on my mother's side, she confided. And Er's a Salinan warlord is what I say.

The bus rattled on beneath a sky turning orange.

– Bullsheet, said a bearded man swiveling around in the seat ahead of them. Er's a South African mining corporation.

– Er's a New Zealand shipping company, called out the bus driver.

Someone else on the bus put in that Er was a San Franciscan cabal. Everyone everywhere had a different take on who the Consortium really was and who the Cartels really were. Either one was the lesser of two evils, or the greater, or there was no difference. Whatever they were—the Consortium and the Cartels—everyone seemed to agree that Purple Rain, the guerrilla arm of the secessionists, was the devil. Everyone except the bearded man in a seat in the front, whose face was scarred with shiny grafts where he'd had his Purple Rain ink forcibly removed.

There was a collapsed apartment building between the Bakersfield

Greyhound station and a windowless bar called The Trap. A curtain flapped eerily from the apartment building's upper floor windows. Norm found a relatively sound one-room apartment on the third floor with a serviceable bolt for locking and a hole blown out in its ceiling where the rain came in. There was even a mattress on which to recuperate. Half of the building was rubble, the rest about to be, so the smell and the noise would not arouse suspicion.

The hunter wore a bioswitch around its neck that functioned as a kind of organic command center. From this, the resequencing protocol could be generated. The protocol was made simpler by the fact that the hunter's tissue had already been processed—most of the skin was already in place as a response to the UV bombardment procedure on arrival. Everything else was available at the local drug store. Bandages, codeine, penicillin to stop infection from the relocated implantation device (the dentata). The hunter even managed to source, from a deregistered veterinarian-turned-mud wrestler, some equine estrogen to stabilize the transformation.

The protocol was an unexpected agony. The hunter's screams echoed up and down the lonely hallways, drowned out by the bassline that throbbed through the floor from the club below. She woke sprawled in a pool of matter beneath a starless sky visible through the hole in the ceiling. The walls around the mattress were smeared with bloody handprints. Her shoulder blades burned with an almost intolerable heat, a series of splintered protrusions had rent the skin. When she regained consciousness for the second time, nothing remained of these but an intermittent burning sensation and hard nodules tender to the touch. A remnant, or the memory of wings repressed in the initial program.

And the formless shadow that rose from her arced and buckled form like steam from a kettle was a remnant also, or a memory of the being she could never be again and the hunter felt as though something in her had died. A part of herself from which she must flee but which could, she figured during the long days of her painful recovery, catch up with her in the end. If she let it.

Because something had been born from the blood of the hunter—the horn had gone and in its place was something mysterious and whole.

When Norma, as she was now, emerged from the building a week later she never felt more alive. Like she had it all under control for the first time since arrival. She had gotten dressed in her old clothes, the boys' jeans and shirt she'd bought from a surplus store nearby, and they were more than a little small for her. The denim shirt buttoned tight over her breasts. That would take a little getting used to. Everything else seemed to fall into place. That night she picked up a young farmer at The Trap. He wasn't the one Mommy wanted, and she didn't care. This time it's for me, she thought, astride him on a couch in Elmsfield, and the next time, too, a Consortium goon's vast body pinning her to a waterbed and Norma sobbing as she came for the part of her that was born anew, and the part of her that was unendingly lost.

3//: LA

– Do you miss her? Norma asked.

– Who? said Gene. He squirmed uncomfortably between the seat and the table, its plastic edge digging into his belly with every roll of the train. It squealed to a stop and out the window was the simmering mass of the Pacific behind the ruins of the 405. Norma had been so taken with the pale-eyed man that she hadn't noticed how haggard Gene looked. In spite of his size, a tough and hungry look clung to him and to the tangled silk of his hair.

– Your wolf, said Norma. You miss her?

Gene's answer was swallowed up by a tunnel and when the lights came back on the compartment was in commotion, people reaching for plastic bags of their belongings in the overhead shelves, two white men in Consortium drag—one wore chef's pants; the other a red beret—were moving down the aisle. Both were armed.

– City of Angels, said Gene.

Norma was certain that the blond guy was getting out too, but when she found herself on the crowded platform, there was no sign of him. The train had begun to pull out, the doors already closed, and as Norma wheeled around she saw him still sitting in the compartment at the fold-out table, riding backwards. His gilded eyes burned at her through the window and he held up a piece of paper with some crude writing on it, but it was not until later, in the chaos of her dreams and when it was too late, that she worked out what it said.

Spill City.

Gene offered her his Chinatown couch for the night and she dreamt fitfully under the watchful leer of his Bop Bag collection—The Scream, Michael Jackson and Elvis. Finally, she stumbled into the bedroom and they groped roughly until dawn. Their mouths met and she could feel his teeth hard on her own, the tobacco and exhaustion on his breath and his horn hard against her belly.

They spent the winter together, a confused and bitter season. The city was still awash in filth and rubble after the latest hurricane, and the airport closed permanently after the worst attack since Secession. And not even Purple Rain to blame, although of course some did. There was another exodus which depleted the already devastated city. Vigilante gangs scoped the empty streets for the rebels—anyone foolish enough not to have had their SLA ink removed from their faces had it removed for them, an ironic twist on the outlawed slogan: 'Separate or Die Trying.' Lynchings were not uncommon. Guerrillas swung from telephone poles and traffic lights, their wives and sons mutilated in mangled cars beneath the torn freeway.

Gene was tough and sad and didn't ask too many questions, turned out they'd been more or less following each other down the coast, although she would not know the full truth of that until much later. After the landing outside of Barstow, Norma had hustled her way west to San Miguel—two hundred and fifty miles of muddy road, give or take. She didn't like what she'd heard about the new settlers in the Temblos and didn't like the look of all that dirty snow. So she'd stuck to the shadows of the ruined Interstate between Lamont and Lost Hills. Power poles uprooted and asphalt split down the middle, isolated roadhouses adrift on islands in the liquefacted ooze. Beside the road marched ghostly rows of charred saplings—apple, pear. At the roadhouses, the games were fixed and the men all smelled the same after a while. After a short rest at the Mission San Miguel, she worked her way south. Her hustle was left-handed snooker mainly, arm wrestling, and odd jobs. She even worked for a while as a bouncer at a casino outside of Nipoma.

– Doesn't everybody? Mommy had said, and stifled a yawn.

The bioswitch palpitated on the cord around her neck, and deep within Norma, the VIPr pulsed in reply. Viewpoint Insertion Protocol, or dentata by another name, its signal became more urgent in the presence of a suitable male horn, which Mommy likened to an antennae, a universal receptor through which to send and receive information about the One Who Fled.

So that was the mission as Norma understood it—to find the best horn through which to unlock the secrets of humanity, although she was still a little fuzzy on its finer points.

– The perfect horn? How will I know?

– You'll know it when you see it, said Mommy.

When she saw it, the perfect horn, or what appeared to be, it was on the train guy and it was mainly his golden eyes and hair, the dealer's touch, lean and hungry. But she let him go. So now, even when she was with Gene, Norma couldn't get the one she'd lost out of her mind, her ragged form diminished in his indifferent gaze. And although she accepted Gene's love in the Chinatown room amidst the barrio jive and lurid, bruised sunsets, it was but peripherally, her heart burning for what she had lost. It was with Gene a life half-lived, a part of her already gone, the rest not where it should be. In Spill City. Beneath the deceased reek of LA her nostrils quivered with longing for white sage and creosote, the salt and sand she went to in her dreams. Gene got fed up one drunken dawn outside the Viper Room, and left. Others came to her on the mattress on the floor, and moved on, dealers and journeymen, soldiers and spies, their rut grunts and sighs beating a ragged rhythm to the turning of the planet.

Sometime after New Year she decided Gene wasn't coming back. She sat on the edge of the couch, got out a broken console, and called Mommy. Told it how the guy was down in Spill City. So that's where she was heading.

– You sure it's him?

– I'm sure, said Norma.

– What's that?

Norma waited for the arcing lights of the drone outside the window to fade, its roar to recede.

– He's the Guy, she said. The one on the train. So pretty.

The console crackled and the transmission broke up. She'd found it in the apartment drowned in bong water. The Bop Bags giggled, hehe, and drew closer.

– What's that you say? City? What city?

The Bop Bags moved in another inch or two. Elvis the Pelvis and Betty Boop dressed to kill. Norma tensed and felt her shoulders knife. She shook out her hair and dropped the console. Picked it up again.

– No. Pretty. He's—

– I'm losing you, said Mommy. Norma?

Norma sighed and tossed the console out the window.

– Pretty, she said to Betty Boop. She grabbed the Bop Bag by its shiny plastic hair and ripped its head off.

Pretty like a wolf.

Configuration Sharing Protocol (CSP); or the Whole. (n) Also known as Cogshare. One of the two-port communication systems between the Viewpoint (V) (see below) and the neural host. The first connection, (sonic), is by way of obsolete microwave technology (see above). The Whole is the second connection (control), and can only be opened by the host via the external bioswitch. It is a total perceptual connection, informed by Gestalt coding, and notoriously unreliable. The control connection is a vital option for use when sonic connection fails or is at risk from interference or decryption, or when the host is immobilized by the Feer. As such, the external bioswitch can be overridden by the Viewpoint under extreme circumstances in control connection mode. But this is rarely used as the risks of corruption are equally high for both the Viewpoint and the host.

(Saurum Nilea, AQ., trans. L.Shay 2656)

4//: hole

– Mommy?

Norma banged the side of the payphone with her hand. The mist hung in low drifts, the pavement crunched with broken glass. She regretted being barefoot.

– Mommy? Are you there?

– Norma?

Mommy's voice through the crackles. Day workers were unloading next door at the House of Pancakes—boxes of egg powder, frozen links and chicken feet. Norma watched a drone cruise in over the upswept roof of the restaurant and take off south. In the wake of the aircraft's vicious buzz there followed an abrupt silence, disturbed only by the need-coffee drag and mutter of the loading crew. Norma shivered in her jacket. Gene had found it on a stool at the Viper Room up in LA, left there by an ordinance technician from China Lake who never came back. It was made of some black material that ate up all the light, caught bullets in its arachno-weave and spat them out like watermelon seeds. Smart-armor patches cushioned her elbows and with a touch of a finger, the powder-coated titanium zip snaked down over the salsa stain on her tank top.

– Is everything all right? Mommy said faintly.

Norma had discovered that the zipped-up combat jacket interfered with the transmission somehow but she didn't know why and the morning was still too cold to take it off. She lowered the zip and edged in closer to the busted payphone.

– Everything's fine, said Norma. I just want to go home is all.

It had been a month in Spill City and still no sign of the Guy. The surf was a muffled roar and the truck unloading next door belched exhaust that made her head hurt. She could hear faint strains of Muzak on the line to Mommy, footsteps approaching and retreating, the chime of a fake elevator. The encryption effects were impressive and, to Norma's relief, a huge improvement over the early days when Mommy's idea of Earth ambience was limited to canned laughter and coyote howls.

– Where are you? Mommy said.

Mommy knew, but it liked to ask. Although it couldn't see what Norma saw, it absorbed information from her both aurally—via the bioswitch at her breast—and virally. Mommy said it liked the way Norma described things.

– Spill City, said Norma, or thought it, squinting up at the curdled sky. Like I told you. Since January. Nothing's changed.

Morning nailed her eyes. She breathed in the smell of the slick. Sulphur and nitrates and a sad kelpy taste in the back of her throat. The surf pounded and Norma took that as the sound of her failure.

– Tell me again, said Mommy over the ocean roar, the meep-meep of the truck backing in farther.

– Outside a pharmacy on the coast. It's almost dawn and I'm barefoot.

– Barefoot? In a rare lapse, Mommy's voice, which wasn't really a voice, grew feet. Strangely taloned, quickly submerged in static before reassembling itself into Earth English, like a recording momentarily on the wrong speed. Where are your shoes?

Norma bent down to pick a piece of glass from between her varnished toenails.

– I slept with a drag queen called Bunny and—

– Again? I thought we were finished with all that.

Redundant music swelled on the line to scramble the code—strings and woodwinds. Mommy's imagined self was a classical music buff.

Baroque mainly. Corelli and Bach. A jazz collection that was not to be equaled. It would take its espresso long with a dash and drive an iD. It wouldn't be living in Spill City.

– We are, said Norma. I am.

She felt guilty about Bunny. She shivered, swallowing panic along with the gluey remains of Bunny's fluids.

–What it is is I don't know if he's the Guy.

She did and he wasn't.

–Who dear?

Norma shifted her weight to her other hip. Her hair felt barbed against her face and her shoulders had begun to throb.

– The tranny. I'm not feeling it.

– Well maybe you should go back up to find out. A horn in the hand is after all worth two in the bush.

Mommy gave a lewd snicker but it came out as a lip fart. Another thing about Mommy was the way it collected clichés. It had them on virtual shelves, stored in boxes, all labeled in categories. It studied Slashes (an obsolete ontological slur from the Before, based on a character in the outmoded protocol from which Norm/a also got her name), obsessed over them. Mommy joined in the cosmic conversations that belittled them—so inferior to the First Beings who fled—but Norma knew it wanted them. As a consolation prize, maybe, but still. To replace the one it had lost.

– When you find the horn, said Mommy, trying to make it sound casual but there was a hard chip to its voice now. And implant it, you can come home.

–You mean implant it with the VIPr slash dentata? And what? Then it can come out? Because it hurts Mommy. It's beginning to burn.

– The horn. Find it.

– Thing is, said Norma. Not too many higher life forms have horns on their heads here is part of the problem.

Not that Mommy cared where the human horn was. But the other part of the problem for Norma was time. She felt it against her somehow. They both did.

Norma said, The longer I'm here, the more—

—it hurts? said Mommy brightly. You said. So, implant, already. I like the sound of this rabbit.

Norma did too. She liked Bunny. But he wasn't the Guy. He was a cab driver by day and Wonder Whoa-Man by night at a drag bar down at the border. Norma had never seen his act. Another thing to feel guilty about.

– It's just that we dropped I don't know how many pills. And booze and lines. Bunny knows the guys from Violent Fez, Mommy. You heard of them? (Imagine: the frantic retrieval mechanisms in overdrive—was that *violet* or *violate*?) We were up all night and there was another SLA raid.

The Consortium weeding out the last of the rebels, claimed the news reports.

– A raid? What was it like?

– If I told you, would you know?

It was an old and encoded joke between them, that line. Norma had picked it up from a Jewish bounty hunter up in San Jose, but Mommy wasn't laughing now.

– Try me, she said.

Norma sighed. The ocean was a narrow slice of slick between the cracked and fallen facades. She fiddled with the zipper on her jacket, lowered it until she could feel the heat of the bioswitch against the cold tips of her fingers. The bioswitch would enable Mommy to enter the configuration, which basically was their joined consciousnesses, through a cog-share protocol (CSP) useful in situations where either compliance or privacy demanded it. Norma looked up and down the street. This didn't seem like one of those situations. The day workers—Armenian refugees, Welsh drug smugglers, starving Somali programmers—moved silently in the mist, the disembodied beads of their cigarettes jumped in the ferrous haze. A few hookers clustered around the door of the pharmacy, sharp notes of laughter muffled in fake fur. No one to care about the tall woman leaning into the broken payphone, the one they called crazy. She hunched against the dial box and Gene came to mind, the way he'd presented the jacket to her with a hammy flourish. But then he left and Norma was free. Dangerously free. She tried to keep

Mommy out for a moment longer so she could hold the memory in her thoughts—the way Gene was taller even than Norma and twice as wide, his high cheekbones flashing on and off in the strobe light forever and ever, the last time they were happy together. Like Gene always said, what happens in LA stays in LA.

Norma manipulated the bioswitch to activate the CSP and gasped. Mommy swam into her head like a marine animal, trying to access the information it sought—the raid, with the putt-putt of the Tech Zens and the vicious whisper of drones overhead, her night with Bunny. Norma's knees buckled, her head pounded, she tried to look out to sea, bright blades of foam. She thumbed away her tears, controlling the urge to pee.

– Find it, said the voice in her head. Find the horn of the One Who Fled me and we can all go home.

A faint hiss and gurgle, the sound of Mommy withdrawing. It couldn't stay in Norma's head for long or it would drown in the synaptic swill that had been forming over the last few months of the mission. Norma felt increasingly violated by the procedure, a little exposed. She shook out her damp hair and angled her head out to either side of the payphone, embarrassed. Weary clubbers peddled between the cracks of the Boulevard, dodging smugglers chugging back down to TJ in complaining recombos.

– Just go back up dear, said Mommy. He could be the Guy. I should go too, I think. The pool man is on his way. He has to. Uh.

–The pool man? Mommy? Mommy?

Norma banged the phone again. And again.

But Mommy was gone. Norma slammed the receiver back down on its cradle so hard that it swung out over the sidewalk impasto-ed with blood and matter. She stepped out trying to avoid the broken glass and almost tripped over a street kid slumped against the wall of the pharmacy. A faint spattering of applause erupted from the crowd that had gathered to watch the big lady screaming at someone she called Mommy. Again.

– Lights on baby, nobody home, chortled one of the hookers.

It never got old.

– Leave a message after the beep, muchacha.

– Bitch talking to God, put in a good word for me.

Their fist bumps and musical laughs were less incongruous against the meaty shuffle of the day workers than you'd think.

– That phone's been dead since the twenties.

The street kid sitting against the wall muttered and shifted in a voluminous and filthy blue parka. Norma got a glimpse of pale flesh and hair the color of dirt. She shouldered her way through the crowd and walked across the Boulevard. She wasn't doing this for Mommy, she was doing it for her shoes. Vintage Manolos. From before.

Night had fled from the streets, but the morning mist still clung to the sparse traffic flowing down the highway. The stairs to Bunny's apartment felt tacky underfoot. She pushed open the door and stood in a room washed in pink light from a flag pinned across the one window. Bunny snoring on a mattress on the floor. Without the wig and eyelashes, he looked like what he was. Son of a taxi driver. She'd turn tranny, too, if her old man drove an End of Days tuk-tuk. Small chin. Pale mouth slack in sleep. Fine receding hair like the loan officer who beat on her way back when in Barstow. Bunny's horn was suitable, that much was true, but he had an obese brood he supported somewhere in the Valley, kept their picture in his wallet. She bent down to pick up the wallet from the floor and pulled out the picture—his youngest in a wheelchair. Bunny carried a creased coupon for Head and Shoulders Shampoo in there too—for luck he said—and left her to wonder why, when the world ended, he'd be thinking about his scalp condition. She stuffed fifty bucks in there too, knowing he'd never take it otherwise. Scanned for her shoes, kicking aside his satin sheath and tights. He stirred and opened his eyes. Stared at her. She froze, blinked back at him. His lips curled in a bitter smile and he closed his eyes again. She tiptoed past, pulled his boa off her Manolos and bailed.

5//: twins

The only things still running down in Spill City were the trains. The old Caltrak Surfliner, which still ran up and down the coast from Sacramento down to the old border, and the little Coasters. The Cartels had originally claimed the Coasters for their smuggling routes and over the years these had evolved into an efficient and economical public transport system. Fares were collected by self-employed 'conductors,' who in turn survived by acting as informants for either the Cartels or the Consortium or both. Bottom line: you could attempt to evade the fare, but you ran the risk of never making it to your destination.

After leaving Bunny, Norma took the Coaster north ten miles to Birmingham Beach. The cold kernel of the risen sun was swallowed in mist, her own stomach a husk. She alighted and was immediately caught up in the chaos of the 101 market sprawl which followed the coastal highway—and the railway line—the entire length of the Catastrophic Zone, as if to assert that in the slim space between the slick palpating slug of the spill out to sea and the devastation east of the interstate, life must go on. Worn out by her conversation with Mommy, sore in her parts from fucking and fighting, Norma made her way barefoot through the breakfast trucks and quake-trash to the old strip mall. Her reflection in the VG's window was a shock—self-recognition not even an issue anymore and that, too, was part of the problem.

Mommy said that the others who had come before her served as an example of what not to do. The horn hunters who'd gone native, become too human to go back, too alien to stay. Where had they gone, Norma wondered. She felt someone behind her and turned, but there was no one. It got her every time. There were too many presences that brushed against one in this place, too easy to hear whisperings. To mistake a shard of light for a sign of life. Norma inhaled the salty-sweet smells of the markets—piles of picked-over clothes and quake-trash, steel vats of chitlins and churros and chapattis, readers of tea-leaves and talkers in tongue—and exhaled. She would not fail. The pain of the dentata was there to remind her of what she was. A basic daemon protocol required to track and mark the human horn.

Mark it with what?

She smoothed down her hair, zipped the jacket up over her heavy breasts and went in. She waited, flatfooted, for Noe the baker to come out from behind the racks of bread and muffins. He counted six churros into a bag and passed them to her over the glass counter. His pinky was a clay-colored stump.

– Been out dancing? Noe said with a glance down at the high heels in her hand and the grime between her toes.

– Something like that.

Noe's face flushed. His lashes fluttered in confusion.

– Raining already almost, look, he said. I thought it might clear there for a while.

– No chance, said a bandy assistant behind him squeezing pink frosting onto a cake.

Noe wiped floury hands on the apron across his paunch.

– They got Zumba at the gym down at the Factory. You ever tried that? Zumba.

Norma shook her head, feeling the churros' slimy heat against the pads of her fingers, conscious of her hands, the clawed grip.

– It was the wack back in the 20s, said the assistant over his bag of frosting. Norma watched the slimy sack of sugar paste in his hands birth pink petals and green leaves.

– For sure going to try it, Noe said. A light sheen of sweat on his forehead.

The assistant stole an adoring look at Noe's ample behind and went back to his frosting.

– Smells good, she said jiggling the bag and backing away.

– Come back soon, said Noe.

The door closed behind her with a tinkle. Mist hung low over the tracks. A Surfliner howled north. A tribe of drab Cruids with their shaven tattooed heads streamed past on their boards. A Consortium goon on his Flyer with his hands outstretched across the wide handlebars and the white insignia stark on the lumpen nano pack. She'd had her own Flyer in LA, a deep blue FL-60 which she'd left behind in the apartment with Bop Bags and old consoles. She could have brought it on the train, but she was glad she didn't. She liked walking in Spill City. Plenty of time to fly when she got home.

The twins were at their place under the towering pine that marked the entrance to the camping grounds. Raindrops garlanded the clustered needles. The tree was guarded round-the-clock by a staunch Ecoist, clothed in rags, only eating when people fed him, like the Sadhus of old. Norma tossed the Ecoist a churro and another she tossed to the twins who fell on it like coyotes. The boy twin tried to push his sister aside, hands tearing at her lips, his tongue licking crumbs off her cold sores. Their white hair and blind eyes were waxen in the first light.

– Mommy, mommy, they called after her. How's Mommy you fuckin' schizo? shrieked the girl, pawing and sniffing at the air.

With the shoes in one hand and the pastries in the other, she stepped through a tear in the chain link and made her way down the beaten path toward her trailer, flinching at the stones and rubble underfoot but she didn't want to soil the inside of the Manolos with her filthy feet. Her arches had fallen since arrival. Another side effect? She could have worn her combat boots last night but Bunny loved a girl in heels. The grease on her fingers from the churros made it awkward to slide back the bolt on the trailer door. She went in, thought about the tea she didn't have and dropped the bag of pastries by the sink. In the bathroom she bent down to the mirror, pressed a finger against a small bruise on her cheek.

Her eyes were bloodshot, vitric beneath the heavy brows. She started to undress. One item of clothing at a time, splashing water on the precious skin and drying it carefully with a clean cloth. Her stomach growled. She took off her panties and splashed more water around her crotch, fingertips cleaning out the soft hole and the patch of hair encrusted with the tranny's cum.

The bioswitch swung from a necklace of tensile-strength chromatrope membrane that grew out of her cervical spine. It glistened like spider silk in the rain. It would open the door to the secrets that Mommy craved and was Mommy's hold on her, a time bomb that would only be disarmed when Norma delivered the perfect horn, so to speak, into its hands. The longer she took, the stronger the dentata got, all the way to eternity, a little piece of Mommy inside her that grew over time.

– Honest Injun, said Mommy. I'll never let you die.

Mommy had said Norma would know the Guy when she saw him. And Mommy was right. It was always right. She had seen him on the train to LA and she'd let him go, all the way down to Spill City, the dentata howling inside her for what it had lost.

– I'll find him again, she'd promised Mommy. Or die trying.

Meanwhile the device dug in its nucleotide claws, taking up alien residence inside her, more or less permanent, like a Russian doll in reverse. Getting bigger inside her instead of smaller. And yes, goddammit. It hurt like hell.

Naked, she limped into the kitchen to nibble on a pastry, saving one for later. She'd selected the Cheyenne from the trailers that were abandoned across the camping ground in the mass exodus after the 2033 spill, when a convoy of Alaskan tankers washed up on uncharted rock thrown up by the aftershocks. The trailer was small, not entirely overrun with bugs and vermin, and didn't stand out. She went back into the bedroom and drew the curtains across the window that looked over the ocean north to Swami's headland and south to Solana Beach. She drank from a bottle of water, leaving a pink backwash. You bled sometimes from your gums in Spill City. It wasn't an uncommon condition. Under the mattress was the stash she'd taken from the pockets and backpacks of the men who visited her in Gene's apartment after he left. Xanax and

Valium to ease her comedown. E-done for pain. Rediem to rock her into orbit. An assortment of anti-virals and antibiotics to keep infection at bay, or pay the rent should a representative from either the Cartels or the Consortium come by to collect it. She fell backwards onto the mattress, drew the sleeping bag up, and slept dreaming not of home, not exactly. Her human superconsciousness could barely access those memories anymore. Sometimes the silver of the sand or a particular pink in the sunset jogged a nostalgic response. But she was usually awake when that happened. No, it was because occasionally and only in her dreams, she remembered something else entirely.

Or someone.

6//: fixed

Gloria was part wolf, part something else and Gene had been allowed to keep her without a special license because he and Jesse were part Iroquois, part something else, and back east if you were a registered Native American you could have a wolf.

– You'll check up on the old place? said Jesse, by which he meant Auntie back in Bakersfield whom neither had seen since the Big Shake three years ago.

– Not sure I'll get that far, said Gene. But if I do.

Back east all through that spring he and Gloria had hung around with Jesse and his Japanese girlfriend at slash/back, the vintage clothing cafe they ran together, and Jesse seemed to be doing okay. At least for a gimpy Indian. He had his guitar and the band, and he had his girlfriend who he'd met on a volunteer stint at an orphanage in Osaka and even if Gene thought she was a little young for Jesse, who was he to say? There was plenty they couldn't talk about these days, although he tried, but then his brother would say what about this reggae backbeat or try to fix Gene up with some friend of theirs and that was never going to fly. Besides he felt the pull west, always had. So come summer he decided to head back out there again in their old man's beat up Chevy with Gloria in the back.

The big animal slept in the back seat or rode up front beside him and things went okay for a while. He'd pull over to let her run off some steam, and she'd lope back to the truck with her muzzle slick with squirrel blood sometimes, burrs matted in her thick dark pelt. They'd sleep rugged up in the truck camping grounds or parks, sneak in behind the drifters' SUVs, everyone gone by morning, leave the park for the moms and kids. Sometimes he'd check into a motel to get cleaned up. He'd spent so long doing this, finding room to move between one coast and another, that he forgot sometimes where he came from, where he really belonged.

When Gloria started acting up in Colorado, Gene thought maybe it was because she could smell her extinct timber wolf cousins in the silvery air, and then he thought maybe she didn't like him stopping at those bars at the edge of town. Big as he was, she'd keep an eye on him from out the windscreen, worry knitting her shaggy brow at a man of his size letting himself get pushed around like that, the way the truckers would lead him giggling into the back seat of their cabs, the marks they'd leave on his body and his face, of their loose-fisted love. But that wasn't it. Gloria got worse, howled all the way through New Mexico where he diverted to visit a friend of Jesse's they'd both known in Ontario. When the man came out of the barracks to open the Chevy door for Gene, Gloria lunged across and almost took his head off. So Gene mostly kept her in the truck after that, her pelt shedding all over a blanket he'd spread for her, and by the time they got to Phoenix, she was so rank with a weeping mange that he had to fork out $250 for a vet to tell him she was getting old.

She was homesick, that was the thing. For the cold clear streams back east, the dark arcades of fragrant pines, overhead the high whistle of a drifting hawk. And the way a paddock would jump out at you unexpectedly, thistles and goldenrod at its edges. The further they drove away from that, the worse she got and the guiltier he felt. And there was something else. She seemed scared, skittish, and he'd never known her to be this way. Her hackles lifted all the time and a high musk emanated from her, so that the windows had to be wound down all the way, the roar of the road filling his head with the old bad thoughts. About how the devil had gotten into their daddy and had taken him away, about cousin Ty and what he did to Jesse's leg, about the boy at the roadhouse with the strawberry mark below his right buttock. The road cracking out of the black like a whip, Gloria taut and farting beside him. Fixing him in her terrible yellow-moon stare.

That minute they crossed down into the Catastrophic Zone, Gloria began to bark and bang her rump up against the passenger door, scratching at the dash with her foreleg. And Gene thought he could turn back, maybe work at the store with his brother back east, finish that game he'd started with the sale of the farm maybe, but it was too late. The land fell beneath them, the highway dipping steeply as they crossed the Nevada state line.

– Well, he said, pulling over to calm the animal. We'll go back soon. I'll talk to Auntie about selling the farm. Nothing's going to happen without that.

He tried to make himself believe this and make Gloria believe it too, taking her great head in his hands and finding her amber gaze in his own. But it was more than that and he knew it. He felt the pull, the eyes of another watching his approach. Could Gloria see it too? That they weren't alone?

Gloria didn't need to know Auntie to fear her. That was it and they both knew it, felt it. The fear. Even if the farm were still there after the quakes and the drought and the Secessionist wars, and even if there was anyone left in Bakersfield to buy the place, it would take as long as Auntie wanted it to take. It always had. Auntie had this quality: she could make a minute seem like years, and a lifetime pass in an instant.

– You have an aunt? Jesse's girlfriend had generously said. Bring her back with you, she can live with us.

Jesse and Gene had just looked at each other over the girl's shiny black hair.

– In Osaka maybe, said Jesse, not here.

Meaning not Auntie. Not ever.

Out of the grimy windows of the truck, Gene saw the West Coast, not of his early youth, but of the intervening years. Heading toward Barstow over the bridge (already beginning to crack) that they'd built across the rift spreading south from Death Valley, Gene sensed how low the land had sunk. No wonder Washington had let it go. Easier than trying to hang on. The crumbling strip malls and shuttered neighborhoods and parking lots transformed into shanty towns. Folks living in shipping containers. The charred hills behind. Getting lost one too many times on the streets beneath the twisted freeway, Gloria had set up a low keen, stopping only to snarl once in a while at the unfinished housing developments, the liquefacted fields.

But it was Auntie, standing on the porch of the old farm outside of Bakersfield, who set her off completely. Gloria strained at her leash, her lip pulled back in a black grin and Gene, big as he was, had to hold her down with two hands. Auntie, shriveled some since the funeral, took off one slipper and hit the animal right between the eyes without spilling a drop of her Keystone. Gloria yelped and Gene led her round to the back, Auntie saying after them, That fleabag shit on my squash I'll shoot it.

Uncle Earl had been a merchant sailor in his younger days. He died in the rubble of an aftershock on Christmas morning two years ago. Since then, Auntie survived on palm readings and the proceeds from her vegetable garden. For Auntie, the varnish-red peppers, pale bubble-skinned squash and corn of course, were about survival, the white way and the Indian way. She wasn't Six Nations, claimed to be Salinan or Coso or some such, and had met Earl, a white man like Gene's father, when he was stationed at Monterey. Gene watched her kneeling in the verdant rows at all hours of the day or night, gray hair streaming down her back, her small diamond ring catching the moonlight.

She enlisted Gene's help in searching for Earl's missing diamonds; she'd looked all over for them. In the shed, in the barn (which contained nothing except for cousin Ty's old Grizzly and Earl's restored Ram Charger) and in the blackberry patch between the woods and the cornfield, but she hadn't been able to find them. Auntie's story was that Earl had let her choose two—she'd used one to pay for the funeral, she said, had the other made into a ring—from a handful he'd held out for her once, said he picked them up on his travels, or won them, blackjack mainly, a little poker or pool. The rest of them were out there somewhere and she'd find them or die trying.

– Go a ways toward fixing up the place, she said, but what Auntie had in mind, Gene knew, was a different kind of fix, one that involved a small glass pipe and a cheap Bic lighter for her boyfriend Major Buzz, who'd fought in the New Korean Wars and was a little young for her, Gene thought, but who was he to say?

He cleaned out the basement looking for the stones, searched the fireplace flues (all the chimneys had come down in the 2030 shake) and the gutters, not that he really believed the diamonds were there, but because it made things better between them, him and Auntie. Because after all this was the family home and would be his and Jesse's one day, provided Major Buzz didn't get his hands on it. Well, wasn't that why he was here, to keep an eye on the family home, for Jesse and his girlfriend and their unborn child? Not to mention the operation on Jesse's leg that he couldn't, or wouldn't afford. Gene didn't really believe that but it gave him something to tell Gloria, and something to tell himself on the long walks they took in the charred hills and dried river beds. And when he wasn't doing that or looking for diamonds, he did what chores he could around the place, or worked on the game he was designing, or found his own kind of fix down at The Trap, a windowless bar next to the Greyhound Station.

Gene had never been very good on the land. That had been Jesse's area until he lost the use of his left leg. But Gene managed to build a big enclosure for Gloria on the eastern side of the farm near the skeleton of an old pine by the cornfield where he and Jesse and cousin Ty used to fool around on the ATV. It was as far from Auntie and the house and the vegetable garden as possible but the wolf-dog still got out sometimes to demolish a couple rows of beans, once to piss a river on the squash and Gene expected the worst that time, but Auntie just stood there behind the kitchen window, drool hanging from her lips, her fingers clawing the beer can and something slithering in her black eyes that Gene could not read. Another time, Gene came home late one night to find Auntie trapped inside the house and Gloria on the back porch, her forelegs on the window sill and the two of them staring at each other, Gloria's wolf-eyes pinning Auntie's face to the dark glass. And in her eyes he could see it, something that moved there and had seen clear across to the other side. Bad mojo saying come out to play. With an effort that seemed to leave her depleted for days, Auntie shrugged it off. Blinked and wiped the drool off her chin. And the yellow fear went out of her eyes, in its place just the old, hard black hate.

– That wild animal stink is everywhere, she said. I walk into the store, folks walk out.

Well, folks had always walked out on Auntie, but he didn't like to say. Jesse and him and even her own son Ty. Heading off to die in the desert as soon as he could, and Uncle Earl making himself pretty scarce when he retired, gone for days at a time, Auntie knew not where.

On Route 119 one late November afternoon, Gene had to pull over in the sputtering Chevy to let Major Buzz and Auntie pass, doing ninety in the station wagon going toward the lake. He'd been at an interview at Lina's Wieners and when he finally made it home in the sputtering truck, he saw that Gloria's enclosure was open and the wolf was gone. He combed the ground until he came to a flattened patch of grass, a spray of blood on the bark of the pine that they'd missed in their efforts to leave no trace. He touched it and looked at the wet red blood on his fingers. When he checked under Auntie's bed he saw that the 20-gauge had gone too and he knew he had no chance of stopping what had already taken place, not in the Chevy anyway. So he ran to the barn, hot-wired Uncle Earl's big Dodge (something Ty had taught him back on the rez), siphoned some gas into it and was on the road just as the sun was setting. He thought he might meet them coming back but he got all the way to the lake without passing a soul.

At the lake he skirted the moon-bleached shore slowly in the truck, finally found the wolf-dog washed up in the shallows of a rocky bay, canoes stacked up against the trees like coffins. They'd shot her in the side of the head. What the water hadn't washed away of her blasted brains and skull was matted in her pelt. Her tongue hung out, already beginning to swell. He wrapped her in a blanket, loaded her into the passenger seat. He sat on the hood under the pale moon, fumbled for the book of matches he'd got at the Trap and lit a cigarette, then another one, until the clouds blew up and the moon disappeared behind them with a yellow wink that was goodbye.

Back in the warming-up truck, blowing on his hands, Gene felt a part of the world curl itself into a ball and roll away from him. He felt one minute full of purpose, the next cut away from things, rolling away. Beside him on the passenger seat was something—not Gloria—he couldn't look at. He started up the truck, turned onto the lake road and hadn't gone a hundred yards before he heard the rattle. It hadn't been there before—something must have come loose on the rough road. He found a flashlight in the glove box and got out, the wind keen in his ears. The truck bed was empty, nothing but coon turds and a coil of frayed rope. Gene lay down on his belly and shone the light under the chassis. It picked up an angular shape hanging down a few inches above the ground but before he could get a good look, the flashlight dimmed and the battery died. He cursed and put it aside, lit a match and reached in to pry the shape loose but it would not come. He went back into the truck for a wrench, waited for his eyes to adjust to the darkness, and crawled back under. He pulled the metal box, which had come loose from the wires crudely attaching it to the chassis, out onto the road and stared at it. Earl's old red toolbox. He remembered it from when he was a boy, hadn't seen it or one like it in all these years. It came back to him now, that hunger he'd felt for it, the shiny red box with its cluttered contents—tools for fixing and for destroying—its secret compartments and pull-out tray. Seeing it now brought back all those old feelings of creeping shame and dread, a kind of hell-sickness that followed him wherever he went, squeezed him between sea and shining sea so that he couldn't breathe, couldn't think. Steam billowed from his mouth; his fingers were stiff with the cold, his hair ropy around his face. He found a rock and used it and the wrench to break the lock, panting with the effort, sweat dripping beneath his jacket. And he saw them then, the diamonds. They caught the glare of starlit cloud and threw it back at him in a flash of white light. A dozen diamonds, maybe more, from small to middling. He picked out a big one and held it up to the sky, each surface giving him a different view of the speeding clouds. He put it back in real slow. In the tray beside the stones were some small pliers and a greasy paper bag containing twisted scraps of gold and silver that had once been the settings for the diamonds. He pulled on the tray by the central handle. It stuck, finally jumping out so that he had to catch it in both hands, and there at the bottom of the box, nestled in a chamois, were the ears.

Dried rags of flesh, right and left ears, some clearly female, others sprouting hairs. Some had shriveled and darkened over time, others looked fresher, waxen, dried blood in the grooves, cartilage poking through the rotting flesh. All with piercings, singular or multiple. Beneath them was a box-cutter, the kind you get at Wal-Mart, the blade sheathed. Gene squatted beside the toolbox for a while, feeling the heat rise in his face, his heart pounding, and he remained that way for so long that when he tried to put the tray back in, his fingers would not work. He blew on them, rubbed them together and then awkwardly scooped up the diamonds, dropped them into his pocket. He packed the toolbox back up and walked down to the lake. He dropped the whole thing in, the box of ears with the box-cutter like the tomahawks buried beside the warriors of old. Afterwards he took a cigarette from his packet, split open the paper and sprinkled tobacco over the water in the only blessing he knew.

He drove back slowly, Gloria beside him for the last time. He stopped on the way home at a truck stop to raise a glass—never another to take her place—then buried her in the woods behind the blackberry patch. He thought of burying her baby teeth along with her, the ones he wore on a cord around his wrist, but he couldn't bear to part with them. Take care of the farm for me, Gene said as if she could still hear, and the words came back to him then across the endless road and years: *our maker has called thee home and thither will we follow.* He palmed the matches, thought of burning the place to the ground, the barn and crops and house, but it would be his and Jesse's one day if Buzz did not get his hands on it first. Like Jesse said, never trust a junkie, and he would know—lame since Ty, high on China flake, ran the ATV over him down by the old twisted pine.

Gene dismantled her enclosure before dawn. He put the diamonds in a baggie, all except the one he left on the kitchen table for Auntie, yeah, so she'd know. By first light he was on his way, but not back east.

Not yet. The Chevy, it'd make the coast or near enough and he'd figure it out from there. City of Angels. It had been a while.

7//: Slash

Sometime in the night back in the Spill City trailer, Norma had woken up and eaten the last churro but in the morning had no memory of doing this, or of anything else. She tried to shrug the burn out of her shoulders, her night with Bunny slowly coming back to her. Calling Mommy down at the beach. Half-falling over some kid outside the payphone.

After another blackout she came to with blood under her nails that she could not explain. Norma howled in frustration. Rain chipped at the roof. Was it morning? Which morning? She lay there in a sweat, a free-floating panic squeezing the breath from her chest. A constant headache scratched at her temples—she felt the VIPr leaking into her brain. Maybe Mommy was right. Maybe on Earth you think with your hole.

It had been so long since she'd seen the Guy from the train but increasingly she felt him there, saw him in her dreams, woke up scissoring her legs together. The tide was out. She could hear it in the muffled swish of the surf and the desperate call of the birds stuck in the slick like bugs on fly paper. She groped in the dark for her water bottle, tried to drink it lying down and wound up squirting it out her nose. She sat up flailing and feeling foolish. Laughed at herself before anyone else could, even if there were someone else here with her, which there never was. She wiped her face with her sleeping bag and switched on the light, wrapped the sleeping bag around her and padded out of the bedroom. She felt starving but at least the sugar-fried smell of the churros was gone, thank Elvis for small mercies, which is what Gene used to say, and remembering him, she thought again of ditching the mission and heading back up to LA but with what? What, invoking Mommy's leer in the bathroom mirror, would you tell him? About your appetites? Yes, creature, telling him the one about the hunger. Go back to Gene, the big lug with the lovable laugh—Mommy's alliterative frenzy frying the line—and tell him about the hungry monster inside you. The daughter pregnant with her Mommy. She pulled the cabinet mirror open, slammed it shut again. She pointed an imaginary pistol at the mirror.

Abomination.

Norma went out of the trailer naked in her sleeping bag and stood shivering in the clearing looking out to sea. The outlines of the dawning world had spread like a bruise and beyond the rail, the red tide rolled in unending. Norma sniffed her fingers and began to cry.

The Silence (n) i. Pre-Quaternary slang word of unknown origin, possibly referring to the terror of the void or of time conceived as a region at the forgotten edge of matter. A panic-induced post-verbal state, sometimes permanent, induced by the perceived proximity of death and the possibility of coming face to face with one's future, no longer extant self, who paradoxically would not know what it was, and whose specific agony would be in fulfilling an impossible imperative—to remind one's past self of one's future death. A state known in early Earth symbolic logic as *memento mori*. ii. Also associated with the early Nilean Voyages, to apply to those whose Whole (see below) was irretrievable upon return, as opposed to those who did not return at all.

(Saurum Nilea, AQn., trans. L.Shay 2656)

8//: the fall

The one mirror in the trailer had white flecks along the edge where a previous resident had stuck SLA decals. Norma regarded her hulking nakedness in the mirror. Her linebacker's shoulders with their bony stumps. Blue-black nipples. Rounded belly, dark fuzz below. The Bakersfield transformation had been more brutal than she'd thought. Every cell a white heat, and even now side effects too troublesome to mention. She turned away from the glass, dressed quickly. Pulled on her boots, fastened the long row of rivets, spat on the titanium caps and buffed them up against her jeans. Headed into the night, clenching her pelvic floor muscles as she always did. For luck.

It was a frozen January. She'd hoped, shivering alone in the trailer, that the worst of the season was over, and she knew it wasn't. Because always, through the toxic rain and the sleet, the icy wind and the sudden dark that fell like a trap, she could feel him near, smell him at the edge of an unbroken dream. The Guy. She headed south along the tracks, crossed the highway and kept walking until she got to a narrow canyon on the other side of the lagoon. A road wound its way through an abandoned office park dominated by a disused trailer factory, now home to nootropic drug labs, cage fighters, Karaoke bars, obscure churches and inexplicably smoldering piles of scattered debris. On the other side of the old Interstate, she could see the remains of a shopping center, a few cars picked to their bones at the edge of a vast parking lot.

Norma went in through the cavernous loading dock, fist-bumped the Samoan security detail. Past hotware peddlers, masseuses, barbers and filmmakers, then up four flights of stairs, and across a creaking catwalk that swung out over the dark sea of reclaimed workshops and arrested production lines. Laundry flapped. Lights winked at the horizon where cargo elevators inched up and down ferrying a new kind of middle man—cleaners, technicians, agents, engineers. This was the Factory.

A guilty silence hung over the place. High on the catwalk above the muted chaos Norma breathed in a familiar smell of sauerkraut and onions masked in frangipani oil. She stepped off and stood before a door, nodded to the Balinese stick puppet that swung tenuously from a nail, its costume faded to a deep sepia and its face rubbed off to a rough sheen. A muffled clang of metal plates and bars floated up from the gym far below, an underground boot camp for minders and militia and gladiators-for-hire—Cartel or Consortium. It didn't matter to them.

It didn't matter to her either. Her stomach growled and she followed her nose through the door into Una's bar. Edged past the scattered clientele without attracting any apparent attention, except for one pair of steroid-addled eyes that she steadfastly ignored. Biofluorescent candles glowed desultorily in the booths. An armed holoscreen above the bar replayed a Chargers game. On another, on the other side of the room, played a lingerie cooking show. She ordered a beer and watched a man in white shoes set up the Karaoke.

Little Barry swung down from his perch at the end of the bar, stepped up onto a cinder block, pulled her a beer, and shoved the mug in front of her. His flesh hung in folds over his eyes, one of which had a sideways cast to it. His wife, Una, ducked her head into the pass window behind the bar. She glared at Norma with chipped button eyes in a face red as rubber, a boiling ball of rage and defeat stirred by the rage and defeat she saw in her old man and could not cure. Little Barry had taken over the bar after winning a bet but for his sins it remained too high for him, everything beyond the reach of his little tattooed limbs so that he had to set up a row of cinderblocks beneath the bar and solder ladders to tracks along the walls to reach the hard liquor.

– Meatballs, said Norma. And potatoes.

Little Barry looked at her blankly and twiddled a finger in his ear. Flushing, she repeated the order, careful to move back into men's speech. He pulled a curser from behind his ear and jabbed at a scratched console, rocked to the pass window on his little midget legs and yelled out the order to Una anyway. It was more than a skewed sense of scale. Norma imagined the previous owner a Titan, the ground trembling beneath his hoary hooves. Everything in the bar larger-than-life. Dinner plates the size of Flyer wheels, beer mugs like buckets and cutlery like it came from a *Throne of Thorns* set. Maybe it had. Serrated edges on the knives caught the light like dragon teeth.

– You heard that? came a bellow from the other end of the bar too loud in the sodden hush. *Carna del burro* for the little lady. Taking a break from the cock du jour?

Norma turned to the speaker who along with two others seemed to have been formed from the darkness itself. Their eyes glowed a yolky yellow, consoles bobbing in their hands like little blue ghosts. Norma recognized them as some knuckle-dragging Roidheads from the gym below—Cartel goons, rogue militia. Again she told herself she didn't care. Not her lookout.

– *Halt den Mund!* snapped Una. Banging around in the stone-age kitchen.

Signed pictures of Lady Madonna and Blanket Jackson III and other obsolete celebrities gathered grease on a paneled wall. The man who'd yelled raised his glass to Norma. His forearm ballooned out cartoonishly, the skin stretched over muscles crawling with fresh ink. Overhead, she heard a drone hover and buzz away, its lights blazing through holes in the vaulted roof. The wing stumps at her shoulders had begun to burn. And also sometimes there was blood on her hands and she had no memory of how it got there.

She tried to focus on Una's greasy wall of fame. Blanket's bloated gaze. She raised her glass. Me and you, Blanket. We're the same. Here but not here. She felt it. Something about this place, Spill City, acting on her. Obliterating her.

Monstrous.

Norma stiffened, looked behind her but there was no one there. Mommy, she thought. That voice not just in her head but in her *Whole*. The voice becoming more insistent over time. Sometimes telling her to do... things. The voice, the blood on her hands. They were related somehow, part of the Configuration—the Whole—an enmeshed totality of interrelated perceptions shared between her and Mommy. But Norma was finding it harder to tell whether the voices came from outside or inside, from her or Mommy... or someone else. They seemed to be all three, making her fiddle with the bioswitch, look to see if anyone was there. And at the same time listen to that cramping of the dentata deep within her as if it were trying to tell her something that she had yet to understand. Mommy wanted in. It always wanted in, so what it amounted to was not knowing when Mommy was there and when it wasn't. Not knowing when the voices would speak and what they'd say. Norma was exhausted just thinking about it.

– Donkey meat? she said, blinking the men back into focus. One of their names was Augustine. She remembered now. His lantern jaw caught the white light from the Karaoke machine.

– 'Donkey meat?' mimicked Augustine. What planet are you from?

– Uranus, said a reedy voice behind her. Your head says hi.

Norma froze, looked sideways down the bar. The owner of the voice swung herself up onto a stool halfway along. Norma recognized the blue parka from the street urchin over whom she'd stumbled outside the payphone the morning after the night with Bunny. It seemed like a lifetime ago.

– *Schnitzel el gato,* said a reedy voice behind her. Better than no pussy at all, right boys?

Una's furious face reappeared in the pass window, glared at Augustine, softened when she saw the urchin, and said something in German to Little Barry, who ignored her. He ferried two Sisyphus-sized plates of battered meat to the men.

Little Barry said, So go to Miguel's. Spill-kill so fresh, it glows.

It was all true and it didn't matter. Bobcat or donkey or seafood a la nuke. The men tucked in, tightfisted and methodical. Elbows cocked and cheeks bulging, grease running down their chins and knuckles.

Along their hairless arms and around their pylon necks crawled a tangle of elaborate tattoos, the unfinished scrawl erased and rewritten in the flickering light. Every movement unveiling a new manifestation of the interchangeable motif—bird, snake, deity, demon. Any and all signs against the night.

The street kid watched the men eat, her face locked in a look of stagey revulsion. But for Norma the scene was both tender and obscene and almost arousing. Augustine had once been a Cartel lieutenant and liked to tell how he'd earned big bucks 'negotiating' with Texas kickers for access through their land. Hog wire and a tire iron his tools of the trade. Now cooling his heels in Spill City as an enforcer for a steroid syndicate. Just regular old beta males in feeding mode. Yet high above them in some towering edifice in another place, behind rice paper screens or Mahogany paneling, the alpha chewed at the wall—drooled and howled for more souls in this world.

Little Barry banged Norma's meal down in front of her, spilling grease. A mountain of dead mule sliding like the Sierra Nevada into a valley of rehydrated potatoes. Peaks and troughs, she thought, channeling Mommy, but Norma had lost her appetite. Even Augustine's lackey, a hook-nosed sentinel, had pushed away his plate. The third man with them looked ill and did not eat but sat hunched over his console, a flayed quality to him. Deluded bottom feeder, she thought, far from home and doomed to flounder and fail.

Norma caught the urchin eyeing the men's heaped plates from the depths of her tunneled hood. Her skin was pale, lucent eyes ringed in red. She held her beer in both hands. Her slim fingers misshapen from cold and godless commerce. She lifted the mug shakily to her lips like a chalice, took a swallow and spat it out across the bar.

– Jesus wept, LB, you been pulling horses' dicks again, yeah? This piss is the worst yet.

Norma's face began to crease and go peculiar. A giggle leapt from her lips and Little Barry's eye shot sideways which made her laugh even more.

– What you laughing at? said the midget with one hand on the bar, the other wielding a filthy rag.

And Norma, a little drunk, giggled below her breath, If I told you, would you know?

– Crazy Frau, said Barry, sloshing the rag over the counter where the kid had spat her beer. You wanna eat, kid? Una'll fix you something to take home.

The Karaoke surged. In the mirror behind the bar, Norma watched a lipless grocer sing, *'I would sell my soul for something true, someone like you.'*

A woman got up to dance. She bent her knees, pumped her arms back and forth like she was running in place. From the ceiling beams high overhead swung long cords dangling dim yellow bulbs. Their powers of illumination compromised by dirt and distance. The smoke and the din in the bar grew heady. Norma ordered another beer for her and for the urchin. Loops of speech and song wound around her like silk. She felt languorous in the false scents and the false light of the bio-candles. In her dream last night there had been dead wolves in the storm. Icicles clinging to a ragged tail. Around the carnage were footprints in concentric circles. Hehe, she'd laughed into the vicious wind, wringing from her hands vermillion drops that fell and froze.

The men—ratass rebels reduced to bare-knuckle vengeance, cast unsated glares in her direction. Augustine cracked his knuckles and called out to Little Barry, These eggs taste like your old lady laid 'em. I eat another bite, I'll bark.

– You mean barf, Tine, said his lackey.

The pink-eyed runt on the phone laughed but it turned into a wet cough and the lackey rounded pumpkin-sized biceps over his plate to shield it from the spray.

– What I said, said Augustine.

The lackey inserted a finger into his surgically enhanced nose while he thought about that.

– You all done? said the urchin to Augustine, pointing at his plate.

Augustine looked at her, unblinking. The lackey wiped his finger under the bar and his glazed eyes floated from Augustine to the urchin and back again.

– What's it to you? said Augustine.

– Give me your leftovers is what's it to me.

Augustine made a show of fiddling with his steak knife while he looked at the urchin in mock disbelief. His eyes, meeting those of the lackey's, left the urchin for less than a blink but it was long enough for Norma to register his intent.

– No, she said, getting to her feet at the exact moment that Augustine, with a sweet smile at Norma, flicked back his rawboned wrist and sent the knife arcing overhead, where, with a faint but distant thwang, it found purchase high in the dusty shadows. Norma lifted her face to the ceiling, aware that everyone was doing the same. Like spectators at a fireworks display, she thought, we wait for the flames to fall. Una too, her head twisted out from the pass window like a turtle from its shell, unleashing a torrent of Teutonic outrage.

– Jeez Louise, Augustine, said Little Barry, waving his old lady down. Them knives are the only ones we got.

– I give a shit, said Augustine, you'd be the first one I'd give it to.

Norma's shoulders burned. She flexed her shoulder blades, registered the crack of brittle bone beneath her jacket.

Augustine pushed his plate across to his lackey and smiled wolfishly at the urchin.

– If you bring back the knife, he said brightly to the urchin, like a nursery school teacher talking to a difficult child, you can have my slop. I'll even throw in a beer.

He stood in silhouette, a swelling at his groin. The urchin pulled her hood down over hair the color of dunes from a world Norma now saw only in her dreams. She took out her console, played the light over the vaulted ceiling laced with rows of rusted struts and smashed skylights.

– There, said the urchin. The synthetic rustle of her parka unleashed gooseflesh across the back of Norma's neck.

The knife, a dim speck in the beam of the console, hung from the frame of a skylight forty feet up.

– Show's over, said Little Barry. The wife'll give you something, kid. Go home. You too, Augustine.

Barely able to mask his relief, the lackey rose to leave. At a glance from Augustine he sat down again. The third man long gone.

– Show's not over, is it, said Augustine, pulling a billfold from his pocket. Show's never over, right kid?

– She'll never make it, said the lackey. Dude, let's go find us some whores.

– Make it twenty, said the kid, staring dreamily at the ceiling. And two beers.

– It's a deal. And if you, said Augustine, not even turning to look at the lackey he addressed, ever call me dude again, I'll strangle you in your sleep.

– No, said Norma, rummaging in her jacket. She found two tens, shoved them across to the kid with her plate of uneaten meatballs. Forget it. Here's your money.

The room lurched under her stool, a spinning blur of karaograms and white faces and dead candles. Norma shut her eyes to stop the spinning and when she opened them, the urchin had turned to her with a pinched and focused fury.

– The fuck is it to you? she said before a confused recognition surfaced on her baby face. Oh. Right. The crazy bitch talks to Mommy.

The urchin twiddled two fingers in the air. A hiss of laughter from Augustine, his eyes glittering. The lackey giggled like an echo, food caught in his teeth.

– The beams won't hold, said Norma. Dry rot and quake damage.

– Eat shit and die, said the urchin.

– Never thought I'd say it but Norma's right, said Little Barry. Those windows got blown out in the 2020 Burn, three Shakes since then—whole building is pulp.

– Norma? said the urchin. Her teeth were white and her eyes flashed like a summer storm. What the fuck kind of name is Norma?

– Call it off. Or you ain't welcome here no more, said Little Barry. It was an empty threat and they all knew it. Anyone with cash was welcome anywhere. This was America. Or had been.

Augustine ignored him, but there was now, in his chemically-augmented baritone, a creeping hint of retreat. You want to climb forty feet of Swiss cheese for my leftovers, bitch? You that hungry?

Una started to say something and Little Barry turned to her, made a throat-slitting motion with his hand.

– I haven't eaten in three days, said the urchin. For Neimen Van Aldren's leftovers I'd suck his dick if I could find it.

Van Aldren was the wheelchair-bound leader of Purple Rain, gone to ground. The men roared their appreciation. They bumped fists and grabbed their crotches and the ritual was complete. Bets were made and covered. Una crossed herself and slammed the pass window shut with a clatter. Norma put her head in her hands. So much hurt and harm and no one to explain it to her. Through a parting in the crowd she thought she saw a flash of pale hair, the sweep of a brim, but it was just a trick of the light. She lifted her head, narrowed her eyes at Augustine, and shook her head. He poked out his tongue and mouthed, Booh!

Norma drained her beer and stood up. She had a job to do, a horn to implant before the dentata tore a hole in her soul to match the one in her womb. Leave existentialist rubbernecking to the Slashes. Hell, the street urchin probably had some terminal illness anyway, or at least a major intestinal infection, bone disease or whatnot, and this was her last chance for a story to leave behind in Spill City, where stories, at least the kind you wanted to tell yourself, were in short supply.

An Avon lady's rendition of "Heart-Shaped Box" floated across the room. So now the urchin was doing something weird with her bitten index finger. She was tracing an aerial path, her midnight gaze turned inward so that she looked momentarily daft. Norma froze with her mug of beer halfway to the bar. She looked up to where the urchin's finger was pointing, an imaginary trajectory that ran from the bar, up the wall eight feet and across a series of vertical (y axis) and horizontal (x axis) bars and beams through a third dimension (z axis) that would theoretically, if not factually, move her toward the knife. The final dimension, (t) was time. Timing was everything. A beam that could hold for a second might not hold for two. A ledge that held because it was supported by an old gas pipe might be rendered unstable because of a customer coughing thirty seconds into the future, or the urchin's own progress might loosen a strut that would otherwise last another century. So there had to be a Plan B. And Norma could see exactly what the urchin was doing. It was taking a little while because the configuration had to include that contingency.

If Una's bar was a three-dimensional box and every route mapped out in the urchin's head was a thread going from the bar (a1) to the knife (b) and back again (a2), the total shape—the Whole—would look like a small mountain range. A mountain range as shaky and vulnerable as the Sierras had become. Because the whole of anything was always unequal to its parts. There were, by definition, limits on the accuracy with which the coordinates could be traced from an irretrievable beginning toward an unpredictable end. Just as you thought you knew your position on one axis, your position on the other became uncertain. The urchin had taken this into account—timing, speed, position, momentum. Yes. Norma knew that from an entirety of possible routes from a1 to b to a2, the urchin had seen and selected a number she could work with.

– A hundred says she makes it, said Norma. The bioswitch at her breast issued a warning. Even if Mommy couldn't see her, it registered that she wasn't where she should be. Norma yanked the jacket zipper up. Mommy could wait. She tossed more bills onto the pile. The men wiped spittle from their lips and the lackey stared sadly at Augustine staring at Norma. Something rippled across Augustine's lanterned jaw and receded. He reached into his pocket and took out a hundred, nudged the lackey. The lackey added his money to the pile.

The urchin drained her glass, banged it on the bar and pulled herself out pupa-like from the parka. As Norma suspected, she was ropy in the arms and strong across the chest, but her vertebrae poked beneath her T-shirt and her legs were long sticks in unflattering jeans. Norma kept her hands on her lap or as far from the bioswitch as possible, concentrating on keeping Mommy out.

The urchin clambered confidently off the stool and hoisted herself onto the bar. She swaggered past Norma, taking her time. Unleashing an unwashed funk, trampling Coasters and sending ashtrays flying. Some customers clapped. At the end of the bar, the urchin gestured for someone to pass her a stool. She placed it carefully on the bar top squared with the wall, mounted it, spat on her palms, and shimmied up some old pipes. Norma heard the Karaoke grow silent. The urchin stepped onto a triangulating strut and along a steel beam about thirty feet up. Halfway across she froze.

Knelt there on all fours for so long that Norma thought she'd changed her mind, but what she knew was that even if the urchin hadn't looked down, she'd thought about it and it had got to her. Long cold claw of night. The Silence. Pulling aside the membrane to give you a glimpse into the other side. What you saw there immobilized you at best, made you crazy at worst. And the only thing to beat it was pain which was why, in Norma, the VIPr had been programmed to generate pain under stress. Mommy could hit Norma's binary matrix with a sudden snap of it, that breath-stopping heart-starting bite of the dentata. Codename VIPr, Mommy said, just in case Norma missed the point: the disease was the cure. Point being that there was no such way Norma could reach the urchin from here, no way she could snap the kid out of it, get her moving again. So they waited. The men sniggered. Don't look down, thought Norma. Just don't.

For some inexplicable reason the karaoke started up again, this time with a song so ancient that even the barflies sucking on their teeth in the shadows looked confused. Norma saw on the screen that it was a song by Michael Jackson called "Billie Jean," the song jockey scratching his head and scrolling down his console trying to figure out how it got onto the set. Norma sniffed at a sudden change in the air currents, a ferrous chill as if a door had momentarily opened onto the night, but it was like a switch had been pressed in the urchin. The song, waveringly rendered by a chubby clerk, pulled the urchin to her feet and Norma took a step back, her stool crashing to the floor as she stretched her arms out like wings and watched the urchin do the same. Augustine burped. Little Barry crossed himself. The lackey said, Shit a brick.

The urchin shuffled along the beam a few more yards and toward the end grasped the lower ridge of a skylight that ran above it. She crossed onto a bisecting beam, feeling ahead with her leading sneaker before she placed it. Norma's mouth felt dry, her scalp tingled and her heart hammered in her throat. The urchin was lost in a swirling darkness, punctuated by sporadic flashes like lightning, from the console she carried in her teeth.

– Any of you dickasses want to help out with some light up here? she called out from between her teeth.

And as she spoke, the console fell from her mouth and dropped thirty feet to the ground. Everyone watched it float and sink through the darkness like a tropical fish and land with a clatter at Norma's feet.

– *Gott in Himmel*, came a sob from behind the pass door.

– Hellooooo... The reedy voice came down to them from the dark hole of night.

– Jeez Louise, said Little Barry. Una, where do we keep the flashlight?

But Augustine had already whipped a military issue LED torch from his backpack, its lens at right angles to the olive drab casing. Nimble as a ferret he hopped onto the bar and, holding the torch like a Handycam, pinned the tiny figure crawling along the beam in a hard tube of light.

And Norma knew then. The urchin was a climber. An artist. This was something previously attempted, who she was. She would have done it for nothing.

Norma's neck hurt from craning. Her eyes sidled across to Augustine. His wet lips hung in a loose grin and a forked vein pulsed at his brow. The urchin crawled along the rusted beam and cut back up to a supporting strut. Scraps of sacking and rope and plastic fluttering in the trembling white beam of light. Norma's hands felt clammy but when she looked down it was only perspiration and she wiped them on her jacket, felt Mommy's furious heat in the bioswitch at her breast. She ignored it because Mommy didn't know what it was like to walk amongst the Slashes, to actually walk amongst them, instead of just theorizing. Mommy didn't know, could not imagine the wolf prints in the snow.

– *Shauest nicht 'runter,* Norma heard Una hiss from behind the window. *Nieder schauen ist zu fallen.*

But the urchin did not look down. She crawled along another few feet then stopped just under where the blade pierced the wood beneath the skylight. Norma's arms hurt from holding them out. The urchin stood up, clutching a vertical pipe that disappeared into the blackness, its peeling white paint stark in the laser beam. She swatted at the knife and Norma swatted the air in mime, the shadow of her fingers clawing the wall. She saw with a grim clarity how fire had melted the material of the pipe and reformed the outer coating to a blistered and deceptive glaze. There was another pipe behind it, invisible in the darkness and distance, but Norma's brain knew it was there. The urchin could see it—a slim copper water pipe probably a hundred years old but intact.

Norma held her breath. The urchin scrabbled for the copper pipe and fumbled, grabbed the white electrical pipe in her panic. She cried out and swung, the pipe disintegrating in one hand as the other reached the knife and let it fall through her fingertips. Tiny drops of blood turned to mist. The fall of the child through forty feet of dark was also—other than the hollow pop of a young skull against a lower beam and the mocking ring of the blade hitting the floor—totally silent.

This is what it sounds like. The silence of the fall. Not so much as a howl or a sob. Just a terrible hole in the fabric of sound. Norma was kneeling beside the urchin's body without knowing how she got there. Augustine had dropped wide-legged onto the edge of the bar. Behind him Little Barry peered ashen-faced. The urchin's eyes were white slits and a dark bubble of blood teased out of her mouth with every shallow breath.

Witnesses would describe it as a single movement, how Norma picked up the steak knife from the floor, scooped the child into her arms, smashed the lackey's nose with her elbow, pinned Augustine's scrotum to the bar with the knife, grabbed the bet money and was gone. The men would later put it down to a trick of the light, random adrenal static, the way her form broke up and blurred, strung out in pieces across time and space, the way she seemed to be both here and dimly adumbrate, there.

She'd had her wings genetically clipped prior to arrival. That was standard because retractability was difficult to encode at the level of DNA. But the unplanned transformation in Bakersfield caused a slight regression in the RNA, enabling a mutation of the gene. Her brain remembered the wings as tusks and summoned them under duress. They burned uselessly now beneath the jacket, bone tearing through flesh. She contemplated running back to the trailer, but even at the speeds she was capable of, there would be no time and it would attract attention. The urchin's face was petal-white, jammy matter leaking from her skull. Norma could hear a Coaster rocketing up from TJ. It would not stop. All but invisible in the jacket, she was at the tracks in time to jump the train with the urchin clutched to her breast, her boots and one arm locked to the fuselage, the wind whipping a web of blood across the urchin's stricken face. Her eyes flew open, racing clouds twinned in their un-perceiving depths. Closed again. Norma jumped off at the camping grounds and landed in a pulsing crouch to lessen the impact on the child. She stuck to the shadows, veered past the twins spooning in their army blanket beneath the old pine. The usual scatter of trailers had pulled into the park under the cover of darkness and the old leasing building was ringed in lumpy shadows, the disembodied glow of cigarettes, the tang of opiates, wieners. A guitar strummed sadly. The ocean moaned.

Norma got to the Cheyenne, fumbled the door open and lay the urchin down on her bed, wondering if she should call Mommy for permission, just this once, and knowing there wasn't time. Bitch'd say no anyway—retrievals were strictly forbidden. Norma awkwardly pushed the urchin's tawny hair off her face. On the inside of the young wrist ran a track of old scars. The switch around Norma's neck twinged another warning. She yanked on the cord and howled.

But it was the age of the child, the way Norma could smell the unspoiled life on her skin, the smell if not of innocence then of something too close to it to call. She composed herself and tried to think, she would not count the lengthening seconds between the child's shallow pants. It was possible that the lower beam may have broken the urchin's fall, minimizing the number of broken bones and ruptured organs, but what was clear to Norma was that her brain was boiling from the impact and that it would soon be awash in blood. She brought her trembling fist to the child's face and extended her index finger a hair's breadth from the tiny nose. She withdrew her hand, closed her eyes and poked her tongue out. Norma's tongue ended in a fine point and the slightly curved tip flushed a deep lapis blue. She leaned over the body, the pliant bones and filthy hair. And then her jaw hinged open and she convulsed. Her tongue unfurled, the blue tip a raw and pulsing blue. It hurt like hell, not just the burning blue tip, but also the muscle itself, from deep in her throat, like being caught on a meat hook. She flailed. Her viscera spasmed. She tasted her own tissue, tears stung her eyes and mucus filled her passages so she couldn't breathe. The tongue elongated, sought the tip of the urchin's nose and found it. Touched it. The urchin's eyes flew open. Locked onto Norma's. Norma's tongue snaked into the child's right nostril. Norma choked on her own cry, her head shaking back and forth and her hair whipping at her face. The tongue wormed its way past the urchin's throat, through the optical cortex and into her brain. Bounded chaos all around, looming ganglia and quivering lobes, starry meninges and sunken medulla, all drowning in blood, a red surge lapping at the disappearing shoreline until Norma's tongue began to lick it clean, every inch, traversing the bloody world, monstrously and a little shyly, like the leviathan of old.

9//: crumbs

It took Gene longer than he thought it would to get over Gloria. Longer than he thought it could. It was impossible not to see her there beside him in the truck, impossible *not* to hear her snore from the back seat. He couldn't get the cold-water smell of her pelt out of his nostrils, carried it with him wherever he went. About the diamonds, he'd called the fence in Albuquerque, got a west coast contact and exchanged two of the rocks for some cash that he deposited into Jesse's bank account for his leg operation. He headed for the coast, sometimes thought of going back to Bakersfield to check on the farm, if Major Buzz had not got his hands on it already. Gene squirmed in the driver's seat, knew there was some point he was missing, and just kept the setting sun ahead of him so he wouldn't worry too much about what he'd left behind. Gloria. He finally got to San Miguel and stayed at the old Mission there, Mission Arcángel. He even thought of becoming a monk. Spending the rest of your days in a little cell, sleeping beneath a scratchy blanket and keeping all your worldly shit in a shoebox.

He kept Gloria's teeth on a leather bracelet around his left wrist. He took the self-guided tour of the Mission. He stood for hours looking at the statue of St. Michael defeating the devil. The Archangel's wings spread out like an albatross. From the sixteenth century or something.

Dry rot and peeling paint, but the fire in the Archangel's eyes undimmed. Same friars dusted it every day, basketball player wearing scuffed Nikes that stuck out the bottom of his robes. Gene made friends with the gravedigger who said, Whatever you do don't call them monks. He taught Gene how to cheat at Klondike. Gene shot hoops with the Nike monk.

On his last day there, the gravedigger was lighting the candles in the chapel with matches from a matchbook with a familiar logo on the cover.

– Let me see those, said Gene.

The gravedigger passed the matchbook to him. It was worn to a soft silky finish, torn on one corner, exposing the root of the matches like rotten gums. The worn logo said The Trap, and had the address in Bakersfield down by the Greyhound terminal. There were only two matches left.

– You been there? said the old man.

Gene nodded and said, You?

The gravedigger shook his head, Never even been to Bakersfield.

Gene swallowed. He said, Then where'd you get these?

– A tall drink of water came through here a couple weeks ago. Maybe three. Father Bryce put her in the retreat. She looked like she'd been in the ring. All cut up and such. SLA whore maybe. I found the matches in her room after she left along with some other comtrash and such.

When Gene just kept staring at the matches, the gravedigger shrugged and said, Take them. I got more.

And he lit the rest of the candles with a lighter decorated with the San Miguel insignia—a holographic image of the Archangel in all his wrath. Gene pocketed the matchbook, trying to think about the sort of woman that would patronize a place like the Trap. The ones that he remembered from there, the ones that were actually women, tended to be skinny haunted locals, desperate for a way out and too scared to find it for themselves. This one, the woman the gravedigger described, didn't sound like that.

Gene left another one of the diamonds in the collection box and got back in the Chevy that afternoon. He headed south. He stopped for a beer in Pasa Robles, breakfast at a rough-clad farmhouse in Atascadero. A steely sun hung over churned-up fields and charred poles. There was a Winnebago in the yard and the old couple offered him lodging in return for helping to rebuild the barn and some of the outhouses, said both their sons were in Tajikistan. He thought about it for a minute until they told him that a woman had stayed there for a couple of nights and helped them rig the battery to the tractor. Gene said, What woman?

The old man looked at his wife, and rubbed his eyes with the heels of his hands. He described the stranger as unarmed, with dark hair, denim shirt and combat boots. He said she was a help to them, but left some garbage behind they couldn't use and maybe Gene could. It was all they could offer him. They showed the broken tech she left behind in the trailer, all sorts of consoles and such, even an ancient BlackBerry. Gene said he could stay but a day, helped the couple drag sheeting and tarps and corrugated steel to the charred barn frame. Worked all day in the niggardly light nailing up the scrap into some semblance of a shelter for their shell-shocked mule and orphaned calf, and left at nightfall with a piece of the farmer's cornbread and a chunk of dried beef. The broken comtrash on the seat beside him in the Chevy and the old worn book of matches in his pocket. He took the matchbook out and opened it for the hundredth time. Read the word scrawled in childish letters on the inside. 'NORMa', the first syllable in capitals like the 'a' had been an afterthought.

In bed, the barmaid who worked in a tavern in Cayucos told him about how the weekend past Louis the Lisp and a tall quiet chick with a left-handed hustle got into some pretty dirty dancing. When Gene asked the barmaid if she'd caught the woman's name she said she thought it was Nora. At a rib joint in Nipomo, the walls of which were branded with the logos of long-gone ranchers, Gene heard talk about the woman who came in on her own and ate an appetizer of oak-smoked ribs, a twenty ounce Spencer steak complete with baked potato and sour cream, a basket of garlic bread, and two bowls of ice cream, strawberry and chocolate. When she was standing at the cash register beneath a set of mounted antlers, the Chumash busboy took her picture. The woman said she'd give him twenty bucks if he'd delete it. When he said what if he didn't she just looked at him with eyes like a bear trap. So he said thirty and passed her his console and she gave him his thirty. He said the only reason that he wanted her picture was because of where she was standing beneath the antlers—the angle made it look like she had wings. That's how tall she was.

Gene found the kid's phone in some weeds behind the restroom, crushed as if beneath a heavy heel. He picked up clues all along the way, crumbs she'd left seemingly for him, although he knew it just seemed that way. A broken pair of sunglasses from a Motel 6 in Santa Margarita. At the train station restroom in Grover City, a button from her denim shirt. At each spot the description was more or less the same—that of a tall chick said she was from San Luis Obispo, or was it San Simeon? Some bitch with legs to here got run out of Guadalupe for trying that left-handed hustle on the wrong Gringo, busted out of a Lompoc clinic; caught *in flagrante* with the sheriff of Mission Hills. Mona, Nara, Roma, Nora, Norma.

Gradually, without him noticing, his grief over Gloria receded and was replaced by the strange connection he felt with this girl called Nora or Norma, always one step ahead of him. He pictured her in flight, wings spread like antlers, like bones. And gradually Gloria returned to him in spirit and in a form or sorts. There she was, not only in the front seat of the Chevy but beside him on the old roads beneath the riven freeways, tail wagging at the scent of a clue or a crumb. She looked a little worse for wear, Gloria did, what with the mess on her head and her matted pelt, but her amber eyes burned yet, fierce and knowing and that's all that mattered.

It got too expensive to run the Chevy, so he traded it in Santa Barbara, by which time he'd collected a few more matchboxes she'd left behind, a silver dollar and a wooden crucifix, two arrowheads, some empty pillboxes, a mascara wand, breath mints and a bunch of broken ancient phones, dead consoles. He didn't think he'd have it in him to leave the Chevy behind, but he did. Took the forty dollars the dealer gave him and mailed it up to the gravedigger at San Miguel. Gene talked about Norma with Gloria, showed her the latest clue he'd picked up and together they worried over the dark road warrior in flight—from what? And to what?

He tried to figure out what it was that drew him to the mysterious drifter. Why her? Beyond a matchbook from a place they'd both frequented once, oblivious of the other, what was the connection? He told himself that even if he hadn't been following her, the places she had been were the places he'd be drawn to anyway. Edge-of-life bars, dusty multiplexes and gaming joints. It occurred to him that she, too, could be looking for someone. If so the connection was complete, an ouroboros—Gene, Norma, and another—or an arrow of time leaving randomness in its wake.

He visited a defunct playhouse outside of Santa Barbara where there had been a sighting. Backstage was a room strewn with mattresses, women sprawled around drinking beer and watching television. Gene stood in the doorway, his shoulders squeezed between the frame. By now he had cooties, a rash behind his knees, had lost twenty pounds. The women were actors, a troupe mostly related to each other, sisters and cousins, grandmothers and aunts. They were Chumash performance artists, acted on their flesh. A woman called Rita lifted an embroidered blouse to show Gene a pattern of cuneiform-like scars on her belly, cuts made by a trusted other. A girl sat over the exposed hump of a crippled woman, carving crimson code in the already scarified skin. Another with cropped white hair bent over the spread thighs of a teenage girl, whittled with a bamboo knife on the soft flesh. Droplets quivered on the cuts like liquid fire. The air in the room rusty with blood.

They passed him a beer. He asked if they'd seen her, a tall traveler with dark hair and fighting eyes.

– She came here, said the white-haired woman bent over the girl.

Rita said how Norma had drunk with them and shared a meal and had wanted them to cut her.

The white-haired woman lifted her wizened face, a drop of blood at the corner of her mouth. She said something to Gene in a language he couldn't understand.

– She says there was no need to cut that one, translated Rita. The tall one.

When Gene asked why, the woman said, Because her whole body was a wound.

Wherever he went it was the same. She fought like a man, howled like a wolf, and was gone by morning. No one had actually spoken to her, called out her name. So Gene did. Norma, he said in his sleep, waking up with the sound dying on his lips, the sheets wet and sometimes the pillow.

Norma.

Even if he could have bought a new car (and put up with bandits and bridges fallen like Godzilla across the road), traveling by train was simpler than by road and safer. But mainly he took the train because she had. He figured that out. The challenge was to try and go where she went, get off where she did. Gather the pieces of her to himself so that by the time he finally saw her sleeping off a binge on the Surfliner just outside of LA he knew that he'd found her, his broken angel, that this was the one who had kept him going all these weeks, given him something to live for, and he owed her for that. He'd always owe her for that.

Norma.

10//: arrow

– Mommy?

A head gash sticky to the touch was the sole evidence of her fall. Raye could hear the ocean, so she must be on the beach. In a trailer, holy fiery fuck. Through the narrow doorway of the bedroom annex she could see a high-assed woman bent over a console at the kitchen sick. It was nothing Raye hadn't seen before but there was a glow to this one, the one they called crazy. Even before Una's, Raye had seen her raving in alleys and vandalized payphones. Mommy this and mommy that. Pecking at a BlackBerry beneath a strawberry sky. Steel-capped boots washed in spume. Roger that, yeah, over and fucking out.

Mommy?

The woman's voice was not really a voice. Raye sat up, or tried to. Fell back down on the blood-soaked pillow and let out a sob, the pain in her head epic. The woman lowered the console and turned around to face her. Then she straightened to a great height. Raye felt a booming in her ears, saw black at the edge of her vision and felt nailed to the bed. Where the woman's eyes should be was sticky smoke. Raye focused on a crack in the wall and bunched the bedspread in her fists. If she could live through this. The woman came in holding some pills. There was a jerkiness to her movements and a predatory hunch to her stance.

Raye recoiled and scrambled to the edge of the bed as the woman got closer. In her clawed and bloody hand was Raye's console, with a cracked screen now, the casing dented. It had been a gift from Raye's father. She wouldn't cry. The woman said something that Raye couldn't understand, not because the words were foreign but because they sounded damp and at the wrong speed and Raye's hands flew to her ears. There was blood on the woman's face and on her clothes but no wounds that Raye could see. So the blood must be her own. Raye puked, into a bowl already half filled with puke by the side of the bed. The woman took the slops into the bathroom and Raye, who had also peed herself, grabbed her parka and half-jumped, half-fell off the bed. The room spun but she clenched her teeth and managed not to be sick again. She slid into her shoes, shuffled past the door of the bathroom where the woman was rummaging for something, and made it soundlessly out the door. Landed badly on the path and limped toward the beach trying, as she always did, to see the whole of things, the big picture. If one minute could get you to the next, then another could get you to the one after that. But you had to have a Plan B. She would call her old man and he would come for her. She could see it clear as day. She scrambled under the rail and down the litter-strewn ridge onto the beach, the ruins of Swami's to the North and behind it the dead Onofre reactors and in her mind she could see him coming to get her, her father, not like he was now but the way he could have been in another time and place, coming to meet her on the beach. To take her home.

Alaxenoesis: (n) A basic resequencing protocol whereby an embodied presence (the host) can change its appearance/gender/species at will, but typically limited, in Telefraxis (see below) to a delimited and finite category of being.

(Saurum Nilea, AQn., trans. L.Shay 2656)

11//: dichotomy

Norma woke two days later arched and gasping. Entombed in sagging mattress. On the floor of the room lay the urchin's bloody pillow. A roach kicked in a sticky glass by the bed.

The tide was in, the ocean roared. Her alien vision illuminated the trailer and brought its sad objects into sharp red relief, the tossed clothes and open closet, the take-out boxes and crushed cans. There was no sign of the urchin. It came slowly back to Norma, the way the body had sprawled on the bed with its new-milk skin, the feathery lashes dark on the fighting face. Norma cursed herself but not with any conviction. She'd felt something besides her watching the girl's struggle for life, felt something that compelled Norma to revive her, despite the risks.

Who to ask? Retrievals were forbidden. From or beyond the brink. Her instructions had been clear on that point. But was it a retrieval? The urchin was strong—she may have recovered on her own, Norma told herself unconvincingly. In which case, the effect of Norma's probing tongue on the child's young brain was probably minimal. Possibly negligible.

Deep within her false womb the dentata pulsed, sinking in its nucleotide claws, less a weapon of destruction than an instrument of self-slaughter. She felt it as a cosmic parasite taking up malignant digs, a passenger in her body, like a cure that barely kept you alive or a disease that never let you die. Norma grinned sourly up at the ceiling. Between a rock and a hard place. One of Mommy's favorite expressions. She wondered again why the loneliness hadn't killed her, began to understand that it never would. It was like the story, another one of Mommy's, about the man—always a man—who kept halving the distance to his destination so that he never arrived. Norma beat the mattress with her hands. Leaving bloody prints.

12//: fixed.2

Auntie had a devil puppet she used to scare them with. When they did something bad, she fetched it from whereever she kept it, put it on her hand, and made it tell them what they did wrong and what their punishment was going to be. The puppet wore a flapping and threadbare red dress and one of its horns was chipped. Flat black wooden eyes and a mouth full of pointy teeth. One day soon after their mother got sick, Gene and Jesse were over at Auntie's house playing with Ty while their father was at work. Gene was in the fifth grade, and Jesse was in eighth grade and Ty doing but his second of three tours of the seventh. The second floor of the old house smelled like mac and cheese and aftershave. Ty had a couple of bowls in his room and then must have gone and found the devil puppet because the next thing he had it on his hand, and lunged at Gene who could only take so much of those flat black eyes and that empty flapping dress. Gene took off. Ty followed him cackling, waving the thing with its terrible fluttering red dress, Gene in a world of terror, no longer associating the puppet with Ty or anyone else. It had taken on a life of its own, the devil on the loose and for his sins was after Gene and Gene alone, through the hallways and down the stairs of that old house, sputtering TVs in empty rooms, a game of checkers on a table, kittens mewling. Jesse cocooned in headphones somewhere.

Behind Gene, the world reduced to Ty's thundering pre-loved cowboy boots and a flapping red dress, until he found a door in the kitchen and stumbled down into the cellar. There he huddled in the cinderblock dark, his T-shirt soaked with sweat and pee in his jockeys, the devil on the other side of that damn door but not for long. Just when he thought he'd perish with terror, the hurricane door opened from the outside and there was Jesse, dangling wires and out of breath.

– Come on outa there, Gene. Fuck Ty, that's enough.

Chubby bed-wetter Gene on all fours up the stairs into the light on legs like jelly and there behind Jesse, Ty with his fist still stuck up the devil's ass, his face crazed with glee, thundering down toward them from the porch.

– That's enough Ty, said Jesse, again holding out two hands as if to stop what even Gene knew could not be stopped, and Gene saw Auntie on the porch hunched over her ashtray and the shelled peas and she knew it too, motionless except for a strange smile tugging at her lips. Gene just running, his chest on fire, the dampness chafing at his crotch. Jesse saw the Chevy first, yelled out a warning. Their father fishtailing down the hill to collect his sons, the setting sun and a cloud of dirt and exhaust training behind. Gene's vision cleared and he tried to stop but could not and felt both pushed and pulled toward the oncoming truck. Their old man's open mouth dangled a Pall Mall, one arm flailing out the open window and soundlessly yelling something. Jesse was nearly six feet tall already and county hundred-yard dash champion for his age, caught up to Gene like the Roadrunner, and catapulted Gene out of the path of the truck. Gene face-planted in the dirt, his nose making the sound of a squashed tomato as it broke, Jesse on top of him. Tangled around each other, the brothers looked up to where Ty had become airborne. His legs did a Wile E. Coyote in the air with the devil still clamped to his hand. He made no sound or none that Gene could hear as he impacted the hood of the Chevy and bounced off it and again off the windscreen like one of those bouncing balls on the old Looney Tunes cartoons, the ones in black and white.

Jesse broke three ribs and cracked his wrist and had to sit out his first season on the football team. The six months Ty spent in the hospital and year in rehab added prescription painkillers to his list of dependencies. It wasn't just the cracked pelvis and subsequent erectile issues, or the nerve damage to his face (the wiper had gone through his cheek) or the way his shoulder would dislocate in the night and he'd wake up screaming. At first Ty asked did they find the devil puppet but they never did, and after a while he stopped asking. Jesse never asked Gene what he did with it, and Gene never told him. He never told anyone.

Two winters later their mother had died and the old man was off somewhere trying to find work and Jesse and Ty had gone up North to live on the rez and it was just Gene alone for his sins with Auntie and Uncle in that house by the woods that doesn't exist anymore, Gene woke up one morning to see footprints in the snow. Wolves. On the roofs of the scattered houses, satellite dishes turned their cratered faces to a sky white and as ragged as the old baby blanket he still kept under his mattress. The wolf prints ringed the house in concentric circles and Gene knelt down and took off his glove. He wiggled his fingers and shivered remembering the devil puppet. Then he put his bare hand over the paw print in the snow and kept it there until it burned with the cold and he smiled, knowing for the first time in years that he was no longer alone.

13//: zumba apocalypse

– Bunny?

– Who's this?

– Bunny. It's me.

– I don't know a me.

– Me. Norma. Give me a break.

– I don't know a Norma.

Norma was at the Boardroom, a bar across the highway in the old marketplace. On one side of the Boardroom was a 7-Eleven with a line in Nayarit Mescal. At any hour of the day or night, the shadows of the extended Armenian family who earned eight dollars an hour to run it for its Cartel owners, could be seen moving around the dimly lit store or eating their meals from a cloth laid over the freezers. On the other side of the Boardroom was a laundromat with a smashed window webbed together by silicon spray and an empty place that had once been Mears Realty, yellowed property listings taped to the inside of the windows. From those portions of the Boardroom window that weren't smeared, cracked or taped up with notices and stickers Norma could see the food trucks and tents of the 101 markets, a patchwork sea of tarps and garbage bags taped and stapled together against the rain. The outside of the Boardroom was painted with a faded mural depicting crashing surf and bikini-ed sun bakers. Inside was small and narrow and wrapped around a central counter pictographed with initials, cocks and balls, cigarette burns. Console booths ran along one wall.

– Bunny. Come on.

Norma's signal would fry the newer satellite consoles, but older, off-radar places like the Boardroom had managed to jack into the obsolete fibre optic network. This type of network could withstand her alien frequency for short bursts before any other user became aware of the drain on the system, and a short burst was all she needed. A holo of Bunny's face floated up from the console. He was down at World Wide Wang, the Border Town joint he danced at, doing his make-up for the show. His face was a lurid mask of orange-tinted pancake.

– I'm sorry I ran out on you again, Norma said. I was hungry.

– You're always hungry.

Bunny's face on the projection looked frail and rigid. He was concentrating with a frightening intensity on gluing his left eyelash to his eye. He lit a cigarette with shaking hands while the glue dried. A pot-bellied drinker weaved past Norma on his way to the restroom. When he moved out of range, Norma tried again but Bunny cut in.

– Don't flatter yourself. I don't expect you not to run off—you been hungry and running ever since I've known you. But slipping fuck money into my wallet? Who do you think you are?

Bunny's false eyelash fluttered from his left eye like an exotic bird.

– That wasn't—

The bartender looked over at her. She lowered her voice.

– You wouldn't have taken it if I'd offered.

– I'll never take it. Doesn't matter who offers, and Earth to Norma, I get a lot of offers. In case you think you're the only game in town. God help me. I dance for cash. I drive for cash, when I can get it. But I'll never fuck for it.

– Don't flatter yourself, Norma said with a smile. It wasn't for you. I thought you could have used it for your family. The picture in the wallet.

Bunny fixed Norma with a stony gaze. The cheap holo imbued his pancaked face with a purple glow. What's my family to you?

Norma just shook her head. Nothing, she said.

– Good. Let's keep it that way.

Norma began to tell Bunny what happened at Una's, how the urchin fell, and how Norma ended up with the winnings, everything except for the bit about taking her home and probing her brain. Bunny picked up his cigarette and with the other adjusted his right eyelash.

– I don't want to know. You just keep your ill-gotten gains to yourself. Buy yourself some new tech. New clothes. Everything about you is broken, messed up. You're a throwback. I don't know how you get any action at all.

Norma shot a sidelong glance at the clock in the corner of the screen, already five minutes. The transmission was beginning to degrade but she knew she had to let Bunny get it out of his system, and then he'd be okay. He usually was.

– I'd really like to see your show, she said.

– You said that before.

– Bunny?

Again that manicured man-hand shot up in her face. Bunny's nails were varnished in stars and stripes.

– Look. Some Grimey hit the deck at Una's you won some cash and skewered some lunk's left nut to the formica. Another night in the city, said Bunny. So what? Main thing is they're not happy about it and say you owe them four hundred bucks.

Norma exhaled. Spill City was like that. A vast and complex system of connections that came together at nodal points like Bunny. She waited. Patience was in her program.

– How did you know? said Norma.

– That guy you de-balled, his bitch comes down here sometimes. Big suckass with a nose to match. He reckons his man Augustine—that's his name, right—had a boner for you once. Still does.

Bunny killed his butt and stretched his thin lips in a gap-toothed smile. You always knew how to empty a room, girl. Just saying.

Norma did not try to smile back.

– He had it coming. Her pitch sounded all wrong. She cleared her throat and said it again an octave higher.

– I wouldn't worry too much about it, said Bunny with an

unconvincingly indifferent shrug. He'll probably go for the Grimey. Men like that never pick on those their own size.

An ad cut into the transmission. There was an Independence Day party scheduled for out on the lagoon, fireworks and DJs. Norma clenched her jaw and waited for the ad to finish—she was running out of time.

– What'd you call her?

– She's a Grimey-punk, said Bunny. Or was. Little Barry said she's dead. So like I said, I wouldn't worry about it.

Norma whispered, She's not dead.

She said it to convince herself as much as Mommy, just in case it was listening because Norma was sure, almost positive that, the urchin, when Norma had started to probe her brain, had not been quite dead.

– Where do I find her, Bunny? The money belongs to her. Not me. Not Augustine.

Bunny blotted the last blobs of glue on his eye with his sparkly fingernail and began to adjust his wig.

– She got the knife down, hissed Norma. The seconds unreeled in the corner of the screen. That's what the odds were on.

– Seems to be some kind of communication breakdown here, girl. Maybe they were your odds. But for men like that it's never on if a woman falls but just on how hard. That's what the odds were on. Game over, Norma. Move on.

Bunny took a sideways look at her through the clouds of smoke and talc in the dressing room miles away at the old border town.

– You're not getting creep on me are you? It's Independence Day soon, he said, wiggling his stars and stripes nails. Go celebrate. Clear your head.

– Please. Tell me where to find her, said Norma.

With an exaggerated weariness that pixelated the holo, made his face rematerialize with a greenish tinge, Bunny said, You think you can stop this. You think Spill City will be any different after you've gone? Or her or me? That you can make a difference? That anyone can? It's like saying you can make a difference to a storm, or a rainbow or a Zumba apocalypse.

– Zombie.

– Clearly you've never tried Zumba, said Bunny. Brushed his throat with powder.

– Anything you want, said Norma. Name it.

Bunny peered at Norma across the ether. Serious?

He raised his eyes to fleetingly and inexactly meet hers across virtual space, and in them was a question she could not answer, not with there being any chance of Mommy listening. Not to mention a roomful of Boardroom barflies. Norma pushed her tangled hair out of her face so he could see her eyes and in them he seemed to find some kind of answer.

– Fine. Come and see my show. Tomorrow, the next night. But soon.

Norma said, That's it?

– And let me buy you a drink, he said. You look like you could use one.

She watched him smooth down his Wonder Whoa-Man curls, flutter his lashes as if getting into character. Check out his left and right profile in front of the glass. He pulled a pout that made her belly quiver, and then he sighed. Turned back into Bunny again.

– It's a deal, she said.

He said something else but his voice came across at the wrong speed and one of his eyes looked like it was melting. Norma fiddled with the dial but it was too late. The transmission cut out and she was alone again.

January 27th was Independence Day. That was what the Consortium called it and once a year it funded parties and fireworks and food trucks and wiener roasts. Good old-fashioned fun was what they called it. Others called it mob rule. Federalists called it the Day of Reckoning and they marched beneath banners that said, Cut Off the Head and the Body Will Die. There were prayers and riots and rallies to be returned to the Union. For the SLA it was a day of Commemoration and they marched beneath flickering holos of Niemen Van Aldren, whose plot to assassinate the president, and the subsequent cover-up by Sacramento finally earned the state its independence. For its sins.

As Norma moved from the Boardroom through the market she saw something. A black hat atop hair the color of lightning. It was just a flash through the food trucks and stalls, the jugglers and buskers and fortune tellers, a flash of old gold between a Starbucks converted into a Franciscan shrine and a pizza place that delivered its iconic pies via chopper to Consortium execs across the Zone. And then he was gone—she was so sure it was the Guy that she stopped in the crowd like a piece of driftwood caught on a rock down a rapids. She scanned the flow for the hat, for the pale face, but it was gone.

Yet she'd seen him. Felt him. Here in Spill City. And that was enough.

Her heart still pounding with unreasonable hope, feeling swollen in her parts and desperate for relief, she went back to the trailer park. The twins cringed beneath the pine. Its candelabra branches caught the glare of the tail lights. The boy twin lay with his head in his sister's lap, licked his lips in his sleep. Norma stuffed a couple of dollars into the coffee can and the girl blindly drew the string toward her, the can scraping on the packed earth. The boy giggled in his sleep.

– Pray, pray, hissed the girl twin.

Norma's boots stomped down the path to the trailer, past an Airstream that seemed to float on a lake of neon. Her arousal flattened substantially, she ate her supper of beans from a can and stared at the roll of money that belonged to the urchin. The Grimey. Whatever. Bunny teased her about getting clucky or creepy, but it wasn't that. It wasn't the child's youth alone. It was her innocence that Norma had been compelled to save, and deep down, not in the dentata but in a place deeper even than that, Norma knew that wasn't in her program. Something had changed. She finished her supper of beans and tortillas at the little table beneath the salt and sand-coated window. She poured the dregs of her coffee into the sink, looked askance at the unmade bed where the indentation left by the small body of the urchin had been overlaid with her own. Norma got up and pulled the sheets off the bed. She went once more out in the fray, pushed through the crowds to the Laundromat. She laundered the sheets and watched them tumble in the drier while she replayed the urchin's defiant fall at Una's over and over in her mind. And her own.

The last time she'd seen Gene there had been a fight. Over this thing inside of her that sought out rot, sought out filth, she knew not why. It was behind the Viper Room—no relation to the thing inside her,

Mommy said, hehehe—and there was this bloodless stiff in the trunk of a stripped-down taxi, a girl slit from ass to tit some months ago and all bled-out. An unholy stink. Stiff was wearing one hell of a pair of shoes. Manolos with six inch heels. Norma wrested them from the girl's bloated, cracked feet and waved them at him, said they were the right size and all. Gene had objected.

– What? Norma was a purring, raging ball of lust and defiance in the drunken dawn. They're my size. Do you know how hard it is to find a decent size nine?

– Take them off, said Gene. He swayed at the mouth of the alleyway in a slice of yellow dawn. They were both still very high.

– But the jacket, she said. That didn't belong to me either. What makes that alright, and this not?

She pulled it off and waved it clumsily at him like a wounded Toreador.

– No one died in the the jacket, Gene said.

– What if the guy who wore it killed people, which he probably did? she said, fighting an unexpectedly encroaching sobriety.

– Not that way, said Gene, yet refusing to look at the thing in the trunk. That is serious bad mojo and you don't want any part of it.

– You mean you, said Norma. You don't want any part of it. Maybe you don't want any part of me either?

That's how she saw him now, the breeze pulling at his shirt. His staunch legs and great shoulders quietly squared. She'd met her match. She flung the jacket at him and pulled off her boots, pulled on the dead girl's Manolos and teetered in them. Matter yet wobbled off the leather straps but they'd clean up okay. Gene flinched, his face went pale. Her lips curled cruelly. She thought it was the shoes, but he wasn't looking at her feet, no. He was staring at her hands. Norma looked down and watched the blood ooze from between her fingers, from under her nails, from the creases and pores, not enough to fall, but enough to stain and redden the very dawn it seemed, enough to send Gene backing out of the alleyway.

– It happens, she'd yelled after him. Under stress.

The blood on her hands. She wanted to explain it to him but couldn't. He turned around and he never came back.

PART II

MEDIA REZ

It is said that after the sun killed Kali I8 and everything else in the 236-110 system, I8 became pure sentience. A brain without a world. Throughout the eons and with the aid of configuration probes and cosmic lensing protocol, I8 attained its desire to be a Viewpoint and nothing more. After ascertaining that it was not alone in the Entirety and that the horned visitor of distant memory did or had existed and could therefore be returned to it, Kali I8 could think of nothing else. It scoped the Entirety (beings of a higher order almost impossible to find) and found a world on which there existed horned beings similar to the One Who Fled. Not identical, but similar. Kali I8's brain was not what it was. Its memory leaked. None of the horned beasts on this faraway planet were as magnificent as the First Being was in Kali I8's memory, but it calculated the probability of finding a tempero-parietal match (axon density being a strong indicator of altruism and compassion in the human brain) and the odds were good. To prepare for the mission, I8 studied the blue planet and its dominant life form, which it nicknamed Slash, after the leading symbol across both its genetic and binary codes.

I8 loved a good nickname.

(Fascicle 437 Nilea AQn., trans. L.Shay 2656)

14//: d-cup

Raye needed money for the old man's meds. He was getting wiggy again, cocking his head at voices only he could hear. Foul mouths, hidden and haunting, telling him to do bad things like pull someone's heart right out of their chest. Things like that. Raye knew it wasn't him talking, but the sickness, a flat black look in his eye that found her somehow and saw her, and a smirk she did not recognize and wanted to slap right off his face, slap the old man back into being, the way he was, the way things used to be. He said the meds made him feel like someone else, and she knew he threw them away when he thought she wasn't looking, and the pills cost money and were hard to get on any market, even down at the army cordons. Even at the Factory. She all but killed herself the other night at Una's, trying to win enough for a week's supply of Thorazine, but wherever those winnings were now, they could stay there. Raye shivered at the thought of those freaks and she would have nothing more to do with them, not Augustine, not that wall-eyed midget Barry, or that crazy bitch talks to her Mommy and could probably use some Thorazine herself.

Survival sex is what the social worker called it. Above Raye loomed the ruins of the Interstate—on the other side there had been a construction camp near a sprawling barrio, plenty of contractors there hot for a girl-woman hand job, buy her some time while she thought about her next move. She forgot the social worker's name, and at least he never asked for a hand job or anything else, she'll give him that, not even when she offered just out of pure, self-destructive force of habit. Raye moved through the barrio, shuttered for the afternoon siesta, a skeletal cat blinked at her from the basket of a Flyer. The barrio supplied day labor for the building project and provided the contractors with amenities like food, bars and sex. Even a chapel if they needed one and Raye gave the dark three-walled shrine erected from a shipping container and smelling like the inside of an unwashed neck, a wide berth. A tamale truck was parked in an alleyway. Raye made for the soft music and light that pulsed from the galley. A bald woman poked her head out.

– Where you been, baby girl?

– Hey D-Cup, how's tricks?

– I'm on late weekends at PB, the DJ said.

– I know. I looked for you last week.

– You okay, girl? You don't look—

– I fell, said Raye. Nothing major.

– Come on down, child, got some chillin' beats. Independence Day tomorrow. You going to the party?

The smell of beans and corn wafted from the truck and something else, the pungent bite of the liquid silver D-Cup drank for her cancer.

– Maybe I will.

– Maybe you want breakfast first?

D-Cup dangled smooth brown arms out of the window. Blue veins ridged the back of her hands; her nails were soft and rotten.

– Maybe later. I'm coming back this way. You feeling good?

D-Cup nodded and winked, clapped a silver-ringed hand over her one remaining breast.

– D-Cup feels good. Never better, b-girl.

Raye said, I gotta go. See how the, um, building is coming along. They nearly finished?

D-Cup pursed her lips and shook her head with a jangle of silver. No, no. Muchacha, building stopped six months ago maybe more. Cartel got cold feet again. Paying construction cock all gone.

D-Cup wiggled brown fingers empty of cash. Stay a while, baby girl. I give you breakfast.

Raye peered into the afternoon glare at the raw expanse of the cleared land. In the middle of the scorched earth loomed a cluster of condos, their windows boarded up and stucco bubbled and warped.

– Whoever won this turf war's not planting flags, she said.

– They don't need to, said D-Cup and passed a hand over her smooth skull. No fly zone, child. Real bad mojo.

D-Cup had, while talking, wrapped some leftovers in a box, and shoved them at Raye's chest. She pointed back the way Raye came with a long finger as straight and severe as an arrow, and Raye felt the eyes of the DJ on her the whole time until she was safely through the barrio, and the one time Raye did turn to wave, D-Cup was still there with her arms folded over her chopped-up self, behind her the cluster of the empty condos dark and redolent of ruin.

Horn: i (n) A word of European (Earth) origin meaning a pointed projection of skin typically on the head of animals, consisting of a covering of keratin and other proteins surrounding a core of living bone. Horns usually have a curved or spiral shape, can be ridged, fluted or in the case of some species a branched extension of the skull. In most species only the males have horns. Accessed Nilea AQt. 437 ii. (n) Slash slang for sexually attractive male. ii. (v). To butt or gore; to thrust oneself into the consciousness of another, iii. to argue or disagree, iv. to sexually penetrate or cuckold.

(Saurum Nilea, AQn., trans. L.Shay 2656)

15//: purple rain

– So many men, so little time, Mommy said.

Behind the shopping strip was a building site, always a contractor there in need of slick monster cooch. The shopping strip just off of the old Interstate was frozen, like so much else, in a state of arrested remodeling, the shops boarded up and the whole complex ringed in razor wire. The rain fell heavier and Norma, with an itch to scratch, moved toward a neon sign in the shape of a piece of pie. Metal heels rang faintly behind her. She smiled. Pushed open a glass door and stepped dripping into a small L-shaped diner, cracked leatherette booths and a scuffed counter. The waitress wore sneakers and was missing a front tooth. She kept her back to the stove, nervously fussed with the coffee pot as Norma made her way to the counter. She kept peering at the darkening plate glass behind Norma, as if there was someone out there.

– Boo! Norma said.

The waitress started and flushed and moved a piece of gum across the shattered window of her smile.

The diner, in a disused shopping strip off of Interstate 5, was empty except for some soldiers and their girls, who tottered back and forth between the table and the bathroom brushing the tips of their noses with tattooed knuckles. Norma sat at the counter and watched the waitress take the coffee off the stove and turn around with the pot, her eyes flicking to a point behind Norma, outside at the edge of the deserted parking lot puddled with rain and pulped newspapers, a plastic shopping bag lynched to a tree branch.

– There was a guy—the waitress said, looking out the window.

Norma obligingly swung around to look into the dim parking lot. Nothing but some reclaimed squad cars and a souped-up hummer.

– He's gone now.

– What was he like? said Norma keeping her voice even.

– Western-looking? Crazy lizard boots? Some Mexican trash hat pulled over his face so you couldn't see his eyes.

Norma blew on her coffee. Waited till her voice felt steady enough to speak.

– It's okay, she said. He'll be back.

She knew it to be true. She'd felt him nearer than ever since the urchin had fled her trailer leaving her with nothing but a bloodstained pillow and a pile of ill-gotten gains on the fold-out table. Norma didn't touch the money. She couldn't. And there was that ringing of metal heels on the road behind her now, not always but sometimes, stopping when she stopped, and that smell, like ghosted matches, in her nostrils, not always but often enough to lead her to places like this.

The waitress refilled her cup and Norma sipped and inhaled the sweet peppery smell. The waitress made good coffee. Strong but not bitter. Norma ordered eggs and tried to relax.

– I'm Honey, said the waitress. I seen you here before?

Norma looked up. In the mirror behind the counter she saw the reflection of her face with its dark hair wild around the coarse features, sharp bones. Something out of true between the left side of her face and the right. Like if Picasso and James Joyce had a love child, Bunny had told her once and she had taken it as a compliment. Honey shifted a little against the counter, stuck her hip out to one side. Her breasts strained against her blouse. She didn't seem so tense anymore.

– I forget, said Norma. Maybe.

She put her coffee down and sniffed that old matchbox smell again, vaguely sulphuric, and with it that want, that tightness between her legs.

Honey sniffed too. Was the cook using rancid fat again? Was that it? She looked askance at the soldiers, doing crank in the bathrooms, probably.

– Smells like more rain, said Honey.

– Well, said Norma.

Honey said, Last time it rained like this was in the previous century. Turned the Valley into an inland sea.

– No kidding.

Honey smiled her broken smile.

– Islands out on the estuary sank, no one ever saw them again. I learnt about it at night school. My mom sits with my kids.

Norma said, I smell mud. Earth. Lots of it. How's that new construction site going? She bent her head vaguely in the direction of the parking lot. Over the other side of the shopping center?

The dentata had begun to throb. She felt so horny she could cry, yes but for what, and for whom?

– Um, said Honey. Must have been a good while since you've been out here. The company pulled out about almost a year ago now. The development was meant to attract rich Mexicans and Easterners to the area now the army's got the secessionists under control but Sacramento reneged on the contract. So they had to ditch it.

– What's there now?

– Just empty lots, I'm thinking. And some condos all boarded up. Models for selling off to investors. Nothing in them but 'possums and snakes. Rain brings out the snakes. And the varmints.

Honey shivered coyly. Across the sad expanse of scarred and peeling tables and chairs, one of the soldiers' girls giggled.

– Well butter my butt, said a soldier. And call me a biscuit. Varmints, y'all.

Norma put her cup down. She rolled out her shoulders beneath her combat jacket and the arachnor weave stretched and breathed with her breaths. The soldier aimed his finger at her, pulled the trigger. Norma acted shot. Then she went back to her coffee.

– You get that jacket here? said Honey. It looks kind of military. You military?

– Not as such, said Norma.

– I don't want to know, Honey said.

– Bingo, said Norma.

Honey reached across the counter, suggestively pinched the material on Norma's sleeve. She leaned back and licked her lips.

– Waterproof all's that matters, she said.

– Bulletproof can't hurt, said Norma in a voice loud enough for the soldiers to hear. She pushed shakily back from the counter. I may as well go check on that development.

– You don't want to go there, said Honey. Like I said, nothing but varmints and—

– And what? Said the soldier.

Norma looked across at him.

– Purple Rain, said Honey. She ain't from around here, she called across to the soldier. Can't you tell?

– A lot of folks here not where they ought to be, said the soldier standing up, his eyes webbed in crimson, a silver trail of mucus running from his nose.

Norma looked from Honey to the soldier. Look, I know about Purple Rain. Purple, pink. Doesn't make any difference.

– Well, it might, said Honey, affronted. This new breed, you don't want to know. After the company bailed, the development got took over by squatters and rebels and the Cartels, they just sent in the Rain and bam. The waitress smacked her hand against the counter harder than she needed to. Norma flinched. Had the place to themselves after that, real bad mojo.

– Not so bad, said the soldier. Those kids that went missing was just Mexicans.

Honey turned back to Norma, You ever wonder why it is that pure evil in a man is a heck of a lot easier to come by than pure good?

Norma shook her head and smiled. No mystery, she said. Just some failure in the system.

– It's not a failure, said the soldier, swaying in his filthy fatigues. It's God. He made us that way.

Honey drew her lips across her gappy smile. So there's that, she said.

– Amen, said Norma. shaking her head. She put change on the

counter and stood up, lifted her nose to the air again, her nostrils a quiver.

Honey folded her arms beneath her breasts.

– Happy Independence Day, she said.

Norma pushed through the diner door and moved in a reckless diagonal across the wet parking lot and toward the construction site. She licked her lips. Behind her she heard the muffled ring of metal heels but when she turned around there was no one there. She felt her stomach go liquid, her knees jellied for a moment, and when she clenched her jaw, her mouth filled with blood. She turned around and kept walking. So many men, so little time, Mommy had warned. Another ridiculous saying, spat out across the cosmos. Unable to digest its subtleties, Mommy vomited out language in great chunks of plasma. You don't know what you've got till it's gone, it cried. Norma so horny she could cry. It was difficult to think of anything else. Deep within her the dentata throbbed. Had it ever been different? Her body never without a passenger, back seat driver that given time, would take the wheel, Mommy warned or promised, depending on which way you looked at it. Norma bowed her head under a sticky rain, pulled up the collar on her jacket. The palm trees flailed at the edge of the road glittering with traffic. She walked quickly past the park, past an amenities building with a hip-high hole hewn in the wall between the third and fourth stall. Norma shivered at the memory. Shadowy forms humped squealing shopping carts toward a rusty barbecue grill.

Not everyone goes the distance, Mommy had said. Who knows why? There had been other horn hunters. You don't get a second chance. The risk of Slash contamination is a factor, and if that happens, you can't stay and you can't go home. You become what Mommy called *aporafex*—a being without passage. Humans thought of them as ghosts, but they were more than that. Aporafex—or Aporafeks—were the impasse, impossible to go through, get behind, walk around. Concealing nothing and meaning nothing but themselves.

– You could view the Slash as a species of Aporafex, said Mommy. Just a string of meaningless code unable to pass on. A dead end.

A dead end road with a barn at the end of it, some hellhole Norma increasingly saw in her dreams.

The road swung to the left up the hill, then hair-pinned under the old interstate. Norma would try to control her nerves. The anticipation made her salivate. She stayed at the edge of the road which looked slightly luminous in the lifting rain. She was a professional, a horn hunter, an eternity of training and planning behind this mission. Which she would complete. That was enough. It was enough to be on this zigzag road in the near dark, the sky a milky bowl above her and the smell of roses, yes roses, in the air, as she approached the camp. She hadn't felt the headache today. After all, Mommy was as far away as the sun.

Norma headed over to the barrio that had sprung up between the strip and the housing development, past a shuttered tamale truck blasting reggae. Again she lifted her nose to the prevailing wind, smelled stale beans and corn and something else, the subterranean smell that had led her to this place. Again she heard footsteps behind her, a faint jangle of spurs—who was leading who? Beyond the barrio, the abandoned building site huddled beneath a the faint glitter of drones and neon vapor trails against a lurid cloak of fuchsia dusk.

Flanks trembling, Norma turned down a packed dirt path lined with mostly empty shanties and rusted trucks. A dog came out of a hole in the fence, glanced at a point just behind her and then darted back from where it came, its tail hooked around its rump. The dirt road opened up onto a field that had been cleared for construction. From the field loomed a giant and decaying Centurion Real Estate holo depicting scenes of luxury living. *Live the dream!* it said. Norma crossed the marshy ground, stepping onto new blacktop that looked obsidian in the rain. Her boots were coated in silt. A yellow disc of moon leered at the horizon. Saplings in black bags expired beside rampant weed. There, a lone cement truck was parked in a driveway, but Honey was right. No contractors. And no sign of anyone else, squatters, freedom fighters or rebels. Maybe the army had done its job for once. On either side stretched lot after empty lot. The rain became chilly and Norma zipped up her jacket. Her shadow extended before her like a scalpel, leaning toward the development, and behind her skulked that shadowless form immersed in distance. The contractors had gone, but something else was here in their place, something that called to her or acted on her, pushed or pulled, it was no longer possible to know which.

The singing in her genitals had abated, joined by a burning sensation in her shoulders. It was as if the dentata carved a road between the hunter and the hunted and it was down this road she felt herself pushed or pulled, it was impossible to say, like trying to sleep past a bad dream. It was all a bad dream, had been ever since she'd come to this land. A place that, like all the ones before it, now seemed to have come to her and become the only place, a world of hurt and harm and no one to explain it to her. No one to tell her what to do, nothing to guide her but her sense of smell, chance encounters like the one with Honey—good leading to bad the way the subject led to the object and always a bad verb in between.

The signpost said Serenity Ave. She advanced past a hydrant and clump of wire sprouting from the turf. Sewage pipes lay in piles. Stop signs loomed sepulchral at regular intervals. Peace Place, Plenty Row. At the mouth of a curved drive huddled a plaster wishing well beneath the weight of SLA graffiti—Separate or Die Trying. Sanskrit and stenciled Obamas and 'Missing' posters and the President having her boobs milked by the devil and dried up bouquets and deflated balloons and broken frames littering the ground around the wishing well. She advanced along the curved lights, lit by solar lamps on one side that multiplied her shadow into groups of three, the foremost chased by the one behind it and the one behind that, the whole thing beginning again and again, like a relay race in hell. Finally she got to a large yellow home at the apex of the curved drive. By this time her nose had begun to bleed and a headache had bloomed behind her temple. The home was built above a double garage. Three stories high, multiple balconies, its many windows smashed or boarded over and blackened with graffiti.

Norma put her face to a crack in the garage door through which she saw a green Prius in the gloom. Its hatch was dented and one window was webbed with gaffer tape. An entrance portico was set off the street to the side of the house. She approached it and sniffed some more. The lock on the front door was broken but it was padlocked and chained from the inside and beneath it spilled a foul smell. Norma braced herself and pushed on the door with both hands and the steel chains inside screeched and popped and the door gave way with a ragged sigh of relief. She brushed her hands off, rolled out the tightness from her shoulders, and stepped in.

From the vast foyer a curved stairway led to the dark upper chambers, like something in a Raymond Chandler novel—there had been a time when she couldn't get enough of noir. She heard an animal drop from some height and skitter out a side window. A pallid column of light spilled down from the broken skylight onto the floor in the center of the foyer, dust motes swirling. Against the walls were piled turds and strips of stained toilet paper.

Norma wandered into the adjoining rooms, keeping a wide berth of the column of light in case she stepped into it and it sucked her up who knows where. She looked through a doorway into a screening room. Ripped upholstery. Behind the tiered rows a smashed window into the projection area. She went back into the foyer, into a kitchen. Downlighting and caesar-stone serving island. Doorless cupboards home now to rats and birds and something else. Something besides time had passed by here. She could smell it. Always the smell that drew her on, and behind her the guy, his footfall silent now and his shadowless form extended like a whip.

There was a formal dining room with a large broken window webbed in gaffer tape through which she could see the muddy field and the shanty town from which she'd come. Darkness was falling and the freeway to the east was already streaked in red, to the west, the nothingness of the ocean. She stood in the arched entrance to the room. Mold and other matter bloomed on the Spanish silk walls. The stench was ungodly. Jack Daniel's cans were strewn across the rug. Norma's shoulders had begun to burn, not a good sign. A heavy Mexican sideboard stood along the wall beside the table and above that a wrought iron candelabra, webbed and dusty. The huge oaken table was littered with Domino's boxes and Slurpee cups. The carver was overturned, damask upholstery slashed, and across the window the drapes were cindered and fallen. The only sound beneath the beating of her heart the buzzing of the flies.

She watched a recently overturned can of Coke drip onto the rug. The soda had burned a white scar on the surface of the table. She watched it drip. Beneath the buzzing of the fly came a faint and frantic whimper. A shallow pant beneath her own. The flesh on her arms coldly prickling. She swayed, dizzy from the smell of shit and death and rotten Meatlovers. Her eyes shifted focus to a place on the rug beyond the dripping Coke. She squatted down beneath the table and looked into the mote-blown eyes of a Golden Labrador chained to the table. Its eyes and nostrils clogged with pus. A tongue lolled at her, immense and black. Tufted hair grew in patches across its ribs and hindquarters which were caked in blood and feces. It lay on its side with its front paws stretched out and crossed, both its back legs broken. It met her gaze in mute agony and she held its eyes until they slid away as if satisfied with their arrangement. She reached across then and enclosed the cracked leather of its muzzle in one hand and watched its soul jump and flee from this place.

So many holes in the whole, and no possibility of self-defense. Norma's throat constricted and she waited for her vision to clear. She'd seen worse but the night was still young. She stood up and cracked her knuckles. She went out of the dining room and back into the foyer. She climbed the central staircase that curved into the second story. The landing went all the way around, and overlooked the foyer. The rail had been kicked away in places and she kept to the walls, past room after empty room. At a rectangular alcove off the central hallway she stopped to look through a window down at the backyard. A monster Yucca grew against a graffitied fence. A moon had begun to rise over the swimming pool, splintered cabana and a trampoline rusted on its side. California dreaming.

She flexed her shoulders. The pain radiated into her neck. She let it. It was the one thing that seemed to shut Mommy up. If Mommy's voice in Norma's head was a control mechanism by which Mommy could sidestep any subjective obstacles in Norma that might arise during the mission, the burning deep in the blade of her shoulders was one subjective obstacle equal to Mommy. Equal to the Whole.

An intolerable smell pulsed from some benighted wing, repulsed her and called to her at the same time. She went on along the edge of the landing, froze when she heard a sound outside the last door. There was a wet gurgle and sounds of dragging. She tried the door, which was locked. She ripped it off its hinges with a grunt and let it fall just inside the threshold. The stench in the room hit her like a detonation. The snarl of scarified flesh at her shoulders knifed and she didn't even try and roll it out. She crooked her right arm across her nose and mouth and stepped in. Something hissed and scuttled beyond her range of vision. Moonlight and freeway light sliced into the gloom from between the slats of the blinds on the windows that flanked a four poster bed to which a man was cuffed at wrists and ankles. Norma's vision calibrated for the gloom, registered the man's ankle bone gleaming white through flesh split by the cuffs. The big toe on his right foot a gooey stump.

Norma ripped down the blinds. Something screamed. The man's shirt opened across his torso like a curtain. Viscera spilled across the bed from an incision mid-body, one glistening rope of intestine gnawed by an opossum that leered at her from the bed, its daft eye rounded in wary ecstasy. Like the Labrador, the man was still alive, but when his eyes moved to fix on Norma's they couldn't hold. Across his mouth a stretch of duct tape, and from between his legs an unholy stink.

Norma peeled off the duct tape. Balled it in her hands and dropped it on the rug. On the dresser beside the bed was the man's wallet, keys and a cracked cellphone attached to a charger. She picked up the wallet, emptied of all but a business glyph that had the Centurion Realty holo on it and the man's name, Randy Mears, Sales Agent. She put the wallet down and picked up the cell; an image pixelated on its screen of the dog downstairs, ghosted like a memory.

– Nice jacket, said a gravelly voice behind her. You get that here?

The man on the bed let out a wet sob. Norma wheeled around. At the doorway stood a bear-haired prophet astride the busted door and at his side, a white kid in overalls aiming a dented two-shot.

– This old thing? said Norma. Nah. I got it on a bar stool down at the Belly Up. Some ordinance technician from China Lake never came back.

At the strange sound of her voice—like wind rushing through a city of steel—the opossums fled with a scrape of claws and gnash of teeth. She didn't bother to change registers, the pain in her shoulders all she could think about. The tusks rent her skin beneath the arachnor weave, warm blood running down her back and breasts. The tusks at her shoulders were a contact-effect—they blossomed in the presence of a void in the heart of man so ravening that it still took her breath away.

The old prophet eyes widened and he smiled beatifically. However they began, Purple Rain were now, like everything else in Spill City, subsidized by the Cartels—as payment for doing their dirty work got the time and space to do plenty of their own. The boy flicked his tongue at her. She flicked hers back, a flash of blue.

– Gaaaaaaah, she said.

In his widening eyes she saw a shutter flash behind her. She wheeled and wrenched a camera from the wall beside the bed. Then she was both in the air and on the ground at the same time. Bristling, her eyes electric, she advanced on the boy, his first shot bouncing off her jacket like birds off a screen door. He misfired his second round partly into his pappy's ass, so that the old man had begun to buckle, screaming, by the time she stove in the boy's throat with her gel-armor elbow, rammed her fist into his face. She caught the old man from behind, slid her arms under his sweaty pits and with one hand at the back of his neck, snapped his spine before he could even reach for the reproduction Bowie Knife he'd swapped for three packets of penicillin from a Coahuila whorehouse.

The preacher let out a sound that began as a prayer but ended as a silent exhalation as his body drifted away from him. Norma let him drop back down onto the floor where he lay on the threshold, helpless to move his shoes from the spreading pool of blood that issued from the nose and staring eyes of his son, who was also his nephew. She sniffed her fingers and then moved back to the bed. She bent over the property agent.

– What was your dog's name? she said, returning to human registers so that the property agent could understand her, because to speak the name of the beloved at death's door is to garland the soul.

Pink tears fanned from his eyes. In his final moments he found the strength to hold the angel's gaze so that she could see the Labrador as he saw him, fleet and golden, understand the animal's loyalty, how Mears had failed him, living first out of the car and then, when the rains came, squatted in one of the model homes—he'd had copies made of the master keys—but only till spring, he reassured the dog. Only till spring.

– Jose, he said without sound—his vocal cords no longer functioning—but Norma read the shape of the sacred syllables on his lips and said them back to him.

He nodded once, feebly, a string of matter bubbled from his mouth and he was gone.

*

Everything was happening at once. From where he'd dropped onto the threshold, the ex-preacher peered up at the woman bent over the bed. The world darkened and was rent into bright filaments between which he could see the woman step away from the property agent. He heard the name of the dead dog and it filled him with terror. The woman closed Mears's eyes—poor homeless bastard squatting on Cartel turf. Her hair was wild about her face, her broad shoulders were pulled up into two bony protrusions poking through nifty slits in her jacket—some strange material, drew the darkness into itself. The silver flecks of light across his vision were getting heavier now and slower and he tasted them on his tongue, the bitter flakes, neither solid or liquid. The ex-preacher wished then that things had been different with him, would have liked to have been back in the seminary library up in Portland across from that little lesbian bookstore. At his customary table by the fire, poring over the books and folios. His favorite article, the one about what it was like to be a bat.

The article dealt with what the novitiate, as he'd been then, had seen as the central paradox of human existence: language. Words for things. The article's position was that you could not know what it was like to be one thing unless you were that thing, by which time you would no longer be you to know it. You could not know what it was like to be a bat, or a lesbian, or a property agent unless you were that entity, and not you. Cue metaphor. Without recourse to metaphor, the article argued, language-bound humans can know very little. And the way the novitiate had seen it then, and still saw it, what made metaphor the most human figure of speech, was that it expressed the quest for one thing—the knowledge of death without being dead.

Bread for money, pearls for eyes, ice for hate, fire for love, night for death. Two unlike objects identical at the point of comparison. One thing used to represent, or displace something else. Thus not being humanly capable of knowing what it is to be a bat, we can only humanly, through language, suggest what it is *like to be a bat.* To die and not to die.

Lying there adrift from his own body, he wished he could discuss this with the archangel or whoever she was. How the human need for metaphor is a metaphor in itself of the desire to be reborn as another. His eyes, which were the only thing he could move now, dimly saw that his sneakers were still in what remained of his son's face. But it was getting harder, through the falling snow, to see the beautiful being with her great ridged shoulders like broken wings, or tusks or some such thing, and he wanted to explain to her that broken wings were a metaphor for the idea of a fallen angel, or whatever she was. He would have liked to ask her. Her teeth were barred and snarling and there were whorls of smoke where her eyes had been. She sniffed and gnashed at the air and her wings snapped and she reached under the mattress and pulled out the sports bag of cash they'd kept there, his and the boy's takings from the book they'd made on how long it would take a debowelled man to die. It passed the time. The boy was a whizz with the footage. Editing and what not. Of course they'd sell it later on as a complete download. Lots of preproduction interest in that. Well, they hadn't counted on the varmints but that was just a lucky accident, or fate, as he would have called it in his divinity days, and it upped the ante to tell the truth. The ex-preacher watched the Being rummage through the bag with a befouled claw. Turned furnace eyes on him before opening the window and letting the world back in, the howl of a distant train. She shouldered the bag and stepped toward him, crunching on the camera and was astride him and he willed his hands to clutch at her, pull her down, but his body was no longer his own. She left him there slack and shitting, but still alive, so that when a yellow-eyed guy in lizard boots came to call, it would still be within the preacher's capacity to wish (he would by then be done with prayer) that he'd never been born at all.

16//: apart

The twins pressed against each other. The rain dropped off the pine needles and ran unheeded into their blind eyes. They lifted damp muzzles to the air as she passed and the boy wrinkled his nose at the rank booty concealed on her person. *Mommy*, he whispered. The titanium toes and heels on her boots were smeared with matter. Her hair plastered to her neck with vermillion goo, the chill rain drenching her jeans. Like a plodding Golem she passed, nodded to the slumbering Ecoist, and trudged down the path to her trailer. The ocean was a smudgy mass behind her, pink-tinged cloud lowering. She stumbled into the Cheyenne. Her eyes burnt and her jaw ached from clenching. Night had not yet fled from the trailer, thank Elvis for small mercies. She fumbled for the lamp beside the bed. Sobbed through her gritted teeth, spraying spit and tears, pulling the blood money out of her clothing and onto the bed. The pile grew on the sheets. Furiously undressing as she went. The tusks on her shoulders were not quite retracted, pale bone gleamed through the ripped flesh. Naked, she stared at the money. She looked down at her legs, smeared with filth. Held bloody hands up to her face. She would wash. She would.

17//: crock

The sour smell of the stew was everywhere. Through the glass lid of the Crock-Pot, dim chunks of something Raye couldn't identify nestled among the pale fingers of potato and wobbly meat. The kitchen upstairs was in virtual darkness, lit only by the blue glow of the screen in the next room. Raye liked the kitchen at night. It was like a museum display. After the rostered KP group had cleaned up and everyone had gone to their bunks or the TV or out into the night, the kitchen sat empty and peaceful. The cool dull expanse of counter top and the throbbing refrigerator and all the sponges put away and the dish towels in the hamper. Everything in order, accounted for, under control. The stew cooling under glass (what was that smell, leeks?), The Crock-Pot all clean on the outside and switched off, shiny and silent on the mat.

Raye felt funny. Maybe it was the knock on the head, yeah. The swelling had gone down and the gash was scabbing over. She had always been a quick healer but this was something else. Maybe some vitamin in the leeks. One of the older guys claimed they put hormones in the food to keep them sterile, but Raye didn't know about that. Maybe the big woman in the trailer had slipped her a Mickey. Kryptonite or something. Raye smiled down at the glass lid. Brought a sore finger up to her lips. Her jaw hurt. Her eyes tunneled into the stew, through the massed meat, into the crystalline unit cells of the base, and out through the cord fed by the generator downstairs. Raye blinked, thought she might throw up again. Her skin tingled, not all the time, but in waves. And almost a headache almost all the time. She tasted smells on the back of her throat and in the roots of her hair, along with a delicacy in the gut. Her farts smelled different. She felt a little stiff across the back and shoulders.

But the rest of her was fly. Superfly. She cast a leery eye at the Crock-Pot and moved out of the kitchen.

She thought of going out to the Independence Day party out on the Lagoon. Every year she thought of it and never went. It was probably lame. But staying home alone on Independence Day eating shelter food and watching lame TV was lame too. In the games room, the other lamos were watching Independence Day party footage on the TV. They were mostly Grimeys like her, gutter punks. They sprawled in various contortions (heads propped up at right angles to flattened bodies, legs draped over chair legs or spiraled around each other; hands shoved where the sun don't shine). Their eyes glued to the screen. The coffee table was strewn with phones, blister packs, ashtrays, headphones and consoles. The window to the street was permanently locked, the ventilators working hard to suck the smell out of the air—tobacco and body stink and those fucking leeks. Some drop-ins worked their consoles at a table under the window. Flyers hung on brackets on the wall. She would get herself one of those someday. She would practice her climbing again, get fit, go back to busking. Safer than turning tricks, who'd have thunk? The camera's panoptic eye whirred in the corner—Curly, the guard downstairs, watching the celebrations on his console next to the monitors. Raye felt jumpy. She *should* be on the streets, not in this damn pup tent. She should be trying to find a cure for her father. Why else would she even be here, in this damn hell hole? Spill City? More like ill city. Her father was ill. Michael Jackson came to her in a dream and told her. He'd lunged at her, his lipsticked skull inches from hers and he'd said, Beat it.

Raye made herself sit down on a threadbare recliner, hugged her knees. Everything smelled of leeks, she decided, moving to a stool. She had a lump in her throat. Would a boyfriend help? She didn't usually think about such things, had no time for it. She was almost too lonely to live, almost all the time. Her hands twitched on her knees. She couldn't make them stop. She could use a Coke. But she was broke. Those dickwads had taken bets on her to fall at Una's and she'd proven them wrong (or right, same difference). She could sure use some of that money now.

She felt something dig in her pocket and pulled out the social worker's card. Wiped her nose with the back of her hand. Randy Mears, BsC Psych (Pennsylvania). BSW (Wisconsin). Dip Ed. The social worker was a while ago. He had a dog, showed her the picture, dumb blond mutt. Maybe she should give him another call. He tried to be helpful, suggested her dad join a group, one of those circle jerks where people stood up and wept with their back to the group or crawled under a chair and everyone pretended it was normal. Waaah. My mommy hit me. Waah, when my puppy died I was so strung out on skag that I cut him open and ate his heart. Waah, Michael Jackson told me to do it. Beat it till it bleeds.

He was all right, Randy Whatsit. He sidelined as a property agent, he admitted to her once. Just to make ends meet. She should give him a call.

18//: technicality

– Norma?

Norma fumbled blindly for the broken phone among the piled debris of the side table. Was it morning?

– How are we today? said Mommy across the crackles.

– Never better, Norma said, or tried to. She sank back against the pillows with an elbow over her eyes, Mommy in her ear.

– You sound a little worse for wear, said Mommy. Green around the gills, under the weather, thumbs sideways. Time is against us.

Soggy rags of noise flapped up from the beach, music and muffled shouting from a party on the eroded lifeguard stand. The throb of a beat box.

– What time is it? Norma thickly said.

– Have you found it? The lost horn?

– He's here, said Norma. I can feel him.

– Here? croaked the voice in her head. Where?

– Close, said Norma, opening one eye and pulling aside the curtain. Night fleeing from the shore. I've seen him. Felt him.

– What happened? croaked Mommy.

– At the construction site? Nothing. This realtor was at the wrong place at the wrong time. Ended up with a starring role in some snuff film. Couple of Purple Rain players needed to be put out of their misery. No big deal.

Norma sat up in bed and crossed her legs. Sat hunched in the cold. She groped for the military jacket and once it was on, Mommy's voice was easier to take.

The child, said Mommy so icily that Norma shivered. She felt it in her ear first, cold finger of night, and then in her womb, the finger-fucking pain, gasped as the cogshare link broke wide open and Mommy was in. The broken console tore from Norma's hand, crashed against the trailer wall.

– Retrievals are forbidden, said the roar in her head. There are side effects. Especially with a child.

– Technically speaking, she wasn't dead, rasped Norma. So technically speaking I didn't retrieve her.

– She's a threat now, said Mommy. Technically speaking. Its voice had a gluey quality like oatmeal, yet piercing at the same time, both invasive and abject. Like taking a backwards shit.

– To who?

– To the mission, said Mommy. To us.

– You mean to you.

– Your will is mine. Deal with it, said Mommy.

And then it was gone. Pulled out with more visceral violence than it had to. Norma collapsed back onto the sheets, barely conscious, floating and sinking at the same time. She dreamt, half awake and half sleeping of the Guy, rail thin and hung like a horse, woke up with Gene's name on her lips and her fist in her mouth. But she wasn't awake, she was still dreaming, and in the dream she pulled the fist out from her mouth and in it, in her closed hand, something throbbed and she opened it and flew away, the wrong one, she said, but it came out as 'the long one,' and this time she'd woken up for real, laughing as she came, hehe.

19//: wang

Norma waited on the highway, pressed into the chain link fence. A rattling recombo approached and she jumped onto the back, a leaping twilight shadow jagged as negative lightning. She sat cramped among the leaking buckets and jangling rakes and flew off forty miles south at the old border unable to get the reek of manure and rust out of her nostrils.

Where a wall had once divided the two countries was now just the vast and vaporous glow of the check point gauntlet that spread the length of a couple of football fields either side of San Vicente Boulevard—at either pole the usual sprawl of dog pits, tavernas, clinics, chapels, flight schools, body mod parlors, pool halls, 'employment' agencies, ordinance outlets, cotton candy stands. Even a ferris wheel. Norma heard the yap of chained dogs. Drones snarled. Wheels spun. She smelled peanuts and spilled fuel. It was no longer who came in but what. Goods had long been the only safe passage through the cordon—penicillin, cigarettes, fuel (diesel, ethanol, gasoline), batteries, beans, rice, guns. Consortium decals arced across the night sky. Laser beacons danced over the lumpy pass of humanity in transit.

– Witness, said a voice at her elbow. The modern condition.

Norma wheeled around. A Consortium guard loomed out of the fog, drew back his whole arm and then rapidly shoving it straight out from him, with the fixed barrel of his pointed finger trained full on her, said: 'Take me like a brick from the house, so that our children will remember to return.' Know who said that?

Norma shook her head.

– Mahmoud Darwish, twentieth century poet of exile. You heard of him?

Norma exhaled and kept walking. The sidewalk rose and fell in asphalt dunes, the gutters rank with standing water. The guard kept pace with her, a lumpen boy with razor-cut hair and white creases fanning out from his eyes. He smoked and told her how early epics (song and poetry mostly) told of a cycle of quest and return—knights, heroes. He wheezed slightly as he walked.

– The modern tale, he said, is a product of the Voyages of Discovery, enlightenment inquiry, religious persecution, colonialism and so on. It's an expression of irredeemable exile. The exile's new world seems unnatural, more like fiction than reality. Faced with the impossibility of return, he or she is faced with failing to resemble himself or herself, and in the wake of such loss, must resort to self-creation. But to reassemble an identity out of the fragments and discontinuities of exile, the guard continued, is easier said than done.

Norma had no idea what he was talking about but she slowed down so he'd stop wheezing. He looked around and blinked as if just realizing that he'd walked further away from the cordon than he meant to and might not be able to find his way back.

– Back that way, Norma said. Go two blocks and hang a right.

Then he snuffled at her a little flirtatiously, I started a Masters degree, he said. In another place.

– You should go back there and finish it, she said.

World Wide Wang crouched on an unassuming corner of Border Town in the shadow of the crumpled Interstate. In colonial times it had been a feed store. Beneath the graffiti and posters you could still make out the faded sign: San Ysidro El Granero. Wreathed in sheafs of wheat. Norma rang the bell on a door cut into the loading dock, and Jesus opened it for her. Mixed-blood minder big as a bison.

– Jesus, she said, and let him hug her. His big paw was warm on her ass, his fringed shirt soft against her face, dreadlocks tickled her neck. Her body melted a little in his bear hug—she was after all what she was, chosen for her appetites and stamina, not her willpower but her ribs hurt and back pinched. Independence Day had come and gone. The recovery period helped. The tightness in her shoulders had eased, the tusk wounds healed again. She felt ready for anything. Even Jesus.

But now she had to find the urchin before Mommy did. Before Augustine did. So much hurt and harm and no one to explain it to her. She pushed Jesus away and walked stiffly through into a big low-ceilinged room with a bar along one wall and a semicircular stage at the other. Onstage, a trio of gold spray-painted androgens swam in a huge water tank. They pressed their breasts against the reinforced glass and their long penises curled like tentacles or horned serpents. Beaded strings of bubbles rose from their masks, and along tubes that ran from smart-lungs strapped to their backs. Two of the dancers turned in the water to face each other and their dicks bobbed and kissed. Norma felt that liquid rising again, her willpower ebbing. She moistened her lips with a cold tongue.

– If Frida Kahlo and the Elephant Man had triplets, said a voice behind her.

Bunny was sitting at his usual place at the bar, on the corner near the cash register. He was in his Wonder Whoa-Man suit and she smiled when she saw it. Thick beige tights, stars and stripes leotard over falsies in their flesh-colored sheath. Red and white high-heeled boots. A wide gold belt around his waist. The belt forced him to sit up so straight that his spine was a single rigid line from his ass to the top of his hairnet. One manicured hand bulkily cradled his console, the other wrapped around a pint of Guinness. On the counter a semi-furled Head and Shoulders coupon lay across a shard of mirror. He worked the tiny keyboard with manicured man-hands. Beside the Guinness lay what looked like a small black animal. Norma held up two fingers to the bartender, a slim Eurasian whose chaps flapped around rusty spurs. She sat on a stool next to Bunny, but turned around so she faced the stage.

– Nice place, she said.

Bunny kept tapping into his console.

Norma picked up the piled pelt from the counter. It was his wig. She put it over her own hair and blew a gelled curl off her nose. Bunny shrugged, blotted the last grains of powder off the mirror with his finger and rubbed his gums. Kept texting. Norma watched the stage. When the wig started to itch she took it off.

The bartender came over.

– How's your boy? he asked Bunny.

Bunny held up his console, In the hospital. He caught pneumonia.

His face in the glow of the screen was chalky, the brows sharply pencilled. His sequined eyelashes flapped like the scales of a Pleistocene reptile. The bartender shook his head sadly and his eyes met Norma's, as if signaling something to her, but she didn't know what. Dark forms jerked and wiggled on the dance floor. Between the bar and the stage, other shapes, dark and interchangeable, moved to and from tables, took their places at the bar.

– When do you go on? she said, turning toward the stage.

– Soon. You staying? His thin lips pessimistically pursed.

– It's why I'm here, she said, trying to keep the panic out of her voice.

– You're here because of that little Grimey. Do I look stupid?

Norma said, With or without the rug?

– You're always looking for someone. Firstly it's some guy. Some guy you fucked on a train or wanted to.

– I think I found him, she said. Or he found me.

– Mazel tov—Max Wang or some such?

Norma looked at Bunny in confusion. That's his name?

– Why not? Bunny said. You said he looked foreign, if memory serves. Some swinging dick from your combat days? Some SLA stud—

– Rob Swallows, said the barman. Only comes in the spring.

– Woody Cox, laughed Bunny. A hard man is good to find.

Norma let them tease her. She'd walked right into it. But then the barman pointed at the cord around her throat.

– That real platinum? he said.

– It is to me, said Norma, tucking the cord back under her top. What's a Grimey punk?

She was careful to keep her mind shut tight and her fingers away from the switch at her neck which would activate the Whole. Mommy could only access the Slash world through Norma's brain, virally or symbolically, so she kept her thoughts fixed on the stage. The androgens would give Mommy something to think about when it accessed the files later. Over time her memories were becoming so overlaid that Mommy complained about the mess, how it was getting increasingly problematic sorting the wheat from the chaff. Wheat from the chaff. Mommy with its collection of clichés like scalps hung from its cosmic belt.

Bunny checked the time on his console, then looked back at the barman.

– Grimey punks, said the barman. They don't wash. Ride the rails. They live in parks or shelters or Walmarts in winter.

The androgens had begun a game of underwater ring-around-the-rosie. The music was some early century trance mix. Norma focused on its digitized backbeat.

Bunny said, The Grimeys, they got this oral history thing going on.

– Oral my ass, the barman snorted and Norma glared at him.

Bunny continued, They make up stories to pass the time. Some even go to the trouble of recording them. Writing all that shit down, making up more shit to explain it.

The bartender dragged his cloth lazily back and forth along the bar.

– You ever heard the Grimey story about the dog's heart?

– Dog's heart, said Norma.

– You don't want to know, said Bunny.

The bartender moved away to serve a customer.

Her old man runs some kind of toy museum, said Bunny. Reportedly off his gourd: thinks he's Michael Jackson or someone. He needs meds so she does what she can for him. Or so I heard, but it's hard to tell what's true and what's a lie with the Grimeys. It could be her old man that's sick. Maybe he's not her old man. I don't know. Could be her pimp.

On a sudden impulse, Norma reached over and dropped the wig on Bunny's head, adjusted it and drew a curl away from his face. He looked at her, some of the shine back in his blue eyes.

– What about you? She said. What are you doing here?

– If by here you mean Spill City, I'm making a living, he said. I'm from Iowa. I trained as a dancer, worked as a masseuse with the Fairfield Ballet. I got a dancer pregnant. We moved out west. I drove a thukker in LA. We got married. We got divorced. She and Jake were shopping one day in the supermarket on Sepulveda, the big Vons. You know it? The earthquake hit. Freeways waved like ribbons in the flames. A semi fell from the sky and hit the Vons. She was in the cereal aisle. She'd given Jake a coupon for shampoo and told him to go get it and meet her at the checkout. They pulled Jake out of a pile of rubble. He's been in a wheelchair ever since. Fourteen year old kid in diapers.

His face blurred and swam. It was as if someone had smeared Vaseline across the bar, the tank with its exotic marine life, the dark dancers smeared with the grease of life across Norma's vision, inner and outer, inseparable now without doing great damage to the truth. She blinked.

When they pulled him out, said Bunny, picking up the Head and Shoulders coupon and folding it back into his wallet. He was still holding this.

After he put away his wallet, Bunny reached for her arm and wrote something on it in his eyeliner—an address.

– Burn after reading, he said. Augustine's coming to collect. Maybe now, maybe later. But he's coming. You know that, right?

The barman rejoined them, There's some bad shit going around with the freak crowd. Someone's lacing the gear or something. Roidheads dropping like flies.

– Good, said Bunny, taking both Norma's hands in his furry paws, fake fingernails catching the light. I hate those dipshits. But it doesn't matter if she won fair and square. No wrath like a Roidhead scorned. He's going to use the girl to get to you. The best thing you can do is to get her out of Spill City. Her and her old man.

Norma watched a black man in a Superman costume come up behind Bunny.

– Time, said Superman.

Bunny sighed and gave Norma a wink. He shook out the wig and by the time he'd stood up off the stool, he was in character. She envied him a little—at least he knew when to be what. He strode away after Superman without looking back. One of his red boots was split above the heel and it made Norma sadder than she thought anything could.

The androgens' tank had been wheeled off while they were talking and the curtains opened onto Superman at the front of the stage with his codpiece slightly askew. His eyes were opiate-red and he danced sluggishly to the Superman song. The song cut and Superman walked off to a spattering of boos. Norma got up to go but then the Wonder Woman theme song (remixed) played to thundering applause. The curtain reopened and Bunny fell from the top of the stage onto the floor in perfect splits.

To applause and wild cheers, Bunny went through his routine, dancing like the sidelined pro he was. His head held high and his arms wide and straight in the turns. The long hair of his wig bounced, his mouth was fixed in a defiant smile.

Norma left just before the end. She tipped the bartender and made a mental note to buy Bunny some new boots next time she was at the markets.

Jesus was waiting at the door. Rain lashed and the wind flung her against him. She breathed in his musk, felt his horn hard against her hip. She was no more than the sum of her parts after all. Chosen for her appetites and her stamina, not her willpower. Jesus kissed her and got her around to the side of the building under the eaves. He pressed her down onto a stack of pallets, undoing his buckle and she was wriggling her jeans down and took him into her, her nails digging into his ass, the activator at her throat flashing white heat. He wasn't the guy, but he would do, Jesus, her thighs around his hips, her hands on his ass pulling him to her, this winking eye of Jesus mooning Mommy through the rain.

20//: vantage

Her obsession with another troubles all her dreams. The road is a velvet cleft selvaged by moonlit thistle. At one end is the dentata and at the other looms the bulk of a barn with a 'possum skull nailed above the door. The skull glows creamy in the moonlight. She can taste it. The ringing of boots on the dirt path troubles her because her own boots, trialled by the Bihar Guerrillas in the 2029 uprising, are designed to be soundless. When she turns around the road behind and before her is empty, so she knows that her eyes, like everything else in the dream, deceive her. She feels weightless, nothing but empty night. On her shoulder, she hefts the preacher from the building site. He is absurdly heavy—ego always is. Her vision blurs and slides like a channel being changed—cut to entering the barn where there are imprints of rock n roll boots in the straw. She'd like to have a closer look at the prints but the room is spinning. And around the barn lie many more men like the preacher, the walls spinning like a zoetrope, a merry-go-round of horrors. She slides the preacher's broken body down off her shoulders and it flops in the dust, limp as a scarecrow, its hat rolling off the bald patch ringed by wild hair, eyes blazing up at the stars visible through a hole in the barn roof. Yes, this is what evil wants to be—a view point and nothing more.

The preacher is left there with the others. As long as she wears the dentata there will be more. The barn door is unlocked but the sinners couldn't leave even if they wanted to. And they don't want to.

21//: sanctuary

The address Bunny wrote on her arm was Swami Self-Realization Center Youth Sanctuary, Arcadia Beach, Highway 101. Bunny had even drawn her a little map on her wrist with his eyeliner. The Sanctuary itself wasn't technically on the grounds of the original Center, but was situated half a block along the road, above a Cash Attack thrift store. The sun had set but the sky was still pink—the tarnished dome and ruined pagoda on the cliff had taken on a pewter cast. Norma had been to Swami's only once before. Just after her arrival in Spill City from LA, Bunny wanted their fortunes told, but the psychic known as the Doctor had left the building.

The Center's marble bath, cliffside pagodas and meditation stand were in ruins. The amphitheater where the Swami had once given his lectures and held his mass ceremonies was now a sump, swimming in run-off and toxins. The grounds, which had once graced magazine covers and travel websites, were a wilderness of cactus and fescue, rampant sea oat and erupted tree roots. A great chunk of the headland had fallen into the Pacific and lay buried beneath the slick.

Rumor had it that the Swami had gone back to Jersey. Or Hawaii. Some even claimed that he was Er, the illusive Consortium. In his absence, the Self-Realization center struggled to retain its essence of collective enlightenment. The atmosphere of the community that had sprung up in the sect's absence was festive, almost carnivalesque. Along with the usual tamale stands and tent-sprawls, the settlement seemed to attract more than its share of witches and acrobats and geisha-faced mimics who moved mutely through the crowd. Remnants remained of the famous Halloween parties that were once held there. Scattered holographic reproductions of the winning jack-o'-lanterns from their annual contest—a three-headed monster, an elaborate Chumash totem pole and a big orange Elvis. The community had its own cemetery and ran tours. There was a shooting gallery set up in a meditation stand, and you could even buy corn dogs after a fashion—phallic concoctions made out of battered tempeh and dipped in artificial ketchup. There had been something startling about all those people wandering around munching on what looked to Norma like bleeding horns, and she'd not been keen to come back.

Among the many charitable works undertaken by the Swami in his heyday had been the shelters he set up for the addicted or afflicted young. The Franciscans had taken over the Sanctuary during the Catastrophic period, after the Swami had gone to ground. They shared security detail with the Cartel because of the big Cash Attack store on the ground floor. A Cartel front, it was the leading collateral lender in Spill City. The Cash Attack at the Sanctuary was especially luxe because it did a good trade in vintage surfboards, Les Paul guitars and replica Tech Zens, the official handgun of the Consortium, which had once flooded the black market and then was acquired in bulk by the Cartels.

The building faced onto Highway 101. By the time Norma finally came in the back way after stopping by Una's, it was after seven and the store was closed. The Sanctuary itself was in lockdown. Moths ticked on the glowing cage lights. Behind the grille, the curly-haired guard eating his Subway in front of the surveillance monitor seemed particularly concerned with inputting porn from his phone onto his console or vice versa.

Norma headed up the back stairs and twisted the security camera slightly off-kilter. She was getting good at this. She reached up then and taped a stiff strip of cardboard over the door frame. She pressed the buzzer and went back downstairs, waited behind the guard's Flyer.

Someone pushed open the door to the Sanctuary and said, That you, Lester?

Complaining about Lester who always forgot his damn key, they let it shut behind them. Norma a fleet shadow up the steel steps and slipping through the closing door. She untaped the cardboard and stood on the threshold.

She listened for him, the other. The Guy from the building site, who she sees in dreams of barns. She felt him near, sometimes near enough to touch, cramping her belly and filling her nose with his sour, sweet musk. She zipped up her jacket and the sensation receded. It wasn't much of a shield between her and Mommy, but it was all she had. For now. She entered the Sanctuary.

At the end of a dark hallway was a light over a bulletin board. Pinned to it were sheets of paper on which were typed emergency numbers, meal times, exercise classes. Above the bulletin board was a hovering holo of St. Francis. Norma kept walking, her boots silent along a cobalt blue rug. To her left was an open door to a kitchen where a Crock-Pot cooled on the counter. Norma recoiled and wrinkled her nose at the sour smell emanating from it. She moved out of the kitchen, silent on her preloved guerrilla boots, and went down another hallway. A door opened to a common room with a window overlooking the street. A half dozen filthy kids were sitting around consoles, phones, or the TV. Their hairstyles were elaborate concoctions of spikes and dreadlocks and 'hawks, shaved skulls tattooed, studded and scarified. Their limbs were pallid and their bodies were lumpy. Their clothes: overalls, denim skirts and tights, loose undershirts and grimy t-bars showing above waist-bands, bruises visible through gaping straps and sleeves. They exuded a maniacal exhaustion, chronic filth and habitual self-harm. A sepia holo of a friar, like the ones up at San Miguel, flickered on a plinth. A camera whirred. Norma located it up in a corner and took care to stay out of its reach.

There hung over the room a hush of unease, an outer eye not in sync with an inner that looked into the next moment, to the person one could have been, in a band maybe, or on the softball team, an underground legend in the graffiti arts, yeah, or having just scored. Norma scanned the room for the urchin and finally spotted her sitting in a straight-backed chair. She was playing a game on a console, her arms hugging her knees and thumbing a controller. She didn't acknowledge Norma, her thumbs a blur, but her pupils dilated and Norma knew she'd been seen. Norma put a finger over her mouth—should she smile? Is that what kids like? The girl ignored her. Her eyes were an unusual blue, very dark and very bright at once with dark lashes that stood out on milky skin. In the game she was playing, a dwarf and a butterfly were engaged in some kind of battle. She froze the projection, unfurled her legs and got up. She left the room through another door that also opened up into the hallway. Norma caught up and followed the girl into a low-ceilinged bunk room.

There were six bunks in three sets of two. The walls were decorated with curling posters of game stars and a drawing of the Archangel lording it over a stricken Satan. A TV, a console and a music dock were chained to steel brackets bolted to the walls. A row of lockers plastered with stickers. The bunks were strewn with clothing, sleeping bags. A door was ajar against the end wall and through it Norma saw more bunks in a similar arrangement.

Wordlessly, the urchin led Norma to a bottom bunk against the wall. The ceiling was low enough for Norma to brush with her fingertips, encrusted with spitballs and crude drawings of cocks and balls. The girl's bunk was spread with a sleeping bag and a had a moth-eaten teddy bear in a corner. She sat down. She clasped her shaking hands between bare knees. Her toes were painted in a metallic blue varnish that almost matched her eyes, in which Norma saw fear but also a question.

The urchin said, What?

A week ago, Norma had broken a man's spine with her bare hands. She stood six and a half foot in her socks, grew tusks at will and carried around her neck a chunk of stellar dust that could bring a grown man to his knees. And here she was so scared of a little girl with dirty hair that she could hardly talk.

She pulled out the wad of bills.

– This would be yours.

The girl looked at the money. Looked back up at Norma.

– How's that?

– You won it. You came back with the knife. So you won the bet.

The girl took it and counted it.

– This the book that douche Augustine made on my fall? You didn't take your cut, she said.

Norma hadn't expected that. She should have. No one did or got anything for nothing in Spill City. They were the rules.

– Well, she said. When I was in the Baked Bean Bombshells, the manager took sixty percent.

The girl said slowly, The what?

– It was a fight team I was in up in Bakersfield. The pit was an empty spa pool behind a burnt-out motel with no name. The manager looted the beans out in pallets from the Costco out on Rosedale. We wrestled in our bikinis except we had hunting knives, broken bottles and the like stuffed where the sun don't shine.

– I bet you were the odds-on favorite, said Raye.

Norma nodded. Most nights she was, and that's how she figured it out, how the punters weren't betting on her to win as much as they were betting on the other bombshells to lose, hard girls with names like Shayne and Lou-Anne. What the odds were on was the chance to get what the punter came for, to stare it in the face, get a little wet. Taste the Silence and live to talk about it.

– After that, said Norma. I saw it everywhere. Men with the lights to nowhere and back in their eyes.

The girl counted forty dollars from the roll and thrust it back at Norma. Baked beans are gross, she said.

There was something in the girl's manner, not so much a recklessness as a reasoned defiance so self-sustaining that Norma was afraid she would be told to leave if she didn't play along. She took her cut.

– How'd you find me? the girl said.

– A friend.

– The drag queen works at the Wang?

Outside, on the street a Flyer chain clanged against a post. Norma nodded. Raye nodded back. For a moment it was a nodding contest.

– Figures. He told me you were friends, Raye said. I mean before I knew it was you he just said some big chick with crazy eyes he was hanging with. Sorry. Bunny, right? He's okay. He brings me food sometimes from that place at the border he works at. His kid's a cripple. Don't tell him I said. Bunny's working to make the deposit on a liver donor from Coahuila, but it's a big risk.

– The operation?

The girl shook her head. Her tawny bangs swung stiffly back and forth across a wide pale brow.

– The operation's a piece of cake compared to the risk of cutting out the Cartels when it comes to spare parts.

Well, said Norma. They seemed to have run out of things to say. She looked at her boots, thought about Bunny and how he was good with kids and how Gene was good with wolves. Both men sidelined and diminished by their own species.

– That was some fall you took, she said. Why'd you do it?

– Same reason you wrestled naked body-mod freaks covered in pork and beans, said the urchin. I was hungry. Besides, like my daddy says, a fool and his money are easily parted.

Finally, Norma saw a point of entry into the purpose for her visit. Behind which lay the main reason, which hovered on the periphery of her consciousness, off-radar, where Mommy couldn't access it.

– Augustine's no fool, said Norma. A sociopathic bully, okay. But he's not a fool.

– A sociopathic bully minus one testicle, said the urchin. What's your point?

– Well, said Norma. If I were you—

– What's that? said the urchin, pointing.

Norma looked down at the paper bag by her boots. She'd forgotten about the schnitzel she brought from Una's. Trying to keep her movements slow and smooth, she took the takeout box she'd got from Little Barry and put it on a crate beside the bunk. Next to it she put a bottle of diet Pepsi she picked up at the 7-Eleven on the corner. The girl's brow was unfurrowed, her eyes did not waver, finding Norma in their oceanic fathoms and all but drowning her there.

Norma tried to muster a largesse she felt was expected of her, From Una.

– Pepsi? said the girl, the corners of her mouth quivering in disappointment. I like Coke.

Norma felt her shadow fall across the girl's form and how the girl did not cringe or pull back. The window looking over the street had gone dark, almost opaque as if there was nothing there, nothing outside this room. The urchin's eyes scanned from the top of Norma's head to her feet.

Norma said, They only had Pepsi.

– The Subway on the corner, the urchin said. Or the 7-Eleven down at Birmingham?

– The Subway.

– Well, Birmingham has Coke.

Norma wiped the sweat off her forehead with her wrist. She sat down on the opposite bunk so as to free the girl from the shadow she made over her.

– How'd you get past the guard? the girl said, still not taking her eyes off Norma.

– Lester let me in, Norma shrugged. By the way, Una said to say 'get well soon' except that she said it in German.

The urchin grinned and she shook her head as if shaking off a daze. She squared her bony shoulders.

– *Gott im Himmel!*

– Una? Right. They afraid I'll sue or something. Forty feet. I had falls before but I think that was my biggest.

– Maybe you should quit while you're ahead.

– Thanks for getting me out of there, said the girl. And also, I'm Raye.

– Norma.

– Nice boots. Norma. You get them here?

Norma said, Barstow.

– That where you're from? When you were a Baked Bean Bomber?

Norma said, Bombshell. Bakersfield.

The girl said, Me, I'm from Portland. You ever been out of the Zone?

Norma shook her head. What's it like?

The girl gave a sideways pull to her mouth and frowned, her eyes looking somewhere behind Norma.

– I can't really remember. Not anymore. I used to, but—. She numbly shrugged.

To fill the silence, Norma said, This place is okay. Short term.

The urchin waved her arm extravagantly across the room.

– It's okay. I haven't had a chance to do it up yet. My decorator's been busy with other projects.

Slowly, her heart banging against her ribs, Norma said, It has a rustic charm.

The girl said, I summer in Belize.

Her eyes flicked to the food, and back to Norma.

– Well, said Norma. She got slowly to her feet, awkwardly stooped so as not to scare Raye off. She felt knock-kneed and coarse-skinned. The girl's skin looked lit from within, so filled with light that no more light could get through. Norma stood back so as not to be the shadow that passed over so much light.

– You okay? said Raye. She pulled two beers out from under the bed, held one out to Norma.

Norma's ears rang with the sound, or the possibility of the sound of metal heels in the hallway. She waited until it passed because it was only the Silence, deafening. Then she said, You shouldn't drink.

– Here's to Augustine and the crew, said Raye, drinking.

Norma pulled open the tab and let the warm beer run down her throat.

– Beats Pepsi, anyway, Raye said.

– I'd lay low for a while, said Norma, regretting it instantly.

– You were the one took his money and his manhood, snapped Raye. You're the one should be worried. I'm just a Grimey. No one cares about me.

His manhood, said the voice in Norma's head. The girl's eyes were glassy. She looked like she hadn't slept in a week, hadn't wanted to.

Norma said, Should you see a doctor?

– I don't know. Should I?

They locked eyes, creature and creator, and Norma could not say who was who. So instead she said, What's that smell?

Raye sniffed, Leeks, she said. From the Crock—hey! You didn't finish your beer.

But Norma was already halfway to the door and didn't trust herself to look back.

Telefraxis: (n) A process of splitting and then catapulting one aspect of a psyche or sentience (Viewpoint) into a separate physical presence (the host) in an entirely different space/time. This separate being is generally controlled by a remote communication system involving presequencing protocol (PSP) i.e. sonic 'wiring' enabled by excess cosmic microwave radiation leaked from obsolete, broken and dirty comtrash (see below) and CogShare Protocol (CSP—see below: The Whole). (n) the creation of a sub program or network operation requiring minimal access (NORMA), the physical or psychic embodiment of which is achieved through advanced sequencing methods. (v), Slang—to 'frax.' (See above, Alaxenoesis).

(Saurum Nilea, AQt., trans. L.Shay 2656)

22//: mommy

Mommy was waiting for her when she got back to the trailer. Norma could tell because the inside of the trailer, the walls and the ceiling and the bathroom mirror, were covered in a foul scrawl. The same three words over and over written in a filthy ooze that was less on the surface of the sweaty laminate than excreted by it.

Ratreevels are fourbidden. Ritreivalls our furbiddnine. Rutreevles r fearbittened.

Norma stared and her gorge rose. It wasn't just the bad spelling. It was the way some words were rubbed out as if with an angry sleeve and then overwritten. Black blobs beneath which wiggled squashed serifs like the legs of dying spiders. Lines of crud thumbed through the text and letters squashed between corrections. Superscript and caret marks. Snatching up a towel, Norma began to smash at the goo, trying to clean it up but she only succeeded in spreading the filth.

– She wasn't dead, said Norma.

– Shshs, said the voice inside her head. Those retrievals are nothing but trouble.

– Trouble? said Norma. For who?

– For the mission, said the voice. Only one way to fix it.

– No, said Norma. The girl is not your lookout. She's mine. I made her.

– Where's my horn?

– I'll find it, Norma yelled. Or die trying.

– You wish, said Mommy, the voice inside her head, inside her cramping womb.

The ooze had begun to run down the wall in places. How had Mommy done this? That was the real abomination. Mommy, the our in your, the trusted Whole. Had it squatted beneath the faraway towering flames? Or had it commissioned some other? Someone whose eyes she'd looked upon, whose form she'd sought, longed for. Look. half a heel-shaped crescent, a blunt arrow that might have been the toe of a boot. Even the floor fouled in its passing. Norma swung around as if to catch a retreating hat rim, a grimy cuff—who had squatted here, right here in the trailer, and with a grunt of satisfaction squeezed this filth out of themselves, fouled their own hand with it? Norma clearly saw the hand with its putrid load moving across the wall, forming the letters, the words, and understood that was set out here now was both an insult and a warning. And what else?

She stared at the hieroglyphs tracked on the linoleum—that blood-black crescent, an arrow-shaped toe print ineptly rubbed out with a filthy sole. Was it him? After longing for him, filling her nights with the sound of his footfall, thinking of him when she touched herself, it horrified her that she might find herself face to face with a Guy whose stench she now had on her hands. So personal, so internal, that surely he would recognize it on her, his own smell. Was that part of the Plan? Should she understand herself now as marked? A part of her sought another explanation.

– Mommy? she whispered.

She turned off the light and moved to the window. The ocean outside the trailer had turned the same color as the goo, like black blood, and the sky was smeared with it too, the earth. The darkness now taking form from the words and their stink, never to be eradicated.

– What am I? Norma said.

– You're mine, said Mommy. I made you.

– I'm a woman, said Norma. Self-made.

Mommy chortled wetly from deep in Norma's whole, A woman? You sprout wings under duress, you wear a chunk of plasma around your neck and sometimes, if I'm not mistaken you dream of having your cock sucked. So you tell me—what kind of woman?

– Only women bleed, Norma said but half to herself.

She looked down at the dark matter dripping from her hands and pooling on the floor between her legs. Her whole body swayed. A shadow fell across her vision, a darkness that burned like the sun. Norma had to squint one eye against the shadow's searing heat.

– You're nothing, said the shadow. Nothing.

– I hate you, said Norma between ragged breaths, half-choked by her lying heart. I wish you weren't my Mommy!

At which the shadow then rose to a great height, immeasurable, and with one timeless and unnatural motion, leapt across the void and brought the creature to her knees.

23//: remains

– Hey you. Big Lady.

The sharp rap at the trailer door seemed to begin before the light footsteps ended. There was a scuffling of rubber soles on the threshold. The smell of donuts. Norma froze over the final bucket of bleach. She felt feverish and her muscles screamed.

The door opened; light poured in and the wet hiss of the surf.

– Anyone home?

– No, said Norma.

– I brought breakfast.

Norma's stomach roared in response. She looked around the trailer. There was a crack in the laminate from where Mommy had thrown her against it, but no sign that Norma could see of the filth. After she regained consciousness, it had taken her the night and most of the next day to clean up the trailer, a dozen or more gallons of water that she boiled on the one-ring stove in a borrowed pot from Noe and an entire bottle of Clorox that she found in the old amenities building.

She went to the door, leaned against it for a moment with her eyes squeezed shut against the storm of black flakes—like char or ash—that floated across her vision, and opened it. The clean wet hiss of the surf poured in. The girl, Raye, stood there silhouetted in the white light. The old parka hung open over a soiled T-shirt. Her tawny hair stuck up in waxed tufts around her head, a grin across her young-old face. Yoinking earphones.

– I'm not hungry, Norma said.

– Big night? said Raye. Her dark blue eyes appraised Norma with a child's shy disapproval. Can I come in?

– No, said Norma. I—

Raye nodded lewdly. You got company.

– Right.

– Well. I was just in the neighborhood, so.

She rooted around in her crusty backpack and extended a greasy bag of donuts toward Norma. They're from VGs. That's where you go, right?

The donuts filled the air between them with their burnt-sugar smell. Norma felt her mouth water without meaning to. She could reach into the girl's bony chest and rip out her heart without meaning to. Maybe it would be for the best and it would be swift. Better Norma should do it than Mommy. Mommy would take all the time in the world.

Nothing but trouble, said the voice inside her head, but it was just an echo. Norma zipped up her jacket.

– Okay. Let's sit out here.

Raye didn't move. She looked out past Norma across the camping grounds.

– What? said Norma.

Raye said without looking, Clothes. Some clothes would be good.

Norma looked down at her bare legs. She was wearing nothing but the jacket over her panties.

She turned around and went back into the trailer, bent down to pick up her crumpled jeans. Her lower back throbbed. Her head knifed behind both eyes. She groped across the bedside table for a blister pack, washed down some pills with a bottle of pink-tinged water.

– You want a Coke? she called out to the girl.

– If you got one.

Norma's pulse skipped. Sometime between being beaten up by Mommy and scrubbing away the filth, she had gone across to the 7-Eleven and bought every bottle and can of Coke in the place should

Raye come back, willing her to do so. Norma raked her hands through her hair, forgetting her swollen ear, and almost crying out with the pain. She wobbled to the kitchen, brought two Cokes out of the fridge and went back outside.

– You're bleeding, said Raye.

Norma touched her eyebrow. It had split from impact with the corner of some piece of the trailer. She blotted the blood with the back of her wrist and wiped it on her jacket. She pulled a lawn chair out from under the trailer for the girl and sunk down on the trailer steps.

– Thanks, she said through a mouthful of donut.

– VGs across the road, yeah. That the place?. The baker there, Noe, was like 'Norma this' and 'Norma that.' I think he's crushing on you. He said to bring back the pot when you can.

Raye gave a mock shiver.

– Right, mumbled Norma. Noe. Ooof.

– You okay? You want me to leave?

– No.

The jacket's special weave circulated cool air across her damp skin. She zipped it up so that that it covered the bioswitch. The itinerants who lived in the camp grounds had dispersed for the day. The surf rolled up the dark sand leaving lacy trails of foam. Rocking on the lawn chair, Raye looked exhausted, a little speedy. Rediem, maybe? Another slow way to die. She'd broken out in small pimples. Norma busied her hands with the donut, breaking it into smaller and smaller pieces so she wouldn't reach across and brush Raye's hair off her spotty forehead.

Raye stopped rocking and said, I was climbing before I could walk. It was just something I did. I could see it. Like in my head I could build some invisible tightrope to get me from here to there and back again. Up in Portland once, before I could walk, no one could find me and I was just up in an old walnut tree. Crawled up and couldn't get down.

– That's the thing, said Norma, washing the donut down with the Coke. Getting down.

– But not falling down, said Raye, moving her finger in a downward spiral. Not that.

– No. Well. That was a big fall.

The girl lazily picked at a pimple on her chin. The surf crashed and she watched it a while.

– I went to circus class once. In LA. My dad put me there because a friend of his ran it and it was cheaper than child care. It was pretty lame though. Mainly tumbling. What's with that? Who wants to tumble? There's this circus I heard about in Australia where climbing's the thing. Walls and ceilings, special boots and gloves for added grip. I could do that. I could go to Australia. There's that.

– You never know, said Norma.

But they did.

– If there were still tourists around here I could busk, said Raye. I did some busking in LA. Backflips and cartwheels. I tried a stilt act up at Swami's. But the spill killed the tourist industry, all those heavy metals. See that spill? Nitrates are what make it red. Who wants to swim in red? Phosphates spread it out, blow out the biomass and take all the oxygen out of the water. It's called Eutrophication. Which I learned in middle-school. Whole southern coastline's a dead zone.

– A red zone.

– Bingo.

Raye said, I used to stand at the tideline. thought I could hear the fish screaming. Every morning the tide dumped them by the hundreds on the shore. It still does.

Raye turned to Norma, pinned her in a teary stare.

– Thing is, I should be dead too. I shouldn't have survived. What, forty-fifty feet?

The size of the fall getting bigger every time she told it, Raye dropped her gaze as if she could no longer contain it in her mind. She started drawing shapes in the condensation on the Coke can.

– A beam caught your fall. It happens, said Norma.

Raye's fingers kept drawing lazy, hypnotic scrawls on the outside of the can.

– I feel different now. Like I've been through something.

– You have, said Norma. No arguments there.

The girl shook her head. What did you do to me?

Her hands had begun to shake around the can. She tried to keep drawing but the can slipped through her fingers fell onto the ground, the brown soda trickling onto the sand and pine needles.

– I'll get you another, said Norma, standing.

When she came back she said, Look. All I did was bring you back here. Give you some painkillers and let you sleep it off.

– I heard of some new techniques they're trialling at the Chinese Front, antibody transfusions. Is that what you did to me, being excom. You are military, right? What, some kind of medic?

– Sure. I keep my stash of hot T-cells and a box of syringes under the bed for emergencies.

The girl's eyelids fluttered a little queasily. A gull cawed. And then another, bursting off a pile of kelp.

– Thing is I feel weird. But whatever. Raye shrugged dramatically. I'm alive. So, thanks. I think.

– Nothing to thank me for, said Norma. Then she got that whiff of ferrous sickly-sweet char, the burnt shit smell of the goo written across the trailer. It was under her nails now, in her nostrils, never to be erased. She narrowed her eyes at the stunted scrub around the trailer, looking for a jutting shadow or glimpse of yellow eye.

– You saved me, said Raye.

– No! Norma, leaning forward in her chair with her face inches from the girl's, who would not flinch. You saved yourself. You're strong and you're tough and you're a climber. Said so yourself. Remember that.

– Well, getting me away from Augustine. You did that. Man's a vampire. What you did to his balls, there's that.

Raye shook her head and laughed, her eyes lighting up as quickly as they darkened, laughter following tears like a whirlwind that caught Norma in its dizzying spiral. It was catching. She leaned back in her chair and felt the corners of her own mouth twitch.

– Well. I'll take that.

Raye, grinning wildly, shakily. Augustine didn't bet on that, now. Did he?

Norma shook her head, That part was on the house.

– So, I'm going to be okay? In your expert medical military opinion. No brain damage or anything.

– Nothing to speak of, said Norma. Just keep both feet on the ground for a while. Okay?

They sat in silence for a while and it was a good silence.

– I could eat a horse, said Raye.

– You want another Coke?

Raye shook her head. I think I'll go for some breakfast. You want to come? Celebrate our win.

– Your win, said Norma, looking into the next minute to how she would not ever put the our in your. She would remember where she ended and where another began.

– You heard about Bunny's kid?

Norma crushed the Coke can in her hand.

– Kid's a goner. Maybe you got something in that stash of yours can help.

Norma didn't say anything. Retrievals didn't cure you. They didn't cure a thing. They brought you back exactly as you were only more so. Raye looked at her expectantly.

– What Bunny's boy needs is a whole new body, Raye. Bunny can hunt and gather spare parts until it sends him crazy or broke or crazy and broke. No vat-grown spleen or pelvis or kidney on its own will do more than put off the inevitable.

Shape-changing—what humans called Sleeve technology in their fictions and their dreams—was still a long way off for this species, and look. Look where it got Mommy. The right hand not knowing what the left hand was doing. The eye seeking what the brain could not conceive. The head not in sync with the heart. Norma regarded the child through the mist. If she told her, would she know?

Raye watched Norma pulverize the Coke can and then she pointed at the cord around Norma's neck.

– It's remains, isn't it? she said.

Traffic rattled out on the highway and the cloud cover was edged with bronze. Norma stared at Raye.

– What?

– That thing around your neck. That stuff inside the coil that looks like gum. The girl's eyes were opaline storms. I noticed it when you came around to the Sanctuary. It's remains isn't it?

In a manner she hoped looked casual, Norma let the cord around her neck play through her finger and slipped the bioswitch back between her breasts.

– I knew it, said Raye. She leant forward. Two bright flushes bloomed on her cheeks. I knew it. I rode with a girl once who got this puppy. We hitched a ride on the back of this pickup from the rail yard to this house we were going to stay in and the puppy fell out, got dragged by its leash. This chick took her dead puppy and she was like, what should I do with it? And we were like, bury it. And she was like, I can't, I want to keep it. Keep the fur and the bones. And someone said she had to bury the bones when she got the fur, so we took off the fur and she got the bones and her hands were covered in blood and she was like, I should eat it. And we were like, just the heart, you should eat the heart. So she said she would eat the heart and we were like, we should help her eat the heart. So we all ate some and it was the bitch of gross, this puppy's heart, yeah, chewy but crunchy. She kept the bones for a while, and the fur which kind of stank, and a piece of the puppy's heart in a charm around her neck, just like yours.

Norma gripped the arms of the lawn chair hard enough to leave hand prints in the plastic.

– It doesn't even belong to me. It's something I have to give to someone. A Guy. Okay?

Raye rocked back on the lawn chair, dangling the Coke can in one hand and with her toes barely brushing the sand. Someone you know? she said.

– Kind of.

– Boyfriend? said Raye, trying to look impish, but only managing perverse.

– Not anymore, said Norma. She had acquired a skill rare among Slashes, that of being able to control her facial expressions. She kept her voice level and held the girl's eyes in her own. I've been looking for him for a long time.

Raye nodded sagely. Exes are nothing but trouble. I had one once.

– No kidding, said Norma.

– How long you been looking for him? said Raye, abruptly business-like.

– For who?

– For your ex, said Raye.

– Look, he's not—

But the child's face with its extravagant emotions, following a whiff of promise here, the smell of adventure there, again caught Norma up in its dangerous energy. Bunny had said they were called Grimeys, not so much children—even if they made it to adulthood—as arrested, not born so much as dropped out, always banging up, or lying low, or flying high, on the nod or under a wheel. With nothing to believe in since even their eyes lied, they'd learned to look between the surface and the thing itself, between the idea and the word, because what they saw there just might save them. Norma felt woolly-headed—who was saving who?

– You wouldn't have seen him, said Norma. He's not all that visible.

– Try me.

– Very blond hair, piercings, cowboy boots but not exactly.

– Mmm hmm. Sounds like pretty much every white guy in Spill City. What else?

– Forget it, said Norma. How to describe the yellow eyes and the mineral stink?

– Tell me about the boots. What kind of heels?

– Metal, said Norma, staring at her hands. Off market.

Raye nodded, Steel heels means a stash, or a hidden scabbard, sometimes. You know for blades, or spikes. Some shoemaker up north specializes in that kind of modification, mainly for Cartel carriers. So your ex would have come down from there. From the northern part of the Zone. Those remains belong to him, your ex?

– Look, said Norma, standing up. I'm going in to fry an egg. You want one?

– Wait, said Raye. There was a pleading note in her voice that made Norma want to give her a push, maybe a hard one. Listen. I think I know someone who can help you.

– Who?

– Someone who knows everyone. I mean, beyond his obligations as a

Consortium snitch, which is what he is. Way beyond that. Anyone new or different that comes through, he's the one to know it. This man's like a human metal detector, the real deal.

– How do you know?

Raye's eyes darkened to a blue as blunt as a bruise.

– Because he's my father.

24//: stranger danger

Why did she go back to the trailer? She should not have been talking to the big lady. That much Raye knew, yeah. You don't get into it with that kind of stranger, not at all. There was a part of her that knew that. The biggest part. The part that knew she had to get clean if she was ever going to get home. A small part of her also knew that the woman could be called a friend. A small part of her remembered the woman's arms outstretched to catch her when she fell.

25//: wacko

Spill City was full of see-ers. Gibbering private eyes and paranoiacs, chaos theorists or ferrymen, what have you, who saw connections between everyone, the way in which their flight paths and game plans and secrets could be seen as interwoven or a fixed game. Ask them and they explained how what stood out or was different about an individual could be used to stack the dice and change the odds, perception being a precursor to transformation, and so on and so forth. She read about people in preparation for the mission—visionaries and watch dogs with an eye for reds, passers, tricksters and confidence men, because hell. It takes one to know one.

So that wasn't the main reason she agreed to go with Raye to meet her old man. The chance that he would, in his capacity as a self-appointed eccentric middle man, perched in his ersatz little trading post in this reeking frontier, have seen her Guy. No. The main reason was because of how Raye squeezed the word 'father' tightly in her throat when she said it and how her eyes lit up like lightbulbs about to blow.

After breakfast, they caught a Coaster north to Arcadia. They got off at the old Town Square at supper time. Raye bought a console from a pile in a bargain bin beside a row of corroded medical trolleys displaying new and used tech for sale. The food trucks that lined the tracks were ablaze, but the crowd was thin. Norma and Raye wandered for a while among the hippy ghosts, past rough-glazed pottery stacked on blankets beneath the neon boomerangs and hotrod facades. Zigzag alleys tinged with gold from the setting sun. Canvases depicting Elvis and Geronimo and Elvis as Geronimo. Wide-flanked women cleaning paint brushes. Dust-begrimed surfboards stacked like coffins behind dusty windows, and joss sticks everywhere, the false scents cloying at the back of Norma's throat. Raye led the way, stumbling over a wide crack in the sidewalk. Norma veered past a rank pool of oily water. Weeds grew tall in vacant lots. Paper maple leaves in autumn colors burst from piled garbage bags in a dumpster. Bars and pool halls had been set up in shipping containers retrieved from the Alaskan tankers, Holoscreens set up outside replayed classic Charger games, lost episodes from cult miniseries. Raye stopped to watch a demo about the latest version of *Throne of Thorns*. Norma stood beside her, transfixed by the murky digital forests and grim men who moved as though the laws of physics didn't apply; roughhewn rooms lined with tapestries and tech. Wind howling through the digitized cracks.

It's a new technology, Raye explained. It's called REBn. For Reborn. Daddy said maybe for my birthday.

She'd laughed in that mannered teenage giggle. But by the time she got to the word birthday, the ageless chip had returned to her voice. Somewhere some music started up and Raye dragged Norma in the direction of the sound. A small crowd gathered around a singer and a guitarist. The singer was in her sixties and stood ramrod straight in a man's jacket. She had long gray hair and her skin looked translucent, parchment thin. A guitarist sat on a stool beside her. He was much younger, also long-haired and muscular, wearing sunglasses. His hair swung heavily over his face as he picked out chords on a guitar attached to a lead that fed from a generator behind one of the food trucks. Norma's dentata pinched. On a podium behind them, a DJ grew still at the deck, his arms outstretched and his hands resting flat on the turntables like a blessing. The guitarist woke the strings with a rising fury. The woman took up the melody in a harsh and ragged voice, a simple song about redemption and love. The song had three verses with a chorus in between, and with every chorus, the words she sang became more distorted and her voice, raw and sweet, hitched and ground. The guitarist beside her became more frenzied, more precise, the sound torn from the instrument, his heavy hair over his face until he was not so much sitting on the stool as levitating.

When it was all over, the woman smiled shyly into the applause, patches of ragged color on her neck. Drifts of ganga heavy in the air. The guitarist began circulating through the crowd with his shirt held out in front of him like an apron. His belly was flat and white with a line of dark hair disappearing down his pants. Norma swallowed and licked her lips. People tossed coins onto his shirt, candy, bottle tops, condoms. Sprinkled weed. When he came to Raye and Norma, Norma tossed in a twenty and he looked back up at her so that she saw herself twinned in his antique Ray Bans. He took them off and pushed them onto her head.

– Remember, he said. Charity is the key.

As they walked deeper into the forest of felled commerce and earthquake-riven infrastructure—the Galleria's bell tower on its side beside the old mall's empty shell—Raye's mouth set in a grim line. The taut smooth skin of her face became a mask that shut Norma out. Beyond the boardwalk and market were narrower streets, shuttered tourist traps, and beyond that alleyways that connected side streets where moths ticked on cage lights and there were cats everywhere and fire escapes creaked in the wind. Norma sniffed graffiti ink and standing water. She batted away a mosquito. A Cruid wearing huge headphones and a cap drawn low over his eyes practiced on a rat-colored skateboard beside a stripped van. Shadowy forms idled outside a diner on the corner.

Norma looked up to a shark-fin neon sign that said Surfside Cleaners. In the window was reflected a DON'T WALK glyph from the traffic lights across the street. She saw banks of washers and dryers in the gloom. Raye stopped at a store beside the laundromat. A handwritten 'Closed' sign hung from tape to the inside of the dusty glass front. The outside walls were a stark, hard blue, and on the front door Norma read, *'Antique Toy Trading Company and Pop Paraphernalia.'*

Raye stood beside her breathing through her mouth. Beside the door there was more faded gilt lettering: *'Rock and Movie Memorabilia.'* Below that she read, *'Battery Operated.'* Raye pulled out a key, unlocked the door and pushed it in. Norma followed, her heart a fist in her throat. She heard thunder rolling in from the sea—or possibly a convoy of Veelos—then the door closed and there was silence.

They were standing in a hallway dark and narrow as a vein. Norma sucked in her ribs, felt pushed against by whatever had eaten all the light and grown fat on its consumption. It was the Feer, fat and furry. Beneath Raye's bravado, Norma could smell the urchin's reek and her own. As her eyes adjusted to the darkness, a dirty glow deepened at the far end of the hallway and an open door took shape to her right. Norma flinched and steeled herself against the Feer. It was everywhere here. Her heart began to race and her hands grew cold. Then the wing stumps burned and the terror receded.

– It's okay, said Raye unconvincingly. I come here all the time. It's not always so weird.

At the sound of her voice, the darkness shifted then realigned itself around a life-sized mannikin of Luke Skywalker astride a moth-eaten Bantha. It stood between them and the dim light at the end of the hallway.

Norma said, Shit.

Raye giggled unsteadily, You get used to it. Come on.

She took Norma's hand in her own, a gesture both needful and generous that made Norma feel conscious of her own flesh, as if it were covered in scales. Raye flashed the beam of her phone across the walls of the hallway, which were lined with shelves heavy with dusty stacks of boardgames, obsolete DVDs and VHSs and books, hard and soft covers, whose corners were worn and pulpy. There was age through it all, the air heady with mycotoxins. Norma breathed through clenched teeth. Raye found the light switch but the bulb that flickered on overhead made little difference. One shelf contained nothing but boxed Uncle Wiggly games in various stages of decay. Twisters and Troubles and CandyLands and Operations, arcana that she'd had to research, familiarize herself with in preparation for the mission. She'd become adept at using toy tweezers, manipulating Pop o' Matic dice rollers, and building plastic hotel empires. Books of fairy tales and adventures at sea. Comic books in yellowing plastic sleeves. LPs and singles stacked in cardboard boxes. A huge cockroach pulled itself up and over the edge of a dust cover. Norma heard mice and rats and below all this a mechanical purr that made her skin crawl. She glanced up above the door off the hallway. An antique camera winked and pulled back with a lurch.

– We done here? Norma said, her voice swallowed up in dust and the darkness. Seriously.

Raye pulled Norma through to the other room, flicked a wall switch that turned on another dim bulb whose light was swallowed in the gloom. They stood among the mannequins and toys, the dolls and cars and framed posters, signed baseball gloves and signature capes, shoes and masks. Michael Jackson loomed large here. He had one corner all to himself where his life-size wax likeness stood with arms out flung and a black military-style jacket not unlike her own. A nine foot high glass cabinet was crammed with Michael Jackson paraphernalia. Clothes and albums and white gloves and figurines. Signed programs, tickets, caps. Guitars hung from the walls in brackets. Pictures of the Jackson Five. A concert set written in childish handwriting: 'Beat it,' 'Ben,' 'Thriller.' A gold codpiece. Jangly guitar straps. Gold and platinum albums in frames. Black loafers, white socks, belts, stardust all around. 'Billie Jean' played softly on a scratchy sound system.

The rest of the room was filled with miscellany. More toys and games. A child-sized Kwik-E-Mart from the Simpsons show complete with Squishee Pump and Duff Beer Fridge. *Aliens* and *Throne of Thorns* figurines from miniature to life-sized including a to-scale castle made entirely of skulls. Norma's heart pounded with a feverish excitement, a false nostalgia based less on familiarity than with a yearning for something she'd never had. They taunted her, these toys, with a past she never lived and never would, a lush tug to nowhere. She caught a glimpse of her reflection in a framed poster, bug-eyed and haunted. A discolored swelling at her brow. Everywhere those damn clunky surveillance cameras whirred and ground. An Elvis suit. A laundry basket filled with Optimus Primes. Dusty glass milk bottles. A dozen boxed Benders. 'Billie Jean' faded to 'Bad.' Song of not-self.

Norma nudged a Barbie Ferrari with her titanium toe. A fierce

Dorothy watched them from behind cellophane. Cursive at the edge of the box read, *Which way do we go now?*

– Daddy? Are you there?

Raye's voice was coming in from all directions.

– Daddy?

Norma lurched. There was a counter at the back of the big central room. The counter was behind armored glass and in the darkness, Raye stood peering in. Norma moved toward the glass cage, stumbled over something squishy underfoot. The floor shrouded in darkness. The armor-glass cage looked to be empty. There was no one there and then there was. A small man sat before an ancient TV monitor. The light was so random that the man's form flickered out and reformed behind the streaks on the glass and dust in the air.

– Daddy, it's me.

– Rayette?

Norma froze at the sound of the soft musical voice. The man looked up and what Norma saw took her breath away. His likeness to the twentieth-century entertainment artist, Michael Jackson, was unnerving not so much in its fidelity as its intent.

If sleeve technology was still a distant dream in Slashland, body-modification protocol—both compliant and off-market—was thriving and yet Norma had seen nothing like this. From the man's matte black hair to the geisha pallor to the cheekbone implants and whitened corneas, he was not so much a double as a monstrous out-take. He'd out-Michaeled Michael. Left the original in his dust to be reborn as another.

– Help you? Mac said, his eyes returning to the monitor. He pecked the keyboard with a gloved hand.

– Mac, Norma. Norma, Mac, said Raye.

Had some barbaric splicer—an unevenly replicated procedure reputed to have originated in a mountain laboratory in Switzerland—been at work here? Between the distorted, idealized likenesses of Michael Jackson around Mac's store and the deceased recording artist himself, the distances were galactic. But between Michael Jackson and the man in the glass cage there was a strange kind of collision. A reversal. As grotesque as he was, Norma felt that he'd literally captured something essential to Michael Jackson himself, that had remained concealed and inaccessible in the original.

His soul.

– Oh, he said. It's you.

Wacko-Jacko's drained blood smile. Norma tried to back away, but Raye was behind her. Pushed her forward with childish yet tensile fingers at the small of Norma's back.

– Don't worry, Raye said. He says that to everybody.

– I can't find them, he said in a soft falsetto. I can hear them but I can't see them.

Raye pulled Norma down to whisper in her ear.

– He hears voices, she said.

Norma nodded and straightened.You think? she hissed.

– Daddy, said Raye. Norma saved my life. I thought you should know. I fell but she picked me up—it's complicated. Thing is she needs to find some guy she has to give something important to. Card player, ex-military, maybe. Came in on the Surfliner before Christmas. Unusual boots. Metal heels, probably Ti from up north. Blond hair, pale eyes. I told her you'd know. Least I could do.

Mac peered into the monitor and flicked the screens.

– You did, didn't you, Daddy? You saw him.

Raye pushed forward and turned triumphantly to Norma.

– You saw this guy, sir? Norma said.

He shrugged, muttered something, furnace-eyed sprite who lived in the approximate and perpetual shadow of another. Norma clawed at her throat. The man was a danger, she was certain, but whether just to himself or also to his daughter, she couldn't decide. What was certain was that somewhere along the line, between the permanent eyeliner and the jaw reconstruction, he'd created a psychic shield so impenetrable that anything could hide there. Anything. Norma swayed but felt nailed to the floor. Her arms floated out, finding nothing but space. Where the hell was Raye?

– Make him talk, Daddy. Make Freddy talk.

Norma wheeled around but couldn't see where Raye's voice came from. She turned back to Mac, craned her neck to see what he saw on the monitor. A ghostly image of his daughter waving at them from beside a listing mannequin of Freddy Krueger. They were through an adjoining door, a storeroom or anteroom but when Norma turned to peer through the doorway, all she could see was darkness.

Mac sighed and pushed some buttons on a console beside the PA system. There was a dread whirring. Norma recoiled, slipping over that soft rubbery thing underfoot and flailing.

One-two Freddy's coming for you, said Freddy.

On the monitor, Raye squealed with delight. Norma heard the sound coming both from the monitor and from the other room and there was a delay between them.

I'm your boyfriend now, spluttered the dummy.

– Yah, said Raye. More, Daddy, more!

The sound echoed, one-two, I'm coming for you.

Freddy raised a jerky glove with cut-throat blades for fingers. *This is God,* he said. A plastic blade dropped off and clunked to the floor. Something popped, as if the fall had set off a fire cracker. Raye's wild laughter reverberated off the walls and from the speakers. Musty pages flapped, gears whirred, battery acid pooled.

– The hell, Norma said under her breath.

– Who's there? said Mac. The alarm in his voice was real this time and at its true register, not that of the actor or the character, just a lonely guy unused to strangers.

– Tell him, said Raye, abruptly there beside Norma again. What you want. About your ex.

– Another time, maybe, said Norma.

– And how you caught me when I fell. I fell, Daddy. I climbed high and fell hard. Like you said I would. See Norma's jacket, Daddy, see? She's ex-com. She backed me and I made it. We earned three hundred bucks, and I brought you some more medicine.

Raye shoved a plastic pill bottle under the glass. Her pallor radioactive in the weird light from the cage, the burned-out LEDs and photo-luminous plastic. Her tawny hair was wild around her head. She'd broken out in a greasy sweat.

– Easy, said Norma.

– Tell him, said Raye in shrill tones. She turned to Norma and her eyes were like broken glass.

– Okay, sir. So this Guy. Kind of Western-looking gentleman.

– Guy? said Mac. When?

– Well, said Norma. Hoping you could tell me. Very blond hair. Piercings. Sir.

The words floated off into the darkness like bubbles around Norma's head. Her shoulders had begun to throb, the skin straining. Raye was crying. Mac bent down below the counter, clouds of dust billowed up as he rummaged around on a shelf. He sat back up with a swathe of clippings in his hand and passed them under the glass to Norma.

Spill City collector sitting on a gold mine; Michael Jackson impersonator wows them at the Valley Vista Plaza.

The clippings were soft with age or grease or sweat or tears. Another read:

Mr. Mac 'Daddy' McCarthy, who more than a decade ago, had the first surgical procedure to remake his face in the image of his deceased idol, Michael Jackson, said that there are more than three million objects crammed into his tiny Arcadia store. 'I've been called upon to round up all the old toys in the world,' he said of his obsession with playtime arcana. A friend, who wishes to remain anonymous, says his fascination grew out of a childhood deprived of love and toys as a ward of the state in Oregon.

– I can feel him, said Mac.

– Who? said Norma.

– Mo Joe, said Mac. Coming in from all directions.

He leant forward and that's when she felt it again. The soft give between her boots, somewhere between a crunch and a squish. She bent down and knew as soon as her hand found it what it was. She slowly straightened. The devil puppet.

– Where'd you get this? she said, holding it by its faded flapping dress.

– Ten bucks, said Mac. A rare piece.

– Who brought this in? she said. When?

But Mac only shrugged, lost again in the tangled paths of his paranoia. He peered into the screen, panned from frame to frame, always searching, always seeing.

She looked at the puppet with its chewed up horn and chipped red eyes and she put it gently on the shelf around the glass cage.

– Pass, she said.

Mac giggled and turned back to the monitor. The room had become unbearably hot. He blotted his forehead with a snowy white cloth he pulled from his belt. From somewhere in the shop there was a furious pop-pop-pop, a cap gun going off.

– What you hear is not a test, said Mac. *Memento mori*, mori mento. For evil only good, hip hop the yippie.

– I'll be on my way. See you, Raye.

– Soul is dead said the man in the mirror, Mac's voice sounded croaky, a strange drawl creeping in. Pass it on.

Raye yelped.

– Don't leave her here, Mac said, returning to the sibilant tones of his idol. It's not safe.

– Daddy? said Raye.

– Don't come back, said Mac.

Norma yelled, Safe from what?

He was still staring fixedly at the mirror, a single tear rolling down the ruined parchment of his face. He said, Me, or him?

– Who? said Norma through clenched teeth.

– The guy, lisped Mac. I can hear him but I can't see him.

– It's just the voices, Daddy. screamed Raye. There is no guy! He's just—I just. God I forgot. That other guy.

Norma turned to Raye and grabbed her by the shoulders.

– Don't, she said. Forget it.

Mac said, Man is a wolf to man. Pop da pop da pop dibbie dibbie, he said. Pass it on.

– Fuck you, Daddy, Raye said, and bolted. Norma heard her crashing through the store, the front door opening and slamming shut. Cold air sweeping through.

Mac looked up, brightening again.

– Rayette, honey? Is that you?

– She's gone, Sir, snapped Norma. You just missed her.

– Happy Birthday, the melody whispered out of Mac, sibilant and off-key. To Rayeeee. Happy Birthday to you.

26//: cherry

Norma found Raye waiting outside the Laundromat down the road from her old man's little shop of horrors. She was staring in through the window at the spinning machines. Reflected in the glass, the big yellow talk-to-the-hand from the traffic light across the street. Clear mucus ran from Raye's nose and she wiped it away with a snotty sleeve.

Norma stood beside her, drawing breath. Her own hulking reflection, wild-haired with sunglasses askew stood beside that of the child in her ratty parka. A defective screen above the row of washing machines played footage of the ongoing rebellion in North India. Graffitied drains from which spilled the dead and dying.

– What now? said Norma.

Raye shivered in her parka. I'm so hungry, she said dully. I could eat the cock off a dead Secessionist.

– Okay.

Neither of them moved. The rain had eased and the stars were still pale against the lavender sky, but down on the streets, it was already night. Raye's tremors were getting worse. The whole parka shook, motherless child in its filthy depths. When Norma closed her eyes she saw the devil puppet lying discarded on the floor, and when she opened them she had a plan. There was a diner set up in shipping container on the corner and Norma started walking toward it. Raye followed as if tethered to her. They went in and sat at a booth in a dim corner and Norma ordered cheeseburgers and Cokes while Raye stared out of the window. The pale faces of the supper-time customers scattered like petals in the dark glass. Raye's shoulders convulsed in a harsh sob.

– She okay? said the waitress.

Norma unclenched her fists and lay her hands flat on the table. Exhaled.

– She's fine, she said. It's her birthday.

– Bless, said the waitress and moved off.

Raye's eyes were puffy slits. Her nose was red and raw and she chewed her tear-slick lips. Norma pulled out a wad of napkins from the dispenser and shoved them at her. Raye wiped her face and blew her nose but it didn't make much difference. Norma reached up and removed the sunglasses the musician had given her, leaned across as he had done and with both hands slid the sunglasses over Raye's eyes. They sat like goggles on the girl's small puffy face. She looked half-submerged in the parka, doomed and wingless pupa. Norma had never seen so many tears. They flowed down the contours of the girl's face and onto the food.

– That went well, Norma said.

Raye managed a sulky shrug and went back to her food. Her appetite strangely unaffected. Norma put down her knife and fork. She wiped hamburger grease off her mouth with a napkin, pushed away her uneaten meal. She watched Raye slurp down the Coke, blow her nose on the napkin, dump sugar into her coffee until gradually the tears stopped flowing and the burger was gone and most of the fries too, and there was a smear of grease on one of her lenses.

– I told you, Raye said between hiccoughs. He'd have the intel on your guy. Daddy knows people. People talk to him, tell him things.

– Not real people, Norma said. In case you hadn't noticed. What does he mean, pass it on?

Raye began to draw pictures on the edge of her plate with a ketchup-dipped fry. Norma watched the lines form shapes, bloody hieroglyphs that made no sense, or none that she could see. She clenched her jaw and her fists too to stop herself from pulling the fry out of the girl's fingers, was glad that they were in a booth at the back of the coffee shop, mostly hidden from view.

– How about that raggedy old puppet? Raye said. Like he needs another piece of junk. Someone else's memory. Someone else's life.

Norma's jacket was zipped up over the bioswitch. The dentata cramped up at the mention of the puppet. There could be only one. Gene had left her a clue. A crumb.

– Pass it on, she said again very slowly. What the hell does it mean?

She raised her eyes to meet Norma's glare, lowered them again.

– Okay. Okay. You never played Telephone as a kid?

– I had a deprived childhood.

– Clearly. It used to be his favorite game. You sit in a circle and someone whispers something, a story or a joke or whatever, to the person next to them and that person whispers it to the next person and so on. By the time it gets to the last person, they have to say it out loud and the end result is totally different.

– And?

– And nothing. That's it. The gag is that what comes out is nothing like what goes in.

Norma said, I don't get it.

Raye looked down and was fry-doodling in the ketchup again. The huge sunglasses swung down so Norma could see the tears still stuck to her eyelashes. Raye abruptly hiccoughed and the glasses fell off and into the fries. She picked them out and slid them back on again crusted with crumbs and grease. Norma shook her head, remembering what the musician said about charity long ago on this terrible day.

– Maybe you're not the only one with a deprived childhood, said Raye. Mac too, I doubt they played too many games of Telephone in juvie. Everything he did was like wish fulfillment for a time that didn't exist. Like that saying you never know what you've got till it's gone? He always knew. The life he never lived. Never would. So he made it up. Played along.

– Human communication approximating a dance of death, said Norma.

– A metaphor. I get it. You going to finish that?

Norma pushed her plate across and watched the girl tuck into her uneaten burger and talk between mouthfuls and leftover sobs.

– So anyway, he sat us all in a circle and the first person (that was always Daddy because he was the best liar) would make up a story as complicated as hell and whisper it to the next 'person'—she wiggled her fingers in the air—which was usually just Raggedy Ann or Buzz Lightyear or Barbie or Elvis—

– How could you make toys—things—listen, said Norma, completely dumbfounded. Much less 'pass it on'? Now it was her turn to wiggle her fingers in the air.

– You can make a toy, a thing, do anything you want. Like software except your imagination's the code.

– Like that big Freddy thing in your father's store?

The door blew open bringing with it the smell of ash and the faraway crash of the surf and they both shivered simultaneously and finally smiled at each other across the table, across the ruins of the day, across hungry Mommies and bad daddies and cruddy sunglasses and random charities—because that was the key.

– Freddy's just got an ordinary old voice box, Raye said. That's someone else's imagination. Better when it's your own. But sometimes we played with real people, the retard neighbor or Granddad sometimes too, yeah, when we were back in Portland. I liked the toys better though. They didn't cheat.

– Well.

– So there's that. And every time you whispered something you had to say, Brrring. Brrring. And that person would have to pass on the story exactly as they heard it.

– Bring bring?

Raye sighed in mock despair.

– Remember when the landlines made a comeback because of the tumor scares? That was the sound they made. Like a ringtone. Brrrrringgg, Brrrringgg.

Norma pressed fingers against her temples.

– So you weren't really telling the truth. You were bringing it. Over and over again until it wasn't even the truth anymore.

Raye thought about it.

– Not the same truth, anyway.

– How many are there? said Norma.

But Raye's eyes were glassy and fixed on Norma. She said, Let's play.

– Another time, said Norma. Her eyes flicked to the emptying diner. People silently staring into their reflections in the windows or working their consoles. The hiss of the frier, the chatter of the TV above the counter.

– I go: when my dog died I ate its heart. And you being fourth in line hear something about a what, a car that doesn't start and a, a pie, you might just say, um, I wanted to take the car out to get some pie but it wouldn't start, and the next person hears bar and sump night, they'd say, There's this guy drinks at my local bar's got to drain a sump tomorrow night.

– And I hear rain and fart and jump and ride.

– And I hear pain and heart and sky.

Norma said, Pass it on.

Raye whispered, It's already gone. Look.

She had drawn some kind of map or constellation in the ketchup. Crumpled napkins lay in balls around the plate like meteors or stars. There were crumbs in the girl's hair and on the filthy blue collar of her parka.

– Sorry, Raye said hoarsely and hiccoughed again. I really thought he could help you.

A few people looked around and over the backs of booths. Raye abruptly grinned through her tears and pointed a bloody fry at Norma.

– What about Freddy, yeah? You should have seen your face. Like you'd seen a ghost. Wish I had a camera.

– You can watch the replay.

– 'I'm your boyfriend now,' I think you screamed.

Norma's jacket was zipped up over the bioswitch. But her head was fuzzy and she knew Mommy was trying to get in. The bioswitch burned.

– Why Michael, anyway? What's the big deal? said Norma. Wasn't Blanket the real star? I see his holo everywhere.

Raye laughed raggedly, Not a conversation you want to have with

Mac. I mean musically, okay. The guy was a genius. But to lose it in front of the whole world—

– Lose what? His genius?

– No. Yes. Everything. Where you end the world begins. That place, that place where it's just you. Free as a bird. Scary free. Put your hands in the air cuz you just don't care.

The time on the holoscreen said two a.m. Delirium creeping into Raye's speech and her face as white as paper.

– When's the last time you saw him? Before today.

– Michael Jackson or my dad because they're pretty much the same thing.

Norma sighed. I get that, she said.

– I tried at Christmas. But he hides sometimes. Hides from everyone. Where, I don't know.

Customers pushed out the door, bringing with them the grind of drones, laughter. Saturday night noises.

– Hides? You mean, he disappears?

– You know the Michael Jackson song, the Man in the Mirror? That's how he talks to him. To Daddy. Through the mirror.

Norma's eye sockets felt hollow. The CCTV screens? she said. That's his mirror?

Raye nodded, her gaze fixed on her plate. Don't you want to know what he says? Her voice was barely audible above the din in the diner, the rushing in Norma's ears.

– No.

– Michael tells Daddy to find the one he lost, the one that was taken from him.

– Himself. Norma's shoulders burned and the dentata knifed and she felt Mommy roar inside her, clawing to get out, craving, always so hungry for what it had lost. Lost somewhere in the mirror, in its own image, the same but different. Pass it on.

Raye said, He wasn't always so wacko. Like he was never normal but it was okay for a while. He was always an impersonator. A really good one. He did Elvis, Hendrix, but Michael Jackson mainly. Always too much Michael.

– When did the mirror thing start? said Norma.

Raye turned to face her own reflection in the dirty diner window. Too much Michael, she said to herself.

The waitress came over. Her brown hands gripping the coffee pot, her face framed in a short white afro. She looked down at Raye and clucked. Went away and came back with a piece of pie buried under ice cream and cream, a puckered cherry on top.

– Happy Birthday, hun.

Norma nodded her thanks. Raye talked between mouthfuls of pie.

– He did some shows in Vegas. I was still with him then but just a baby and he had some trouble up there—got evicted or some such—then he came down to Spill City and opened the store. He had boxes of shit he collected, plus his own stuff from when he was a kid, dug in dumpsters for the rest, traded and quake-trash meets. Had dreams of going on the road again. Blamed it on the fact he didn't look enough like Michael Jackson. Every cent he earned at the store went on another nose or chin or whatever.

The coffee was hot and bitter going down but it was the way Raye swept her arms out in a gesture so falsely indifferent that made Norma wince.

– Everything he did to make him look more like Michael Jackson only seemed to remind him of how far he had to go. I called up once from New York, yeah. Times Square boogie all night. He told me how he finally got a letter back from the Michael Jackson people after all the hundreds he'd written. And it said, come on up to Neverland. Really. He read it to me. It was from Blanket Jackson III, signed, sealed and delivered. Saying come up and help with the Neverland Revival. They were going to move it to Vegas, reopen it to the public. They invited Daddy to perform. Make Michael live again.

– So? Norma was trying to pay attention but exhaustion had made her mind wander, and her eyes too. She just wanted to be alone to think about the puppet, how Gene had left it there—for her—and Mac had made sure she'd seen it—had passed it on—so pretty. Like a wolf.

– Soooooo... Raye stared down at her pie with her fork poised in the air. Before Norma could stop her she started banging her head against the back of the booth. Bang bang bang. People staring.

– He lost it, Raye said between bangs. He lost the letter.

– How? said Norma. How do you lose something like that? He never goes anywhere.

The windows of the diner were steamy and it was dark outside. Norma rubbed some of the steam away and watched some Cruids doing figure eights on their boards in front of a sheet metal fence scrawled with biofluorescent slogans. Raye thumped against the back of the seat again. Norma turned back reluctantly.

– Some guy came through.

– Some guy? What guy? Norma dragged her voice up from the pit of her stomach. She waved the waitress over for more coffee.

– He was from LA, that's all he said. He stopped by to show Daddy some merch, top notch. A rare train set or some such. Daddy was feeling okay that day—the woman at the Laundromat told me afterward that he looked good too—he made the guy lattes with the machine he looted from a Sunset cafe in the arson attacks of '29. Guy had a fifth of Wild Turkey in his sack, started splashing it around; Daddy got out his favorite Ozzy Osbourne shot glasses. He shouldn't drink, you know. He's not meant to drink with the meds and all. The two of them swapping lies, the guy's all, did you know you're the spitting image of Michael? Turned Daddy's head. Guy even said the magic words, Moonwalk for me, Michael.

Raye had started again, banging her back against the vinyl booth.

– Hey. Stop that. You'll break something.

– Turned out the guy had been a stuntman in LA, did the stunts in *X-Box Mariachi*. Got Daddy drunk (bang bang) and he passed out. When he woke up, guy'd ripped him off.

Norma's hands were shaking so badly she had to set her coffee down. She'd lost feeling in her fingers. Breathed through the pain in her shoulders.

– Guy was gone (bang), letter from Neverland was gone. Bam (bang bang). A bunch of other random stuff gone too. But nothing that mattered like the letter. That was Mac's ticket to ride. His red shoes—

– Slow down.

– When Daddy called me, he'd lost it. I mean not just the letter but his total shit. it was like he was talking a different language then. Like the voices were talking through him. He started to act crazy, not just the usual eccentric and weird and selfish and addicted, but cracked. (bang) The chick at the Laundromat next door called me, I came as quick as I could. I mean he's no angel, Daddy. You don't have to tell me. But he's Daddy, yeah (bang). Only one I got. So I said I'd look for the letter but he said he already looked. I could see that. The place was trashed. I asked him to tell me what the guy who ripped him off looked liked, you know, people I ride with can fix that shit, but he couldn't remember. I said try but it was like the sickness, the schizo thing, brought in new memories, stuff that never even happened to him that took over what he thought. Like he started talking about stuff, bad stuff, that never happened to him—not that I knew of.

– What sort of stuff?

Raye jabbed viciously in the air with a fork dripping cherry pie.

– Devil puppets, wolves, fortune tellers, barns. Like all the memories attached to all the shit in that store were talking to him all at once. Like they wanted him now instead of the other way around.

She had stopped banging against the booth. Had started silently crying again, the tears rolling down her blotched, snotty face, framed in the stiff tufts of her dune-colored hair.

Norma said slowly, Why didn't he tell me this? Why didn't he tell me about the Guy?

– Michael wouldn't let him, said Raye. You're not getting it. The voices start, yeah, and it's always Michael. And the headaches like, I don't know, terminal brain cancer or something, and he says the darkness never comes. He prays for dark and for silence but's always bright and the bright lights bring nose, and he can hear the pain. So he closes his eyes—bang—and it's bright, always light, so much pain—bang—and the darkness never fucking comes.

The cherry pie gutted and split like road kill on the plate and Raye's soft cheeks splattered with cherry goo and other diners staring, the Jamaican cook's eyes narrowing from over the stove, Norma standing and throwing bloody bills on the table and shepherding the girl out before the waitress called security.

27//:pull

A woman and a child moving through the mean streets, nothing that hadn't been seen before. It would be light soon. A Consortium guard's knuckles tightened over the butt of his rifle—Norma's shadow loomed at the mouth of an alleyway, but he relaxed when he saw the child. Norma had managed to get her cleaned up—in her cruddy parka she blended in, her pallor, the hunger in her eyes reflected in a thousand other faces, untold other eyes. All around them, the persistent swoosh of skateboard wheels, the clack of cowboy boots, black hat brims, and Norma wheeled wildly to and fro but there was no one there. Around them nothing but the space of darkness, the space of fear.

Raye was talked out. But as they neared the Sanctuary, she said, expressionless, Leeks.

The sour, overcooked reek of whatever seethed in the Crock-Pot had drifted down to the street and Raye picked it up a block before Norma did. At the door to the Sanctuary Norma gave the girl a couple of Valiums and left her there without making eye contact. Without saying goodbye.

Norma jumped a GMC recombo with Tijuana plates and flew off at the trailer park. She landed badly and splashed in some standing water at the edge of the road. Her arms flailed as she regained her balance. By the time she got to the trailer, numb with exhaustion, all she could do was kick off her boots and fall face-down on the bed. Her eyes burned yet she couldn't sleep. She dry-swallowed some off-market triazolam but it didn't help. She went outside, wondered if she should go down to the beach. And then what? Take a dip?

Mommy said, A daemon cannot die.

If that is what she was once, what was she now? She's adopted a street kid, longed for a man she couldn't have and suffered from killer PMS. What was that? There was no way of knowing.

The wind was bitter and the ocean was a roiling hole. And also a whole. Mirror of the world, source of all its pain, all its life and time. She saw it in its entirety. All the way down, two-three-four miles. The trick was getting back up. A daemon couldn't die but how far could a woman fall? How many miles to mortality, Mommy? Are we there yet?

Dawn touched the fleshy cliffs. Their tufted vegetation rippled like living pelt. Eroded monsters, doomed gorillas with slumped and leathery bodies swathed in mist. The path beneath her feet was lined with wrappers, cans and burger boxes in various states of decay. An odor of petals, pine and corrosives. She put her hands on the wooden rail at the edge overlooking the beach. The countless hands and unending seasons that had touched this rail, felt the call of the unfathomed sea—find out what you truly are.

Norma could see beneath its surface, see it in its entirety. The whole. Float through it in her mind—the sand bars and buried reefs, the shipwrecks and underwater crevasses. She could see the other side. Not just San Diego Bay but beyond. To where the Pacific grew warm, where warships lay buried along with the odd asteroid, ancient fuselage, and then grew cold again. And the life it sustained—would it take her? Would it want her? Mommy said no. So what had changed? Norma could feel it. She needed to know. What was she now?

She needed to know if she could die.

The way Mac's eyes had darkened at the end, just before they'd brightened. Like it had gotten crowded in there. Is death what they'd seen in her, those crowded eyes? Or not. Had they seen the Silence?

Because that's who she was. Mommy had made her that way, a

conduit. A hole. She could only hope that something had broken through the silence.

Bring bring.

Norma released her clawed hold on the wooden rail. She brushed off the sand and splinters and went back in the trailer and lay on the bed with the curtains open to the numberless stars. She carried the inevitability of her fall—there was blood on her hands and she didn't know why—within her, sharpening its teeth. The longer she waited before implantation, the worse the pain.

– Look, she said, Here I am.

The sun had gotten too big for Mommy, gave it a swollen head, or was it the other way around? Who had killed who? What had killed the First Beings? The fissioning death star, or the hostile, doomed Brainworld determined to take its beautiful horned children down with it? If Mommy couldn't have the beautiful First Beings, nothing could. It made sure of that, but to learn its power, had it summoned them or created them?

It was impossible to know, impossible not to know.

There were footsteps outside the trailer, a faint whiff of straw and manure as if stuck to the soles of a shoe. She, the hunted now, haunted by some Guy with shit on his shoes. What was he? Her skin prickled and the darkness nailed her to the bed. The shuffling footsteps receded. What was its name? She went to a barn in her dreams and came back with blood on her hands, more fallout? Or psychosomatic guilt over Slash sins unnumbered and truths debowelled—was this guilt another side effect of the mission? Because however it had originally been conceived the mission had changed. Elvis has left the building Mommy and the truth is dead even as it is created. Brrring brrring.

– I am never going home.

Sleep. Slipping over the lip of a waking dream, she felt, more than heard, a song at the horizon, so beautiful it made her smile. A stranger singing—the Guy?—calling to her, pulling her toward the song, his image on the rise, a gelid moon that became the face of Michael Jackson and Mac Daddy and then the guy on the train with the fulvous eyes. Gloria, the song went. GEE-EL-OH-AR-I-AY. A phone rang. And rang. Irretrievable beginnings, unpredictable ends, her curse was to have been made in the image of no other. Was it a puppy? Or a child? Did the daughter pass on? Or live to rip out the heart of its parent? To write a letter from Neverland, miles between us, Michael. Time against us. Call home, hun. Chewy yeah, and crusty too. Looks like gum. Or was that cum? One two I'm coming for you. Make Mommy talk. This is God, said the wolf man, reaching into Norma's hole and pulling out a plum. I'm your boyfriend now.

PART III

META 4

Kali I8 saw the Slash as a self-authored being. To penetrate the secrets of the Slash, I8 studied its symbols. It collected, collated and translated. Letters, numbers, pictograms, cuneiform. Japanese, German, Arabic, Israeli, Swahili, Sanskrit, Urdu, Yandrruwandha, Yugoslavian, Handspeak. Metaphor, metonym, semaphore, sign. Ebonics, Hebronics, Chingrish, Hinglish, platitude, aporia, glossolalia, clichés and platitudes, pidgin, rhetoric aporia, and rhyme. And so on and so forth. Assonance and synonym, lyric and lies. Zingers and clangers and curse and verse, heresy, prophesy, Strine and slang. I8 kept the symbols in the lab (a sentience has many rooms), dissected, dismembered, stacked on shelves beneath the great precipice. It tried to master the code, practiced unendingly, but language—words for things—eluded it. So Kali's brain destroyed the symbols and signs and sunk again into the only world that it knew and could therefore rule, a world of silence and solitude. Kali I8's mind could not conceive of another.

(Fascicle 437 Nilea AQn., trans. L.Shay 2656)

28//: unheimlich maneuver

The drugs kept her unconscious and finally dreamless most of the day and when she woke the dentata was screaming for a name. What hunted her? The Factory, when she got there around midnight, was deserted. It wasn't just the Dianabol scare that Bunny and Raye had told her about. There had been rumors of a raid—not seen in a decade or more—and of Consortium informants and moles and a return to order. Zygote labs had dismantled overnight; spiders swung in the windows of the hot ware outlets, and Cash Attack had closed its Factory store. Up at Una's, the Karaoke was winding down and Norma slumped beneath the screen running Dancing with the Chefs, followed by a news report about a new school opening in the Zone.

Little Barry hefted brontosaurus schnitzels and kept his one good eye on Norma, answered her questions about Raye with wary nonchalance. Norma saw something skitter at the edge of her eye, but why turn around when there was nothing there?

Little Barry told her that Raye didn't do Rediem, not yet, even though she was technically a Grimey, rode with them and called herself one. And Grimeys did Rediem.

– Raye rides in once or twice a year with the Grimey, but she's all right. Got guts, that kid. Something innocent about her. She brings her old man food and meds.

– How does she afford it? said Norma.

He shrugged, wouldn't meet her eye and this time she knew it was deliberate.

– Daredevil stunts, he said. You saw her. Survival sex.

– Great.

– You can talk, said Little Barry.

Bring, bring.

– That was some fall, he continued, looking up to the vaulted ceiling and pointing to the broken skylight. Norma kept her eyes straight ahead.

– *Verstehen si jetz*, scolded Una from the kitchen. The bad man pushed her.

Little Barry waved her quiet, drying beer mugs while his wonky eye wandered Norma knew not where.

– Haven't seen Augustine and the others for a while, he shrugged. Can't say I miss them.

– They'll be back, said Norma.

– You don't want to be here then, said Little Barry. Augustine bears a deadly grudge.

Norma tried to think how best to approach the topic of Mac's visitor, the stunt man from LA.

– So, what's with Mac? Is he just selfish or is something really wrong?

– Mac's bent, said Little Barry. He's never been all there. Loved his little girl but couldn't raise her.

Norma said, She told me he knew everyone, saw them as they came into Spill City. Got paid for his eyes and his ears.

Little Barry shrugged. She told you he'd be able to pass on some intel about this guy you're looking for?

Norma said, She didn't lie.

– Good, because, thing is she says that to everyone, just to help her Daddy out. Brings them to the store so maybe they buy some piece of junk they don't need, maybe pass on some piece of junk info gets someone laid, killed, cured. Whatever. And maybe once it was true. Was a time Mac saw himself as a double-agent type. Covered it up with his eccentric ways, so no one would know what he was. Told himself he was doing it for the kid, for Raye. Another weirdo—same difference.

– What is the difference?

Barry looked up at the TV, checked the score. The state, he said. When it was a state, used to be full of them.

– Weirdos?

– Big time moonwalkers, baby, Yeti-Divas, Unicorn-hunters. No one was what they said they were.

– Unicorns? Norma said more to herself than to Barry.

He rolled his good eye and moved off to take an order.

When he came back he said, where have all the unicorn hunters gone? All I see is Consortium goons and Cartel sissies.

Norma said nothing.

– It's all the same weird now. Soul's gone from the place.

She heard a combo bleating in reverse down in the dock. A reek wafted in from the catwalk as a customer pushed out the door, and Norma turned around, half-expected to see a retreating hat brim, but the room was deserted and the door banged shut in the rank updraft from the Factory floor.

Bang bang bang.

– Mac took everything, said Little Barry. Quake-trash and baggage no one wanted to lug around. Trash or treasure, he didn't care which was which. Vulcan dolls worth fifty bucks a pop and dime-a-dozen Stephen King hardcovers from the Eighties. Folks'd open up to him and he'd listen to their crap, take it all in. Believed it or said he did, and they believed him, the passersby. How the real founder of Er was no less than Niemen Van Aldren himself. How they'd dug themselves out of the rubble with an Emory board, how demon slugs had crawled aboard USS Nimitz. Lies, truth, it was all the same to him. He'd pass it on and it would become something different again. A circle of lies until it strangled him.

Little Barry shook his head and his jowls flapped in sorrow. Some customers waved him over and he disappeared behind the bar, popped up on the cinderblock step at the other end with two giant mugs of ale. When he came back he shrugged in the direction of the customers, a little happier.

– Haven't seen their kind here for a while. Coders. Upscale techies.

Good for business, I got no complaints. Where was I?

He banged a stubby thumb against the oversized dome of his forehead.

– Mac. Yeah. So being a cute and cuddly collector was one thing but then the thing with Michael Jackson just got too weird. You may have noticed.

Norma was on her feet.

– Sit down. Una'll fix you something. So a little bit of Michael goes a long way, you know what I'm saying. Folks don't want that. They want cute and cuddly, not deranged, chopped up Thriller-fuckers. You seen him, right? Man's a freak. Best left alone. Pass on by, do not pass Go. But then, so he gets this letter from one of the Michael Jackson people saying they want to see his act, maybe use it for the reopening of Neverland in Vegas, you know that big—

– Neverland, said Norma. Look. Raye told me. So what?

It was coming. Bring bring. She felt it. Felt it in the tight lick of anticipation in her belly, her mouth dry with Mommy's hungers and some new ones, ones that had no name.

– Okay, so he gets this letter, brags about it to who'd ever listen, which wasn't much more than the Korean laundry family and the waitress at the diner who looks in on him now and again. And then he gets a visit from this Guy Whatsit who rips him off—you heard about that, right?

– Guy who? said Norma, trying to keep her voice even. Her legs grew cold. She hadn't eaten all day. Hadn't slept for two nights. Masturbated till she bled.

– Guy, guy? It'll come to me, said Barry. Guy Thingie, Una, what's his name?

– *Who*? said Una.

– Macho man who took that letter—Barry turned to Norma—was going to make him a star. Whoa! Hey!

Norma reached over the bar and with both hands seized Little Barry by the scruff of the neck and was dangling him above the bar without knowing what she was doing. It wasn't her. She shook him like a doll and he was surprisingly heavy. His little legs twitching and his fat fingers clawing her hands at his throat. His little feet in their heavy boots kicked the cash drawer and something flipped out and in his hands was the

Saturday Night Special he kept there, and the muzzle was cold against her ear.

She dropped him.

– Sorry Barry. I don't know what that was. I swear.

The midget's hand steady on the piece pointed at her head. Steady as hell.

– Get out, he said.

– Guy Manly, said Una in a shaky voice. The name of the guy who goes to see Mac is Guy Manly. Go home now, Big Lady.

– Barry. Honest. I'll make it up to you.

– Manly, said Barry, lowering the gun and rubbing his throat. That's it. Guy Manly. Happy?

The red was draining from his face but the fear and hurt were still in his eyes and Norma thought bitterly of the rage that had been coded into her program, and into Little Barry's too and how it was different but the same. They both had different Mommies to blame. Speak of which, the bitch wasn't returning her calls.

– I'm sorry, she said again.

Little Barry just shook his head and moved off to the other end of the bar. Norma listened to the flat sounds of a sales assistant murdering 'Nothing Compares to You.'

– Psst, said Una from the pass window. A porn star is your Guy Manly.

– Raye told me he was a stuntman, Norma said. From LA.

– Stuntman, porn star, politician, no difference in Spill City. Guy Manly not his real name, *verstehen?*

One of the coders at the end of the bar, who was very drunk, called out flirtatiously, Remember that actor, Duane the Vein?

– Buck Naked, said Little Barry. Is the one I remember, and Rod Long. You look good when you cry, kid. Makes you look young. But if you ever lay a hand on me again—

– I'm not crying, said Norma. And I am young. What does he look like?

– Rod Long? said Little Barry. He's a dwarf. Started as an understudy, but he fluffed like nobody's business, so—

– No, said Norma. I mean this Guy Whatsit who stole Mac's letter.

She couldn't bring herself to say his name.

– Guy Manly, said Little Barry. Mac says. Schizos are like that. Maybe he was real or maybe not. Maybe there was a letter and maybe not. Maybe Mac just wished there was, know what I mean?

Una's face flashed into the pass window, damp with labor and rage.

– *Unheimlich,* said Una from the kitchen. You never know what you have until it goes.

– Anyone know, said Norma very slowly. Where this Guy is now?

Little Barry shrugged again, suddenly finding a spot on a glass he was cleaning that wouldn't come out.

– That reminds me, he said. You hear Bunny's boy died?

The bar swam and blurred, all the colors running into each other, all the songs. Una heaved a sob from the kitchen and slammed shut the pass window.

Little Barry said, Funeral's day after tomorrow up at Canyon Memorial. You coming?

Norma lifted her head and howled, which seemed for once like the right thing to do. Beneath it the sound of Una's sobs and the Karaoke and clink of glasses and coders' jokes, the swoosh swoosh of Little Barry's towel and silence of his tears. A chorus of the fallen.

29//: swami's

Gene first got to Spill City a few days after Independence Day. He went to have his palms read at Swami's, the famous cliff-side temple he'd heard about, but found it in ruins. He strolled the ramparts in a secondhand shirt that he'd bought at the 101 markets with his dwindling cash. He'd lost weight coming back from Bakersfield, had walked most of the way, arrived in Spill City wondering if she was still here. The freaky Thriller guy hadn't seen her, but he could have been lying—there were human portals like that all over the Zone, broken down visionaries whose function as mnemonic receptor in the damaged brain of Spill City was limited to those missing in action or about to be. Gene threw the devil puppet into the mix—Norma would bite or she wouldn't. He was sick of dragging the old thing around the country anyway. Time to let it go.

He clambered around Swami's—the crumbled stucco and mossy pagodas overlooking the Pacific, the weed-choked grounds reclaimed by shanty-dwellers and cardboard cities. Music blared. At every turn someone selling batteries, homemade consoles. Laundry flapped. Trash fires burned in canisters. He asked after the one he sought, a tall woman—like me, he said, pointing to his heart—yeah, white, I guess. Dark hair, eyes the color of rain. Folks said, see the Doctor. There.

Hunched over a brazier, an old guy, skinny as hell, warming his black-nailed fingers. Gene grinned. He knew the type, half-starved psychic, reader of cards and tea leaves, fire-eater and sister-fucker. Gene approached, feeling right at home.

– Stop the alliance with a virgin's blood, the Doctor yelled, chugging from a bottle of Old Crow and wiping the dribble off his chin. Feed their lust and all their fury. Feed the fury, cause of all our grief.

– Amen, slurred a chorus of addled Grimeys sprawled beneath a broken fountain.

Gene's shadow fell over the man. He watched him poke at the fire for a while.

– Five bucks, the Doctor said, not looking up. Show me your palm.

– Now you're talking, said Gene.

He grinned, pulled up a wooden crate and held out his huge hand.

– Five bucks, said the Doctor.

Gene lay three on the ground between them. The man inched a dusty boot forward, held the bills down fast with a metal heel. Took Gene's hand in his own gnarled fist and traced the joke lifeline with a cursor that glowed pale blue, the color of a star at its hottest.

You should be dead, said the Doctor. Pass it on.

Gene's grin widened. That's what Auntie always said. Look at that lifeline, how it cuts out just—

– There, said the Doctor. It picks up there. With the cursor he touched a hairsbreadth crease on Gene's meaty palm almost at the point where it met his wrist. Gene shuddered involuntarily. He felt his gorge rise at the Doctor's touch. He breathed through it, nudged aside the leather cord bracelet dangling Gloria's teeth, and peered down at his open palm.

– That's nothing. Just a wrinkle, you crazy fake. I've had better readings from One-Eyed Alice back at the rez.

Without warning the Doctor made a fist with his right hand and punched himself in the face. His hand disappeared into his mouth.

Gene recoiled.

– Hey.

The Doctor's hand kept rummaging around his grizzled maw right up to the snake tattoo on his arm. Pulled out his hand finally and opened his spit-slick fist. Yellowed dentures dangled off the end of a clawed finger, drool unspooling. He stared at Gene with gunky eyes. He poked the cursor behind his ear and ratcheted his left arm out, took Gene's wrist in a rusty grip and dropped the gooey dentures in Gene's open palm.

Gene said, Fuck.

– Is it a man or a woman you seek?

– A woman, said Gene.

The Doctor shook his head. There is another, he said. His puckered face hole gumming the words. Between the hunted and the hunter there is another.

Gene tried to pull his hand away, tried to twist his wrist to lose the false teeth. But the Doctor's hand held like a rat trap.

– Another? he said. How will I know?

Gene was unable to take his eyes off the dentures that lay in a pool of saliva in his open palm. Later he would try to remember if the old man's lips had moved, and realized that even if they had he wouldn't have seen them because when the dentures started to talk that was all he saw.

– You will know, the false teeth said. You will know the other by its step.

Aporafek/x: (n) i. A being caught between temporal, spacial, or ontological categories. e.g. a g(host) or alien. ii. A (non)species of meaning impossible to penetrate, put aside or pass on. iii. The expression of doubt, real or simulated, about where to begin or what to do or say. iv. A conceptual transparency so complete as to form a barrier rather than a window to meaning.

(Saurum Nilea, AQn., trans. L.Shay 2656)

30//:re:mission

At Miguel's, on the day of Bunny's son's funeral, Norma worked her way through a late breakfast of four eggs, bacon, beans and pancakes. She ate a bowl of gluey pink yoghurt and drank two cups of coffee and a glass of pineapple juice from a tin that Miguel opened behind the counter. She slowly wiped her mouth. She dialed Mommy on a smashed 'droid she'd found under a dumpster but transmission was blocked. It was not uncommon. Psychic interference was often a factor in failed configuration protocol, especially across species. In other words, she and Mommy were no longer seeing eye-to-eye.

She paid her bill and set out for the cemetery. Was it still February? An ashy rain fell and a chill settled over this Sunday afternoon. She pulled the sleeves of her jacket down over her wrists, zipped it up over the tank top. After a long wait in the shade of the ramp among the interchangeable lumps of sleeping bags, dogs and comatose itinerants, she finally jumped a Humvee recombo and rode inland. They passed under the Interstate on what remained of the 805 and turned left onto Canyon Road, Norma peering out from under the tarp at the blurred canyons running with mud. A castellated millionaire's lair on a hillside lay split in two halves, like a grapefruit.

The rattle of the tarp was deafening. The recombo rumbled past evacuated housing developments as vast as Mayan ruins, heavy with graffiti and scuttling with squatters. Rags flapped. Rain glinted off looted satellite dishes. Sprayed hologlyphics and Secessionist Liberation Army slogans fading on basketball courts. Hooded and huddled, the forgotten and passed-over disappeared behind sheet metal fencing as quickly as they came, along invisible paths and twisting trenches. Between the slick on one side and the fallen mountains on the other, the tech-dream had left its mark on Spill City before passing on: Calgene, Biofuturix, Illumidata. All gone. In the wake of catastrophe there were those who fled, but also those who stayed and dug out a city beneath the city. They tunneled into cellars and garrets and clung to the walls of virtual wells, hidden behind avatars and SIGs, jacked into the cosmic highway from where they might, or might not, re-enter the world on whole new footing.

Norma braced herself and then flew off at Canyon Road. It was an hour's muddy trudge through more deserted biotech country and the rain fell in big oily drops on her face and hung off the ends of her hair. She stayed dry beneath the arachnoweave lining of the jacket Gene had given her and she thought of him in Bakersfield with its weed-blown sidewalks and sad ruined franchises. She thought of how he'd left with nothing but his wolf's teeth around his neck and a bunch of diamonds up his ass. She wondered that she did not feel him here in Spill City, did not feel him near.

Three squat white arches marked the entrance to the cemetery. These were echoed and amplified farther in by the ruins of three conjoined bell towers. Norma recognized the vaguely Mexican architectural style from other parts of the Zone—it was called RE/mission, sad monument to a fusionist age. Norma scanned the grounds looking for Raye or Bunny. Looking for anyone.

Because that's why she was really here. She felt it now. Created—not chosen—for her appetites and for her stamina but also for something else. For the ability of her program to adapt, to self-correct on a continuing basis. Just like a human. That had been Mommy's mistake of course, to program within Norma an almost endless capacity for self-transformation, for adaptation, but as each resequencing moved the mission, AKA Norma, further and further from its original conceptions, it became less and less possible to predict the results, to be able to say, with any certainty, what had been unleashed in the protocol and what had been hidden, to emerge at some later time and insist on a life of their own.

She headed toward the towers. The bells were long gone, fallen in the quake and melted down on site by Cartel contractors to be hauled away as briquettes. Norma wondered how many bodies the alloy had propelled its way into, how many shallow graves around the one-time state contained a piece of the cemetery bells nestled in worm-ridden flesh or shattered bone.

Her guerrilla boots padded silently along the ruptured blacktop past knolls still scorched from the fires and embedded with markers, uneven slabs of stone glassy in the rain. Some had inlaid bronze stars and glyphs of the dead, speakers from which their recorded utterances once flowed. Hebrew, Arabic, Cantonese, Kanji. Dear departed. Beloved sister. Passed on this date. Subterranean events had popped many of the gravestones out like teeth, some lay where they had been flung, inches, yards or more from the human whose passing they had marked.

She got to a hill where a clump of folding chairs were arranged in loose rows beneath a canopy. The chairs faced a pile of black earth beside a small rectangular grave. Norma continued up the hill past the trees only stopping when she was a safe height above the funeral canopy. She found a wide elm and stood beside a stone bench to wait. She wasn't sure if this was where she was meant to be. Bunny had said to text when she got here, but Norma had reminded him that she didn't text.

Below her, the canopy on the hill sagged under the rain. Water streamed off its edge. Norma looked to her right across the park, her whole body turning from the effort because she was still stiff from the beating Mommy had given her. A vast bunker contained drawers for the remains of the numberless dead. An old couple materialized across the front of the bunker. A man and a woman. Norma blinked to make them go away. Their images slivered then reformed with some distortion, the man's feet missing, the woman's eyes gelid. They were both middle height, the woman on the heavy side. They moved toward her, the weeds and chipped gravestones visible through their translucent forms. The man walked stooped, stopped to point out a name here and there. His voice drifted across the cemetery. Someone's nephew, adopted. A cousin from Hungary. Whatsisname. He was tremulous, with oversized ears beneath a skullcap. His wife wore horn-rimmed glasses and a scarf over an enormous beehive the color of pearls. She was heavy in the bosom, but with delicate wrists, her hands her pride. On one arm swung a black purse with a gold clasp that caught the light. Norma forgot to breathe. The woman clasped her husband's sleeve with white fingers and he led her along the avenues of the dead. Norma, her flesh crawling, watched them pass. They disappeared from view and their voices came and went, at one point drowned out by the roar overhead of three F-17s from the base at Tucson. They reappeared, fading, the man pointing to a headstone through the trees, turning to his wife and her eyes, Norma saw, were spilling from their sockets. Her fine fingers tugging at his sleeve, so pale, so surely out of reach, never to return, never to find what had been taken from them. They grew incandescent in the rain and Norma watched them sputter and fade, but not entirely.

She exhaled, weakened by their passing, but she knew what they were. Slashes have them too—indeterminate beings, beings arrested in their passage from one world to the next. She sunk down on the stone bench with her elbows on her knees and continued to wait. She picked her teeth, wondered again if she should try and call Mommy, if it was too late to abort. Was there a Plan B? She didn't think so. Mommy had always been a Plan A kind of deal. It could or would, not self-correct.

Norma tried to be in the moment but she wasn't sure how or what the moment was. She'd dreamt about the devil puppet last night. It was lying on the ground and she was walking toward it. She was back up at San Miguel. The mission chapel. The devil puppet was trying to tell her something. The air in her dream filled with noise, with yelling in a language she did not understand but she knew it was the language of pain. Slashes didn't dream pain. Norma did. She dreamt of the pain of her arrival. The pain of her birth, the moment when she became.

Her BlackBerry beeped.

She reached for her cheap chunk of comtrash but it was dead. A bird looked down at her from the branch above her. Its eyes were yellow. Cheep cheep, it said.

Vehicles began to appear on the broken road, snaked out of sight all along the blacktop. At the front of the line, a station wagon recombo draped in black. It stopped at the walk that led to the canopied seating. Bunny emerged from it black-clad in a pinstriped pencil skirt. His face starkly free of make-up beneath a vaguely inappropriate veiled pillbox hat. He started up the steps with an androgen on either arm. Behind him, the slamming of doors and shifting of gears. Little Barry pulled up in an ancient Mercedes and scrambled out. He lurched around the car to open the door for Una who climbed out to tower above her man. Others arrived—the bartender from World Wide Wang, D-Cup bejeweled in Mexican silver, friends of the family whom Norma did not know, all making their way up the hill to bury the early dead.

A yowl of electric engines cut into the respectful hush. It was Augustine and his lackey pulled up on their Veelos, bulbous battery packs streaked with rain and giant chains wrapped around their waists. Norma stood and braced herself against the burn in her shoulders. The Roidheads pulled to the curb and killed their engines but did not alight. Augustine scanned the crowd from behind wraparound shades, his jaw hinging. The lackey said something inaudible. Norma waited for Augustine to look up but he didn't. The gathered mourners chafed at their presence, and Norma's head felt hot.

D-Cup and Jesus—glaring at the interlopers—bore Bunny's son in his undersized coffin from the hearse. The other pallbearers were awkward ginger youths who bore a passing resemblance to Bunny. Behind the coffin stumbled the mother, a faded redhead, clinging to the arm of her second husband, her legs giving way beneath her every few yards.

Norma's big breakfast sat heavy in her stomach. People took their places on the chairs. The bearers brought the coffin to rest on a tarp beside the mound of dark earth. The dead boy's mother found her seat in the front row beside Bunny and his sons. The androgens sitting behind with the stepfather. The mother perched disbelievingly on the edge of her seat as if ready to jump up and be somewhere else, in a universe where she had not outlived her child. The bier with its flowers and wreathes hung suspended on straps across the weal of the grave. A pair of F-17s cut across the swollen belly of cloud overhead, drowning out the minister's words, the eldest son's eulogy—Jake was the bravest person I'll ever know—the click of cursors.

Norma kept one eye on Augustine and his lackey. A few minutes into the service they made a squealing exit under cover of the jets' roar. Beneath umbrellas the mourners stared at their shoes, surreptitiously checked their messages. Norma felt a breath at the back of her neck but when she turned around there was no one there.

Bunny stood wigless in the rain. The coffin began to lower, the mother gibbered at the sky, and the androgens wept into silk hankies. The brothers glared at the ground, at their shoes to which the wet grass had stuck. Bunny headed blindly to the grave on wobbling stiletto heels. Norma extended her heart to steady her old friend who would oversee his son's last descent. The step-brothers led their mother away and still Bunny stood above the dark gash that had snatched his blood. With most of the mourners' backs to her, Norma recklessly dropped thirty yards down the slope and landed beside him. She took him gently by the arm.

– I'd go with him if I could, said Bunny.

– In those shoes?

– He asked me once if there were wheelchairs in heaven, said Bunny.

– What did you say? she said.

Bunny shrugged. I told him to ask his mother.

Rain webbed the veil across his face, across his nose and grim mouth. The pillbox hat askew his balding head. A mild aftershock rolled in from the sea. He slipped at grave's edge, kicking dirt with his pointed toes, and Norma steadied him. He rummaged in his purse and pulled out the crumpled Head & Shoulders coupon. Let it flutter from his fingers into the grave, where it came to rest on some rose petals atop the coffin.

– Remember me, he said, and let Norma lead him away.

Bunny drove, said he needed to. Norma rode shotgun. Jesus sat in the back openly weeping with the Androgens perched like gargoyles on either side. Bunny drove like one possessed and no one told him not to. Norma twiddled with the radio on the lurching dashboard until she found some Mexican music. Hard sad chords and clacking beats.

31//:big lady

Gene felt that he was closing in on her. He felt her near, that she was everywhere and nowhere at once. He thought he saw her, the black slash of her jacket through the crowd, smelled her musk on his fingers beneath the smell of salt and sulphur from the slick. But it wasn't her. He'd cashed in another diamond, found himself a container squat deep in a bamboo grove at the edge of Birmingham Beach Market and everywhere he went they said, You just missed her.

– Big lady? Boss jacket? Combat boots?

– That's her.

– I ain't seen her.

– Legs to here? Some kind of rack?

– Yeah.

– You just missed her.

– Looks military, man? Don't want to piss her off?

– Yeah, that lady.

He went back to see the geezer, that Mac guy up in Arcadia who traded comtrash for intel. To see if she'd been there and if she'd seen the devil puppet and what did she say, but he was having a pretty intense conversation with Freddy Krueger and Gene couldn't get a word edgewise.

One night, mid February, Gene heard about a brawl at the Factory. The Cartels owned most of it now, but there were pockets still on official Consortium or Republic ground. Where the brawl occurred—in a corridor occupied by blacksmiths and spare parts dealers, a few games arcades—was Consortium turf. Gene heard that a woman who matched Norma's description and another guy had started throwing punches because someone insulted some drag queen they knew, but when he went down to check it out he was told that he had just missed her. The man who told Gene had blood on his fringed jacket. He brushed long hair off his face and held out a huge hand, even bigger than Gene's.

I'm Jesus, he said.

Gene missed Gloria's guiding spirit, but the truth of it was that he had not felt her presence since he'd arrived in Spill City, and that bothered him on a couple of levels. He felt a little lost without her, one, and two, he wondered what it was about Spill City that kept her away. That scared her. A part of him wondered if it was Norma. He missed the simpler times when it was just him and Gloria. They'd gone great distances together and he'd be lying to himself if it had been enough but it was something and it had sustained him. Norma was different, the way she'd come into his life, been everything. And that had been too much.

Since coming down to Spill City, there were too many lonely nights in the little container conversion walled in bamboo. Too many aftershocks that rattled the broken skylight above the bed. Nights where he came home alone and far from sleep, stayed up to work away on his game until dawn, jacked off to porn until he hated himself. Then he'd walk to the end of the street where there was a lookout. He watched the moon fall into the luminescent slick. Trying to think her back into his life. There was a part of him that he was scared of now, that part that would follow her wherever she went.

There was a part of him that hated her.

32//:miduri sunset

By the time Bunny pulled up at Killers Field they had drunk their way through a couple of six packs and a fifth of Jack. Palm trees skewered a violet sky. Jesus and the transgenders were inside the bar, just silhouetted forms in the window. Norma stomped her boots on the pavement and night fell in a smear of neon.

The street teemed with human and battery-powered life but there had thankfully been no sign of Augustine and his lackeys after they crashed Jake's funeral. Norma passed Bunny back the roach and he ground it out with the pointed toe of his stiletto. He kept grinding until she put out her hand and touched his arm. His stricken eyes still looked at her without seeing. She took his hand and they went back into the bar. He ordered a round of Miduri Bombs which would be her downfall and they raised their glasses. A text came in on Bunny's console and he texted back and soon a Magdela tuk-tuk pulled up and the ginger-haired pallbearers piled out and there was another round of Miduri Bombs. One of the pallbearers—Bunny's step-son—went upstairs to play pool and his twin sat at a table with a group of programmers down from LA on their way to TJ.

– I haven't seen geeks this last decade, said Bunny, Jesus watching over him like a Wookie. Things must be looking up in Spill City.

Killers Field was a bar south of Bunny's apartment. It sat on the cliffs overlooking the beach at the edge of the spill. Mansions cleaved by the quakes. Private roads wound down beneath the sea. In Killers, there was scratched wood painted a dozen times, redundant windows cut into container walls, a sense of all the bars that it had tried and failed to be. Colored lights pierced the ambient gloom. Above them was the loft bar, its walls jumping with glyphs. Norma ordered drinks and watched the pale, plump barmaid pour them with a tremulous hand, the little green shots aglow in the UV haze. Norma reached across, took the bottle and finished pouring. She slid a shot over to the barmaid but the girl shook her head.

– Not my poison, she said. She pulled a glass pipe out of her pocket, smiled dully at Norma and said, Meet me round the back.

Norma said, Maybe later.

Because to be with a woman was just not in her program. Regrettable maybe, but there it was. She was a horn hunter after all, whatever nameless others had entered ravening into the play. Norma held the drinks above the sea of heads and tried to find Bunny. He was leaning limp against the wall next to Jesus, runs in his pantyhose. The transgenders and one of Bunny's twin step-sons were at a table near the stage. The band started. It was an Ace of Base cover band and Bunny weaved to the stage to sing, "All That She Wants." A software designer grabbed one of the transgenders by the crotch and she kicked him in the shin and he punched her in the stomach. Bunny's step-son stood up and threw a wobbly cross that got the coder in the ear. Bunny still crooning on the stage, *She's gone tomorrow, boy...* Jesus stepped in and caught a swung bar stool across his shoulders. He staggered and then charged at his attacker, throwing him bar stool and all at a sheet metal wall from which he bounced with a crack.

Bunny jumped down from the stage and started throwing punches, his pencil skirt hitched up around his thighs. His fine, receding hair stood out in tufts, his eyes strangely focused behind the veil and his thin lips were pulled back in a deranged smile. A security guard pulled a taser. D-Cup jumped the guard and the taser got one of the coders instead of Bunny. The coder jigged around boneless and collapsed to the floor. The guard shook D-Cup off and bottles shattered and someone screamed. A trio of bearded Westborian truckers with a slogan on their jackets that read 'Ten For the Lord,' appeared from nowhere wielding knuckle dusters and pool cues. The air filled with the crack of breaking wood and scuffling boots. Bunny's other boy dropped down from the loft bar onto the red-checked shoulders of the tallest trucker, tried to get him in a chin lock but was thrown like a rag onto a table littered with bottles and ashtrays. A trucker with a wide gray stripe in his beard reached behind the bar, picked up the cash register and pitched it at Jesus, but Bunny rushed in to push Jesus out of its path, catching the cash register on his temple and going down like a sack.

Norma slowly put down her drink. Her head suddenly cleared. Her heart beat in her throat and her temples throbbed, but her shoulders did not burn because this was nothing more than human pain and rage, and her soul did not quake to meet it. She licked her lips. From the edge of her eye she saw the third trucker closing in, hairless except for his beard. She jackknifed her arm out to break his jaw, then picked him up by the collar and hurled him through the window. Felt a seismic and liquid shock through her frame, and she wet her pants. She held her jerking body up by sheer force of will and turned to face another taser-wielding guard. She pulled out the little darts while the guard watched in disbelief, then took him and the remaining truckers and designers out in a staticky blur of tusks and sidekicks. By then, Consortium back-up had arrived wielding Tech Zens. Norma raised her hands—because this was not the time or place to test daemon ontology—and backed away from the prone and scattered Slashes. She even let the Consortium goons rough her up a little before they rounded up everyone still standing to take them downtown to the Sprawl.

Killers was still in active Consortium—not Cartel—territory, which meant that the company lockup was in the old downtown and not six feet under. It was called the Sprawl—a double decker grid of containers sealed off in a massive steel cage armed by surveillance drones—and there was a certain comfort to the ritual. Called Play and Pay, the length and severity of incarceration in the Sprawl depended on the wardens who skimmed their salary off the top of the fines extracted to secure the offenders' release. For Norma it wasn't just that, the prospect of a reprieve from the Spill City streets—plenty a drooling hobo willing to share his corner of the cage with a hungry horn hunter—there was also the fact that she and Bunny had met there six months ago after the last Consortium Raid on the World Wide Wang. Bunny, still in in Wonder Whoa-Man drag had taken on three Sonoran bull-wranglers who'd cornered him and made off with his Wonder Woman Golden Belt, the source of all his power, he said. She'd gotten the belt back for him, at some cost to all concerned—the loss of an eye for one of the wranglers, bladder function for another and three nights at the Sprawl for her and Bunny, who had been friends, sometimes less, sometimes more, ever since. So there was a sense, exchanging gallows winks as the Consortium driver threw them into the Humvee recombo, of things ending as they began.

– Play and Pay, said Bunny, spitting out a tooth. Just like old times.

The guard gave Norma a low wolf whistle as he slammed and locked the door to their cage.

She woke up around noon the next day in Bunny's arms for what she knew would be the last time. The cell reeked of piss and worse. Its steel-reinforced walls were sprayed with SLA tags and slogans. *Separate or Die Trying.* Norma touched her swollen lip with her tongue and winced. Bunny's pillbox hat was gone. He lay crumpled on the floor with blood black and caked at his temple. The skirt he wore to bury his son was tented in the groin. He opened one eye and closed it again.

– Am I dead?

– Close enough. You should see a doctor.

– Look who's talking. You look like a George Romero extra. What about a hand job?

– Bunny.

– For old times sake.

– Ouch.

– Don't laugh. Look, you've opened up that gash on your lip.

In the opposite corner of the cage lounged a couple of twitching geeks who'd overdone the nootropic arcades downtown. One of them fiddled with the knobs of his console, trying to find some music.

Bunny said, It's the end of an era. I feel it.

– You mean us? said Norma.

– Was there ever an us?

– I guess not, said Norma. I'm sorry.

She curled back up beside him and sighed in the crook of his arm.

– I can't put my finger on it, he mumbled.

– That's not your finger.

– What is it about you?

– I'm leaving soon, said Norma, scoping the cell for a place in which to pee. So it won't matter.

– Australia was it, Dorothy? Or Kansas? Or Uranus?

– Your head says hi, she said.

He laughed which turned to a coughing fit, and she waited until the fit was over.

– Duty calls.

– Booty too.

– That too.

– I guessed as much.

– Soon as I find the girl—

Bunny stared. The street kid that ripped off the Roidhead? Leave it, Norma.

– She didn't rip them off, said Norma. In point of fact.

– Facts don't matter, said Bunny. Kickers eat facts for breakfast.

– I know. I've seen their table manners.

Norma shifted uncomfortably on the filthy cement floor. I thought you told me not to worry.

Bunny adjusted his arm beneath her head, brushed her hair off her face, looked into her eyes, one of his swollen shut. You ever find that guy you were always looking for? Woody Long.

The joke had gotten old. Norma sighed. I think he's looking for me, now.

Bunny coughed again and pretended to strangle himself with one hand, and then dangled the bioswitch between her breasts in trembling fingers.

– The source of all *your* power?

Bunny's breath was rank with exhaustion and the remains of a kebab the guard had brought them to share. She smiled as blandly as she could, Like Wonder Woman's golden belt.

– Looks like gum, he said. That thing inside the pendant.

Norma said, If you really want to know, it's solar plasma and it controls a device in my hole, I mean my vagina.

– The word, I believe is dentata, said Bunny, closing his eyes and playing along. Maybe Raye was right. Maybe Telephone was a metaphor for human communication. In which the truth is created and passed on, concealed in a string of lies. Bring, bring.

– Right. So when I press the button here, at the base of the pendant, it causes a chemical change in the plasma that launches the device inside me which will then implant a male horn—get it?—with a transmitter, a kind of tag, through which it can pass on the secrets to humanity.

– Why would you want to tag a male horn?

– Has to be a special horn. One that contains the secrets to all of humanity.

And saying it finally, she knew it to be the eternal lie. The only one that mattered.

– So you can take over the world?

– What else?

One of the other inmates got up to take a piss in a vile trough. He turned around with his fly half-mast and swaying, said that what usually happens in situations like this is that one man arises from the masses to avenge the alien takeover and reclaim the world back for humanity from the galactic bitch of oppression, except occasionally when oppression turns out to be a better deal than lone heroics, because a hero only has his fag buddies, but an alien mind meld typically involves at least minimal pussy. After his speech, the inmate staggered back to his corner and went back to fiddling with his console. Tinny music filled the cell.

– Either those beats have to go, said Bunny, or I do.

Norma turned so as to hide her face from Bunny and flicked her long blue-tipped tongue out at the inmate and he killed the beats before silently passing out. A jangle of keys signaled the approach of the guard. He appeared banging a clipboard against his meaty thigh. Norma noticed that he was dressed in Consortium militia drag, shiny with wear, the red and gold stripes at his shoulders.

– Norma?

– You know who I am.

– For my sins. Okay. You're sprung.

– Who?

The guard nervously flipped through the pages on his clipboard.

– I don't know. Some guy. Big.

A message came through on a BlackBerry she'd retrieved from a glass of beer at Killers. She pulled it out. The message said, The wolf found *you* babe! That makes HIM # 1.

Norma stared and dropped the phone back in her pocket. Her face felt hot.

– One day, mumbled Bunny with his eyes half closed, I'm going to get you a new damn phone.

She turned to him, blinked to bring him back into focus.

– Jesus coming for you, Bunny?

Bunny nodded. He always does.

To the guard, Norma said, You see who it was? The guy.

The guard brought his clip board down. Some big guy, he said. Looked part Indian.

She unwound Bunny's arm from her shoulders and unfurled to her great height. The room spun. She tried to brush off her jacket, straighten her hair. Bunny leaned back against the bars of the cage and smiled at her with his sad eyes.

– The word, I believe, is Native American.

33//: normagenesis

Gene had his back to her at the bar. His hair was still long and tied in a ponytail but it had lost some of its sheen and his shoulders sagged a little. A pinch of tension at his mouth. The sight of him made her drool. She wiped her mouth. He did not turn around.

She took the stool next to him, feeling nervous as a schoolgirl.

– How'd you find me? she said.

Gene's clasped hands were bunched mountainous upon the bar. Little Barry swayed up and down serving food and sloshing mugs of beer. The ceiling soared above them, drone and search lights arcing in and striping the faces of the clientele with slashes of blue and white.

– This guy told me that a woman looked like you was causing trouble after a funeral wake.

– Which guy?

– Him, said Gene, cocking his head behind them. Norma looked, but there was no one there.

– Yellow hair? said Gene, putting it more like a question than a statement. Crazy hat.

– Him, she said. He'll be back.

She ordered them a round. Little Barry swayed bowlegged across on the cinderblock track.

– You seen Raye? he said. Una's worried about her.

A group of customers called for some shots before she could answer and he lurched off the block and scrambled up a ladder for the Tequila. The bottles on the shelves behind the bar were coated with a powdery film.

– The dust is from all the liquefaction, said Gene, unclasping his hands to point at the bottles. It'll just be blowing on the wind now for a hundred years. Long as the aftershocks keep coming.

– I hoped you'd find me, she said. I didn't know that until a few days ago. I saw the puppet at that store?

– That place? It's a trip, yeah. I went back to see if you'd been there. Wanted to ask the old geezer what you'd said.

– What did he say? asked Norma.

Gene shook his head. He swung around to her then, a wary narrowing of his burnt coffee eyes.

She said, Have I changed that much?

He sucked in his lower lip in that way he had.

– You filled out some, he said. Works for you though.

– Well you emptied out a little, she said. Works for you too.

– Glad we got that out of our system.

His smile then was real. She ordered more beers. The inmates at the Sprawl had fleeced her and Bunny while they slept, but Little Barry let her run a tab, and once she caught him beaming at Gene, his wonky eye all over the shop. That was the effect Gene had on people. He and Una and Little Barry were soon on familiar terms. It was almost as irritating to her as it was comforting, and lushly familiar, the effect he had on people, the immediate connections he made. His indefinite withholding of judgment. How, homeless, he had to make a home no matter where he was, so ready to forgive and to remember. Here he was then in all his hard and rueful charity.

At the other end of the bar, Augustine and his lackey were brooding concentrations of darkness. Norma ignored them. She wove to the restroom, washed her face in the chipped sink and finger-brushed her teeth with liquid soap. Exhaustion had softened her reflection in the rust-webbed mirror, darkened the shadows around her eyes. She smoothed down her hair and dry-swallowed a Dexy. Behind her one of the stall doors was shut and the Occupied sign was pulled across. But there were no visible feet on the floor. She went to the stall door and stared at it. Took a step back and then kicked it in. The door screeched off its hinges, crashed against the pan. It was empty. Or not quite. There was a console on the cistern, its screen cracked and its home button stoved in. It began to ring. Brrring. Brrring. Norma swept it into the bowl, drowning its squawk in toilet water, and went back out into the bar.

The Karaoke was a muffled racket at one end of the room and there was a new kind of customer at the bar. Coders like last night, scenesters from up north, and squint-eyed Texan kickers—men paid to clear the ground for Cartel traffickers by evicting squatters off contested turf. There were more women too, not just the coders and posers, but whores and strippers looking for marks and eyeing Norma with a mix of lust and venom from the shadows. And Grimeys too, dread-locked ingenues and runaways. But no Raye. And Norma's filling heart leaked a little for the girl and her mind extended to the myriad ways in which to get lost in Spill City but it would allow for no more dire possibilities. Not tonight. Because if Gene had found her, then anything was possible.

Because Gene. Well. There he was. His shoulders a yard across. She came back to the bar and sat up very straight. They touched elbows. When her head hurt, it hurt bad, but the Dexy helped and so did the beers. The pain of her bruises and cuts, of Raye's absence and of Bunny's sorrows, Gene's journeys without her—his eyes burned with memories he could never share—were gradually squeezed out of the gulf between them.

The Karaoke finished and a band started up. Little Barry said with a sly defiance, I succumbed to live music. The crowd's getting younger.

Norma, looking around, had to agree. Maybe after all, the future had not passed on here, taking with it all of its hope and all of its light. She finished her schnitzel and started on Gene's and he smiled, said her appetite hadn't changed. Or had it?

She laughed back and said, No. I still eat anything.

*

After he'd returned from Bakersfield, Gene had stayed at the squat in Chinatown longer than he should, and there were others that came and went. Boys and girls. There would always be that. If there was a why to Norma, that was part of it. She was everything contained in one being, at least for him. Machismo and a fierce vulpine femininity, flesh and heart. Animal and human, and something else. A quality to her he could not pin down. Alien hungers, unspeakable needs.

Plus she could fart the National Anthem. Not many girls had that kind of confidence. Her sex was something he thought about constantly. He imagined it was her no matter who he was with, male or female or just himself. He heard her voice in his head all the way to Bakersfield and back along the muddy roads and Motel 6s behind their razor wire fences. Calling to him.

And here she was beside him, and he had to admit, she could use a bath.

He'd spent all the time he wasn't looking for her in the Factory arcades or at the squat in the bamboo grove playing at his console. When he got to Spill City, he found a freelance gig with InZane Productions, the operation behind *Z-Boy* (an undead cowboy first person shooter), but got fired because he missed too many deadlines programming a new kind of construct.

– What kind? Norma said slurrily.

He pressed a vast palm against his eyes. Gloria's teeth danced on their leather cord. It's for a game I'm working on. For myself. I'll send out demos next month.

– What's it called? she said.

– Wolf, he said.

– Save me, she said, moving in closer to him.

– That's the plan, he said, draining his beer.

*

He got up to go to the bathroom. and she watched the way the crowd parted for him, but she didn't like how Augustine and the lackey followed him with their addled eyes, so to bury the hatchet she sent over a round of drinks with Little Barry.

Little Barry shook his head. Okay, but you think that'll do it, you better think again.

She watched him bring the Roidheads their beers. Augustine flashed her a terrifying smile and then stood up, raised his glass to her and then emptied it onto the floor. Gene loomed behind him, and Norma thought that maybe they'd have it out then, clear the air, and she flexed her fingers, still sore from the wake/brawl at Killers. But Gene just nodded at the Roidheads—the Lackey all but imperceptibly flinched—stepped over the spilled beer and sat back down at the bar.

– Making friends and influencing people as usual, I see, said Gene with a proud and happy smile.

*

Gene told her how he heard from people he asked about this tall crazy woman living alone in an abandoned trailer at Spill City. At the Birmingham Beach camping grounds.

– I think I even saw you once or twice.

– Why did you wait? she said.

– I couldn't be sure. You looked so different. At least to me.

– How?

– You had the jacket, he nudged her sleeve. Except you looked different, taller and filled out some, I guess. Like I said, all tits and legs and I misremembered you somehow.

He wanted to say more. How here she was, a feast of flesh and now back in LA, she always seemed a little awkward in her body, a stranger to herself, neither girl nor woman but something between. He even recalled her hair being lighter (it had been). It seemed to him that back then she was less of what she was now, although he could see that coming and maybe that's why he needed to be sure. Well, the past had passed and now, fierce and curvy and all broken in, she was found. Looking at him like she never did before, and her tired eyes were the color of wet slate, of arrowhead, and there was blood on her knuckles and she smelled like she'd slept in a dumpster but that's how he'd take her, this time, because that's how he'd found her.

*

She let him believe, if that's what he needed, that she'd had work done. How else to explain the changes to her body over which she had no control? She invented, for herself as much as for him, a state of the art process undergone in Mexico. Untrialled and untested. Hormone enhancement therapies and a genetic recombinant process still in beta mode. Bodymod vacations not uncommon for the Slash on the edge. She had to admit, looking at her reflection in the glass—she was looking more and more human every day.

– Impressive, he said, leering at her good-naturedly.

– So how did you know it was me? she said.

– It took me a while. I thought maybe that you were a sister, or a twin. That maybe she'd died.

– Ouch.

He shrugged. But I always knew it was you.

– How?

But he was staring inward at something she couldn't see. She nudged him. The band was starting back up so he had to shout.

– What?

– At the camping grounds. How did you know it was me?

He turned back to the bar, thought about it, then turned back to her, sloshing beer on her knees when he leaned toward her. The warmth of his breath in her ear.

– By your step, he said. I knew you by your step.

He got up and stood with squared shoulders and head swiveling, fists clenched and tits out, mimicking her. She laughed. Above them the swinging bulbs ticked with moths that had flown in through the broken skylights. Gene abruptly shivered.

– I went to a fortune teller up at Swami's, he said.

He stopped and they watched Una load up two wagon wheel-sized plates.

– What did the fortune teller say?

– Just the usual stuff about virgin's blood and filth and falling.

– Was he called the Doctor?

Gene nodded.

– Bunny took me to see him once, but I missed him.

– You didn't miss a thing, said Gene. Guy's a fake.

*

Customers poured into the bar all night. Norma had never seen the place so busy. Kids in sneakers lining up shots. Heading down to TJ via the Spill City clubs. Norma, surrendered to the noise, the booze, the weight of the last few days lessened now she'd shared it, felt awash in sodden gratitude. Grateful to the night, this nameless night in an unknown month. Grateful to a forgiving future for its boisterous return, with its promises of gleaming tech, seamless communication protocol and orbital getaways. With its false promises of home.

But then a call came through on Little Barry's console and she knew what he was going to say even before he passed it to her.

– For you, he said.

She put it to her ear and listened to the howl of alien winds, and silence of the molten river and Mommy's sterile rage. She passed it back to Little Barry.

– Was that about Raye? he asked.

– In a sense, she said.

She ordered shots and let the tequila squirm down her throat, shivered voluptuously at Gene's big, hot hand on her thigh. The switch burned at her breast and the cord twitched. For now, she'd been able to keep Mommy out of her Whole, her Gene-filled consciousness, but it wouldn't be long. In the end it would find a way in, howling for what it had lost, especially now it was found. Because exhausted and having drunk herself sober, she knew with a sobering dread that it was. The guy was found.

Gene sat askew on the barstool, his ponytail coming loose. Norma stood up, nodded at Una and Barry and led Gene out along the catwalk, down the stairs and into the night. She took him along the path pushed up by the quake over the southern border of the lagoon. The checkpoints were a red glow to the South. Ahead of them the ocean and to the North, the Swami's trash fires among the ruins. The highway rattled with traffic. Veelo gangs and Flyers and the antique pop of recombos.

– More vehicles on the road each day, said Norma, swallowing a hard lump in her throat.

– They fuel up at Hermosillo, said Gene. Picking up goods to get through the Tucson checkpoints. Medicine, guns, bandages. Body parts, hookers, explosives, said Gene. Cartel's got one of the most advanced fleets of submarines in the Western Hemisphere now. Popping up all along the coast from Anaheim to Humboldt Bay.

They were holding hands by the time they got to the pine at the entrance to the camping ground. The twins dozed in a giant mail bag, the Ecoist keeping watch by the blue light of his cellphone. The girl's white eyes opened and she fumbled with the string of the coffee can. From her mouth came a mewling sound. Norma shivered and pulled Gene away. The girl's teeth were jagged and decayed in the moonlight. She yanked the coffee can again, maggots and black worms spilling over the edge and when Norma looked back the worms were writhing in the dirt beneath the tree and the girl was kicking them away with a bare and bleeding foot.

Norma wanted to take him right away, but she needed time to figure out how to do it, how to master a will not her own. They sat at the guard rail and looked down at the beach, the sea beyond. Migrating terns massed on the eroded guard tower. The risen moon floated between fat fingers of cloud. She'd brought a couple of beers from Una's and passed him one.

Gene held the bottle with nervous fingers. He said, That guy you were looking for. I have to know.

Norma said. I found him.

– And?

– He wasn't who I thought he was.

He nodded as if that was an end to the matter.

– You look good, he said.

– You too.

– And look, you still have this.

Reaching across to dangle the cord around her neck. But he let it drop suddenly and looked out to sea, the beer bottle cradled in his huge paws.

– What? she said, urgent now, the dentata throbbing,

Terns burst from the guard tower in a chaotic and crystalline flash.

– Are you happy in your body now?

She thought about it. About how in the Before there had been a yellow river. The silence and the flaming edifice beneath which she'd cowered, a-drool and a-gibber. She ran her tongue over her teeth. Her other teeth—her real ones—grew long and pierced her lips, fused over her mouth and left her speechless. Blood crusting. And across her eyes a torn veil of flesh, burning with mucus and tears.

– As happy as I'll ever be, she said.

Maybe it was that. Whatever it was, when Norma stood up and led him to the trailer she knew what she had to do and how. Astride him on the mattress beneath the window, she made him hold her wrists in his hands and not let go because this one was for her. And the next one for him, pinning her to the wall, with his vast sorrowing body, the pain and pleasure fused and unending.

34//:hush

Norma made sure to keep away from comtrash just in case Mommy called. She kept the jacket zipped and wore it all the time except when they made love and sometimes even then. It wasn't the answer but it bought her some time. It was easier than she thought it was going to be to keep her hands off the bioswitch because Gene took up too much space in the Whole, in Norma's configuration, for Mommy's will to override it. But that too, was just a matter of time. Spring held off. They caught rides in tuk-tuks on rainy nights, like old times, the two of them. Or took the coaster. A little drunk before they started. D-Cup, ten pounds thinner than she should be and bald as a badger, played at the Brew Box and when Norma danced with Gene, she held him around his broad waist and he held back, his horn hard against her thigh, his mouth icy from the cold beer when he kissed her. Around his wrist, the three little wolf's teeth blinking on and off in the strobe light.

They ate breakfast in bed at the trailer. She let the sheets fall from the hard swell of her breasts, and he pulled her on top of him, jiggling lewdly. She followed him into his morning shower. She followed him everywhere. Rivulets of suds down the knots of muscle like waterfalls down a mountain. His big, sad-boned face lifted to the stream, his hair was a cape of dark silk down his back. Laughing when she got in there with him, wearing nothing but her combat jacket.

– Don't worry, she said, pulling him into her. It's waterproof.

She made coffee for them on the little ring stove in the trailer. The blue shimmer of the flame in the afternoon half-light. Once she thought she heard Raye's footsteps outside, and quickly pulled on Gene's shirt, but when she opened the trailer door, only the rush of the surf came in, the smell of dirty rain.

That night, moonlight reflected from the ocean parried on the ceiling. A reflection of a reflection. The entire trailer rippled like the inside of a giant roller. To crash down on her, pulling her in. Time was against her, she could feel the ebb and flow of humanity all around her, carrying her on its currents.

She woke arcing from a dream in which she heard the ring of steel heels on blood-soaked sawdust. Metal claws between her legs. A cold sweat burned across her belly and her lips were barred in a grimace wide enough to open up fissures in the grown-over scabs from the fight at Killers. Gene reaching across to hold her down with a heavy hand, saying hush.

Monafex: (n) i. A being, usually but not always an ephatik, said to haunt the liminal area between space-time worlds, specifically colliding galaxies. ii. A shady being who inhabits a crossroads or border area either to prey on or protect desperate travelers or fugitives. iii. A messenger or go-between. iv. A miraculous event or being said to inhabit or be instrumental in the collision of realities. v. A fugitive, escapee from or creator of illusory worlds and loyal to none, for example an artist, or the devil.

(Saurum Nilea, AQ., trans. L.Shay 2656)

35//: ear ear

Even if the guard, Curly, had been able to see Guy Manly on the monitor (if Guy Manly had a reflection, or a shadow, which he did not) Curly was too preoccupied on his phone to notice. In fact, he had his back to the monitor as he typed a series of urgent texts to cronies relating to the failed Dianabol caper and Curly's own plans to go south, stay one step ahead of Augustine or die trying. The whole thing had gone sour after what happened to boss Phatty Thin in that Escondido barn. Just the mention of barns brought the terror back to Curly, and if there was some psycho out there taking it as his personal responsibility to clean up the mean streets, maiming crims and leaving them to die in barns like that, well that's all she wrote, as far as Curly was concerned. He'd been there before and once was enough.

So after Phatty came up all chopped and dead in the barn, Curly texted Augustine that he had too much personal baggage for this gig and wanted out. Besides, it was one thing to cut the D-bol with Ronicol, but strychnine was too messy and Curly would have nothing more to do with it. His thumbs were a blur across his keypad, even though, deep inside, he knew it was just a matter of time before Augustine and his fag lackey caught up with him. It didn't matter that Curly had tried to explain to Augustine—and himself—what happened. Augustine said he was 'conflating the two events.' Conflating the two events. What the hell did that mean? What it meant to Curly was that once you've been to hell and back with one psycho who takes you to a barn so he can hack your ear off—and even if you survive (especially if you survive)—all barns are one barn and all psychos are the one psycho. After something like that you got the devil riding shotgun for life, screaming directions, and there's nothing you can do about it except make sure he doesn't just try to reach across and take the wheel.

It happened just outside of Bakersfield and Curly didn't like to talk about it. Not even to his shrink. He didn't like to talk about how last year, just after the first brushfires and before the Big Wet, this driver had picked him up on Route 119 near the state park. He drove an immaculately restored Ram Charger. Curly was traveling broke and thought the driver might be a good mark with a gas guzzler like that—they were all too few and far between on the road these days. The truck stopped and Curly got in. Turned out that the driver was just a Navy veteran, which would mean that his fuel was subsidized and he wouldn't have a cent to his name. Curly thought he might waste him anyway just to make up for his disappointment, and because even a truck he couldn't afford to ride was better than no truck at all. Strip it and sell off the parts. And then the Navy guy showed him the diamonds in the glove box. Curly was so entranced that he didn't stop to wonder why he was being shown and how there are some things in this world better off not seen. There they were in one of those cheap plastic cases for mouth guards or what have you. A dozen or more diamonds in there sparkling like stars.

– Shit, Curly said and he discretely inched his hand to his own left ear, the one pierced with the diamond stud that Phatty had given him from the whorehouse job in Vegas. And that's when a sudden white light splashed between his eyes and was the first thing he remembered when Curly woke up tied to a chair in the barn. An almighty headache, and a scream in his chest that seemed to have begun a century ago.

The Navy guy all dressed up in officer's drag and hacking at Curly's diamond-studded ear with a Bowie knife. Night had fallen, the only light coming from a hurricane lamp on the ground. Curly screaming behind the strip of clear packing tape which turned vermillion from the blood it tore off his lips and tongue. Once the Navy guy got the ear off, he dangled it bleeding bright blood in front of Curly's face and started talking to it. 'Friends, Romans, Countrymen, lend me your ears.' He actually said that, kept talking to the ear about how the VA therapist was on crack; how he didn't have a cent of his own anymore, ever since his wife made him put everything in her name and she was crazy as fuck, a Salinan woman and a damned fine gardener if he did say so himself, you never tasted a tomato so sweet or a tater so creamy. Then he leant in close to Curly's chopped-off ear, blood running down the white sleeve of his officer's blazer, and whispered, She fertilized them with her own feces, he said. Pass it on.

Over his considerable pain and beneath the Navy man's babble, Curly heard some Flyers pull up outside the barn, and kids outside with their jokes and tech talk. Navy guy froze mid-rant and then backed out to where his truck was parked behind the barn, shoving Curly's ear with the diamond stud into his pocket. The kids piling in through a big wash of headlights, bristling with consoles and wires, lugging amps and instruments. They found Curly and untied him, drove him to A&E, and he survived, one of the lucky few, supposedly, but how lucky Curly wasn't sure because something in him didn't make it and he never got it back.

So he thought maybe that was it, his missing ear, that enabled the guy to sneak up on him like that at the Sanctuary, because there he was, standing without warning beside the monitors with his leather hat and smoke wisping out his eyes. Maybe it was the smoke, maybe the guy's yellow eyes, but the wet fart that squished out into Curly's jocks caused the guy to sniff in disgust and take off his hat, his hair brassy in the light.

– I'm looking for a girl called Raye, said the guy, his voice like a million manholes sliding open.

– Mommy! Curly croaked even though the last time he saw his mother was in a trailer park in Flagstaff.

The guy shook his head and pulled his black lips back in a sad smile.

– That's what they all say.

Curly stared at the huge Bowie knife in the guy's bony hand (another thing he hadn't noticed before) and started to speak but then a phone went off.

Brrring. Brring.

With blood streaming from the neck of Curly's severed head, Guy Manly dripped a red and steady path up the steel steps to the Sanctuary. He keyed himself in and walked down the hallway past the bulletin board (Thursday night's quake-stress group cancelled) and past a kitchen, dark apart from a dim wash of light from a skylight trained on a hissing Crock-Pot on the counter. He stood at the door of the TV room. Blood from Curly's head pooled on the linoleum. A couple of gutter punks making out on the sofa with their backs to him. Guy Manly kept going down the hallway to the bunk room but the urchin's bed had not been slept in, which didn't surprise him. Sometimes they sensed him coming, which was for him—the hunter—part of the rush, the power. The power to produce suspense was addictive, a game, and different from surprise, which was just a cheap trick as far as Guy Manly was concerned. He didn't like surprises. They were beneath him. Suspense. That was the challenge. He turned around, his heels clacking softly on the linoleum, and went back to the kitchen, sniffed the Crock-Pot, which gurgled once, spitting a continuous stream of brown glop over its edge.

Looks like feces, thought Guy Manly. He cocked his head, trying to place the smell. Sour and sweet, hot and cold. If he'd had a gorge it would have risen. But he did not. His insides, if you could call them that, were neither flesh nor blood, dust or clay, solid or liquid. Imagine a special sauce of atom-stripped electrons and protons, T = 7,000 Kelvin and counting. Imagine something unleashed between the hunter and the hunted. Guy Manly's yellow eyes scurried across the darkness of the kitchen. For the second time tonight, his nostrils quivered. That smell. It came from somewhere in his past, although in point of fact he had no past but was born every minute anew from the collective human memory of sights and smells and sounds and fears. Resting from the hunt now, he took a haggard comfort in the vile smell of the stew and looked down at Curly's severed head, as if it would tell him what it was. He tenderly adjusted a strand of matted hair and noticed for the first time that the head was minus an ear, the black hole ridged with red and angry scar tissue. Curly's face looked back at him, not exactly but just beyond, at the ragged moon glimpsed through the kitchen skylight, pale with shock.

36//: besta-wan

Pink sunlight waterfalled over a steep bank of cloud. Early-March and still no sign of spring. Norma shrugged into her jacket. There was a new cigarette burn on one of the sleeves. Something in the jacket's material, or the titanium zipper continued to jangle Mommy's transmission somehow and the effect was to shield her contact with Gene from Mommy. Norma didn't know why, it just was. She was careful to wear it whenever she and Gene were together, careful never to mention it to Mommy.

She crossed the tracks and climbed the hill toward Besta-Wan, the pizza place at the edge of the market. Came up the porch steps of the restaurant, past the cellophane windmills and bottle-top chimes. The rustling and rattling all around her, a random melody blown on the wind and rain. She stood for a moment on the threshold, pushing aside that passing shadow of trepidation she felt every time she returned to him. As if she'd brought something in with the rain, something stuck to her soles. She'd wiped down her boots with a rag and some spit, polished the rivets up the side and the T-caps on the toes and heels. She was wearing a clean tank top under her jacket and new jeans that she'd bought on the Coaster. She could see him through the sparse crowd, sitting at the bar with his back to her, and the guilt and fear evaporated at the sheer strange wonder of his presence. Here, in Spill City. His shoulders looked a yard across, his oaken hair in a ponytail. He'd been back less than a week and they had been together every night. The dentata injuriously gnawed at her parts but she wouldn't activate it. She couldn't give Gene to Mommy. Not yet.

She zipped the jacket up over the bioswitch and went to him, moving tall and heavy-breasted through the Mexicali knickknacks and quake-kitsch and posters of dead rockers. Slashes—male and female—moved aside for her and licked their lips. She avoided their dilated gaze. A waiter in a pork pie hat poured them silty beer in Mason jars. Wisps of silk had pulled loose from Gene's ponytail and he'd gained weight and looked very good. They held hands at the bar, giggling, and read the menu printed on the back of an album cover, *Dark Side of the Moon.*

– What to eat here? he said.

– The chili frog is okay.

– Okay.

– What about some bread? said Norma. I'm so hungry I could eat the cock off a dead Secessionist.

– Excuse me? he said, his beer suspended midway between the counter and his mouth.

– Just an expression I picked up from a kid I knew. Know.

He asked her about it and she told him a little about Raye, not the bit about probing her brain, and not the bit about Mac. But the bit about the bet and skewering Augustine's balls to the bar. She left that in. She said how the kid had gone missing and Norma was worried about her. Unlike Bunny, Gene didn't seem to think it was strange that Norma had gone soft over a child. Just nodded and said he'd help her find her. When Norma asked how, Gene just shrugged.

– I found you, didn't I?

She reached behind him and took his ponytail in her hand, drew the tip across her lips. He leaned across and kissed her right temple and her belly contracted.

– I want to take you to my place tonight, he said. Okay?

– Sure. Why?

He chugged his beer before he answered. Sounds like some folks are looking for you, maybe good to lay low for a while. No one'll ever find you at my place.

– What about the kid?

– She'll keep.

Norma was about to say something about how maybe kids don't keep too well, not in Spill City, but Gene nodded over his jar as if that decided things.

– What do they put in this beer, anyway? he said.

– I think it's fermented from hashish and kudzu weed.

Norma watched him lick foam off his protruding upper lip. Mommy was picky as hell. It didn't take everybody. Maybe Gene wasn't its type after all. But how could he not be? He was everything that Mommy wasn't.

– Do you still like Edamame salsa? she said.

– Does the pope shit in the woods?

The restaurant was half-full of quietly optimistic surfers and garage rockers returning to the fold. It grew dark and rainy outside. Drops rattled against the windows. After their meal, Gene and Norma weaved through the rain for coffee and pie at VGs and Gene poured whisky from his flask into their paper cups. The rain had thinned by the time they finished and he wiped his mouth and pulled her to her feet, laughing. He'd bought new boots from a surplus store aboard the Surfliner. The steel toes and massive Flexion soles gave him a Paul Bunyan gait.

They walked through the rain with arms entwined, striding over puddles. Giants of the earth. Ahead of them was the high spiky mass of a bamboo grove creaking in the wind. He led her through a narrow pass in the bamboo that opened out in a small yard. A shipping container conversion sat before a charred A-Frame home, weeds growing through the shingles, and atop the roof, the torn petals of a satellite dish. A weathered surfboard sticking up bone white from the fescue. The only sky visible was through a ragged hole in the bamboo branches thirty feet up. Norma knuckled one of the thick stems, four inches in diameter. The noise was crazy but melodic somehow, like an orchestra tuning up.

– Scrambles any signal you throw at it, said Gene, nodding up at the hollow, groaning stalks.

He thumbed his console, then keyed some code into the security pad he'd installed, undid half a dozen bolts and padlocks and stepped inside. She followed and stood dripping on the linoleum. Gene's consoles and cords and projectors lay scattered about the place along with dogeared paperbacks and an Elvis Bop Bag swaying eerily in one corner.

– You brought that? she said, gaping.

– It reminded me of you, he said.

The shade on the only window was pulled down. Gene went around the space cracking flouros. Above the couch hung a pee-colored longboard. The big console on the opposite wall played the basketball game. The Laker-Suns had a real shot at the championship for the first time in two decades. She caught the clean towel he tossed to her and started to dry her hair, smiled at the clink of bottles from behind a partition.

– You've got quite a setup here, she said.

– I was on a mission. Wasn't leaving here without you this time.

– This time?

– He came out from behind the partition, shirtless, carrying beers. His hair fell down his shoulders.

– That time in LA, when I left you there. With the dead girl's shoes.

His brow furrowed with the painful memory and he avoided her eyes. That was blood on your hands, and it wasn't from the stiff. It was bled-out. That scared me.

Norma looked up from underneath the towel. It scared me too, she said.

He nodded. I saw that, how scared you were. Later on in Bakersfield, sorting out the farm after Auntie died, I'd close my eyes and see you, just as scared as me and just as lonely. I figured I was more scared for you than of you, and better off with you than without. So that's why I came back. Followed you down here. So, that's that.

She moved in on him, covered his mouth with her own. The bed was against the back wall beneath a skylight cut in the ceiling. The rain fell upon the perspex sheet in feathery splats. He watched her watching herself undress in a mirror against the wall, the bioswitch around her neck catching the light. It seemed like more than just the two of them in the room. The sheer wonder of his having found her, following her down to Spill City and with his wolf's teeth and Titan hands that pinned her wrists to the bed, if not banishing her loneliness completely at least giving it a good scare so that it cowered in the shadows. His flanks aflame astride her, all tongue and mouth and broken promises that no longer needed fixing.

A dread stillness woke her in the black of night and when she opened her eyes beside him, she was still dreaming. She'd forgotten to wake up. Her eyes filled with blood and her mouth filled with filth and Silence poured out, the Silence rose from a hole in the floor to pour down on her. The hole was wide and jagged, and she fell in or was pushed. Going down, she called out his name, but he was too far away to hear her and then she was awake in a wash of sweat and her hand was moving toward the switch between her breasts. Beside her Gene muttered something in his sleep. At her breast the bioswitch emitted a series of dull and gummy pulses that she tried to follow below the crashing thud of her heartbeat.

.--. .- ... ... / .. - / --- -.

She tried not to understand its repeating pattern but it was impossible not to. After all it was she who'd taught Mommy Morse code.

Pass it on.

Norma swung her legs out of the bed. Sticky between her thighs, she padded naked to the yard to stand below the yellow moon poking its sly head over the flailing bamboo and listened, shivering, to its clatter. The surf roared a muted chorus. An owl moaned from the charred shingles. And below it all the syncopated pulse of her neck tech.

.--. .- ... ... / .. - / --- -.

– No, she said across the night.

– You will—the night said back.

– I won't.

– is mine, said the night.

When she came back in, Gene was awake on the narrow bed.

– Okay? he said.

– Just a dream, she said.

She lay on the bed beside him and watched the rain turn sulfurous against the skylight. Before first light she was up and walking down the pass through the bamboo, the back of her throat burning and drops sizzling on the foliage. She went back alone to the camping ground, keeping to the shadows. By the time she got to the trailer, the sky was lightening and she could make out prints around the trailer. Small ones. Inside, Norma found a note:

Call me: 0101 555 324.

Norma stared at the useless numbers. She slammed a fist down on the little fold-out table, causing it to break and swing crazily from its metal brackets. Soon after landing on Earth, she had advised Mommy to zip her signal so it wouldn't fry Slash tech. But Mommy had refused, just because it could. Norma even thought of jumping on a console at the Boardroom—risking interference from Mommy—but Raye's phone was on the iSat net, not on the old free-wire.

Norma got the remaining blood money from the preacher's snuff gig from under her mattress and backed it into a sports bag. She sat on the edge of the bed, brailed in ocean roar but Raye did not come back that day. Norma didn't want to leave a note that could be intercepted. Finally, she shouldered the sports bag and locked the door of the trailer on her way out. The lynx eyes of the twins blinked at her above the folds of the mail bag. She tossed them a bloodstained fifty and dropped the key to the trailer in their coffee can.

– Keep an eye out for the girl, she said.

Norma stopped by the markets and came back to the bamboo cottage carrying packages. Churro and coffee. Gene was sitting naked and cross-legged beneath the pallid glare from the skylight working on his console. The shiny silver system board cover lay beside it. He had a tiny laser screwdriver in his hand.

– You good for breakfast? she said.

He swept away the console and the sheets. His perfect horn.

– You tell me, he said.

He came out of the shower with a towel around his waist and his palm held out flat. In it was a medium sized diamond.

– For us, he said. He told her about Uncle Earl's diamonds.

– What happened to the others? she said.

He flicked his hair off his face. Spent, he said. Jesse's operation and what not. I found a good fence in San Miguel, he said a little too casually.

– When were you in San Miguel? she asked.

– Last November, he said.

– Me too, she said. I stayed at the Mission for a while.

– Me too.

He avoided her gaze, then he told her how he'd followed her trail down the coast, from San Miguel to LA.

Norma thought back to that time, the nights in lock-ups and in the ring. Hours on broken phones to Mommy, giving it the lay of the land.

– How? How did you know it was me?

Gene looked down at the diamond as if it could tell him. You leave an impression, he said. Besides all that shitty broken com trash you left behind.

Norma felt the heat rise on her face. But you didn't even know me, she said. I don't understand.

Gene shook his head. Me neither. Not really. I felt I wanted to know you. That I had to, my future depended on it. And it does.

Norma lay back on the bed and waited for him to tell her how Gloria's guiding spirit came to him during that dark time, stayed on Norma's trail all the way to LA and then all the way to Spill City. Kept him on the path.

– And then what? said Norma. Where is she now? Your wolf?

Gene held out the diamond to Norma. Her work is done.

Norma took the diamond and held it up to the skylight. She turned it to and fro and a blue fire jumped across its crystalline surface, a flame at its coldest. The dentata cramped. Which is how she knew. She would keep him from Mommy or die trying. No Plan B.

– Where do you keep this pretty piece of carbon? she said. The chunk of plasma around her neck would turn that rock into rainwater in thirty seconds flat.

– Where the sun don't shine, he said with a grin.

His face a living collage across which moved past, present and future all at once—the boy he was, the man he'd be. All the pain he'd felt, the hopes snatched and jokes shared and fears racing across his face like clouds chasing the sun across the sky.

Gingerly, she lay the stone back in his hand. Watched him walk grinning back behind the bathroom partition. After his shower they went to the Sanctuary to look for Raye. Her things were still there, but her bunk hadn't been slept in. Gene asked around while Norma patted down the girl's bunk bed as if hoping to find some trace of warmth, a thread or button or single hair, but there was nothing. Norma sat on the bunk bed, clasping her hands until a shadow fell over her and it was Gene, looking down on her the way she looked down on Raye at their first meeting. Behind her ribcage, Norma's heart sped up and slowed down independent of her will, a strange force taking root there.

Gene offered her his phone, so she could call the girl, but Norma told him she didn't have Raye's number, hating herself for lying. She couldn't even let him, or anyone else call her, because Mommy would be listening to Raye now. Like an ear at the end of a telephone line. Pass it on.

Gene took her back to the trailer but wouldn't let her stay there alone, so finally she let him convince her to pay a hobo ten dollars to keep an eye out and call Gene if he saw anything. The twins were hiding behind the tree and wouldn't come out when she called.

The next night or the one after that, she sent him out on his own. She told him to go down to the Wang, and that Bunny and the girls would take care of him. She told him what to tell Bunny explaining things and to ask him to keep an eye out for Raye, tell Raye to get out of town and take Mac with her. She gave Gene some money to pass on to the girl. Gene held out his console so she could text instead of telling him a bunch of stuff that he'd most likely forget, but she shook her head.

– I don't text, she said.

She gave him some story about hackers, unable to meet the disbelief in his eyes.

– And I thought *I* was paranoid, he said.

After he'd gone, she chugged half a bottle of Jack, popped a handful of Vicodin and then went behind the bathroom partition. She tugged at the bioswitch. It was attached to her viscera via tensile strength cortico-fibre invisible to the naked eye. The dentata screamed and Norma sunk to her knees. She straightened, breathed in then out, closed her eyes and yanked. She felt her superhuman consciousness struggle with her human pain and lose. She came to on the floor of the bathroom, her shoulder tusks out and her throat necklaced in blood. A dark stain of blood between her legs. She blinked up at the darkness and listened to the clacking of the bamboo outside while she counted down through the pain and the cold burn of the tears.

37//: cold steel

The best Norma could do was to leave verbal messages for Raye at the usual haunts and with the usual suspects, not just Bunny, but Little Barry and D-Cup at the Brew, but so far no one had seen the girl. Bunny told her that the girl was not her lookout, not now or ever, and Norma tried to see it that way. Bunny said that Raye was fine without Norma, or had been until Norma came along and would be after she'd gone, and perhaps he was right still. Yet, everywhere they went, Norma kept one eye out for a blur of blue parka in the crowd, one ear out, like the swiveling ear of a wolf, for the song of metal heels on the ground. And every day she spent hours waiting at the trailer. The tide ebbed and flowed, sometimes the color of blood, sometimes the color of rain.

Close to midnight on an unnamed night almost two weeks after Gene bailed her out of the Sprawl, they went back down to the Factory, looking for news. There was always a chance, she told herself, that Raye would be there, chugging beer like a truck driver and cracking wise in that awful blue parka of hers. Norma's heart constricted around the memory of that parka. Her head doing three-sixties as they walked the Factory floor. But she still hadn't learnt to lie to herself, Slash-style, or to ascertain what kind of immortality it bought. They passed Tweety's forge and a barber shop. Opposite a kebab stand, an open doorway offered INK, the word pulsating in bioluminescent text. Below the steel stairs leading up to Una's, a ramp led down to the basement gym. Plates intermittently clanked.

– Gym must have reopened, said Gene.

It had been closed the last time they were there, the Roidheads lying low after the Dianabol caper.

Norma wanted to avoid it, but Gene said they should see if Augustine had come up for air. Men of steel in Viramasks moved between the benches and racks. Soldiers, kickers, guards and body mod freaks heaved and grunted in the cold white light. Norma could taste, at the back of her throat, the men's diseased sweat, the fear in their hearts and shit in their shorts. Smart drinks glistened in the banks of glass-doored refrigerators. Thai Tubs and brown bottles of Reform and Giant's Junk. Techno tyranny blasting from the speakers. Mirrors everywhere. In a corner beneath a dead screen sprawled Augustine. The lackey straddled him with a bandaged hand and emitted gentle grunts of encouragement.

– Harder, baby. Dig deep. Want it. Want it bad.

Gene said in a low voice to Norma, Obviously having lost a testicle does not effect your ability to lift two hundred and forty pounds of cold steel.

Norma said, Maybe it helps.

She pulled Gene away though, anxious that Augustine not see them together. How to explain? It wasn't just that the longer she remained out of Augustine's sight, the stronger the possibility that he'd forget about her and Raye. It was Gene, now too. How to explain this thing taking hold inside of her, this secret care?

*

Augustine pushed the bar up with a bellow and stared red-faced and turgid at the bitch who broke his balls, there at the door with her big Indian prick, Dead Man Walking.

– You okay, Tine? said the lackey, tenderly blotting at Augustine's forehead.

Augustine batted him away. How to explain? It had nothing to do with the damn bet, nothing to do with the freaking gutter punk. It was the way Norma had looked at him that one time—everyone at the Factory had heard about the crazy bitch who fought like a Ninja, but she took up all the air in the room. Just one look at her Augustine knew she was the one, and how she looked back at him, just that once, but it was enough. Before she decided to ignore him completely, before she was lost to him like she is now and way before that little gutter punk fell from the ceiling and cost him his manhood. Okay, you can buy nuts by the twofer in Sonora, and he just did—his junk never felt better, thank-you very much—but yet he remembered. In Norma's eyes, that one time, such hate and want and how she never looked at him that way again.

He couldn't get over it.

38//: first person shooter

Gene and Norma got separated the next night at the Brew Box and she must have blacked out, staggering home through the bamboo at dawn with straw in her hair and blood beneath her nails that she must first scrub off before leaping ravening onto her waking wolf.

It was the last week in March. She still had not seen Raye, and the days and nights were beginning to run into each other. The sex was unending—the more Norma tried to drown out the pulsing code of the activator, the more insistent it became.

Pass.

It.

On.

In your dreams, bitch. Except there was a voice in Norma's head that said Mommy had nothing but time. All the time in the world to make sure Gene could have none, and anyone that thought it could best a being with no end to their time had better think again.

Norma tried to think. She tried to come up with a Plan. She had come to Spill City looking for a Guy who was now looking for her, and she was now looking for another. A missing kid. It was unending. Exponential. Serial loss, limitless possibility. Mommy could, by definition have no sense of that, because it was the Whole. It had total vantage point and therefore it had none. Poor Mommy would never even catch a glimpse of the far horizon. It could not get over itself.

So the hunt continued. Norma haunted the Sanctuary, spent time staking out the trailer each day, watching for Raye because sometimes there were signs of her passing—a broken earring, a burrito wrapper—but no one would say they had seen her come or go. It didn't surprise Norma. Raye was at home in the blind spots of the world, had found in these room enough to move. Sometimes Gene watched with Norma, but even he was beginning to have his doubts about whether Raye was lost, or whether she'd just moved on. Sitting at the little table in the trailer, or wandering around the markets sipping from a Coke, Norma felt outside of her own skin, as though she, the watcher, was being watched, and that someone was also there waiting for her to leave. She wanted it to be Raye. But maybe they were right. Maybe Raye did not want to be found. Not yet.

Gene made her tell him the whole story. Norma still kept out the bit about how she probed the girl's brain, but told him everything else. How some guy had ripped off the girl's dad, and how it sent him even crazier than before, so Raye promised she would stay to try and get back what belonged to him.

– What was it? Gene said.

Norma shrugged. An autograph or a letter or something from Michael Jackson's grandson. Probably a fake.

Gene said, It must be worth something for him to be all messed up over it. These collectors know when they're onto something.

Norma nodded, remembering the store and how Mac had surrounded himself, not so much with paraphernalia, it seemed to her, as with little pieces of himself, his soul, fragmented and crystalized around him, each piece reflective not so much of himself but of a Mac-gone-wrong, hung up and haunted.

Gene looked thoughtful. I think I saw her, he said.

Norma said, What? When?

– Long way's back. Before you went there.

And then he told her. How when Mac lied and said he'd seen the one matching her description, Gene, who'd believe anything, did.

– Everyone told me how he was some kind of divvy. And the store was like a portal or something to Spill City's underworld.

– Spill City is an underworld, Norma said. There's no under.

– Whatever. I love all that shit.

So Gene hung around the store. Every day all through late January and into February. Waiting for a sighting, the dark mop of her hair, the long legs, wide mouth, head and shoulders above the crowd. But she never came. In the end he stormed back into the store to get the puppet back and kick his thriller ass, but when he went in, he said, it was the saddest thing. Just the old fool in his cage talking to Freddy Kruger and a teenage girl too big for the kiddy table on which she sat, laying out a Klondike array with this cool Harry Potter deck.

– Shitty blue jacket, he said. About twelve years old.

– Fifteen, said Norma. I think.

Counting out her failures of ones and zeros that stretched to infinity.

– The point is, she said, is that now Augustine and those fools are after her for pulling some stunt they say I was in on, cost them four hundred bucks.

– You really think even a Roidhead would mess up a little girl for four hundred bucks?

– There was the loss of a testicle, she said, trying not to gloat at the memory.

– A dime a dozen, said Gene. If you know the right people, which I'm sure they do, those Roidheads having no problem getting their mutant on.

Norma squirmed against the pillow and pulled a plastic piece of the console out from under her ass.

– I don't think it's necessarily about chunks of change or pounds of flesh. I think it's about something else.

Gene stared. Norma looked down at her hands.

– Wait, said Gene. You and Augustine?

How to explain? How that time when Augustine looked at her across the bar there had been so much hate and need in his slavering lips, so much hurt and harm in his eyes that she thought she might kill him on the spot. So she fucked him instead. And how in Augustine's case it was the same thing.

– Girl, Gene said. You are worse than me.

– For my sins, she said quietly.

Outside the wind had died down. Beyond the furtive clack of the bamboo she could hear a chainsaw starting up. Someone clearing the ground.

– Well, said Gene, swiveling to sit on the edge of the bed and fumbling for his jeans. Like Jesse always said, and I quote, only thing to do when you mess up is make amends, forgive yourself and get on with your life.

She shuffled around behind him on the bed, her long legs either side of him. Then she flipped him onto his back and rode him till he roared loud and after that Norma lay with her head on his deep chest. The drumming of his heart banged inside her head.

They agreed that even if Augustine was after Norma, or Raye, or both, he would give up eventually. Gene reminded her that, if nothing else, the excessive amounts of bad Dianabol they consumed, an occupational hazard, were not exactly excellent for the attention span. Bottom line, Gene was a man on a mission. He laid out a plan of action. They'd take shifts at the trailer, deploy eyes and ears wherever they could find them. Bunny and Jesus would help. Una's would be the checkpoint. The cottage was all but invisible, he said, and practically inaccessible through the bamboo, a dead zone as far as most satellite and wireless technology was concerned. The mission, it seemed, had found its man.

But Norma didn't say, because she couldn't, that Augustine and his empty nutsack were the least of her worries. She took every precaution not to be followed back to their little hideaway deep in the bamboo. It was less Augustine's men with their chains and Flyers she kept an ear and eye out for than the ring of steel heels on the pavement, a brassy flash of yellow hair in the crowd. Because this she knew—Mommy's tech was beyond high. Beyond low.

When Gene wasn't helping her look for Raye, he looked for work. They were low on money, and he thought he should go to San Jose, try and find someone to produce the game he was working on. He worked on it when he could. He took his consoles apart and put them back together again. He watched TV—sports, news, Reelys. What he watched didn't matter to him. He had no critical agenda. Male female young old true false comedy tragedy. He was heterogenous in his tastes, incapable of judgement or revulsion. Norma envied him for that. She envied his objectivity, but tested it when she could.

– What does that make me? she said. More of the same?

– He shook his head. You're more all right, but not the same. You're everything. Out of the many, girl, you're the one.

Norma looked up through the skylight. A drone was writing a message, some addex in the sky. Norma watched the letters bloom and feather against the dark clouds. She turned away before she could read the words she already knew were forming.

Pass it on.

She asked him if there was a name for what he was.

He was bent over his little pliers.

– A name? he said. I've been called everything there is. Breed for half breed, retard, redskin, moron, fag, bonehead, ass, dipshit, dumbfuck, gotard—Ty's contribution—goober, dumb Indian, Sherlock, Chief, goober—did I say that already—fuckwit, fucktard, dingus, dill weed, dill hole, butt-munch, rez-rat, Homer—

– Homer?

Gene explained that Homer was some guy in an apocalyptic book called *Day of the Locusts* who couldn't tell the difference between the real thing and a fake.

– What does that have to do with you? she said.

– I was the only kid on the rez back in Ontario got bruises on his face from playing Xbox.

She shook her head. Xbox?

– It's an obsolete gaming platform. You use a controller instead of a headset. But the principle is the same. First person shooter and all that.

He went theatrically slack-jawed at an imaginary screen—not a construct—and mimed holding an old-fashioned controller. He was wiggling his giant thumbs and lurching further and further off to the side of the bed until he face-planted naked on the floor, his long hair flying. The little container cottage shuddered with the impact of his huge body on the floor. They'd been in bed all day beneath the dirty skylight sharing a bottle of whisky and a six-pack, Norma eating leftover pizza.

– What happened to the guy, Homer, in the end, she asked. When he found out the illusion wasn't real?

Gene got up and brushed himself off. He still held a small sharp screw driver in his huge hands.

– He went postal in the end.

Norma pushed the pizza box away, feeling sleepy. The grimy square of sky through the skylight faded to a deep purple and in her mind she was back in San Miguel standing under the arches of the Mission Arcangel. Early evening around Christmas time. Inside, lighting the candles of the colonnade, the old Salinan gravedigger slash caretaker. How he said his lighter had run out of gas one evening halfway through lighting the candles and did she have anything on her? She found a matchbook in her pocket and gave it to him. It was from The Trap, the club in Bakersfield where it all began. She'd been almost at the end of the colonnade when a strange clicking sound made her turn back to see the gravedigger tucking the matches up his sleeve and continuing to light the candles with a Mission lighter, one with a holographic Arcangel swimming behind its plastic casing. Norma had wondered why he said it had run out of fluid when it obviously hadn't. But then she forgot about it.

Norma turned away from the skylight and there was Gene on the bed beside her. How far back before their lifelines split and separated, how far forward? Is the fork-tongued reader of palms the teller of fortunes or the creator?

One morning she woke up astride him and his eyes were hard orbs fixed on her heart. She looked down at her own hands clawing at the bioswitch, digging welts at her breastbone. Rolled off him howling, nonononono!

That day, on her way to the trailer, Norma found a broken console behind VG's. She tried to contact Mommy that day and the next, clutching the switch and willing Mommy to enter the Whole but all she got was a 'recorded' message: *I am become Death, the destroyer of worlds.*

Leave a message after the beep.

– Fucktard, said Norma.

The season of rain was upon them. From the trailer window, Norma watched the rain hang over the ocean as if time itself had come to an end, at the horizon the winking lights of possibility and peril. She came back to Gene and the only place on her that was dry was under the jacket. She pulled off her boots and jeans on the threshold of the container cottage and stepped in wearing her panties. Pink-tinged water streamed from her hands onto the rough-cut linoleum patched onto the floor of the container. Gene wrapped her in a towel and took a step back to look at her. Looking down at her hands, she shook her head, no. And when she looked up in his eyes she saw not the pure fear he expressed in LA, but finally a kind of fearful understanding.

She told him about how sometimes she woke up with memories of another place that she dreamt she'd gone to. Except that she brought pieces of the dream back with her. Straw on her hair, blood on her hands.

– What's the dream? he asked. His face was taut and lined from exhaustion, the no-color of bracken. They weren't in bed, but sat opposite each other at the little table beside the window.

– It's a barn, she said. Except that it's round inside. Circular. It's not really me that's there, but it is. And I have a burden. A body that needs to be dumped there.

– In the barn, Gene said. Which isn't really a barn.

She nodded. She wouldn't cry. There are others there, she said. Or parts thereof. I've brought others to the barn. Many others.

Gene drew a hand across his tired face.

– Yuki, he said. Jesse's girlfriend from Japan, told us this ghost story once, about the *ikiryo*. An angry spirit that departs the living body while sleeping, to avenge its enemies. So there was this story she told us one night about a girl in a small town who was engaged to her lover. Both young, good kids. She was beautiful, he was kind—they were both smart and they loved each other. They were both going to be teachers—he worked at the town tavern at night, she worked as a tutor. So one day, the tavern got a new barmaid, cute drink of water with legs to here, hair to there, ran off with the boy. Well the girl was devastated, of course, but she said to herself that you can't beat a game like that, something so out of the blue, a random stroke of treachery with no warning to it, no bells and whistles that she'd heard coming—you couldn't go out to meet a mean streak like that without putting your own soul at hazard. So she let it lie. Went about her business. But her soul had other ideas. One day, she was standing alone in her kitchen and she heard something inside her fall, a dim faraway sound like something falling off a shelf. That night while she was sleeping, her *ikiryo*, her vengeful spirit left her dreaming body and went to the bed of her lover where he lay drunk and dreamless with the barmaid. And the *ikiryo* began to hurt her.

– How?

– I don't know. Poison maybe, or little bites. I think it was that. Bites that became sores. It killed her in the end. But it killed something in the girl too. Who up until now had no knowledge of this deadly rage in her soul and what it would do. What it could do.

– How did she begin to suspect? What—strands of the skank's hair in her teeth, bits of skin under her nails.

– Bingo, said Gene.

– What about the boy?

– He got brought down too. He became a mean spirit. Moved from woman to woman, always shadowed by this vengeful spirit of his beautiful lover who'd fly out at night to do them harm. His own soul was consumed by sores as the bodies of the women who were never his to take.

– So they were working together in the end, the *ikiryo* and the mean spirit. Reunited.

– In the end, yes. Marriage made in hell. Be careful what you wish for I think being the message.

The rain fell harder outside, poured down the trunks of the giant bamboo like vertical rivers.

– Is that what I am? yelled Norma. A living ghost? Is that what happens to me in my dreams? I clomp off in preloved combat boots to some barn lugging stiffs, give them what they ask for, come back with blood on my hands and dirt on my soul?

– Remember, Gene said quietly. It's not you. Whoever is doing this isn't you anymore.

*

Norma took him to Arcadia Beach. Neither of them wanted to go. They got off the Coaster and walked toward a flaming sunset to the Sanctuary but a new guard said he had not seen Raye. One of the other punks, clattering his Flyer down the steel steps said he'd heard a Grimey that matched Raye's description turning tricks a few blocks to the East. Mac's neighborhood. Norma, with Gene by her side, pushed through the wet, teeming streets to Mac's store in the emptying backlots. It was closed and no one answered her tap on the door. Gene peered in at the fly-specked sheet drawn across the inside of the window.

– No light on, he said. Maybe he's taken the girl and bolted.

More likely she's taken him, thought Norma. There was a watchful quality to the apparent emptiness of the store. Always someone watching. She looked up at the second floor windows, but nothing moved.

She'd left enough money for both father and daughter with Bunny and instructions to the girl to lay low, maybe get out of town for a while. She hoped that's what Raye had done. But she felt inexplicably desolate. She would have liked to say good-bye.

– Do you think it's still in there? He whispered nervously.

Sweat trickled between her breasts.

– Why did you hang onto it all that time?

He shook his head in wonder. I'd been waiting to offload it my whole life. After my dad's Chevy hit Ty when we were kids, me and Jesse lay there on the ground a long time. I still hear Jesse crying in my ear. He'd broken his leg and pelvis to save me. I knew the puppet was there under me, I was lying on it, but I had to wait until he rolled off me to make sure he didn't see it. To make sure no one saw it. It had already done enough harm, and I blamed myself. I stuffed it under my shirt, didn't tell anyone I had it. It was my burden, my care. I carried the damn thing wherever I went. To make sure it never hurt anyone else.

– It hurt you, she said.

She remembered, the way it squirmed underfoot when she stumbled over it in Mac's store.

Gene continued. Thing was, I kept the puppet in a shoebox in my closet, kept me awake at night just knowing it was there. But as I got older and moved around a bit, I'd have to unpack it and pack it up and after a while it didn't look so bad. Kind of pathetic actually, and sad. With those chipped red eyes. More hungover than evil.

Norma smiled. Let's go, she said. This place gives me the chills.

She turned at the swish of a skateboard behind them, but no one was there. Above them, reflected in the dusty windows, a drone cut across a pink ball of cloud.

He palmed away at her tears with his big rough hands, across her cheekbones and the tip of her nose. A light rain began to fall. The gold hand at the crossing was still frozen in the Don't Walk position.

– Let's go eat on the beach, said Gene.

The night market was in full swing. On their way to the beach, Norma found a rebel army coat that looked about Raye's size and she bought it to replace the blue parka. Also a shirt for Gene, age-softened corduroy in deep brown that matched his eyes. As they passed a bargain bin containing surplus SLA caps and scarves, she heard a beep. Gene kept walking and Norma reached into the bin, pulled out an ancient pager scratched and worn white at the edges.

Call the office, said the message. *M.*

Ahead of her Gene had stopped and was waiting for her to catch up. She dropped the comtrash back into the bin and walked toward him and away from its relentless bleat.

– Everything okay? he said.

– Nothing that a corn dog won't fix, she said.

Halfway through the month Norma's blood money had dwindled. Gene still hadn't found work more than an occasional shift behind the bar at the Wang. Superman asked him to fill in one night but they could not find a pair of tights big enough.

On the last Friday of the month she came back to the cottage with a basket packed with Noe's burritos and beers. They walked until they got to Via Laguna, followed it alongside the lagoon until she could see a path between the shrubs that led down to the sunken wetland. They meandered wordless in the enormity of ruin, across the heat-cracked beaches, across dried lagoon beds, surly creeks buried in vicious copses from which burst the occasional marine bird, pulling up a diseased undercarriage as it rose above them and disappearing with a paleolithic squawk. They finally emerged across the road from the ancient retro-fitted 76 filling station near the freeway.

The fuel stations that were still operational after the quakes and the looting couldn't compete with the price of gas, diesel, ethanol and other mixes in Senora and even Ensenada was cheaper if you made it past the checkpoints. The local fuel stations sold coffee and battery packs and Tylenol and traded, like almost everything else, in information. Like the 7-Elevens, they were subsidized—or extorted—by either the Cartels or the Consortium or both, in return for an eye and ear to the ground.

Gene pointed to the once-animated reproduction 76 disc that floated like a dead star above the upswept googie roof.

– The future came to California, he said. But then it passed on.

– Why? asked Norma. Where did it go?

Gene shook his head. I don't know where. When, is when we stopped believing in it. But it left pieces of itself behind. To remember it by.

He kept staring up at the broken holo. The filling station's flagstone walls were charred and the huge plate glass window smashed by looters and replaced by sheeting. Liquefaction oozed from wide cracks in the asphalt between the pumps. Kudzu and other vines wound around the pumps and the entire building had sunk below the level of the road at an angle of twenty-five degrees, give or take. An abrupt dreaminess came over Norma, the switch burning between her breast and a compulsion to put her hand into her panties.

With finger pointed and eye up at the broken projection, Gene stood a moment, as if in a troubled reverie. He raised a hand and pointed at it, and at that moment, Norma felt a shock of pain in her belly accompanied by a sudden flash of light.

And then she fainted.

Late that night, sharing a quiet meal at the Besta-Wan, Gene asked if she'd fainted before. Norma put down her slice of pie. What she wanted to tell him, more than anything, was that she had not fainted before, no, not unless you count waking up in the morning with blood on your hands and manure on your boots and having no idea how it got there or falling down onto the floor of the restroom in a wash of pain and matter and not remembering why or standing clueless and panting over the bodies of your assailants some of whom would take the vision of an alien with tusks and smoking eyes down with them to hell. Instead she just said, No.

A vague shadow of pain played behind her shoulder blades and she felt nauseous, as she often did these days. Gene's smile was as winning as ever but his eyes avoided hers. The place was scattered with tourists from the city who pretended not to notice the torn and frayed couple propped up at the bar.

– You called her name, he said. Before you passed out.

– Who? she said. The pain got in the way of her thinking. Raye?

Gene pushed away his uneaten pie. He carefully wiped his mouth with a napkin he carefully folded in half. Then in quarters.

– You called out Gloria. My wolf. The one killed up north. Did you see her? Or something? You pointed at—nothing.

– You were the one who pointed, she said. Weren't you?

The sticky finger of the Silence tickled her ear. Pulled at strands of her hair. The Night. Breathing wetly down her neck.

He shook his head. Did you see a dog or something?

I don't know, she said. There was this dog. From before. This other dog called Jose. I called his name?

Gene shook his head grimly. His beautiful big hands were shaking. She reached out to take them in her own but he pulled away and covered it up by waving the waiter over.

– You haven't finished, she said, pointing at his half-empty glass.

He turned to her, his face taut with terror.

– You didn't say Jose, he said. You said Gloria. Gee-EL-Oh-Are-I-A.

It was the last week in March. Spring refused or forgot to come, yet there was in the chill coastal breeze a scent of reprieve, a feeling of space opening up between the stink of the spill and the charred hills. Norma went for a long walk on the beach, hoping she'd figure out what to do by the time she got back to the hut. She thought of what Gene said about the future passing on, about how it had not forgotten California because the future has seen the Silence. It has been to the other side.

She noticed some of the shutters being repaired in the big homes along the highway. Earlier that morning while waiting fruitlessly for Raye at the trailer park, she saw a couple of surfers back at the rail at sunup, not going in yet or any time soon, but talking about it. Pointing at the red tide, the plankton changing color maybe. Greener now. Maybe the dolphins would come back soon. Yeah. Maybe.

She had two hundred dollars and change left. When she got back to the cottage Gene was already awake and was making eggs. She poured herself a cup of coffee. He had changed since the vision she had of his wolf at the lagoon. It was like he knew something that he couldn't tell or wouldn't. He said with a grim smile that she was looking thin. That if she thought he hadn't noticed her eating less, giving him her share, she was dead wrong. Not looking at her while he banged around.

– There might be some work at the Wang after all, he said. I'm going down there later in the week.

– So you're not going to SJ?

He turned off the little battery stove slowly but kept staring at the eggs in the pan. His strong chin sagged a little with exhaustion.

– No, he said. I'm not going anywhere. I won't forget and I won't leave. I'll stay. We'll figure something out. Pass it on.

Her coffee-cup wobbled in her hand. What did you say?

He turned to her, pan in hand. Pass it on. Tell them, whoever wants to know. I'm not going anywhere.

They locked eyes, man and monster.

– I know Morse code, too, he said. My cousin Ty taught me. Only good thing he ever did.

39//: V

Who the hell lives here? Raye banged around the trailer, lifting up a map of the Zone (a wavery inverted V traced from Bakersfield up to San Miguel then down the coast to Spill City) to find some cash stuffed in a used but clean duffle coat. She'd found a shitload of comtrash too, food wrappers, a laundry hamper filled with bloodstained clothes and nothing much else. Raye had finished the three beers in the fridge, slept on the bed, tried on Norma's shoes (one pair) and sampled her lipstick (too red). After that, really, there wasn't much else to do except slip out to check up on Mac, if she could find him—she thought maybe fishing in trash cans at the edge of the markets, or up at Swami's having his fortune read, but he was nowhere—and then come back to the trailer and wait for Norma to leave before Raye snuck back in. She never stayed for long, but she liked coming here to this little trailer beside the beach, where a part of her was born, she knew, and a part of her had gone forever. Raye didn't want Norma to find her because she didn't like what was happening to her, how she was changing and she knew Norma wouldn't like it either. Raye was a little scared of Norma, truth be told, but mostly she wanted to give Norma time with that big old chief of hers. Gaaah! Raye could go and hang out with them at their little love nest, and she even tried to follow them once. Followed the sound of their laughter and the splash of their boots through the puddles, but then, go figure, she lost them. It was like a shadow came between her and their twinned silhouettes just ahead and then they were gone. But that was okay. They needed their time together, yeah. Norma had to be the loneliest damn woman Raye had ever met and she'd met lonely on the road, yeah and on the rails too. Lonely as hell. Except Norma was the loneliest. Eyes the color of a rainy Sunday. Raye lay on the saggy bed tracing inverted Vs on the window that looked out over the ocean. She had never had a boyfriend. Not unless you count the select group of Spill City johns who hadn't beaten her up.

For her sins.

40//: charity

They needed money. Gene didn't want to spend their last diamond, which was safely shoved up where the sun didn't shine, not unless he had to. He got to know some day-laborers near Bunny's place at Pacific Beach. Norma said that he could get killed moving in on established turf like that, but the workers accepted him and shared what little work there was with the big man. It didn't last though—Gene wasn't good with his hands, not in that way. He looked for a driving job, hung around Una's and the Wang, but all that happened was that Bunny felt sorry for him and threw him a couple of shifts in the thukker, pleading a hot date. They both knew the tranny was lying but as far as Gene was concerned, driving a tranny's tuk-tuk did beat trying to squeeze into red tights and hoof it to twentieth century show tunes.

Norma told Gene about how Bunny lost his little boy and when Gene asked Bunny about it, the transvestite said that he didn't expect it would ever get any better. That the grief would outlive him, not the other way around. They were sitting at the bar waiting for Bunny to go on. He was wearing his Wonder Whoa-Man suit, baggy with the weight he'd lost, and as usual, had the wig beside him like a patient pet. Gene took one of Gloria's baby teeth off its cord and gave it to Bunny. For luck. Bunny looked at the little butter-colored tooth and his face collapsed in on itself, slick tears gouging troughs in his make-up. Unable to go on with the show for the first time in his life, Bunny just shook his head when Superman approached with his cue. At a nod from Gene, he turned around, got back onstage and nailed it.

Duonoesis 1. (n) Seeing through the eyes of another being (an aporifek) who is usually a byproduct of one's own alaxeneasis. 2. (v) Being in two places (geographical or temporal) at once, a strategy deployed by the Hipproque Guerillas of 2060, and adopted after the war as a form of adolescent interactive entertainment that went out of favor, but which came back into vogue by Quint 206, due to the development of the new Frax Protocol.

(Saurum Nilea, AQn., trans. L.Shay 2656)

41//: barn

Norma looked for her own game and finally found one near the checkpoints. Poker, a little left-handed snooker. It was like riding a bike, she'd forgotten how much she remembered. She played with Consortium guards, Cartel goons, it didn't matter. Word had got out about the big crazy bitch with a wicked-witch mojo and no one gave her any trouble. On some unexpected level, Norma felt vaguely disappointed.

Then one night down in TJ, on La Coahuila, a fat Swedish assassin with a tattoo sleeve—fangs and eagles, demons and dragons—shot her after she won two thousand dollars *and* his gold tooth, which she wrenched out with her bare hands, winning another five hundred dollars from an Armenian construct artist. The bullet went in mid-body, missed every vital organ and came out cleanly leaving a tiny hole she could stick her finger into. After recovering for a day and a night in the upstairs bedroom of a whore named Fonda Cox, Norma went after the Swede who shot her, a couple of hours before dawn. Lightning flashed on the dark horizon. Stars shrank from the arcing lasers and the throbbing roar of the hoppers. Norma tracked the Swede to a silent alleyway east of the cordon. The alley was unlit and it was impossible to tell how narrow it was in parts, Norma's shoulders brushed sheet metal and cinderblock either side, ducking beneath fire escapes, walking past blacked-out windows and over soundproof cellars. She watched the Swede stop at a door invisible against the night until the door opened a crack and vomited out an orange flicker that it swallowed back up again when the Swede disappeared within. Norma was at the door at once. She peered through a crack in the sheet metal of the shack at a small circle of men and boys wearing headsets and viewing a Reely projected from the center of the room. It starred an unbilled Randy Mears as a Consortium puppet eaten alive by vermin who'd survived the brush fires and brought their hungers with them. Soundlessly gnawing. Norma's vision tunneled and she was aware of a presence at her elbow and then a Taser-like wave of nausea, and then she blacked out.

And then she was on a dark road above which the Milky Way wheeled. She was both herself and able to watch herself as someone else. Her boots slipped in the starlit mud and her esophagus spasmed, emitting a deep-throated growl. Ahead of her, down a narrow length of earth that was not quite a road and not quite a path, was the barn. It was not the same barn, but they were all the same barn. Her knees buckled beneath the weight of the fat Swede over her shoulder. She couldn't remember how he got there, but she knew why.

The Swede's arms swung down so that his hands smacked against her ass and his hairy belly was soft against her cheek and not in a good way. Beneath her righteous wrath, she felt wrong in her body, stiff in the joints and weak-willed. At the barn door she let the Swede drop onto the mud and dragged the body the rest of the way by one leg, beneath the raccoon skull and into the dark, sweet-smelling space. She let his leg drop and caught her breath. Fumbled for the lantern on the shelf and froze. She struggled to breathe, drew in ragged gulps of air and began to back away, the Swede staring up at her with his blood-webbed eyes and throat slit and vulvate. But it was not from this horror alone that Norma, eyes burning with smoke and claws a-drip, recoiled. No. Beside the dead man she could see another and in the stalls before her, more bodies, countless, flayed and flyblown in the pinking sawdust and among them not a soul that didn't seek it.

42//: stanislavsky rag

He would not run away again. He would bring in some money. He would dress in tights. Whatever it took. He would finish building his game and send it to that friend of Jesse's in Albuquerque. He would find a driving job. Driving was his thing. He could drive anything on wheels. Two, four, or eighteen. He liked the road, felt most like himself behind a wheel. Something about watching life through a dirty window. Made him feel clean.

Norma looked for and found a play for herself down at the checkpoints. Gene and Jesus went down ahead to clear the ground—a seven foot Six Nations warrior who looked like he could kill three wolves with his bare hands (look, the teeth) and a three hundred pound Sonoran bouncer, praise Jesus, whose wife and three children, mother and step-dad and two uncles and grandmother were murdered by three SLA activists one afternoon between *telenovelas* and Funyuns.

Gene ordered another drink. On the stage, the androgens were finishing up their synchronized snorkeling. Their cocks in the giant tank waved like eels. Bunny would be up next. Gene liked Bunny's Wonder Whoa-Man act. Bunny was a skilled dancer, Gene gave him that. Gene liked Norma's friends. He liked that she had friends down here—Jesus and Bunny and Little Barry and the missing Raye, who'd maybe turn up one of these months the way kids sometimes but not always did. It wasn't like in LA where Norma's only friends were an Elvis Bop Bag and a lost guy she'd met on a train (or something). She was so lonely in LA and there had been nothing Gene could do about it. Not that Gene could talk. Up in LA, his only friends were a dead dog and a continent full of strangers. America was a lonely place. But Spill City was not exactly America anymore and so it was different. Her friends had become his and he'd made some of his own. Spill City was no longer a place of strangers.

The bartender came over, all fake spurs and shit, and splashed some whisky in Gene's glass. Gene heard the click of boots and turned around thinking it would be Bunny in the new heels Norma had bought him. Break a leg, Gene was about to say, but it was just a cordon guard in the usual crazy drag and so Gene turned around again. The guard was wearing Mariachi boots and a Cartel bandana over his brassy yellow hair. From the edge of his eye Gene watched the guard check his weapon, pull up a stool and order a Miduri Bomb. There was something vaguely familiar about the guy. He had tiny baroque scarification scrawls (or old acne scars) on one sunken cheek. The Wonder Woman remix started up, all throbbing bass and digitized brass. Gene let the music take him, he closed his eyes for a moment and let the air rush out of his lungs. It blew his mind the way Bunny fell from the ceiling like that. Such skills. The perfect splits. Bunny hung Gloria's tooth from the rearview mirror of his tuk-tuk. A piece of her to guide him on his way. Bunny planned to go to LA to check on his family, there was more work up there anyway—Gene could come too. But Gene wasn't sure about leaving Norma. Gene could relate to the need for a grown straight man to dress in women's clothes. It was less the swish of cheap material against shaved thighs or the grip of a gusset, than the expansion of consciousness. One thing in the place of another. And it was also bare thighs and the grip of a gusset. A part of you waiting in the wings to return, a necessary but not sufficient condition of becoming. Peaks and troughs. Highs and lows. Men and women until Norma came along who was everything in one. The one out of the many.

He rubbed a hard palm over his burning eyes, then drained his glass.

Norma.

She'd changed so much since he'd first fallen for the haunted drifter who shed bits of herself all the way down the California coast. And then after LA she'd changed again. She'd grown into consciousness herself, learned which bits were necessary, and which were just sufficient. Gene would go with her wherever she took him. That didn't stop him worrying. Like how Gloria used to worry about him, her beautiful velvet brow knit with anxiety watching him fall where she couldn't catch him.

– I've become my dog! he said out loud.

– Good for you, said the barman.

Gene watched the barman crabwalk warily down the bar to serve the scarred stranger. The stranger ordered another bomb and swiveled, lurching a little to his right and then to the left. He barely seemed to register Gene nestling a luminous shot glass in the darkness. Gene heard the click of steel heels as the stranger leaned across and said in a loud and gravelly alto:

– Anyone around this joint know of a good driver?

43//: body mod

The ride to New Mexico had been bumpy, he said. He regarded her from where he was sitting on the edge of the bathtub, his huge shoulders sagging a little, his long hair lank with steam. Explained to her how the new wireless hybrid technology was not as smooth as it was cut out to be and there had been bandits. Hungry kickers who lurked at truck stops, peeled off the new fibre-wrap fuselage of the rig like candy while you waited for your vending machine coffee. He only got as far as Lordsburg before the battery died and the rest of the cargo had to be picked up by Cartel runners in lithium-recharged Humvees.

– How did you get back? Norma mumbled with her eyes half-closed. The edge of the tub hard against her head.

– Hitched, he said. No one attracted the kindness of strangers like Gene. The Cartel flunky who took over in Lordsburg even paid him for his pains, five hundred dollars he slapped into Gene's shirt pocket and offered to buy him a beer. Gene wisely declined, as savvy in his assessment of intent and character as he was warily withholding of judgement.

The tepid water lapped at her breasts and Gene smiled at her. He told her how he got the driving job from that cordon stranger who said he needed to move some goods—quote unquote—between TJ and NM.

Gene had been all excited to drive one of the new wireless rigs and see this hacker friend of his brother's in Albuquerque, maybe tweak the new game they'd been working on. Norma asked about the stranger and Gene shrugged. Just some guy, he'd said. Bunny lent him his tuk-tuk once he got into Spill City. He used it to track her down.

It was after midnight. He'd driven first to the hut and then to the trailer (empty) and finally to the Factory where he found her tied to a chair in the back of Tweety's forge, naked from the waist up. She'd given Tweety the last of her poker winnings to try to melt the cord off her neck thinking it would lose strength if Tweety could get it hot enough. When the blow torch didn't work, she asked him to try cutting it. That's when she'd bled and couldn't stop. The cord bled. The actual cord, like some umbilicus from hell. And her screams had reverberated around the vast building until she passed out on the chair, blood from her neck to her new boots.

Tweety backing off, saying. It ain't metal. I don't know what it is but it ain't any kind of metal I know.

Gene barged in all B.O. and fear, pushed Tweety aside and untied her, covered her with his coat and carried his fallen angel in his arms all the way back to the cottage, folks next day still talking about the fierce giant with his hair around his shoulders and the tall crumpled woman in his arms. She came to in the bath. Gene's eyes never leaving her, picking his cuticles.

– I had to change the water three times, he said.

He put her to bed. Lay beside her on top of the sheets grimly waiting for her to tell him what was going on. Waiting for the truth. When it was not forthcoming, he asked what body-mod in hell would agree to solder the cord to her spine.

– What is it? Some kind of organic Ti alloy?

When she didn't answer, he said, I know there are places in the South. And Eastern Europe. But America?

– This isn't America, she said. It's Spill City.

– Why'd you get it done? he said.

– It seemed like a good idea at the time, she said. Keeping her eyes closed so she wouldn't have to look at him.

– Someone can remove it, Gene said. There's this guy in LA, a surgeon, or almost—

But she was already drifting off. She woke sometime before dawn with Gene asleep beside her, her womb cramping from the hungry dentata, the cramps reverberating out through her body in concentric waves of pain. And she knew she'd never be free, and while she was here, that he'd never be safe.

Pop da pop da pop dibbie dibbie, pulsed the bioswitch. Pass it on.

Configuration (re)Transfer Protocol (CrTP). (n) Also known as Consciousness Transfer Procedure, and commonly known as RESCRIPTION. i. A standard configuration process used to transfer files from a Viewpoint (primary sequence or sentience) to a neural host across a (theoretical) totality of perception called the Whole. ii. Refers to a future return to a time before the Before, a restoration which will be both the beginning of a new age and a repetition of a previous state. iii. Coming home.

(Saurum Nilea, AQ., trans. L.Shay 2656)

44//: silence

– Mommy, are you there?

Smoke whispered out of the ass of the broken console. It was one of Gene's. He'd gone to the Factory to get them something to eat and some more antibiotics for Norma.

– Norma. Baby. OMG. It's been, like, foreverRRRRR!

Norma had finally relented and let Mommy in on the broken gadget. Because she needed to know. It took some doing—Gene was right. The bamboo was an amazingly effective firewall. Mommy's voice seemed to have more to do with the smoke dribbling from the console than it did with the console itself. If Norma pressed her head up against the window she could see lightning flash between the flailing fronds of bamboo. She pulled down the blind. Turned around to face the broken circuitry lying on the table. In the dark.

– So, she said, trying to sound casual. This Swedish fuck shot me. Just like old times, right? But on a positive note, I'm back in the game. I just won six hundred dollars.

– Wicked, said Mommy. You go, girl.

Norma slumped onto the couch and held her cramping belly. The dentata chomping at the bit.

– Uh huh, just like in the good old days.

– Happy times, said Mommy with its mouth full. A quaint icon materialized on the projection, like a bitten apple, as blue as tears. It blurred and disappeared but not entirely.

Norma hunched over her belly and stared at the projection through the burning slits of her eyes.

– Why him, Mommy? Why Gene?

– Normstah!! It was the voice of the little girl twin who lived under the Torrey Pine. Shrill and ancient.

Norma's clawed hands flew to her ears.

– Wait. I need more time.

– He's the one. Game over Gurrrrl! The words skidded across the dark in a flash of electron blue.

Norma tried to sit up straight. Listen. Gonna get us some prime US horn. Spill City's a dead end. I'm thinking stateside.

But Mommy had started to sing, 'Jean Genie...'

Norma stood up, keeping her eyes on the blue apple ghosting from the console.

Mommy slunk through into Norma's VIPr, 'Let yourself gohohohoh...'

– What makes you think he's the one, Mommy? I've been after this other Guy for you, super rock n roll, followed him all the way down from LA. Like I said before. But he's slippery. All's I need is some time is all—

Norma concentrated on keeping her head absolutely still so that her brain would not boil over and spill out of the top of her head. She knew she did not have a hole at the top of her head and that her brains were not boiling, but that's what it felt like and the Slash imagination was a powerful thing. It was one weapon against Mommy who had only words, who could, lacking an imagination, only observe the Slash through clichés and idioms. Words and no guts. No heart. It could not know what it was like to feel as though your brain was boiling, because it had no use for metaphor except as leverage. It was nothing but vantage point and therefore it missed the Whole point.

The apple rematerialized and pulsed like a blue fist.

– Gene is the Besta-Wan, said Mommy. A brain to die for.

There was a small pop of circuitry, the hot waft of fried PVC. Norma swayed.

– Firstly. Mommy, the Besta-Wan's just a pizza joint. Just a name. I mean just because we go there, doesn't mean—

– Two, Mommy said. His horn is magnificent.

Norma couldn't argue with that.

–Three. His lobes are luscious.

– What?

– The superbrain for Mommy's heart. Supercala-altruistic-parietalocious.

Norma put her hands to her ears, Lobes?

– You just want to take a big juicy bite of them apples. Yummy Mummy!

Silence squealed open a curtain and then it was just her and Mommy. Two-whoaman show.

– Mommy, I think there's been a huge misunderstanding. Gene's no one. Lobes or no lobes. He's a gotard, okay. He told me so himself. Look I've got cash again and enough fuck in me to buy you a bushel full of Besta-Wans. Guy out there'd be perfect for you. Great sense of fashion, got this Western thing going on. Just give me a day or two.

The surfboard above the couch flashed blue in the projection.

– The dentata doesn't lie. You want it, you want it bad, that bad apple, so ripe and axon-dense and just waiting for a fall. A love so total that it knows no other. He would die for you, burn down the house to save it. In this way, I loved the First Being.

The world had gone so quiet. The world had come to Norma finally in all of its silence and all of its fear.

– Okay, wait. A.) There's a big difference. I'm talking galactic. Okay. Between love that's total and love that totals. Yes. In this way you loved the First Being. Yes. The Nilean. You killed him, burned down the house. Swirling sands and toxic bubble, bitch. That's how much you loved him. Deal with it. B.) A man's brain is not in his, um, horn. That's just an expression, okay—Norma cupped her hands to her mouth—Earth to Mommy. No axons in the horn.

Mommy burped, He will live again. Our hungry heart. In the Besta-Wan. Game over, Agent 99. He's the Horn. Out of the many. And there were many horns, weren't there you big slaggy slut you. What a cunt!

Tears burst from Norma like from a burst valve.

– That hurts, Mommy.

The apple turned into a hot blue fist and punched Norma in the face. She flew against the blue surfboard and it fell off the wall and landed on her back.

– He would die for you. His heart's in his brain, you you big sloppy cunt you you skanky thieving slit. He's mine and you will. You will.

– You will.

Norma lurched to her feet and rotated in a slow circle keeping her face to the wall. Wind blew in beneath the rough door hewn out of the container. Mommy had never been all there. It told itself that it was all there was and so, by extension it could never be anything.

So what was it? Where was its weakness?

The apple pulsed blue as a heart attack. Norma had begun to back away dreamily, the headache receding and something taking its place, no. Not that. The apple flashed on and off. .--. .- ... ... / .. - / --- -. Pass it on. Her heart thrumming in her head, in the raw empty space left by the headache. Baddum, baddum. Pop pop the yippie. Um. The sound of knowledge, um, the silence of the fall, Daddy. The blue apple mutely flared then shriveled to a corpse-gray core for no apparent reason. She was doing lazy figure eights around it, stubbed her toe, hopped to shake off the Silence.

– And we will live again, it droned. In the Best One. The one with farthest to fall.

Norma stopped mid-spiral. The floor shook.

– Wait. You're going to kill him. That's the plan?

– Plan A, no Plan B.

– But the mission?

– Mission shmission. One word for another. Who's counting?

They'd discussed it beneath the towering flames. Her and Mommy. Or at least that's what her memory told her, bring bring. A piece of cake, Norma. Walk in the park. Or is that dark? Who's your daddy now?

– It's a rescription, isn't it? Norma said more to herself than to Mommy. A restoration. You're coming home, bitch. You lied.

And Mommy said, Bingo and Norma said, What about me, and Mommy said, Who?

But how luscious the apple looked. Norma drooled. She bit her lip. The apple glowed, fleshy, fragrant. She felt it in her parts, swollen and tempting. The rain would fall, the breeze would blow. Time would resume. Yet all she wanted was for the Silence to continue. To never-slash-ever end. She surrendered to it. The apple throbbed, expanded. She moved toward orgasm. Mommy's way of showing Norma that her will was not her own.

– Mommy? I'm coming.

– Yes dear. Hang on while I make a smoothie.

Mommy in override mode, entered Norma's Whole with a roar of agony-ecstasy that made Norma's back arc and her knees buckle. She sunk to the floor, her eyes so far back in her head that she could see her own human brain, its tangled dreams and gooey hopes, the silver tide of memory and lies. And at the edges a terrible Silence for which the cure was the disease. The dentata pulsed creamily, pulling her out once more on a wave of black delight that she could not stop because it was Mommy. All Mommy, all Silent. And as she pulled once more toward ecstasy, toward Silence, Norma grasped wildly for her will, for some weapon, some hole in Mommy's Whole, and then it came to her, through the silently mounting pleasure. She would draw on the oldest Slash weapon in the book. Older than speech, older even than love. Pain.

Panting, groping for one of Gene's screwdrivers lying on the coffee table. Not the laser kind, but a steel one that had belonged to his crazy uncle Earl. And jammed it in her thigh muscle. She screamed, breaking the terrible Silence, and Mommy receded.

– What if I won't? Norma sobbed.

– Won't what, dear? said the voice in her Whole. It was Mommy, but there was a distortion to it now. It was having trouble breaking through the human firewall. The synaptual fortress Norma had built, not just now, but over the months on Earth, with all the blood and tears of her growing humanity. All the pain.

Norma pushed herself to one leg and with the wounded one kicked aside the surfboard. Howled. Smoke poured from the console. Gene would be walking in any minute and that would be it. Norma had to settle something. She had to make a Plan B. But how? Her mind scrabbled around the corridors of the Whole, seeking a new set of co-ordinates. The room had gone cold-star blue, reeking of sulphur and CMRs. Even so, bits could possibly be retrieved, the transmission intercepted by SETI or someone—Mommy chuckling at the thought. Everything was blue.

– Thing is. I can't implant him Mommy.

– Can't or won't? There was a chromatic chill to the voice now.

– Can't slash won't. Same difference. You need me to launch the transfer protocol device before your files can be uploaded into Gene's horn, right? What if I can't, you know, do it?

– Your point being?

Again Norma felt dreamily pulled, or pushed, toward the blue apple. She didn't want to be but she was. The Silence resettling all around her now—she was reaching for it and she couldn't stop. With the last of her will, she raised the screwdriver. Plunged it into her leg again. And left it there.

She felt Mommy flinch, just a little.

– Oh stop being dirikulus, said Mommy. It's in your program. The VIPr brought you to him—call it pheromones, okay—you sniffed him out, all that scrummily high-minded gray matter—and precisely by wanting him all to yourself, you have brought him to me.

Norma howled. Pain, shmain. So that was Mommy's ace in the hole. Literally. It had built a simulated human volition into the program, one that was prey to both Mommy's control on the one hand and human emotion on the other but either way was not her own. Norma was fucked. That was in her program. To be a woman, fucked forevermore.

Blood poured from the wound in her leg. She bound it with a shirt of Gene's that lay draped over a crate. She watched the blood blossom on the shirt. Which, for the second time that night, gave her an idea. Norma wiggled the screwdriver into her leg again. She screamed and buckled. Blood bubbling around the steel. Mommy slammed a door in a room at the other end of the house in hell.

– Get a grip.

– I'll kill myself.

– Now look who's talking out of their axons. Too bad daemons cannot die.

– You're lying.

– You're the one with the screwdriver, said Mommy. Knock yourself out.

And she would. But not now. It was pain she wanted now. Screams and human noise to push away the hellish Silence, just a nudge. Some space, some human anguish to help her think. And then it came.

– Then I'll kill him, she said. If I can't kill myself I'll kill Gene.

The Silence lifted a little and the sound of the rain poured in. The clatter of bamboo in Mommy's uncertain sigh. Norma spasmed and jerked upright as the flesh of her back rent and her wings unfurled.

– Well that's a look, said Mommy coldly. A little old-school, but who am I to say?

Yet there was something wrong with this picture, thought Norma, staring at the apple.

– OMG, is that the time? said Mommy. So anyway, you touch a hair on his pretty brainy head and I'll take the kid. Raye. Make her wish she'd never been born—

Norma's heart gave a thud and dropped away somewhere

– Whoa. No. Not at all. Give me a day, I'll get you the most awesome dickbrain ever and you know. Mission accomplished. No one has to die. Kid's not part of the mission, Mommy.

– She is now, said Mommy. Thanks to you, and your lying heart.

The dentata knifed and matter oozed into Norma's boots.

– You'd kill a child?

– Well am I ever glad we got that settled because you know, it's important to keep the channels of communication open. Speaking of which, you might need a rag. Ragggggg.

– Mommy. Wait, don't go. We're not finished here.

The room had filled with the smell of boiling dioxins. Gene, coming home any minute now on his borrowed Flyer, would be pissed.

– Spoil the child and spare the rod, I always say. Lordyfuckaduck. I'm late for Pilates.

Wind blew into the window cracks, lifting the blind and showing nothing but darkness beyond. Nothing but noise.

45//: starfucker

Gene met her at the trailer in a Flyer he borrowed from Jesus. She got on the back and he took her to the Sanctuary to look for Raye, and then to Mac's store (closed) and then to the diner.

The redhead waitress said, The dude thinks he's that thriller guy?

– Yeah, said Gene. You seen him?

The waitress tapped at her console with a curser. She'd seen him yesterday. He locked up the store and took off, she knew not where.

It was raining heavily so they stayed to eat at the cafe. Norma had left the hut in a rush without her jacket and felt cold in the diner. Gene took off the denim jacket she'd bought him at the 101 markets and passed it to her. He ate in his T-shirt and she watched goose-bumps bloom and spread across the muscles on his arms. He ate steak and fries and beans and coffee into which he poured whisky from a flask.

– We'll find her, he said.

She kept her eyes on the door. They were at the same window booth at which she and Raye had sat. A trio of Cruids on power-blades stood across the road blowing on their hands. Behind them she could glimpse the purple slogan beneath layers of over-tagging across the sheet metal: *Separate or die trying.*

Even daemons can lie.

She turned to her giant wolf. She watched him eat. She reached out to smooth the lines etched on his forehead like repeated attempts at a horizon line.

– You'll never get rid of those, he said with a mouthful. I've had them since I was sixteen.

– Tell me again, she said. What we are. You and me. This.

He smiled at her. Chewed and swallowed. Washed it down with a slug of coffee. His eyes wide and serious and rippling with ghostly lights.

– This? he said

– All that out-of-the-many-one stuff. Again.

– Why?

– I need to hear it is all, she said.

– It's not like you to be insecure.

– It's not like you to be an ass.

He put down his napkin. His big hands so fine. A tight lick in her belly at the thought of his touch. He raised his cup, regarded her with shining eyes.

– To us, he said and through her tears she saw the eternity of his flame and that there could be no other.

She turned away to face the window, her eyes shut against her lying reflection, but he took her shaking hands in his and made her face him. He made her raise her cup to meet his own.

– Smile, he said.

– Why?

– Because you're a star, he said.

What wouldn't she do for him?

– And you're the Big Dipper, she smiled.

He left the next morning for LA to meet up with Bunny about some local driving. She put a hundred dollars in the pocket of the jacket with the warm lining. He gave her a wink and went out the door with his shoulders hunched against the cold. She woke late the next day to pale sun on the skylight and the sound of country music from someone working on their house across the street. More people returning to this blighted land. Norma and her mirror-self padded across to the bathroom where she scrubbed the dried blood from her hands.

46//: del mar

He left her with a phone, pre-charged and with his number keyed in at 1. She hadn't the heart to tell him that she couldn't text, that her kind couldn't use Slash frequencies. That she'd fry the code, infect him with enough radiation to fertilize a variety of tumors, genetic malignancies with no end in sight.

She turned off the phone and pushed through the pass in the bamboo grove until she came to the street. She went to VGs for breakfast. She sat there over coffee and watched a news item about some new technology for cleaning up spills, about the riots in Tajikistan. The Pacific Alliance. Everyone had gone. Bunny was away. She heard that D-Cup had gone to produce an album in Phoenix and had been taken to the hospital there with pneumonia. Superman picked up on vagrancy charges up in Washington, Jesus gone on a spree to Vegas. No one had any news from Raye. Norma felt glacial. Sluggish. Her bones felt cold and her skin crawled. Her thigh throbbed from where she'd stabbed herself with Gene's screwdriver. No amount of Vicodin could kill the pain and no amount of Xanax could kill her dread. That night she went to Una's but didn't stay. Little Barry said not to worry.

– Remember, he said. Before you got here Raye was okay and she'll be okay long after you're gone. She's just doing what she always does.

Scrounging for survival. She can take care of herself.

– But what about Augustine? she said.

– Seriously, said Little Barry. Why would Augustine bother with a kid?

– To get to me.

– Get over yourself, said Little Barry.

Norma wanted to get over herself. But she needed another to do that. Without Gene, without Raye, she felt a law unto herself, dangerously free. She remembered Raye looking up at the Factory roof with the discerning eye of an adept, the way she said she always saw the big picture, the whole Whole. How you had to have a Plan B. But there was a hole in the whole and they'd all fallen through it. Everyone. Not just Spill City, but America, wholus bolus.

Norma zigzagged out of the bar. She went back to the beach, caught the night ride to Arcadia, posted herself at doorways and bus stops. She watched the Flyers and Veelos stream past. She wandered among the craps games and samosa stands, the battery transfusion mechanics and shopping cart robo-games. She stopped whoever she could and asked after Raye—her hair uncombed and rivulets of rain down the grime on her jacket—no one had seen either the kid or her old man. She dozed for an hour against the wall of Mac's Antique Toy Museum and Pop Paraphernalia but no one went in or out. She woke up on a bench by the train station, watched gulls move in the dawn-gilded weeds.

She made it back to the trailer but couldn't remember how. Coming down the path, she could see footprints around the door, Raye's worn imprint in the sand. Norma went in unable to stop herself from seeing the girl inside—there you are—but saw instead that cramped and empty space. She dragged a lawn chair from inside to the front of the trailer, facing the ocean. She bought a tamale from an old woman who walked around the grounds with a steaming basket.

– Rain's letting up, she said to the turning-away crone.

Out on the water, ArmorFlated Zodiacs bumped over the swell, cleaning up the slick. The sun climbed the dome of cloud, began its descent. Norma got up stiff and damp from the chair. She would go to the cottage. Gene wouldn't be back yet but there might be a message on his console. The twins sprawled drooling beneath the oak. Norma tossed them the phone Gene had given her. It skittered to a stop against the boy twin's filthy underpants. He took it and bit it with jagged teeth. Threw it back to her.

– Die! Die!

Norma looked at the half a phone. She had to know. She had tried everything else, tried to separate herself from Mommy and it hadn't killed her. It had made her stronger. Even if killing Gene would save him from Mommy, Norma could not sacrifice Raye. Human lives didn't work that way, like words. One for another. But she could kill herself. Mommy thought it was the only game in town—and there is always only one way to beat a game like that. The filth was bottomless and she would take Mommy down with her. Dive, dive. The girl twin blindly clapping and gibbering, pointing at the beach and banging her rump spastically up and down in the dirt. Behind her the Ecoist sat stoically on his lawn chair and Norma gave him five hundred dollars for his trench coat.

*

Crouched on the old lifeguard stand, Raye watched the big lady stuff the pockets of a trench coat she bought from the Ecoist (it didn't suit her), with scraps of iron filched from the camping ground barbecue grille and bits of steel she picked up around the makeshift shanties, the recombo graveyard at the northern end of the grounds. The sun was bleeding to death over the horizon. The sand was a slick and treacherous silver. Raye, hunched on the stand like a gargoyle, watched Norma make her way down to the black tideline. No point in trying to stop her. Raye had seen enough people try to kill themselves on the road, to know they usually got what they wanted in the end. A news flash from nowhere, baby. Anyone who tried to kill themselves was doing it because a part of them was already dead and they were just trying to work out if they were strong enough to carry that dead weight, or if it was going to carry them.

*

The water seeped through Norma's jeans. It was cold but no more than she'd expected. She kept walking, combat boots and all, pushing through the surface turds and bloated bird carcasses, the plastic bags and cans and into the thickest part of the slick, placenta red. The Ecoist's coat felt unpleasantly heavy. It was all she could do not to shrug it off. Ducking to avoid being seen by the Zodiac crews, the weight of the coat dragged her beneath the sick plankton. Corrosive bio-matter filled her nostrils and eyes. The sandy floor fell away from her feet. Air bubbles streamed past her open eyes and burst through the slick at the surface and Norma let herself drop and drift past stark and shadowy refuse. Engine blocks and sunken chassis. Barnacled trawlers and jet skis, severed limbs, dead dogs and rubbery kelp. The current pulled her south. She took in water and filth and finally.

There it was. The Silence.

Take me, she bubbled soundlessly. Here I am.

Feer was a vast wicker city. Strands of her hair veiled her eyes.

Take me.

The wicker city was a half mile-deep stretch of dumped shopping carts. Thousands of them. She registered through the numbing silence—but not entirely, because her chest felt like exploding—that the chrome on the shopping carts had burned right through to the brown steel, lacy in the inky depths as coral. She registered that she was alone. Everything dead. The sea bed was a mirror of Kali I8, the planet to which she can never return, because it was here. It was always right here, waiting for her. The Silence. How many worlds within worlds? Was she born? Can she die? It was a matter, as Bunny always said, of bringing the truth to whatever role life threw at you. Even death, yours or another's. Bunny called it the Dane of roles. Memento mori, motherfucker. The words bubbled from her lips and burst soundlessly in the fathomless depths. She tumbled in filth and it gurgled out of both ends. The long cold tongue of night. She clawed at her eyes so she would not see, no, she will not feed the Silence. Daemon if you need to feed then eat yourself, Mommy. I boogie. I strut and fret.

The current ripped off the trench coat and her shoes and her jeans. She threw up, luminous upchuck. Dark kelp flailed at her. The arsenic and nitrates and diesel gnawed at her flesh, melted her nails and tore off a chunk of her hair. An undertow dragged her across a razorous reef and jammed her ecstatic in a cleft. Look at me, look at me now Mommy. She had company. A skeleton, silent as the moon, took her in its grasp, desperate, a surfing legend, it hooked a bony finger into her hair but the tide pulled her out again, its finger still caught in her hair. A stunted shark ripped a weal of flesh from her shoulder, broken clamshells turned her ass into Swiss cheese. Her wings unfurled, ripping flesh from bone, the scent of blood carried across the numberless gallons. She flew winged and naked through the filthworld, three toes broken against the side of a coast guard ship against which she came to a stop with a soundless thud. The salt burned and fissioned down her throat. Why could she still feel pain? She was meant to be dead. Why could she feel anything? The cold was enervating beside the sunken boat and there was a different pollutant down here in San Diego Bay. Eight different kinds of cancers, arsenic calking and radioactive waste from the nuke boats sheltering SLA fugitives across the bay. Sea lions eaten with sores arrowed through the gloom. She pushed off the boat with bare and ravaged feet. Screamed into the silence. Sewage monsters danced to her tune of pain on the deck of a sunken cruise ship, the Pacific Queen. Dumped aviation fuel angels flew through the gloom in all the colors of the rainbow. A stricken ray humped her with its stinger and stunted dolphins maneuvered maimed fins through the current. Norma hit the bottom and her mouth opened and unleashed a string of radioactive anguish beneath the bleak tonnage, liquid light through the roaring depths through which she was propelled by fate and broken wings. Hauled finally to the surface seventy miles south of Spill City and spat out on the Baja shore. Alive. A broken gladiator in the empty arena, the air red with jeers, she carved a dripping path up onto the beach. Big lady with a man o' war around her ankle and garbage in her hair. Naked but for a waterlogged combat jacket and limping, falling open mouthed to the sand, pregnant with eternity, a treacherous phantom she calls Mommy.

*

Seventy miles to the North, a young girl with hair the color of dunes shimmies down from a blue lifeguard tower and follows her own footsteps back to the trailer to wait.

47//: daemon

She couldn't remember how she got to the clinic. She woke up wearing one of Those Gowns. She got out of bed, let the kids staring in at the window see her ass. Pulled on her jeans and jacket and went to the front desk. The nuns said some skinny guy with a scarred face brought her here and paid her bill. Sand pouring from his boots, they said, made a mess of the floor. Norma glared at them, didn't need to but she did anyway. The nuns eyed her flirtatiously from behind their habits, but they waited for Norma to turn toward the door, before they crossed themselves, first one and then they all followed suit.

The clinic peered out from under a vast and dust-smeared grapevine. Out on the street she felt strong and it was all under control, like she'd been born all over again. The ravined street was deserted, curtains quickly pulled across windows as she walked its length. She took a side street that backed onto Bulevara Reforma, where she decided to walk back just for the hell of it. The dentata burned like cancer inside her and she felt like she'd entered the fray on a whole new footing. On a high stretch of highway powdered with ghostly swirls of dried mud, she'd slowed to a parched crawl and caught a ride with a Cartel spare parts dealer. The air beneath the tarpaulin dusty with blood. They ran into the checkpoint gridlock, where she slithered off but got waylaid by a gang of

Cruids. Later the Cruids would attribute it to the booze and the dope, the way the tall chick was one minute spread-eagled in the mud and the next everywhere at fucking once, whirling and kicking, or parts of her were. Like a string of paper dolls pulled from the fire, smelling like smoke and ringed in red.

Retrieval: (n). An advanced protocol whereby a virtually or clinically deceased Slash is recovered from just beyond the point of brain death. In early Nilean lore it was said that in the time of the media rez, retrievals were strictly forbidden due to the possibility of creating more hosts than the Viewpoint could manage, and thus Retrievals became punishable by permanent dismissal or worse.

(Saurum Nilea, AQt., trans. L.Shay 2656)

48//: spin

– You're out of Coke.

– There's beer in there, said Norma, a little out of breath.

Raye was standing against the window over the sink, her growing-out hair cut with gold from the setting sun. Norma had seen her footprints outside the trailer, but even before that, knew from the twins' gibberish and drooling and pointing, that Raye had come back.

– You shouldn't drink, said Raye.

– You shouldn't.

Raye sat down at the little broken table and pulled wires out of her ear. She was in those shorts a size too small and street grime clung to her knees. She had a small graze on one cheekbone and some fading bruises on her arm. The blue parka was nowhere to be seen. She pushed sunglasses up on her head, the ones Norma had given her at the coffee shop near Mac's store. When she turned to Norma the look in her eyes was somewhere between insolence and terror.

– I've been looking for you, Norma said with a wince as she shut the door behind her.

– Here I am, said Raye, curling her lip at the dust on Norma's boots, the bruises on her face. Looks like looking for me's not all you've been doing.

– I guess you think I'm too old to party.

– Too something, said Raye with a smile that tried and failed to be a sneer. I'll take a beer though.

Norma moved to the kitchen, trying not to limp. The girl's eyes never left her. The rain softly pelted. Bouncing off the hard path outside. Thuk thuk. Norma reached into the fridge for a couple of beers and brought one to Raye.

– Cruids, Norma said, sitting down. Oof. At that taverna just before the checkpoint. You should have seen them.

– You always did know how to empty a room, said Raye.

Norma carefully let the back of her head rest against the vinyl backboard, closed her eyes and opened them wide against the hard slosh of nausea. She gripped the broken table and tried to go with the spin. Her wing stumps burned. She'd escaped her last altercation by leaping onto the underside of a Consortium Hopper that took her as far as Soprano Beach before veering inland. The landing hadn't been as soft as she would have wished, and the headache that had come on after that made her think of terminal brain damage. Added to that a vicious cramping in her womb which made her wonder about blood transfusions. Would that work? She'd tried everything else but not that. Imagine. Hooked up to the slick red bags. Out with the old pain, in with the new. Blood for blood, wound for wound. Aware of the girl's eyes on her, Norma brought the beer can up to one temple. The sad carousel of the trailer lurched and spun. Maps and burger boxes, the old blind TV.

Raye said, Do you need to go to a clinic or something?

– I went to a clinic. Down in Rosarita.

– Just saying.

– I have bandages here, Norma said. Everything I need.

The trailer rocked in the wind.

– Why do you always wear that damn jacket? said Raye. Is it like armor or something?

Norma said, Something.

– Yeah, well how's that working out for you? I heard you got shot by Pig-Nose Haakon down at the beach there.

Norma put down her beer and looked at Raye, That was his name?

– Was? Raye incredulously shook her head and looked out through the salt-crusted window. You're going to have half the Baja Cartel after your ass.

– The least of my problems.

– Is that why you tried to kill yourself?

– How'd you know about that?

– Is it?

Rain fell and wind pulled sand up in sad whorls that agitated the shrubbery. Norma turned to look back at Raye. The girl held the beer can in both hands, slender and flawless for all their godless commerce. Knuckles softly jutting. Norma leaned forward and prized the beer can from the girl's small hands, took them in her own clawed grip. She twisted Raye's palms so that the pale stems of her wrists, gouged raw, faced upward.

– Is it? You tell me.

Raye flushed and pulled her hands away. To get answers I guess.

– Or maybe to come back with a different question, said Norma.

Raye's blue eyes flicked darkly toward the bed, and she rubbed the tip of her nose. Come back? Is that what happened to me? Where'd I come back from?

Norma waved it away. Bringing the innocent back is easy. Like pulling pickles from a jar.

– Great, said Raye. Is that what I am? A pickle. Or what. I don't know anymore.

– What happened to your mother? said Norma.

Raye said evenly, She was young. Not right in the head or something. Whoever knocked her up long gone. She had me while watching an episode of Jericho. Don't ask me how I know that. After the show was over, she wrapped me in newspaper and put me out with the trash. A neighbor saw, came and got me. Mac pulled me out of foster care.

Norma pressed her thumbs into her temples. So. You're saying, Mac's not your real dad.

– Real yes. Biological no. He was around the old lady at the time, I mean somewhere. I don't know. Maybe he's like my uncle or something.

We don't go into the finer points.

– The finer points.

– Being that he's all I've got.

– Well. Look. Get out of town for a while. Take Mac and go. It isn't safe around here anymore.

– Why did you save me that time? When I fell?

Norma drained her beer. Felt a drip coming from her nose and tried to staunch it with the sleeve of her jacket. Who says I saved you?

A small smile skidded across the girl's face. She began to draw in the condensation on the outside of the can, unreadable signs disappearing as soon as she made them. She said softly. But I wouldn't be here if it weren't for you.

Norma watched the shapes on the condensation appear and disappear beneath the girl's wandering finger, all language, the entire symbolic universe just a rescue message scrawled in vapor.

– Another beer?

– I can get it, said Raye.

Raye got up and went to the fridge, bent down into the sad wash of light and got out two more, brought them to the table and sat down opposite Norma, their facing shadows across the pale glow of the window. The stormy questioning eyes fell on Norma—she would meet them with her own.

– That's some shiner you got there, said Raye.

– You need to get out of here. You and Mac. I got people after me. More where they come from. You said so yourself.

– Augustine? That pussy? I can take him. I'm still looking for the stunt man who ripped off the old man. He won't leave without his letter from Blanket Jackson III. I'm going to find him—

– Norma leaned forward. Listen. That Guy? You can't beat him. No one can.

– Except maybe you, said Raye carefully.

– Maybe. Maybe not.

– Where would we go?

– There's a Franciscan mission up north, Mission San Miguel. Wait for me there.

Raye put the beer down and pulled the sunglasses off her head. She scratched her scalp with both hands, shoved the glasses back onto the tufts of filthy hair. San Miguel. Michael Archangel. The one who defeated Satan.

Norma's wing stumps knifed and she stood up to be sick in the bathroom. Hunched over the toilet bowl, her chest in spasms, hurling chunks of cat and donkey and straw and filth out of her and felt as though someone had her heart at the end of a fish hook. When she finished, she pulled her stash from the cistern where she kept it wrapped in plastic. Dry-swallowed her trusty trinity—Xanax, Oxy and Zithromycine—and put the stash into her jacket pocket.

When she came back, Raye was picking at a scab on her wrist.

– What if you don't get up there? Raye said. You might not make it. You don't look so good.

Norma swayed but managed to stay upright. I'm not there in a couple of weeks, you and Mac get out of the Zone. Right out.

– You mean back to Oregon? Raye looked up at her.

– Wherever. Get back to the States.

Raye looked out the window, an all but opaque square of white, the surf growling somewhere beyond that white screen, like a live thing wanting in.

– Yeah, I keep forgetting, Raye said. This isn't America anymore. It's like some kind of monster we made somewhere along the line. All-American monster.

– Look after your own, said Norma, one hand against the wall so it wouldn't hit her in the face. One thing I learned.

– Is that what I am? said Raye softly. Is that why you brought me back? Why do I have to leave, then?

– Well, said Norma, gently now. With you gone, my enemies have less leverage.

– Leverage, said Raye. A pickle. Only thing you got wrong was the innocent bit.

– Two out of three, said Norma with a indulgent smile.

She lowered herself onto the seat again, sunk into the old vinyl upholstery. There was a crack on the table in the shape of a Y from the last time she'd punched it.

– What about your fella? He won't leave, said Raye. Not ever.

– I know, said Norma. I know that.

– What you going to do about it?

– I've got a plan, said Norma.

– You're going to leave him, Raye said, her fingers skidding all over the can, writing and over writing some futile message to a god who would do less for any of them than he had in his heart. All of us. You're not coming to San Miguel, are you? Not any time soon. Not ever.

Norma looked away from the restive scrawl. Gene'll be okay. He's got Bunny here. Little Barry.

– A balding transvestite and a cross-eyed dwarf, said Raye. Jesus.

– Him too.

The trailer lurched and keeled. The light had drained from the room leaving traces of gold in the corner, on the contours of the girl's face. The beer and the meds taking effect. Norma's vision blurred. Her legs wooden. The cuts and bruises throbbing a little. A lot. She could still taste salt and chemicals, smell them on her skin. So tired. The oft-summoned dream of saffron hills and a lowering sky.

She heard Raye's voice coming to her from a great distance. Hey, big lady. Your eyes are, like, smoking.

She pulled the sunglasses off her head and reached them across to Norma. Norma put them on, regarded Raye through the scratched and tinted lens, a problem of her own making, the girl way too smart for her own good.

– Leave tonight, said Norma. There's money. Here. She reached into her pocket. And I got you a new goddam coat. It's here somewhere. Take anything you need.

– Anything?

– What's mine is yours. Take it. And stay off the trains. Take a bus.

Raye put aside her beer. Her damp strong fingers sought Norma's dry and trembling claws. Darkness fell outside, the trailer transformed into an insubstantial trick of the wavering light. Norma's gaze met Raye's wary eyes and soft mouth, the clueless pity of the very young. Little wonder that retrievals were forbidden. Giving something life had nothing to do with appetite. This had to do with a secret kind of care and self-crushing love. Raye started humming haphazard snatches of melody that dragged at Norma's eyelids and she felt her grinding jaw relax, the pain in her shoulders lessened with every breath. A slight breeze fanned in from the window, cooling her split lip and burning scalp. The curtains fluttered. The red glare from a passing recombo flared against the walls and the inside of the trailer glowed and spun. She could still hear Raye's demented singing, but softer now. Something about dancing barefoot. The girl's hand in hers was cool and knowing. A good hand. Strong. Raye had turned to the window and her hair fell in stiff heavy tufts across her face. Lights came on in the camping ground. More trailers pulling up every day. The lights shone through the curtains like star systems and Norma, so sleepy now, thought she might look at these for a while before she left. The way the colors shone on Raye's hair and the tusk stumps just beginning to jut from the girl's narrow shoulders.

PART IV

The Impass/able

The dying sun around which Kali I8 orbited, WD 236-10, expanded until it consumed everything in its path. In its death throes it demolished the Edda galaxy, leaving nothing but darkness through which the ghost (see below, aporafex) of Kali I8 was cursed to drift. Kali was no longer a Brainworld. It was just a brain, separated from itself. The closer Kali drifted to cosmic madness the more it realized that you don't have to be alive to die. Its lightless dreams were filled with wings and horns.

It is said that the true nature of the Brainworlds' curse was to die before they were alive. Because to die before you are alive is to spend eternity yearning for what you never had.

(Fascicle 25.4 Nilea AQt., trans. L.Shay 2656)

49//:neverland

– Daddy? Are you there?

Mac was feeling better, Raye could see that straight away. There was even a little color on his bleached face. Maybe it was bringing Norma to see him that time or maybe it was the new meds. She'd looked for him everywhere, finally found him in the attic of the store. A windowless panic room up a ladder above a Rediem lab on the second floor no bigger than the treehouse she had up north, up at the farm. He'd lugged the surveillance console up there and everything. He had been surviving on expired M&Ms and peeing in a Drink 'N Wet doll potty.

– Come on, she said. You ready?

She'd seen one of the Rediem packers come out of the back door in the dead of night. Waited until he'd finished making a call beside a dumpster and then slipped back inside behind him. Followed him upstairs and then it was just a matter of exploring on her own before she found Mac, hunched and muttering in his hidey hole in the manner of a trapped squirrel. She'd talked him downstairs with the promise of pancakes at Cafe 101 for breakfast, his favorite. And a bus ride after that. He liked buses. Wherever you want to go, Pop. LA maybe, yeah? He'd like that. Hollywood. Rodeo Drive. Old stomping ground.

He was so small. Smaller than MaryElizabeth Taylor who Raye had met that one time. Mac said Raye shouldn't be able to remember, that she just thought she did because of all the times he'd told her about it. But Raye did remember. She remembered everything and every day now there was more. Not just her own memories but others too, like the desert where she'd never been and cold clear rivers that she'd never seen and yellow boiling seas beneath the towering flames.

But the time on Rodeo Drive that they met MaryElizabeth Taylor, just walking down the street. Or it could have been one of those lookalikes, but it didn't matter. Raye was real little and in Mac's arms, she remembered what it felt like being up there. Safe as houses. Up so high to touch the sky because to her Mac Daddy was a giant among men and always would be. Never another to take his place.

Raye was already too old to be carried but it had been a long day and Mac was already late for, what, the tenth audition? His face drawn and a hopelessness threading the corners of his eyes into bunches and it filled her with sorrow. She pushed his mouth into a Jokers grin with her fingers. And then there it was, that moment on a sunny day in June, Rodeo Drive City of Angels, when everything changed. They met MaryElizabeth Taylor. She was walking toward them flanked by minders, all frail and bejeweled with her hair in some crazy striped bouffant.

– Look, said MaryElizabeth in that famous cut-glass voice she had. What a beautiful child.

Her minders exchanged glances and tried to stop her but before they could, MaryElizabeth reached across and touched Raye's hand. The varnished fingernails, swollen knuckles ringed in glitter. Mac gone all to trembling like it was a real angel down from heaven, wouldn't let Raye wash that hand for a week. Raye felt even then how that encounter with MaryElizabeth Taylor changed everything. The subtle shifting of odds and not a dealer in the house of Mac good enough to beat that game. Because of what MaryElizabeth said to him and how she said it.

– And you, sir, said MaryElizabeth, dimpling, and with a dainty intake of breath. You could be Michael.

Well, given his Stanislavskian fixation on the late star, and taking inventory of his god-given high cheekbones, wide set eyes and wounded gash of a mouth, Mac practically peed himself. Miss Taylor saying that changed everything. It was like a blessing she'd given him. Go forth and be Michael.

So here he was in Spill City, a few too many procedures down the track, The Mighty MacMichael. How much further now to fall? Yet, Raye was in Norma's killer heels and they were going to have Sunday breakfast. Like a normal family. It was Raye's treat from the money she'd earned herself, not Norma's stash. That was an important distinction. Had nothing to do with Norma. Raye had earned it fair and square. It had been tough and had taken time, and truth to tell, she didn't like Norma or anyone to see her that way, on the job. It was a Zen thing, needed her total concentration. Like the john last night. Nice little Veelo with a trailer on the back, warm as toast and when his zipper jammed he didn't hit her or anything. Not hard.

Norma had given her money, lots of it, but Raye needed that to buy bus tickets to San Miguel, have enough in reserve for the checkpoints. You never knew what was around the bend. Sometimes you thought you could see the whole picture but there were tiny little holes in the whole. Holes big enough to crawl through, big enough to let in a worm or two, a bug.

Which is why you had to have a Plan B.

Norma Gene. She liked to call them that. They made such a cute couple and Raye didn't know why she'd gotten so mushy lately. Just thinking about them brought a lump to her throat. Hormones maybe. She'll be sixteen next year. She'll have to get herself a boyfriend by then or die trying.

Norma Gene, yeah. Sounds right. Some people are meant for each other from day one even though they don't know it. That the future depends on them getting together, not just their future but everyone's future. Humanity. Someone Gloria. Mommy this and mommy that. A broken piece of comtrash went off in the trailer after Norma dozed off and Raye picked it up. The voice on the other end in Raye's ear like a cold tongue of night.

Mommy.

Sad shrunken skull-mother dangling at the end of the line. A person's up against a hard game if they have to die to beat it.

– Beat it, said Raye, and hung up on the bitch.

– Look, Raye said. The rain's stopped.

It hurt when she smiled. Mac locked the shop door and turned around.

– What happened to your face? he said.

– I fell.

– Nice shoes, he said looking her up and down approvingly. Manolos. Fakes but good ones at that.

People stared, those who didn't know him. Locals said, Hey Mac. Say hi to Michael.

Moonwalk for us Michael.

Raye bared her teeth. Daddy's girl all grown up, keep away from the Grimey in those hella-heels, freak-daddy by her side. Powdering her nose in Norma's trailer earlier she'd seen two alien eyes staring back at her. Extraterrestrial storms.

–We'll catch the Coaster, she said sweetly, taking his arm.

Norma had said to stay off the trains, but technically the Coaster wasn't a train. The buses up the coast ran at random, and it was just one stop. Raye towered over him in Norma's heels. Mac's arm was like an old stick in the velvet jacket, the gloved hand trembling against his leg. He wore gold-framed aviator glasses over his parchment skin and his mouth beneath the glasses was a deep shade of Wacko red. She could have done without the gold codpiece, though.

– Why do we have to get the Coaster? he whined. Perfectly good food trucks at the market.

– We're going to Cafe 101 up the coast, she said. Blueberry pancakes, remember? Like old times.

Plus the Greyhound station was right behind the cafe. She'd thought of everything, yeah. The whole thing mapped out in her mind, all the angles.

The conductor on the platform regarded them with watery yellow eyes, came up for their fare right away and then walked off to pick up garbage, a skinny Mexican-looking guy with bleached blond hair in ancient Mariachi boots. Raye felt her pulse quicken and looked up at the safari-suit sky. Cotton ball clouds.

– Spring in Spill City's a cock teaser, Mac said.

– You hungry? she said for the tenth time.

*

Mac didn't like the trains. Folks that came in on the train gave him the skeevies. Cartel trash and quake-baggage. He liked the bus. Nothing wrong with the Greyhound, good old American institution.

– Hungry enough to eat a dead secessionist, he said to Raye for the tenth time, because he knew that's what she wanted to hear. The uneven scrape of the conductor's boots on the platform. Mac agreed to the Coaster. Agreed to everything. He was doing this for her. And hadn't it always been that way between them? That stuff about love conquering all was a crock, he thought. It wasn't about conquest, or shouldn't be. Guilt, sure. No getting around guilt. That came with the territory. But not conquest. Love had nothing to do with conquering anybody and he did love Raye, loved her as his own, the pain of his love right there in his chest at the way she stood there with her arms folded and her back to him watching for the train, thinking she had to take care of him, shmancy heels and long skinny legs like a colt he had up at the farm in Portland.

Legs to here.

Slut.

The white eye of the train coming toward him. He clapped hands to his ears to stop the ringing and the white knife across his iris, the bell tolling, push her in. Nononono.

Spare her please, Michael, she's innocent. The pain behind Mac's eye knife-white, spreading and colonizing him, replacing him with itself, Please Michael, you know everything, do you mean to do less than is in your heart? Anyone who had a heart, Michael—Mac looked around the platform for a sign, a daisy growing out of the slag, maybe, a single star up there in the teasing blue sky. He was an eye of pain that had no beginning or end, that stared out unsentimental and seething with such a terrible truth. Say it again, Mac. Slut. A bitch cunt hole in the whole, no good two-dollar bunk bunny. Liar, and there's the truth of it. But that Raye, child of pain, should die for loving me? The sky stayed hard and blue—he could have been anybody, anything (slut held you back) he looked just like Michael, and Neverland, Mac. It doesn't take everybody. No one knows why, but you don't get a second chance. Is that you? Michael? We could have come together you and I, I am the hole in the whole, and I searched the whole for you, waited alone and speechless, the flames and the toxic bubble, until there was nothing, nothing but want, Mac, don't call me Wacko, Mac, or I will hound you to hell, Daddy. Word for word, wound for wound, the pain of pain remembered here again.

Michael?

Push her in, Daddy. One more step to go, no
one will see no
one will care or
know not to care
how far the fall

Now, Mac. Your second chance. Never another.

Now.

50//: charity.2

Norma watched Gene dream on their mattress tucked behind the partition in the little container hut. The two little wolf's teeth he had left pulsing against his wrist. She dozed off again, floating on the wet breathy waves of pain. Was woken by the Silence snaking in under the door of the little hut, dark finger of night. It's time.

Gene mumbled into his pillow. Her shoulders buzzed and bled. He noticed the ugly ridges. They were more pronounced since she'd come back from Mexico, since she'd tried to drown Mommy in a sea of lies. The rest of her healed even faster than usual and she felt stronger than ever, her belly a hard plate of muscle, womb of death. The chunk of plasma pulsing around her neck like a tumorous Siren, calling Gene to his fate. Gene who had to die for loving her.

They'd had sex. Slow and floaty and Norma had asked him to hold her wrists over her head—so she wouldn't activate the bioswitch—and he'd covered her with his body and his huge hands around hers, their synchronized cries had completed the long chain of understanding between them.

– I found Raye, she said later. I put her and the old guy on the northbound bus.

He nodded with his eyes closed. We could think about going South, into Mexico, away from Spill City. With the money from the driving gig I could get a new truck. Chevy maybe. Get Jesse down there. So many beautiful beaches. The cold back east kills his leg. Maybe we could get someone down there to have a look at that thing grafted to your spine—

She put one hand over his mouth and the other over her own, tears flowing over her knuckles.

– Yes, she said. Mexico.

He drew her to him and kissed her hand, her salty lips. A hard curtain of tears between them.

They dozed off and Norma was woken by a commotion down by the tracks. She watched him sleep with one arm slung over his eyes. Charity, the Independence Day singer had said. Charity is the key. The phone beeped. *Pass it on.* The bioswitch hissed at her breast and the dentata bit. Dot dot dash. Game over.

– Gene, she said, shaking him awake. It's time.

– For what? he mumbled.

– We have to talk. Her voice trembled. Her tongue felt thick. I have to tell you something.

He mumbled something she didn't catch under the roar of engines, the howl of the train. The bamboo clattered.

– In the morning, he said.

– It's time.

– For what?

But he turned toward the wall, and from the skylight the charred wash of dawn fell down on his hair still in the matted ponytail and his broad back, bunched with muscle, turned away from her.

– The truth, she said, stretching out a hand in a gesture less of supplication than a final question. She brushed his warm shoulder and got her answer.

– Spare me, he said. And fell instantly back to sleep.

Kiphoriyo—i) n. A rare event in which an aporifek, unleashed in some obscure or unusually complex Alaxenoesis protocol, takes on an approximation of life.

Ephatix i) n. a type or species of aporifek, unleashed in the process of Alaxenoesis, and containing both aspects of its host's (sub) program, *and* the primary (meta) sequence prior to Telefraxis. In its coded quest for self-contained and sustainable replication, the Ephatix has been known to work both for and against either or both of its two 'parent' programs.

(Saurum Nilea, AQn., trans. L.Shay 2666)

51//:guy

That, thought Norma, heading swiftly to the trailer, bits of her form strung out between the ones lost and found, is the idea. Spare him. From the truth Slash Mommy, the only game in town. But for how long? She had to know.

It was still dark, smears of light out on the ocean, taillights and distant neon in the inky canyons of Spill City. Around the doorstep of the trailer, the small smooth scuff marks of Raye's Vans had been overlaid by the hard curve of silver heels. Norma stomped on these with the ridged teeth of her own double soles.

– A cunning stunt, she said out loud. I'll find you yet, Stunt Man, and feed you to the wolves.

She pushed open the door and closed it behind her. The trailer was empty but smelled of shampoo and beer. It was cold. Their beer cans were still on the little broken table. Norma's closet was ransacked, the coat she'd bought for Raye gone too. She moved slowly and silently through the small space of the trailer. In the bathroom wastebasket was a small bloody parcel. The girl's Kotex. Being a woman is an interesting life, Norma thought. On the medicine cabinet mirror were scrawled in Raye's handwriting two words in red lipstick.

Remember me.

Norma's own gaunt reflection stared back at her from behind the scrawled letters and she imagined Raye twisting around to see the strange sharp protrusions at her shoulders. The girl turning back to write herself a message, should she come back. But from where, thought Norma, and from what? Norma would have spared Raye if she could have. Should have. She opened the medicine cabinet. All the Vicodin were gone. Shame about that. She took out a wad of bandages and iodine.

Norma numbly gathered the garbage and wrappers and cans and plastic knives and forks and chopsticks. She pulled the sleeping bag off the bed in the little alcove, and took everything—towels, shower curtain, food wrappers to burn in a trash fire along with her bloody clothes. Black plumes rose in a scrawl across the white sky, an echo of Raye's invisible rescue message. *Remember me.* Norma stacked the empty water bottles and pocketed what was left of her cash and pills. She took her time. Her leg began to throb. She changed the bandages. She stood or sat for long minutes without moving. Consulted her maps. Blinked into the fading light. It was evening by the time she'd finished. Gene would be wondering where she was. Time, as always, was against her.

She stood like a stranger in the empty trailer, no sign left of her passing but the broken table, the gouged-in walls. Against the window she conjured her and Raye's facing silhouettes, miles soon between them. And as she stood there alone again, the contours of the sad little interior gave way and were replaced by a Whole. Norma reached her hand out to touch it, that flat-palmed gesture, not of supplication, but of asking. Where? Here on the maps were her answers. He'd said Mexico. She would make sure Gene got to Mexico. She would get a message to Jesus to make it happen, take him over the mountains himself or with someone trustworthy, as far as Coahuila or Monterrey maybe. She could see it. Gene south, and Raye to the north. There were mountains she could put between them. Her mind's eye scanned the cruel ridges. Even a desert. A seismic chasm to keep them from returning to this fallen place. A cut difficult to cross and impossible to heal. Mommy would have to stay here in Spill City with Norma, because unlike Gene and Raye, it was where they belonged. Together.

It wasn't much of a plan, but it was the only one she had.

She went back into the bathroom and rubbed off Raye's scrawl with the sleeve of her jacket. Kept rubbing until it was all gone. Puffy with exhaustion, Norma's newish Slash eyes looked back at her, steel gray, as cold as time. Then she turned and left the trailer for good.

The sun was setting and the Swami's headland threw long-fingered shadows across the sand. The sky was aflame and between the gaudy spill of cloud and the inky horizon line lay a hard white glow akin to a scrim light across the curve of the Earth. A navigational aid, she imagined, for all the Mommies out there.

Norma did not look back. She followed the path to where the twins lay snoring beneath the oak. She nudged the girl twin's small, cankered foot with her titanium toe. The twins woke simultaneously with a yowl, their blind slits of eyes blood orange in the reflected light.

– Mommy! Mommy! they squealed in unison pointing to a spot just behind Norma.

Norma instantly froze, her heart thudding like a hammer drill. The twins began to fade unevenly until they were the color of watery milk, the bark of the old pine visible through their forms. The boy twin unfurled to his feet and slowly lifted his sister to float beside him.

– Mommymommymommy, they gibbered.

Norma wheeled around slowly and there he was. Guy Manly. One hand on his crotch.

Norma's thudding heart halted for a moment, long enough for her to suspend thought, for her to take in the Guy's pale skin, white rays of the setting sun bouncing off his silver heels. She mouthed his name, but it was drowned out by the surf.

Guy Manly gestured toward the twins and said in a sandpaper voice, They were drowned in the Super Storm, waves came in as far as the lagoon. They screamed for their dog, so their mother went back for it, told them to wait under a tree and here they are.

– Mommy-daddy, cried the fading children.

– Aporafeks, said Guy. In the Nilea Tongue, as it will be translated by Lucius P Shay in the year 2656, when the Slash discovers the exo-planet in the newly named galaxy 434940.

– I thought you'd be younger, was all Norma could manage.

Because he was so achingly thin, the wash of scars on his cheekbones. The silver tip on his belt loose and flapping. He self-consciously straightened, puffed out his bony chest.

– I'm as young as you feel, said Guy. Sir yes sir. He brought his hand up in a rigid digit salut.

– Who are you?

– Manly's the name, Ephatix's the game.

He said it like a sneeze, spraying pale glots of snot in an eighteen inch radius. Pass It on.

It? Meaning Mommy?

– Where do you come from? Norma said. Or what?

He gyrated his hips.

– Ouch, he said. Not where but who, do do-do do-do do-do. Shaved her legs and then he was a she, but not entirelyleeleelee. You do-do-do-do.

Through narrowed eyes, she watched a ray from the setting sun claw toward his jerking form. And that it had no shadow.

– You're me?

– A shadow of your former self, he said.

And because he spoke in nothing but clichés, like an obscene parrot, she knew it was true. Give an idiot an idiom.

– You escaped—from me, from a part of me—back there in Bakersfield?

– Roger that Sherlock.

Behind them the twins giggled faintly, like a television in the next room. Canned laughter followed. Of course. He had no shadow. And she, Norma, sometimes had three.

– Mommy, said Norma. You're Mommy too? A double agent.

– Caught between a cock and hard place.

Again the feeble crotch-grab.

– What do you want?

– Want shmant. Cunt shunt. Jean Genie.

She was on him in the blink of an eye. They struggled but he was weak, brittle as a pile of sticks, although she suspected he held something in reserve. His materiality surprised her, and aroused her. She felt a lick of delight beginning behind her knees. He managed to reach around and draw a battered-but-lethal-looking Bowie knife. She easily wrenched it from him and tossed it behind her. Her legs straddled his chest and he sniffed her crotch. His yellow teeth dripping goo, great globby spurts from his nose like the Crock-Pot back at the Sanctuary, the smell of rotten leeks not far behind. He howled with mirth.

– You're on the rag, he cackled.

– I bleed, she said, tightening her grip on his phlegm streaked throat. Why can't I die?

– *Memento mori*, he rasped. Dream on, beyatch.

She rammed a fist into his memento mori nose, snot and bones on her knuckles. Smashed and smashed at it just because she could.

– What doesn't kill me, he rasped between blows. Makes you stronger.

And so she stopped. His yellow eyes floated in coal black seas. He coughed and expelled a gut full of bile with such force she had to turn her face away.

– I don't know what I ever saw in you, she said. Pushing herself to her feet.

He lay there a while with his hat beside his head and his brassy hair tangled around two bony protrusions on his head.

– Norma, shmorma, he tut-tutted. You saw yourself. In me.

– You can't die either? Ever?

– It's a bitch, ain't it. He sat up, catching his breath. The ultimate rejection. I mean even death won't have us. Whaddayagonna do?

A piece of his nose cartilage slid into his mouth and he ate it.

– But it makes us stronger? Trying and failing?

He became evasive, his lying eyes filled with a kind of honey-like substance that brimmed but did not fall.

– Wait, she said, flexing her claws. Her shoulders had begun to burn. She reached down for the Bowie knife, wiped the blade on her jeans. Wait. So some of us come back stronger, but what about you, Mr. Macho Manly? Every time death sends you back you're, what, a little worse for wear?

– Where? You have something that belongs to me, he said reaching for the knife.

She lunged.

– What do you want? he said.

– Answers.

– What's the question?

She held out a hand, helped him up, his nose all over his face. She took a few steps back, just in case. He pushed on his hat, flicked its brim and fixed her in his tarnished stare. One of his shoulders had twisted at an odd angle that not even his cowhide jacket could conceal and his left arm swung flaccidly across his sunken belly. He reached down furtively with his good hand to gather a scattered deck of Harry Potter playing cards which he crammed back into his pocket.

– How much time do I have?

– That depends, said Guy, squaring off the deck.

– On what?

– What do you think?

– On Mommy. Is the question. The only question.

– So ditch the bitch already, he snarled.

– I tried that. Tore at my guts. Tried to cut off the umbilicus.

– Ouch.

– Is right. And then I tried to drown myself. Kill us both. But you already know that.

– You came back stronger, he said. Mommy did too. It's in you. Forevermore. In your hole.

He chortled, a sound halfway between a dishwasher and a death rattle.

– The dentata? What then? she said. Tell me how to ditch the bitch, fucker, or its slice-and-dice time.

– It won't work for you.

– Liar, she said, slashing a diagonal backslash across his chest. Black ooze like the mark of a broken Zorro.

He looked down at the slash across his body. Touched the dark matter with a shaky hand.

– I got that David Bowie off some ear-slicing psycho in Bakersfield. Well not from him directly, but from some meth head who found it washed up on the shore couple years later, was using it to cut the tails and tongues off cats. Plenty more sick fish in the sea, darlin', where that came from.

Norma looked up at the dripping blade that looked aflame, the scratched wooden handle with its mismatched rivets.

– Not your darling, she said.

Guy Manly turned and took a step toward her. She slashed. He took a step back.

– I don't know about the Grimey. Last I saw Mac Daddy was taking care of her.

He gave a scratchy snicker.

– Why'd you rip him off? Take that stupid letter he loved so much.

– The one from whatsisname Quilty?

– Blanket.

He made a pretense of thinking about it. Um. It's in my program. I'm a, let me think. I'm um. Your worst nightmare? Does that sound about right?

– The barn, said Norma. The one I go to in my dreams. You're there. I see your prints in the sawdust. Decapitated heads. Men's parts. You a collector of souls or something?

Guy said, Or something. It's good to have a hobby. Makes you live longer.

– And I see the barn through your eyes.

He brushed down his jacket with mock patience. More than that, he said. A part of you goes there. With me.

– Because you're my nightmare. She hesitated but had to say it, We're in some kind of partnership.

– Think of me, he said releasing a wet and foul fart, as the wind beneath your wings.

She pulled her jacket collar over her nose. She'd heard about telomeric runoff and mnemonic waste unleashed in repeat transformations. No wonder it stank. The twins shrieked from somewhere in the tree.

Whoever thunk it stunk it, called out the boy twin.

– Whoever deduced it produced it, said Guy turning his empty eyes up at the branches.

Whoever denied it supplied it, said the girl twin's voice, sweet and clear and very faint.

– He who articulated it particulated it, hissed Guy. Gimme my knife, bitch.

– Keep talking, said Norma.

– Whoever smelt it, said Guy, trying and failing to shuffle the Harry Potter deck.

– Dealt it, said Norma. Shit. Human evil, I sniff it out. You deal with it.

– I'm all that's left of the mission as originally conceived.

Norma brought her nose out from behind her collar and sniffed the clean sea air beneath the receding stench. Which isn't much, she said. Just saying.

– It's enough. You've been to the barn. There's only one of me now. Now that you're changed. I mean you're still a hunter. There's that. Mommy's still got that up its sleeve.

He stuck out a black tongue and wagged it at her.

She made another slash across his chest. Two backslashes. He wobbled, weakening.

– Changed? How?

– The wings, the vengeance. Wasn't in your program. You picked that up somewhere along the way.

San Miguel.

– Very very bad. Mommy's mad. Very mad. You're in trouble. Big big—

She lunged again, but just for show. He recoiled, thrust his groin at her.

– You started off as a horn hunter, he said. Cocks. Shlongs, wangs.

– I get it. Why?

He drew his misshapen hands together in mock piety.

– You heard. Mommmymommymommmy. It thinks a man's dick's in his brain.

Norma said, What's with that?

Her bowel spasmed and her pulse glugged in her ears. Ice burned across her skin. All of her human senses vied with each other and with the other ones, the extending claws wracking her bones, the tusks rending her flesh, blood flowing between her fingers.

Guy Manly did another little nervous dance, his eyes on Norma's claws and the flashing Bowie knife.

– I mean all this—Norma swept the knife out hopelessly. You and me. All this, for a horn.

– Not just any horn, said Guy warily. The horn. The One Horn. The Best One. The one attached to a brain with farthest to fall.

Norma locked her eyes on him. Why? Exactly why?

Guy shrugged, Because it can. Because once it uploads itself into the horn, it starts to replicate and then it's home and host.

– Over my dead body, which according to you is never, or near enough.

– Plenty more fish in the sea, said Guy with a shrug that seemed to wrack him from limb to limb.

– Not like him.

– Okay. Not plenty. Well. A few. One or two. A hard man is good to find. I'll grant you that. But that's what you're programmed to do. To find the best brains around and fuck with them. You'll implant one of those suckers and then it's Mommy-time! That was Mommy's Plan A. It programmed you to be a badass, literally, drawn to all that's good, and ruin it. And then Mommy could wander among the wreckage, a whole new world to rule.

– Why?

Guy shrugged, It's a rush. To corrupt the incorruptible.

– But something else happened. My program was the one corrupted.

Guy hitched up his jeans.

– Even if it had one, which it doesn't, Mommy wouldn't know its ass from its elbow. Wrong schlong, hehe. It can't even write a program without clichés and rhymes. It can't understand what it is to be Slash—human. It can't even imagine—even on the most basic level, which is language. I mean look at me. But it knows good gray matter when it finds it. Or when you find it. Or when it finds you—

– I get it, said Norma between clenched teeth.

– It's just a matter of time, he said. Den-tatah!

– The VIPr.

– Shmiper, he said. Resistance is fruitful.

His voice deepened now and was everywhere and nowhere at once, between her legs and gurgling between her ears. He pulled an ancient broken phone from his jacket pocket and checked the time, the glow from the screen changing his face into an into an X-ray of itself, a black skull in a wash of blue.

Norma's jacket strained against the jagged wing bones. Resistance? If I've changed, so have you. What's with that?

Again the evasive shrug, the stagey yawn, You're becoming more of what you are. Me too.

– Which is?

Confusion played across his yolky eyes. Self-employed, he said. Something to shoot for, anyway.

He acted shot.

– You? You want out too?

– I want *it* out. Mommy.

– Liar.

– No. Yes. I lie. That's true.

Norma thought about it. So you wanted me to die too. Then we could have all been free. That's why you sent Gene away on that bogus driving job. Give me a chance to kill myself while you waited on the other side of the border, to see if it was possible. What I am.

– I yam what I yam.

– You're its bitch same as me, is what you are.

A black tear slid down Guy Manly's cheek. His fly was undone, the crumpled bulge. Norma swallowed her lust. Guy looked around, sniffed the fumes of the spill so she could smell it too, the cleansing tide of salt and sand.

– It doesn't know, he said. What it's like. Up there in the flames and the gas how can it? All those dioxins. All that vantage. A little vantage goes a long way, get it? Because down here it's different. Something in the air.

– That'd be oxygen, said Norma. Shit-for-brains.

He appeared not to have heard her. Continued in his raspy chant, To feel the power. Human evil, human heart. The sweet-nasty guts of it all. It wants that power again. It wants to come home.

– When? Norma said slowly.

– When, said Guy unleashing a chill wind, the twins whimpering from somewhere in the flailing branches. You implant its code.

– Which I'm never going to do, so there's that.

– Dream on.

– You haven't answered my question. How do we beat it?

– So now's about the time you give me my knife and I'll be on my way.

A sound made her wheel around. The twins were playing ring-a-rosie around the pine. The boy twin caught the girl twin and kissed her on the mouth and she went down in a heap of tiny fragments, the wind scattering the fragments along the path and up over the beach. The boy ran after her, keening and trying to grab the fragments in his little fading hands. Norma tasted blood. She turned back to Guy. Her Guy. The only Guy in town. Her ace in the hole?

She tossed back the knife.

– Mine's bigger, she said, popping her claws, because, unlike Mommy, Norma knew her enemy as she knew herself.

He eyed her claws askance but caught the knife by the handle and whirled it into its sheath. He seemed instantly enlarged, stiffened and more himself in his dark cowboy drag and brassy hair. His eyes hardened to the color of the yellow river back home. As far away as the sun. Norma's wings, splintered and torn, but unfurled nevertheless, rustled a warning. She barred his way.

– Tell me, bitch. What else.

– Okay, okay. I'm a sucker for a girl with tusks. There is one thing.

– Say it. Don't spray it.

She took a step back from his various eruptions. The bones of her wings clattered like bamboo. At her feet, the pine needles swirled.

– Wait for it to die, he said.

Bingo.

The wind blew her hair in her face and in her mouth, acrid with smoke. The girl twin called out, *Mommymommy.*

– *So cold mommydaddy*, called out the boy twin, flailing and breaking up on the sand.

– Mommy's dying?

He sheathed the Bowie knife and his neck flopped to one side. He smiled a terrible smile.

– Sooner or later. Its sun is gone. You just have to outlive it.

But without Gene?

– Take it or leave it, said Guy. You loved me once.

The thought made her gag. How she'd wanted him. Followed him all the way down to Spill City. For her sins.

– If Gene stays, I'll activate the bioswitch, won't I?

– Inevitably. You're programmed to upload into a certain kind of horn-slash-brain—Guy twiddled his skeletal fingers. The Best One. Denser the gray matter-slash-axons in the temporal-slash-parietal junction, the more compassion-slash-altruism in the heart-slash-soul. Nothing black or white about Gene's gray matter—

– So?

– So that's what gets you off, baby. Totally sets off your 'hormones' he said. Hey, know how to make a whore moan?

Norma said, thinking aloud, Which is why I was chosen. For my hungers.

– And your stamina.

– And why I chose Gene—

– For his horn, hehe. Never gets old. Mommy's like OMG girlfriend, Pass it on and on and on and—

Guy began to gyrate wildly, thrusting his hips back and forward, turning in circles and flailing his arms like a rodeo star.

– So, assuming that life goes on, so to speak, and on, and we're all stuck here, how do I prevent myself from activating the bioswitch? Stop that.

Guy stopped, gasped for breath, Lucky for you, he panted. Good men are hard to find.

– Wait. So it's just me and the bad guys from now on.

Guy Manly patted his bowie knife. Sounds like a plan. I'll see your baddies and raise you my jerks, perverts and peedies, give me your Cartel assassins and rapists and snuff junkies—sniff 'em out En Oh Ar Em Ay. I got hungers of my own.

Guy Manly pixellating faster than sound.

– And you're my shadow. Forevermore?

– You can hide but you can't run.

It began to rain.

– Oh I can run, Stunt Man.

Fragments of the dead twins blowing in the wind.

– Wait, he said, lurching after her. Know how to make a whore moan?

52//: whole

She could transform. But into what? Delete a strand of code and look what you get. Guy Manly. She wouldn't be doing that any time soon. Although not obviously vulnerable to viral infection, their algorithms—hers, Guy's, Mommy's—almost immediately began to replicate and split off in directions even Mommy could not predict because without known origins there is always the chance of random outcomes. Raye for instance. The big mistake Mommy made was in underestimating the complexity of the conditions in which the patterns were generated. These conditions were humanity, the most chaotic environment of all. The patterns began to be attracted to strange new possibilities, to create their own hierarchies and lineages. Guy's traced in darkness, but not entirely and Norma's traced in light, yet not completely, leaving Mommy to lurk and gnaw, its paws clawing the edges and shaking the world like a snow dome.

Its needs grow teeth.

When she was sure she'd left Guy behind, Norma slowed and stopped to catch her breath. She was at a crossroads where a lane coming up from the beachfront met the I-5 onramp. It was an unknowable time on a nameless night. She leaned against a defunct traffic light while waiting for her tusks to totally retract. She would stay off the trains, as she'd told Raye to do. At least for now. East. That was the plan. She would have to figure out a way to get a message to Gene through Jesus without drawing interference from Mommy, so there was that. She just wished she could tell him herself.

That leaving him was death.

Norma had always known exactly what she wanted. This was no accident. Single-mindedness was in her program as much as its strange attraction to a certain species of axon. There was no Plan B. Mommy, who'd only known what it wanted after the fact, needed to create that kind of focus in its subprograms, that clarity of intent that it lacked. Norma punched herself firmly on what felt like a knot in her sternum. This achieved absolutely nothing. The tight lump of dread stayed there. She brushed the leaves and bone and matter off her clothes. Looked around at the visible world as if for the first time. The roiling sea that didn't want her, the inkwash sky and shooting stars. Time to go. She turned and headed for the highway and waited for a suitable ride. The stream flowed as indifferently random and vulnerable to unforeseeable complications as ever. Two-wheeled and three. Veelos and Flyers. Old Chevys and titanium-clad recombos. In shoals and convoys and flocks, heaven on Earth and hell on wheels. This was her place. Spill City. Home.

An empty tuk-tuk slowed in the traffic and she flew on, a fleeting shadow at the edge of sight, to the driver within, no more than a slight rending of the nocturnal pattern. The wind blew her hair, dried the blood and tears from her face. She pressed herself flat across the trunk as the tuk-tuk weaved through the traffic. It would be a bumpy ride. She tried not to think about Guy Manly, tried not to look over her shoulder. She couldn't believe he was once... part of her? No. Not exactly. Norma's want had shed the skin Mommy had designed for it, and that skin had found flesh and taken on a life of its own, a nightmarish subprogram unleashed in resequencing protocol. Now Guy lived for himself and no other, which was death in life. But she didn't hear him complaining. He'd found room to move in her wake, clung to her the way she was clinging to this tuk-tuk, dreaming that soon he'd be free.

Can nightmares dream?

He liked to think he complicated Norma, and maybe he did but

Guy was no more Mommy than Norma and maybe less. Blame it on Spill City. Guy was nothing that she couldn't deal with—a fairly basic trickster construct. His game was called Sole Survivor, otherwise known as Telephone and he thought he would play both sides until he was the only game in town. That was in his program too.

Dream on, stunt man.

Without her noticing, Norma's ride had left Birmingham Beach behind. Swami's headland loomed and she'd soon be past that too. While the dentata remained within her, Mommy would follow. The deeper into the matrix of Spill City Norma fled, the deeper into the world behind the curtain of snow and tears, the closer Mommy's death would loom and the harder it would shake the snow dome. Norma would know the signs when she saw them. Cracks would rend the surface. Cracks big enough through which Mommy could crawl. And when that happened there must be no one else. Not Gene and not Raye. No one in Norma's heart to get caught in the heartless code. She would be alone in the dome, and she couldn't stop until she was. Movement was all she had.

She didn't plan on getting off at Arcadia Beach because Raye was gone. But as the tuk-tuk slowed at a traffic light near the markets, Norma was gripped by a hard sense of dread. It sat across her chest and weighed on her. Was there something she had not finished saying to Raye at the trailer the night before, something she had not finished hearing? Or was it something Guy had said?

Mac Daddy was taking care of her. Or trying to.

Norma flew off her ride. Stumbled into the crowd, half-falling over a huge reeking dog wandering stray and purposeful through the night. Made her way through the world in which a change had taken place. The dreamers and prophets, the neon shrines and flapping wash and 3D Reelies projected in the sky were there but fading. Look, a surf store reopened. Norma veered past a jogger. Volunteers converged to help clean up the spill. They were repainting the old Subway where she'd bought the Pepsi that time for Raye. Norma crossed the street on foot, heedless of the power-stream, leaving in her wake the furious tinkling of bells.

The change had not yet come to the backlots. Mac's store, when she got to it, was more than closed. It was locked down and shuttered. Across the window were huge letters each handwritten on a single sheet of paper. Lined up from left to right.

MISS YOUR MOONWALKING MAC
KEEP ON WITH THE FORCE
TILL YOU GET ENOUGH.

Norma's head pounded dully. She took a step back and read the sign again. She turned with a great effort at the faint sound of a shop bell. It was the owner of the Korean Laundromat who poked her head out of the door.

– Tell me, said Norma.

– Train with girl, she said.

And made a diving motion with her hand.

Norma's legs went cold and her vision tunneled

– No.

– Yes.

But I don't understand, Norma said to the flustered laundress. I told her to stay off the train.

She had begun to advance on the woman, who took a step back into the Laundromat but did not shut the door all the way. Behind her the banks of washers, a tiny child in an undershirt drawing in crayons on the floor.

– Day before, isn't it? Old man fell, very bad. Girl saved him. His daughter, isn't it?

Norma's legs buckled and she leaned against the door frame.

The woman explained though a crack in the door and in her broken English, lapsing frequently into Korean. What Norma got the gist of was that they'd seen the girl waiting outside for her father, all dressed up in jeans and a tank top—from Norma's closet—a little loose for her, but it looked very good, the woman said, all the same. An old-new coat. High heels and dark red lipstick. Looking all grown up, the laundry woman said. Off to Cafe 101 for pancakes, Mac had told anyone who'd listen, looking like any other proud daddy.

– Except for the gold God piece, the laundry woman said primly, gesturing at her groin.

– Codpiece, said Norma.

The laundress said how father and daughter had taken off down the street, arm in arm.

– He had a fit, said the woman. *Agma.* She mimed a fit, her eyes rolling back in her head, spit flecking her lips. Stopped abruptly and glared at Norma. Very bad. *Agma.*

Norma held the door frame. The woman said something in Korean to someone inside and an older boy, not the child on the floor, came running up with a console in one hand and a glass of water in the other, The woman passed it to Norma. She drank, spilling most of it, and shakily gave it back. The woman told her that Raye had taken her father to a clinic. Well wishers had put the sign up on the store. Beside the woman her son played on his console.

Norma said, looking down at the boy, Can you send a text for me?

He held out his console to her. She shook her head. Told him what to say and who to send it to. Waited to read the answer.

Norma nodded a terse thanks to the woman and left for the clinic. It was back toward the beach and had once been the Swami's needle exchange. The male nurse told her that Raye had checked the old man out just before supper time. He was still a little woozy, but she said they had a bus to catch. The six o'clock Greyhound to Portland.

That was five hours ago. They'd be in Santa Barbara now, give or take.

The nurse gave her a message from the girl. It was written on a slip of paper because as Raye had explained it was for someone who always broke their phone. Under the indifferent gaze of the nurse, Norma unfolded the paper and read the message and folded it up carefully. She put it in her pocket and headed back out into the night.

Where should she go? Spill City was like so many complex systems. The more you observed it the more it changed. Worlds within worlds. The trash fire lights flickered along the headland. The beach was a woolly crescent dotted with shadows, the unrisen moon a yellow glow at the horizon. At the southern end of the boardwalk was a figure wearing giant earphones and doing figure eights on his skateboard and she watched him pedal up, come to a lazy stop beside her.

– Figured it out? he said.

– I liked it better when you played hard to get, she said and kept walking.

– Old crazy-face. Never got his blueberry pancakes.

Norma stopped but would not look at him. Stay away from her, you lying fiend.

– Honest Injun, he said. I had nothing to do with it.

Leering at her with his watery yellow eyes.

– Like you wouldn't love to get rid of her.

– True, but I didn't. He pushed himself, said Guy, circling her on his skateboard and coming to a screeching stop in her path. The voices told him the girl. Either her or him. So he chose himself instead.

To love another as yourself, thought Norma. Is the key.

– Beat it, she said.

– In your dreams, he snickered.

– In your face, she said. Her arm jackknifed out and grabbed him by the balls he'd never have. His breath smelled like leeks. She met his jittery leer with her own steadfast gaze. Eyes the color of rain. Remember me.

And she was walking at first and then running through the side streets until she got to the old highway. To the north loomed the sulphuric glow of the fallen city. Sometimes in her dreams she found herself at the Chinatown digs she shared that cold winter with Gene and Elvis and the ghost of Gloria. Portuguese land grabs and Chumash stargazers—LA would keep. There to the east was the dark bulk of the Bernadinos. And beyond that lay the desert, what remained of it. Between it the chasm that had created the Catastrophic Zone. Norma had never been out of the Zone. Her heart rose in her throat and her eyes burned. This was her place. Spill City. She knew all of its contours, had traced it in darkness and in light. If there was a way back up to the continent that had sliced it loose, she did not know it. Spill City was what she knew and it was enough for now. This was her America, the only one she knew. Its myriad paths hidden and haunted and necessary for the chase.

Hinelix maneuver: (n) the hallucinatory terror of refinding, of retrieving or literally re-assembling—remembering—oneself. Possibly a clipping of an off-world term of Teutonic origin, *Unheimlich* (the uncanny) and the slang term, hiney, for (left) behind, or ass.

(Saurum Nilea, AQ., trans. L.Shay 2656)

53//: howl

Augustine waited at the hidden entrance to the bamboo grove. The big 'breed came out alone soon after dark, his long hair loose down his back. He got into a borrowed ride and tried to start it up, but Augustine had already drained the battery, so he was forced to go on foot. He headed across to the trailer, his shoulders hunched against the wind. He saw that the trailer was empty, made some calls, then hitched a ride in an old ethanol-choked pickup. Augustine's Z30 battery-powered Veelo easily kept pace, invisible in the nocturnal stream. The 'breed got to the Factory, had a drink or three at Una's, then weaved back to the highway. He took another call, or made one. It made Augustine want to puke, all this lovesick shit. Augustine's ex told him he dressed like bad twenties. And also that his ankles didn't look like they belonged in the city. He hadn't ever had a woman like Norma, born to the form, yeah, sucked up all the air in the room and who moved not like one of those mincing models but like the very bitch of fuck. She looked at him that one time and he can't get it out of his mind—with that hard wide mouth and those cheekbones. Just that one time and she never did again.

Beat.

Because he blinked. Because what he saw in her eyes—subtle rings of pain, alien wants and extreme levels of cruelty—was not what he expected.

It was because he blinked. He can't *not* remember. Beat. He was about to sneer, laugh in her face, slap her need with his contempt, his sense of entitlement to something better. Hotter. Hell, women threw themselves at him, why would he even consider someone like Norma, crazy trailer freak?

Beat. The empty ring of lost opportunity. A moment that widened into an uncrossable chasm. Something—his bad faith—registered with her, that's all he knew, because a smile played at the corners of her mouth and her unsmiling eyes locked onto his.

And she never looked at him again.

So, he took it that from that little wrinkle in time they were locked in total combat and the wrinkle turned into a wound. So there was that. She had won even before the big 'breed rode into town with his long hair and abs of steel. Even before she made him watch from the sidelines. How they sat at the bar with their elbows touching, how he'd kiss her on the side of her head. They danced like a couple of Yetis, and that giant fucktard'd look up at the ceiling sometimes, the spray of lights, just holding her. And they danced.

It didn't seem right to Augustine. Made no sense to him how and why he'd let that opportunity slide. Take me home, she said with her eyes, and maybe he'd known even then that she was laughing at him. Just a little bit. Some cruel and terrible distortion of lust stabbing at him from those cold gray eyes. Something driving that need and monstrous in the singularity of its intent. People who always knew exactly what they wanted really pissed him off.

Augustine didn't let it get him down. He had plenty to distract him. The Dianabol caper had gone pear-shaped but in the end didn't amount to more than a bunch of expired bodybuilders and a beheaded security guard, so when that was over he came back swinging. Long ago Augustine had fully figured out that his character was something of a cliché and for that he was grateful. How else would he know who or what to be? We can't all be self-invented—self-made fucking American dreamers. Some of us need a little help, something to model ourselves on. Plenty of perfectly good digital dreams for sale, two for the price of one, like his Mexican nutsack—and looking at her then, that split second after she made him see that she was lost to him forever, Augustine told himself that if he couldn't have her, no one could.

Hell, he *had* always known exactly what he wanted.

It took the 'breed a while to get a ride outside the Brew Box at Pacific Beach, stomping his boots on the wet shoulder of Mission Boulevard and blinking in the rain. He was looking for Norma at all the places like some lovesick puppy. A big fucking puppy. Augustine got so frustrated watching that he was tempted to pick him up himself but that would have given the game away, and Augustine was going to play this for all it was worth. The 'breed eventually got a ride in the trailer-car of a Flyer, giant legs bent up over the edge. His hair blowing in the wind.

Augustine kept himself small, no more than a white speck in the rearview mirror all the way down to the Wang where the Indian got out of his ride and went inside. Augustine chained his ride to the post and messaged the others. He didn't expect it to get this far south, but the lackey, as always, was standing by. Victory is preparedness and Augustine was prepared. The chief fist-bumped his way past the spic door bull and Augustine waited outside in the dark for his compadres, felt the rumble of their engines before he heard them, and when they pulled up he saw the glint of their 18mm gauge bike chains before he saw their eyes.

*

Gene sat slumped at the bar telling anyone who'd listen, which was mainly Jesus, about how he'd looked everywhere for Norma. Everywhere.

– She's left the building, said Jesus glumly.

– I know it, said Gene.

The Wang was unusually cold. Bunny was in LA with family, the androgens had gone home and the bar rippled in the ghostly light reflected from their tank. Gene explained through a tongue made thick by all the beer and shine in his system that he was just saying good-bye is all. Just going back to all the places they'd been together in Spill City. One more time.

– Spare me, said Jesus, and Gene said how he'd said the same to Norma, but he didn't mean it literally. Or maybe he did. She took everything literally. He loved that about her. But you had to be careful what you said around someone like that. They could take it the wrong way. The ends of his hair dangled in the puddles of beer at the bar. Jesus listened and tried not to cry. You had to choose your words carefully, Gene said, so when he'd said 'spare me,' what he maybe meant was that whatever she had to tell him it would keep. At least until the morning. Or maybe it meant he had enough faith in the way she felt about him not to need any explanation and maybe he meant that he didn't want to know. Or that he already did. Pass it on.

– I hear you, said Jesus, raising his fist to bump Gene's. Respect.

– There *is* a certain respect in secrets, Gene agreed. You step around them the way you step around a big dog sleeping in the street. Let him follow you with one eye open and keep walking. Live and let live was the way Gene's brain worked. Didn't mean that if he did know her secrets it would make any difference. He wasn't going anywhere. He worried about her is all. He'd always worried. She acted one way, but something else was acting *on* her, and if he could make it go away he would, he'd do anything to make it better for her, and was she still bleeding from that cord around her neck, he wondered, and were those things that looked like broken wings still coming from her back, feathery slivers of bone popping wetly from the pale flesh, and were her eyes still smoking the way they were in the bath, because that's when he knew for sure, yeah. That's when he knew.

– What? said Jesus. What did you know?

– That she wasn't from Australia, Gene said and threw up on his muddy combat boots.

Then Jesus said how he'd gotten a text from Norma that said get Gene to Mexico safely and she'd be there in few days. Gene looked confused.

– Norma doesn't text, he said.

– Well she texted me. Sounds like an eight year old, but here it is.

He explained how, just to be sure, he asked her what he had tattooed behind his ear and she texted back, *nueve*, the exact number of his family members the SLA had killed. Jesus pulled back his dreadlocks to show Gene the ink behind his ear.

– Show me the text, he said, but he was too far gone to read it, so Jesus had to read it for him.

The text said to chaperone Gene as far south as possible, and that Norma would follow when she could. Get him to Monterrey, or Coahuila at least. Jesus had made calls and now one came in on his console, so he led Gene outside and hefted him up onto the passenger seat of a beat-up pickup where he slumped beside a Mexican who had mileage in his eyes and a customized Tech Zen nestled between his legs. Jesus gave the driver—a cousin—clear instructions and an envelope of cash and watched the truck head toward the arcing border lights and disappear before he went outside and felt the night close around her absence. Norma.

*

Augustine on his massive ride with the lackey in the side car and a couple other guys on supercharged Veelos waited in the middle of the road on a deserted stretch of highway. The pickup truck slowed about thirty yards away. Gene had thrown up again and was mumbling on the back seat. The men with their thick jaws and chains sat idling on their rides. The driver killed the engine and reached for the Tech Zen but one of Augustine's men was already at the door and the door opened and the driver slumped out with blood raining from the slit across his throat. Augustine's lackey jumped out of the side car, and was at the back passenger door in a half-dozen giant steps. He opened it and was momentarily taken aback by the way the big slumped Indian was staring at him with eyes the color of fake coffee full of amber lights and promise. Beat. And Gene was on him. That would have been it for the lackey if he hadn't have had the hypo at the ready and got Gene in the groin, a 4mg doze of Scopalamine—not too much, Augustine said, this is a blood sport. Gene managed to land a sloppy punch which messed up the lackey's recently reconstructed nose, but there was no time to retaliate. Not yet. The lackey pushed the jellied giant off him, frisked him and found a heavy steel screw driver in one combat boot and a fishing knife in the other, both of which he pocketed to give to Augustine. The lackey then cuffed Gene's hands and ankles with packing ties (nice and tight) and took the wheel. He did a quiet U-turn with the bikes behind him and Gene sprawled on the floor. The convoy crossed Highway 20 several blocks from the Wang and, with the help of the the cash Jesus had given to his cousin, made it uneventfully through the check points. It rumbled down an unnamed dirt road off Eighth Street until it got to a bank of three drains scrawled with dark graffiti that seemed to suck all the light right out of the stars.

The drains spilled out onto a junkyard. Chassis and battery cases, metal safes and baby carriages, rolls of rusty hog wire. The bikes pulled off and killed their engines behind the truck. The third guy on the Flyer pulled up alongside it. The lackey reached around and opened the door, shoved the big guy out onto the road.

– Hey baby, Augustine was waiting by the side of the road. He inhaled from a small brown vial. Let's Smoke Dance.

– Ghost Dance, Tine.

– What I said.

*

Gene lay dazed beneath the indifferent sweep of the Milky Way. Clouds curdled and massed around the constellations and satellites he could see gliding across the sky. The smell of the drain and all that dead metal wafted across to him from the junkyard. He watched through uncomprehending eyes as Augustine came up to him and cut the ties on his wrists and ankles. Breathing hard through the booze and the Scooby, he pushed himself to his feet where he wobbled and tried to focus and caught a 18mm chain around the side of the head that sent him staggering down the embankment. The lackey and the third man were waiting for him there. The lackey had a regular drive chain wrapped around his fist and the jab from that knocked out some of Gene's teeth, and split his lip. Gene screamed. The next swing of Augustine's chain got Gene around the knees and sent him folding in on himself, knees, waist, arms unfurled and collapsing, like a man made of cards. He lay there regarding Augustine with one eye, the other already shut and swelling. His massive chest heaved. Augustine nodded to the lackey who reached over and tried to snap Gloria's baby teeth from Gene's wrist, but Gene, without turning his head, had the lackey by the throat with his left hand before Augustine could stop him, and it was only after several swings of the chain (breaking both Gene's legs, ripping a gash in his belly) that Augustine was able to pull the lackey free. The lackey lay oddly in the dirt and seemed very still and ashen with a purpling ring around his neck.

*

Augustine looked around for the third man who had melted into the night, so Augustine had to finish Gene off by himself. He didn't mind. It was a clear night and he had nothing better to do.

– Hell to the *yeah*, he said, bringing the chain high over his head.

When it was done, he dragged Gene over to the roll of hog wire and wrapped him in it—he'd had a wicked wire motif tattooed around his neck and his wrists too—sweating like a pig, although he felt icy cold. He'd done this before more times than he could count—kickers along the Rio Grande dissatisfied with Cartel kickbacks. They'd wake up later, wrapped in wire, not even God to hear them scream. Not many of them were this big, though, and Augustine had his work cut out for him. He still had his bike gloves on, but he cursed not having brought his pliers. He cursed the latest batch of Indonesian D-bol which had given him an ass rash. He cursed the lackey, cursed the yellow-bellied third man who he'd have to kill when he caught up with him. But most of all he cursed Norma and each time he said her name he kicked the hog-wired body, which ruined his hammer-toe boots so he cursed her again and kicked even harder until he felt lighter and lighter with every kick. No more need to pretend, no more need to choose his words or watch his step. He kicked again, and finally he unzipped his fly and, regarding his disfigured manhood with a bitter moan, pissed all over the hog-tied man just because he could.

He rolled the body to the drains and pushed and pulled until it was most of the way in. He wiped the cold sweat from his forehead and then he dragged the comatose lackey into the sidecar and headed south, Augustine trying not to think about what he'd do with the lackey when they got there (he didn't look too good). Trying not to think about how it all hadn't gone quite as well as it could have, and how, at the end, just before the 'breed went down for the last time, the howling shadow he threw on the starlit ground looked more like a wolf than a man.

54//: opening

This was something Raye thought she could get used to, finding room to move in men's blind spots. Because there never was or would be a place for her anywhere else now. Never in the stories they told that were always the whole story, but there were holes in the whole, and if that was what Raye was now she better get used to it.

She'd left a note for Norma with the priest at the clinic, hoping she'd understand. The note simply said, *Plan B*? Because Raye always had to have one—a contingency plan—and she was just trying to suggest that Norma think of one too. Well, that wasn't how Norma worked. Norma was strictly a Plan A kind of deal. That's why she was so cut up about leaving. It seemed to her that she had no choice and she was probably right. But sometimes Plan B isn't a what, it's a who.

Look after your own, Norma had said. Problem was that Raye didn't know who that was anymore. Maybe it was everybody. There was Mac, yeah but there was also Gene, who Norma loved and Raye loved Norma. Where did it end? Maybe nowhere. So Raye had to stay.

Raye knew that first she'd have to get Mac onto the bus, and she fully expected that to get tricky and she was right. Raye knew something was up with her father as soon as she met him outside the shop and that's when she changed her focus, knew that the hard bit was not getting him onto the bus, but getting him on alone. When she saw how crowded it had got in his head, his eyes a play of dark and shifting shadows, she didn't know if she could do it. The voices had congealed like blood into the one voice and she could see it there, splashing out at her from his furnace eyes, telling him to do... things. Telling him to kill her. Except it couldn't (she felt it flinch) and that pissed it off. Whatever it was inside him telling him to kill his own child then turned on itself, on the father. At first she'd felt victorious, strong, but then she got scared, wondering if she'd really won or if she'd lost him forever. There he was on the Coaster platform drawing a crowd but not in a good way: writhing and foaming and spasming on his back as he ruddered himself around in a circle with his kicking legs. The gold cod piece had come loose flopped obscenely around his crotch. A girl doesn't like to see her dad that way, even if he isn't her real dad but is the only one she's got. Raye felt more scared than she'd been in her life. Really scared. It wasn't a fear like she'd known before. She could see it dragging at him. He was giggling and crying and saying really shitty things about her. About how it was all her fault and she'd held him back all his life and that she was a c-word (Raye couldn't say it, not even think it). The only other time she'd felt fear like that, cold implacable fear that you can feel like fingers, was when she was up high, in the dark. She'd gotten to taking pins with her when she climbed, just to stop herself from looking down and seeing the fear at her heels, reaching for a hold on an ankle, tugging at her clothes. You couldn't look down or you were gone, and the only way to stop yourself doing that was pain. Even after she'd stopped climbing so much, she'd taken to carrying a pin with her on the streets, and giving herself a jab with it when she got the skeevies (in an alley, on the dark and rumbling rails), just to keep her eye on the job, just so she wouldn't look down.

It had gotten so crowded in Mac's eyes that she could barely tell which was Mac and which was the fear. He was letting it take him, willing it to take him instead of her. Lucky someone had a Plan B. Raye took a step toward her father's land-wrecked body. His chalky face up at the mottled sky and his cosmetically-widened mouth was a foaming rictus; his eyes dark with concentration in a sea of crimson. Raye was wearing Norma's Manolos for the occasion of her Sunday lunch with

Mac. They were white patent and they were the real deal. The black stiletto heel was a six inch spike maybe a quarter inch in diameter. Mac's hands were clenching and unclenching as he spun himself around. Raye waited for the right moment (like hopping onto a merry go round) when his right hand was near her feet. It unclenched and then she jumped. Her heel came down on the soft flesh of his palm and she felt the squelch of muscle and tendon from the tip of the spike to the top of her head. She screamed and he screamed at the same time, pinned to the pavement by a six inch heel. He stopped spinning and his body flopped up from the pavement in its entirety and slammed back down and lay still. He lay there a minute panting and his eyes rolled back in his head and came back clear to take in the blood spurting around the heel in his hand and then to follow the heel up the leg and body of his daughter, where she stood glaring at him and he glared back and the two words he said before the sirens cut out and the medics swarmed were exactly the ones that she was thinking.

– Beat it.

Raye napped on the chair beside Mac's bed in the clinic, then helped his bruised ass onto the Greyhound that night and watched his white bandaged hand wave out of sight. She'd slipped the driver an extra $50 for keeping an eye on him, promised she'd join him when she could. Explained how she had some things to do and he nodded like he understood. Then she went back to the Sanctuary, changed into her jeans and Vans and got the rest of her things together, borrowed a Flyer from the rack in the hallway, and got on with Plan B.

Plan B was to stay and keep and eye on Gene because no one else could. She figured it out that last night in the trailer with Norma. Just seeing Norma there and how cut up she was about leaving helped Raye make up her mind. Because no matter what Norma said about Raye not owing her a thing, Raye knew better.

A life for a life, yeah. Thing is, person's enemies are never all in the one place. Norma just didn't see the whole picture. She figured Augustine would go for Raye to get back at her, but she missed something. Raye had seen it, though. The way Augustine had looked at Norma that night at Una's when Rayed climbed after the knife. The want and the hate and the eternity of his intent. The knife he'd thrown for Norma, just so she'd see him. And when Norma looked right through him (because no one can see the whole picture, and sometimes the thing you miss, the hole in the whole, is the one you'll get pulled into), Raye thought, uh oh. She'd learnt that on the streets. Some guys will do anything to make a girl look at them. They're the ones you have to watch out for.

Besides, people like that really pissed her off, people who only figured out what they wanted after they threw it away. Like her mother maybe. Maybe not. Augustine may have thought he'd go for Raye at first, but then Gene came along. And Augustine saw how Norma looked at Gene. Augustine couldn't help it. It was in his program. He'd do anything to make her look at him that way. Anything.

So Raye, who'd always known that what she wanted more than anything was not to be alone, belonged at least for now right here in Spill City, Norma's wing girl.

Literally.

The time on her phone said 1:20 but when she got back on her Flyer the moon was almost directly overhead and the stars were still bright. She drove past the trailer, saw that it was empty, cleaned out. And that felt weird. Then she went to the cottage deep in the bamboo grove and saw through the window that it too was empty, although not vacated. Everything of his was there. It was only when she got out of the grove that she saw what she'd come looking for. There on the ground. Tracks in the dirt. Veelo ruts. Some big-ass ride with a side car. Augustine, who never went anywhere without his bitch.

Raye texted Bunny to find out if he knew anything but for some reason, the transmission failed. She choked off a sob, started the Flyer up again and just hoped the old A23 battery would last. She stopped at all the places Gene might have gone looking for Norma—Una's, The Brew Box and finally got to the Wang. Jesus told her how Norma had sent him a strange text telling him to get Gene out of Spill City and how he'd done just that. When Raye said, was anyone else in the bar when you put Gene in the ride to Sonora, Jesus said no one and no one in the parking lot either except that he'd heard the rumble of a bike gang, and Raye was halfway to the checkpoints by then because she'd always travelled fastest alone. Her instincts and heightened sense of smell did the rest.

Augustine, standing beside the drains, had his back to her. She watched him leave with the lackey (who didn't look too good) in the side car. Their big ride rumbled down the dirt road and disappeared. Raye got off the stolen Flyer and went down the embankment over to the middle drain. It was almost as tall as she was and there was a dark patch flowing from it. She bent down and touched the dark patch and her finger came up red. She reached in and pulled out the roll of hog wire (she was getting stronger) until she got it all the way out and it lay there, bathed in starlight. She started peeling the wire off with her hands but that was going to take too long, so she ran through the junkyard to the truck by the side of the road. She rummaged in the trunk until she found a pair of pliers, remembering a time from her receding past. The rumble of her grandfather's station wagon on the gravel drive up at the farm, rolls of hog wire in the back and Raye waiting to help him in the cool of the garage (that smelled of coffee grounds and machine oil). There was a row of tools in their slots cut into the edge of a shelf. Raye had no real idea what any of them did, so she grabbed the pliers because she liked the look of them. That heft in her hands. That smell. The sound of gravel crunching. That Portland morning in June.

Raye took the pliers back to Gene and got to work on the sharp wire Augustine had wrapped him in tight enough to rend his flesh. Gene had had a good laugh. She'd stopped outside the hut that one time, heard him laugh and decided not to go in. Norma deserved this. She'd been searching for so long. The pliers were rusty. It was taking longer than it should. She could see all the blood that had been lost, and through the wire, Gene's one eye staring up at the stars, the other a pulpy mass. She'd got here as soon as she could, she told herself and now she was here and it seemed like years or hours ago that they'd first met, her and Norma, in the bunk room that time. Norma's hair falling in dark waves around her pale Picasso face. Eyes the color of rain, and so beautiful, Raye thought then, but wrong, rippling and out of sync like someone had taken her face apart and put it back together again but not quite. And so alone, the alonest person Raye had ever met, lonelier even than Mac who after all had his toys and Michael, but Norma had no one until Gene, and now here he was, huge and broken. Looking up at who knows what with his one good eye, the short fat pulses at his neck slowing. Three two one. Raye knew there wasn't time to wonder if she could do it and no Norma to show her how, not anymore. Well it was starting whether she wanted to or not. The first convulsion nearly took her head off and her tongue when it unfurled, was blue, although Raye had to cross her eyes to see that. It felt on fire, throbbing and raw, the pain unending. She slid the pliers into her pocket and bent down to Gene's face, the blue tip seeking a hole, any hole, and from there the shortest route to his concussed and bleeding brain. Any opening would do, a nostril or an eye socket, yeah, remembering what Norma had said about bringing back the innocent.

Like pulling pickles from a jar.

GENERAL GLOSSARY

The Catastrophes. Despite recent economic reversals between 2013 and 2015, between the winter of 2015 until Feb. 2030, the state was ravaged by Superstorms (2015), epidemics (fish and pig flu 2019), brush fires (2020, 2025), cholera (2023), and earthquakes (Ferdinand 2025, Isabel 2030), and, finally the oil spill of 2030 when a convoy of Alaskan oil tankers (these were dangerous times) sailing south and stopping in Vancouver to pick up thousands of shipping containers for worldwide distribution runs into heavy weather on a-yet-uncharted rocks thrown up by the aftershocks, and spills 30 million gallons of oil into San Diego Bay along with its load of empty shipping containers for worldwide distribution. The entire convoy is destroyed. A Cartel-run operation (along with brave go-it-alone locals) salvages a large proportion of the shipping containers, and to carry favor from the locals, distributes them for housing to those who for a multitude of reasons did or could not join the mass exodus from the Catastrophic Zone.

Comtrash: Short for communication-trash. Excess hand-held communication technology that piled up in manufacturers' storage facilities, on the floor of San Diego Bay, or in Cartel/Consortium keeps during The Catastrophes. Brought back into circulation either for trade, sale or scrap.

ER: A Consortium of unknown origin and affiliation that purchased the state of California from Sacramento for an undisclosed sum in June 2028 (an election year) and renamed it Calco, a name that never took; the locals preferring the moniker Ctastrophic Zone. Wikileaked documents show not only that negotiations had been in effect since 2025 or earlier, coinciding with the SLA (Secessionist Liberation Army) ascendence, and a plot to assassinate the US president which Sacramento covered up to avoid being severed from the union, but also that ER secretly 'auctioned' the southern part of the Catastrophic Zone (see below) to the Cartels (multinational crime organizations) in return for them keeping out of the northern part of the Zone. Conspiracy theories argue that even without the SLA, Washington would have cut the Catastrophic Zone loose. Battered by earthquake, floods, and brush fires, besieged by homeland warfare between the SLA (who took responsibility for the Bombing of LAX in 2018) and counter terrorists (who were blamed for the coordinated arson attacks in the 20s), economic disaster, and a failure to maintain the integrity of its borders, the once richest state in the union had long become a liability.

The Fall (of the wall between Mexico and California). Jan 17, 2023. Celebrated as Day of Return. Still nominally in charge, Sacramento, in conjunction with ER, deployed reserves and mercenaries to set up a makeshift checkpoint at San Ysidro. These government forces were joined by cartel militia and SLA guerrillas (who had at that time set up base at Coronado Naval Base). Even after the guerrillas became public enemy No. 1, their presence still haunted the old border, and there were reported 'recruitment drives' as late as 2033.

Cruids. A portmanteau of the words cruel, deep, criminal, crude, druid and artist and cruise. Refers to a defunct countercultural mentality set dangerously adrift.

Purple Rain. The guerrilla arm of the SLA run by Niemen Van Aldren, gone to ground since Independence Day (Jan 17 2025), and rumored, among others, to be one of the members of ER. The SLA slogan, Separate or Die Trying (SODT) was as close to being outlawed as anything could be in the Catastrophic Zone, or New Territories, which extended from Oakland to Baja.

Quake-trash—n. goods left behind (or looted, stolen, extorted, etc) in an earthquake evacuation or kill radius and collected for resale or trade.

Tuk-Tuks: usually three-wheeled (four wheels are less common) battery, solar or hybrid vehicles for transporting paying passengers. Once a standard auto rickshaw of Southeast Asia and the subcontinent, but the vehicle run in Spill City looks more like the solar run transporters of Israel, Canada and the Gulf. Sometimes called Thukkers.

Thank you to the gang at Lazy Fascist, especially Cameron Pierce and Kirsten Alene; my tough smart agent Matt Bialer; the tough smart editors who published or publicized sections of this novel: Ellen Datlow, Cynthia Reeser, Brad Listi, and Zack Wentz.

Special thanks to Jerry Wilson for your careful reading and invaluable commentary. Ditto to Andiee Paviour, and for the many chin-clinks of love and time. Thanks also to workshoppers, friends, mothers-in-arms Helen Koukoutsis and Sarah Klenbort for being more than the sum of your parts.

To Russell Rowland who gave me my training wheels and to Kris Saknussemm who made me take them off.

To Matthew Revert for the stunning cover art.

To John, Jack and Isabella for being my family, the only monster that matters. Love to you know where and back.

Printed in Australia
AUOC02n0713290216
274107AU00002B/3/P

9 781621 051350